Christian Brothers

Advanced Reader

Specially prepared to Elicit Thought and to Facilitate Literary Composition

Christian Brothers

Advanced Reader

Specially prepared to Elicit Thought and to Facilitate Literary Composition

ISBN/EAN: 9783742860163

Manufactured in Europe, USA, Canada, Australia, Japa

Cover: Foto ©Andreas Hilbeck / pixelio.de

Manufactured and distributed by brebook publishing software
(www.brebook.com)

Christian Brothers

Advanced Reader

CHRISTIAN BROTHERS'

NEW SERIES.

ADVANCED READER,

SPECIALLY PREPARED TO

ELICIT THOUGHT

AND TO FACILITATE

LITERARY COMPOSITION.

———⚬●⚬———

NEW YORK:

CHRISTIAN BROTHERS' DEPOSITORY,

50 SECOND STREET.

1893.

CONTENTS.

Lessons in Poetry are indicated by a *.

CONTENTS.

PREFACE.

THE ADVANCED READER and the other numbers of the New Series have been prepared to comply with the requirements of our Method.

This METHOD demands not only ability on the part of the teacher to give his lesson in an interesting manner, but also exacts a special preparation of each lesson.

Apart from religious instruction, there is no subject that requires so conscientious a preparation on the part of teacher and pupil, as Reading— so numerous are the topics included, so varied the questions suggested. This is especially true of our method, where questioning is so urgently insisted upon, and legitimate curiosity encouraged with such fostering care.

Good teaching demands that the pupil be taught to co-ordinate his information ; that his knowledge and intellectual activity be brought to bear upon every new subject ; that his attention be secured by the attractive manner in which the lessons are given, thus securing the healthy development of the pupil's mind and the harmonious exercise of all its faculties.

These ends can be attained only where the varied

aspects of the subjects are considered, where suggested ideas are discussed, and the historical, moral, and practical bearings of the subject are brought before the pupil.

By following this method, Reading will not be a meaningless utterance of words, but an intelligent expression of ideas, in which not only memory will be exercised, but the understanding developed, the will strengthened, the imagination guided, and the spiritual sense cultivated.

Owing to the limited time that is at the disposal of the children to learn the elements of composition, these Readers are so prepared as to lead the pupils almost instinctively to the knowledge of this essential branch of education.

To fully realize the plan adopted in these Readers, parents and guardians should take part in the preparation of the HOME LESSONS suggested under the form of QUESTIONS and COMPOSITION.

The object in issuing this New Series is not to increase the number of Readers already before the public. Our motive has been simply to prepare Readers that meet the requirements of a system that has the experience of two centuries in its favor, and that has received the unqualified approval of the ablest minds at home and abroad.

THE BROTHERS OF THE CHRISTIAN SCHOOLS.

READING.

———o———

ITS METHODOLOGY.

DEFINITION

EXERCISE OF THE FACULTIES.
{ The eye and the mind, — sense of hearing, — organs of speech, — intelligence, — feeling, — moral sense.

IMPORTANCE OF READING.
{ Besides its educational influence, reading is the key to study, and the most powerful means of instruction for youth, after leaving school.

DIVISION.
{ *Elementary Reading.*
Fluent Reading.
Expressive Reading.

ELEMENTARY READING. { *Principles.* {
1. Teaching of reading, writing and spelling inseparable.
2. Preliminary exercises in reading, writing and spelling.

READING

---o---

Definition. — Reading is the vocal and intelligent expression of thoughts, written or printed.

Exercise of the Faculties. — The art of reading claims the attention both of the MIND and of the EYE, for the apprehension of the various cháracters. It exercises the sense of HEARING in determining SOUNDS, INTONATIONS and INFLECTIONS according to the rules of harmony, as regards EUPHONY, CADENCE and RHYTHM. It trains the ORGANS OF SPEECH by the correct emission of these sounds; it cultivates INTELLIGENCE by exercising thought; it develops the FEELINGS when it appeals to the sentiments of the heart; finally, it strengthens the MORAL SENSE when it tells of deeds and quotes sayings in which the great moral truths are correctly applied.

Importance. — Reading is the key to knowledge, for in each specialty the scholar must privately study the lesson that has been publicly explained. Even religion can be but imperfectly known without it.

After the knowledge of the truths of our holy faith, there is no qualification more agreeable and useful to offer the pupil than reading. It quietly opens to the student the intellectual labors of the greatest geniuses, the productions of the greatest authors. By reading we

husband and preserve the lessons of experience. The
mind is thus stored with numberless useful subjects of
information that cannot enter into the programme of
ordinary schools. Reading opens the book of the past,
with its noble lessons and reminiscences; the pages
of the present, with all its teachings, its aspirations and
its needs, at the same time that it procures instruction
and amusement for one's hours of leisure.

Division.— Reading may be considered under three headings,
viz.: ELEMENTARY, FLUENT, EXPRESSIVE.

In ELEMENTARY READING, the child distinguishes letters,
pronounces and unites the sounds represented by these
letters, so as to form syllables and words, and constructs
sentences.

In FLUENT READING, the pupil reads a succession of sentences connected by their meaning, CLEARLY, DISTINCTLY,
TO THE POINT, and with SUFFICIENT RAPIDITY, — pronouncing
the words CORRECTLY without HESITANCY or REPETITION,
giving every LETTER and every SYLLABLE its proper sound
in the word, and observing the proper pauses.

In EXPRESSIVE READING, the pupil marks by the INTONATIONS,
INFLECTIONS, and the SHIFTINGS of his voice, the different
ideas of the piece, and the various sentiments expressed
by the author.

The perfection of EXPRESSIVE READING presupposes,
together with the attributes of FLUENT READING, the
following conditions on the part of the reader:

(a) An INTELLIGENCE apt to conceive the sense of the
piece read.

(b) A practised EYE.

(c) A delicate SENSIBILITY.

(d) An accurate EAR.

(e) A VOICE agreeable, ample, yielding and sonorous.

(*f*) A TASTE sure and prompt in discerning literary beauties and defects.

In one word, a good reading is a complete literary analysis.

To read well implies:

1. INTELLIGENCE to grasp the meaning.
2. SOUL to feel.
3. TASTE to express in an agreeable manner.

To EXPRESS PROPERLY one must feel; and to FEEL one must thoroughly UNDERSTAND.

To UNDERSTAND THOROUGHLY is:

1. To grasp all the shades of meaning expressed in every sentence.
2. To note the connection of the sentences with each other.
3. To note their relation to the whole subject.

Frequently, reading is a mere mechanical exercise: words enter the pupil's eye in the shape of characters, and escape by the mouth under the form of sounds, while the mind plays no part in the operation. The memory does not preserve the slightest trace of the ideas expressed. This is proved by the meaningless phrases the pupils at times read. Results far more deplorable than mere slovenly reading arise from such a habit. From thoughtless reading the pupil goes to listless memorizing: from hearing without listening, to acting without thinking, knowing not what he says or does. To prevent this, even the child learning the first elements of reading should be taught:

1. To associate the idea with the words which express it.
2. The judgment must bear upon the different propositions contained in the lesson.

3. The exactness of the thought as contained in its form of expression.

This leads to thinking while reading, and to reading in thinking.

How to Understand thoroughly. —

1. A portion, or the whole of a lesson is read fluently, expression not being yet exacted.
2. The scholars are then required to give the general drift of the portion read.

To assure the proper understanding of the subject, let the pupils:

(a) Replace difficult words by their synonymes.

(b) Give the meaning of figurative expressions.

3. The sense of each sentence must be determined by well selected questions.
4. Leading thoughts must be given in the pupils' own words.
5. The relation of thoughts should be resolved, as well as their reference to the general object of the composition.

To Feel fully. — This consists in being powerfully penetrated by the sentiment which the author desires to express, or by the particular form of thought he seeks to establish.

How to Feel fully. — Let the pupil study:

1. The particular emotion caused by each passion.
2. The tone of voice corresponding to the expression of the passion.

Thus :

(a) In joy, the voice is full, lively and elastic.

(b) In combat or struggle, defiant and bold.

(c) In reproaches, vehement.

(d) In prayer and supplication, soft and timid.

(e) In counsel, premise or consolation, grave and sustained.

(f) In fear, feeble.

(g) In compassion, sustained.

(h) In complaint, broken.

(i) In narration, free and fluent.

Agreeable Expression. — To be PERFECT, reading must be NATURAL.

For this purpose the pupil should :

1. Pay close attention to the emotions or feelings the selection suggests.

2. Give due attention to the vocal tones called for by the selection.

3. Lay special stress on those points that are to attract the attention of an audience.

4. The reading should be accelerated or retarded, the volume of voice increased or diminished, to express the progress of thought or sentiment, or to conform to the requirements of imitative harmony.

5. Inverted and elliptical phrases must be duly noted, showing the logical relations of these phrases to the main subject.

6. A tone-coloring should call attention to certain figures of speech, that might otherwise pass unperceived, such as *allusion, irony,* etc.

This power of tone-coloring may be greatly increased by judicious musical vocal exercises. These

(a) Form the ear.

(b) Give flexibility to the voice.

(c) Strengthen the vocal organs.

7. Judicious selections of prose or poetry should be memorized. These, recited aloud, will

(a) Store the pupil's memory with representative composition.

(b) Furnish him with increased resources of language and style.

This exercise makes the student fully identify himself with the meaning of the author, and is the best method to become an accomplished reader.

Simultaneous reading of such memorized selections is recommended. Correct simultaneous expressive reading is not more difficult than the proper recitation of an ordinary prayer.

The following are examples for the study of tone, corresponding with the rules *a, b, c,* etc., on pages **x, xi**:

(a) O *day* of *days!*   Shall hearts set free
No "minstrel rapture" find for thee?
Thou art the Sun of other days,—
They shine by giving back thy rays.

(b) And first I tell thee, haughty peer,
He who does England's message here,
Although the meanest in her state,
May well, proud Angus, be thy mate;
And Douglas, more I tell thee here,
Even in thy pitch of pride —
Here in thy hold, thy vassals near,

    *   *   *   *   *

I tell thee thour't defied.

(b) Oh! shame beyond the bitterest thought
That evil spirit ever framed,
That sinners know what Jesus wrought,
Yet feel their haughty hearts untamed;
That souls in refuge, holding by the Cross,
Should wince and fret at this world's little loss

(d) Lead, kindly Light, amid the encircling gloom
    Lead Thou me on!
    The night is dark, and I am far from home—
    Lead Thou me on!
    Keep thou my feet : I do not ask to see
    The distant scene, — one step enough for me.

(e) Then why dost thou weep so? For see how time flies,
    The time that for loving and praising was given!
    Away with thee, child, then, and hide thy red eyes
    In the lap, the kind lap, of thy Father in heaven.

(f) O Heaven! methought what pain it was to drown!
    What dreadful noise of water in my ears!
    What sights of ugly death within my eyes!
    I thought I saw a thousand wrecks ;
    A thousand men that fishes gnawed upon :
    Inestimable stones, unvalued jewels,
    Wedges of gold, great anchors, heaps of pearl,
    All scattered in the bottom of the sea.

   (g) The old man held one languid arm in his, and had the small hand tightly folded to his breast for warmth. It was the hand she had stretched out to him with her last smile, — the hand that had led him on through all their wanderings, Ever and anon he pressed it to his lips, then hugged it to his breast again, murmuring that it was warmer now, and, as he said it, he looked, in agony, to those who stood around, as if imploring them to help her.

   (h) If thou also hadst known, and that in this thy day, the things that are to thy peace ; but now they are hidden from thy eyes.

   (i) The lives of a hundred unconscious passengers hung on the issue of the next minute. The ground trembled at the old woman's feet. The great red eye of the engine showed itself, coming round a curve. Like a huge, sharp-sighted lion coming suddenly upon a fire, it sent forth a thrilling roar, that echoed through all the wilds and ravines around.

THE MODEL MAN.

Rev. Isaac Thomas Hecker was born in New York, in 1819. In 1845 he became a convert to Catholicity, and in 1849 was ordained priest by Cardinal Wiseman. After a few years spent in the Redemptorist Order, he obtained permission of the Pope to found the new society of missionary priests known as the Paulist Fathers. His writings are chiefly doctrinal, controversial and philosophical; they are addressed to thoughtful minds, and in a great measure directed toward the enlightenment of our Protestant brethren. "Questions of the Soul," and "Aspirations of Nature," are the principal of his published works; their gifted author is more widely known through the influence of the "Catholic World," of which he was the founder, and for many years chief contributor.

MAN needs, as a perfect pattern of life, one who unites in his nature both God and man, one whom he can see with his eyes, hear with his ears, touch with his hands. One to whom the human heart can easily attach itself in a way fitting its nature, and can love with familiarity. One who is visible to the mind and accessible to the senses, and in whom both soul and body can find their hopes, their proper objects, and their beatitude. In one word, man needs as his model a God-man.

This is no new idea: there is no nation in which the birth of a God-man was not expected. The ancient patriarchs sighed for his coming; the prophets announced his reign; the sibyls chanted his victories; and the poets sung his praises.

The universal convictions of the conscience of humanity are the voices of the divinity. The expectations of men were not doomed to disappointment. In the fulness of time there came from heaven an angel and announced the following message to a spotless maiden in a humble cottage: "Hail, full of grace;" "blessed art thou amongst women;" "the power of the Most High shall overshadow thee, and thou shalt conceive and bring forth a son, and his name shall be 'Jesus the Son of God.'"*

This wonderful child was born in a stable. The moment he was born, angels spoke to men, and said: "This day is born to you a Saviour who is Christ the Lord,"† and from the clouds angels were heard chanting the hymn,—"Glory be to God in the highest, and peace on earth to men of good will."‡ A new star at that time appeared in the heavens, and the God-child was adored by shepherds and kings.

According to the custom of the Jewish people, the babe was brought to the temple, and an old priest receiving it in his arms, in rapture exclaims: "Now dismiss thy servant, O Lord, in peace; because my eyes have seen thy salvation which thou hast prepared before the face of all people; a light to the revelation of the Gentiles, and the glory of thy people, Israel." §

At the age of twelve years he re-appears in the Temple of Jerusalem, "astonishing the Doctors by the wisdom of his questions and answers." ‖

Twenty years more elapse; the child becomes a man: while the waters of Jordan are poured upon his head, a spirit in the form of a dove descends upon him; the heavens are opened and a voice is heard saying: "This is my beloved Son." ¶

The Baptist, a man of austere and holy life, pointing to him, says: "Behold the Lamb of God, behold

* Luke i.   † Luke ii.   ‡ Luke ii.
§ Luke ii.   ‖ Matt. iii.   ¶ John i.

m who taketh away 'the sins of the world!" *
John, his beloved disciple, gives the same testi-
ony. "The Word," hɔ says, "was made flesh and
welt among us, and we saw his glory as it were of the
nly begotten Son of the Father, full of grace and
ruth." †

Peter, enlightened from on high, makes the same
onfession, and says: "Thou art Christ, the Son of the
iving God." ‡

The doubts of Thomas, on beholding him, are all
lispelled, and he exclaims unhesitatingly: "My Lord,
and my God!" §

Paul tells us that in him dwelt the fulness of the
Godhead corporally; that he was the brightness of
God's glory, and the figure of his substance.

This man has the unheard-of boldness to stand up
before the whole world and say of himself, "I came
forth from the Father, and am come into the world,
again I leave the world, and I go to the Father;" "All
things whatsoever the Father hath are mine." ǁ

Increasing in boldness, he fears not to tell us that:
"He that seeth me seeth my Father also;"† and adds,
"I and the Father are one." ¶

Finally, and to leave no room for doubt, when the
high-priest put the question directly to him, "Art thou
Christ the Son of the blessed God?" ** he falters not,
but unhesitatingly and emphatically replies, "I am." ††

To confirm his assertions he works wonders; he
multiplies bread, cures the sick, raises the dead, calms
tempests, walks upon water, and crowns all by saying to
his disciples, "He that believeth in me, the works that I
do he also shall do, and greater than these shall he do."‡‡

* John i.   † John i.   ‡ Matt. xvi.   § John xx.   ǁ John xvi.
¶ John xiv.   ** John x.   †† Mark xiv.   ‡‡ John xiv.

He is condemned and executed because of his daring to proclaim himself God. At the moment when he expires all nature is in mourning. · The sun becomes dark, the earth trembles, the rocks are split, graves deliver up their dead, and the veil of the temple is rent. Unable longer to resist the universal testimony and the voice of nature, the Roman officer present at his execution cries out to the world, "Indeed this was the Son of God."*

He is dead and is placed in a tomb, a rock is rolled before its entrance, it is sealed, and a guard of Roman soldiers keep watch. All now is still, his disciples are cast down and discouraged, his work is ended. Not so! It is but now to commence.

The third day he rises from the grave with a body all resplendant with glory; he enters the room where his disheartened disciples are assembled, while the doors are closed; he encourages them, eats and drinks with them, commands them to preach the Gospel to all creatures, promises them the Holy Ghost, and in the presence of hundreds, he ascends into heaven and disappears in the clouds.

On the day appointed, the Holy Ghost descends, with a noise like a rushing wind and in the shape of fiery tongues, upon the apostles. They who had been so timid to truth, now publish his gospel, in spite of menace and opposition, to all the world. They speak in different tongues, work miracles, and men of all nations believe in the name of Jesus and are baptized.

These timid and illiterate men, now bold as lions, and confounding the most learned scribes, preach the gospel, and in a short time, spread it among the Greeks

---

* Matt. xxvii.

and Romans. They seal their testimony to the divinity of their Master with their blood.

Three centuries of persecution pass away. Millions of men, women, and even children shed their blood like water, as witnesses of their faith in the Godhead of this man of Nazareth, and as a mark of their love for him. The religion of the Nazarene becomes the religion of the Empire.

Conflicts, progress and triumph, from the day when it was said "Hail Virgin" to the present, attest the divinity of the founder of Christianity, and thus is fulfilled the prophecy, in which he is foretold to be "The Father of the world to come."

> "In Him thy God, O Plato, dwelt on earth,
>   An open Presence, clear of earthly ill ;
> The Life which drew from him its heavenly birth,
>   In all who seek renews his perfect Will."

> "But 'mid thy countless forms of being,
>   One shines supreme o'er all beside,
> And man, in all thy wisdom seeing,
>   In Him reveres a sinless guide.

> "In Him alone, no longer shrouded
>   By mist that dims all meaner things,
> Thou dwell'st, O God! unveil'd, unclouded,
>   And fearless peace thy presence brings."

COMPOSITION.

Write the following sentences in two ways : Copy the 17th paragraph.

(a) He that believeth in me, the works that I do, he also shall do, and greater than these shall he do.

(b) They who had been so timid to truth, now publish his gospel, in spite of menace and opposition, to all the world.

(c) When the high-priest put the question directly to him "Art thou Christ the Son of the blessed God?" he falters not, but unhesitatingly and emphatically replies, "I am."

Commit the following to memory:

> Jesus is God! Alas! they say
> On earth the numbers grow
> Who his divinity blaspheme
> To their unfailing woe.
> And yet what is the single end
> Of this life's mortal span,
> Except to glorify the God
> Who for our sake, was man?

familiarity	rapture	assertions
accessible	enlightened	menace
beatitude	dispelled	illiterate
universal	unhesitatingly	Nazarene
convictions	corporally	reveres
conscience	emphatically	shrouded

VENI CREATOR.

John Dryden (1631–1700) occupies an important place in English literature, both by the number and general excellence of his productions, as well as by his influence upon poetic taste. His dramatic works are exceedingly numerous, but at this day, of comparatively small literary value. They are disgraced by indecency and immorality. His controversial poems, "Religio Laici," and the "Hind and Panther," the latter written upon his conversion to Catholicity, are the finest examples of argument in verse. The translations of Virgil's Æneid and the Satires of Juvenal and Persius are standard classics in our language. His lyric productions though few, are excellent, the Ode on St. Cecilia's Day being considered the finest in the English language. Dryden's prose works are chiefly critical essays prefixed to his poetical works. In prose as in verse he showed himself a great master of English, and his style, vigorous, idiomatic and harmonious, did much to improve the diction of the language.

CREATOR Spirit, by whose aid,
     The world's foundations first were laid.
Come visit every pious mind;
Come pour thy joys on human kind;

VENI CREATOR.

From sin and sorrow set us free,
And make thy temples worthy thee.

O source of uncreated light,
The Father's promised Paraclete!
Thrice holy fount, thrice holy fire,
Our hearts with heavenly love inspire:
Come, and thy sacred unction bring,
To sanctify us while we sing.

Plenteous of grace, descend from high,
Rich in thy seven-fold energy!
Thou strength of his Almighty hand,
Whose power does heaven and earth command,
Proceeding Spirit, our defence,
Who dost the gift of tongues dispense,
And crown'st thy gift with eloquence!

Refine and purge our earthly parts,
But, oh! inflame and fire our hearts:
Our frailties help, our voice control —
Submit the senses to the soul:
And when rebellious they are grown,
Then lay thy hand, and hold them down.

Chase from our minds th' infernal foe,
And peace, the fruit of love, bestow:
And, lest our feet should step astray,
Protect and guide us in the way.

Make us eternal truths receive,
And practise all that we believe:
Give us thyself, that we may see
The Father and the Son by thee.

Immortal honor, endless fame,
Attend th' Almighty Father's name:
The Saviour Son be glorified,

Who for lost man's redemption died:
And equal adoration be,
Eternal Paraclete, to thee!

Questions :—Who is the "Creator Spirit' here understood? Who are "human kind?" From what are we to be made free? What means, besides prayer, will then make us free? What are the "temples" meant in the last line of first stanza? What is a Paraclete? Whence is a heavenly love to reach us? What can grace do for us "while we sing?" What is the "gift of tongues?" Who received this gift at Pentecost? In what two ways may this gift have been bestowed? Which would have been the more convenient? Explain why. What is eloquence? What is meant by our "earthly parts?" What are our frailties? Name our senses? Who is "th' infernal foe?" Why must the Holy Spirit "protect and guide us in the way?" What spirit does this for good children? What is asked for the "Eternal Father's name?" Why do we ask that the "Saviour Son be glorified?" How do we pray that the Eterna' Paraclete may be adored?

| kind | plenteous | proceeding | frailties |
| Paraclete | energy | eloquence | fame |

———o———

GROWTH AND REPAIR OF THE BODY.

THE human body is often compared to a house. When a man builds a house, he collects a great variety of materials. He gets timber of different shapes, as beams and boards. He buys bricks of the brickmaker. He gets lime from one place, sand from another, and hair from another, and mixes them to make the mortar to hold the bricks together.

He procures stone for the foundation and the steps, and various other purposes. He provides glass for the windows, paper for the walls, and paints of various colors. Besides these, many other things must be collected to complete the building. And then, how many things are required to furnish the house after it is built!

Now the house that your spirit lives in, the body, with all its variety of furniture, is made of only one material, the blood. And it is also kept in repair with the same material. You can see how wonderful this is if you observe how many different things there are in the frame-work of the body. Think a moment about this. Look at the outside of the body. There we see the skin, the hair, and the nails. How different these are from one another! But they are all made out of the same material, the blood. You would think it very wonderful if a man could make bricks, and boards, and nails out of the same thing. If a man should say that he could do it, you would set him down as a crazy person. But bricks, and boards, and nails are not so much unlike one another as your hair, skin, and finger-nails are. And how entirely different these are from the blood out of which they were made!

Look now at the eye. How different it is from the parts of which I have been speaking! But it is made out of the same blood with them. Look at the various parts of this beautiful organ. See the firm, white eye-ball. Then see in front what a clear, thin, round window is set into this ball, like a crystal in the face of a watch. Look in at this window, and see the delicate iris, which has so many different colors in different persons. Then there are parts which you cannot see. There are three different kinds of fluids inside of the eye. There is a nerve which spreads out its little, fine fibres all over the back part of the eye inside. There are muscles, also, that move the eye about so quickly.

Then, too, there is the tear-factory, or gland, that keeps the eye moist. Is it not wonderful that all these parts, so different from one another—the eyeball, the window, the iris, the three fluids, the nerves, the muscles, the tear-gland and its tears — should be made out of the same thing, and that, too, a thing which is not like any of them?

Look now at the mouth. Would you suppose that those hard teeth are made out of the same material with the clear window in the eye, and the delicate iris, and the soft tears? It is even so. See how different the gums are from the teeth. It seems almost impossible that they are both made out of the blood.

Then, inside of the body, out of sight, are a great many different structures, such as the bones, the red muscles, the white, silk-like, shining tendons, the glands, the firm liver, the spongy lungs, the stomach, and all the various fluids, as the saliva, the tears, the bile — all are made from the blood.

Even the very vessels that carry the blood, and the heart that pumps it into them, are made out of the blood itself! This is no less wonderful than it would be to have the walls of a canal or an aqueduct made out of the water that runs through it.

But you will want to know how the blood is converted into so many different substances, and who the workmen are that do it. It is not the arteries. They only serve to carry the material everywhere. They are the common carriers of the body. Through these the heart, as it pumps away, seventy times a minute, sends the blood to every part of the system. And in every part there are multitudes of workmen that take this material, thus brought to their very doors, and use it to manufacture various things. Some are bone-makers, some nerve-makers, some muscle-makers, some makers of teeth, some eye-manufacturers, and so on.

All the workmen work in separate companies, and very seldom interfere with one another, though they may be in the same neighborhood. The bone-makers, for instance, that make the socket of the eye never get mixed up with the eye-manufacturers.

Once in a while, however, the bone-makers get to work in the wrong place, or rather, some workmen that ought to make something else go to making bone. But this does not often happen. If it does happen, it always produces deformity, and sometimes destroys life.

The workmen all work so well together that it would seem as if they must understand one another, and agree together just as men do about the way of doing their work. But we know that they do not understand any-thing; and how it is that they work together so well is a mystery to us. A mystery that teaches us the great power of God. But I have not told you who, or what, these little workmen are that are so busy in using the blood for the growth and the repair of our frame.

All that we know of them is, that they are very small vessels between the very smallest of the arteries and the very smallest of the veins. The blood comes to them in the arteries, and they use what they want of it, and then it passes into the veins, by which it is returned to the heart.

What can be more wonderful than the formation, the growth, and repair of the human body! How strange that the simple red fluid which we call blood should be formed from such a variety of substances as we eat, and that out of it should be made such a variety of organs and structures as compose the human body! Who can contemplate the mechanism of his own body, and not admire and adore the wisdom of the Creator?

Questions :—To what is the human body often compared? Mention some of the materials necessary to build a house. How is mortar made? What is the use of hair in mortar? What is the house the *soul* lives in? Of what is it made, and how is it kept in repair? Mention some things on the *outside* of the body. Mention some of the parts of the eye. What are nerves? What are tendons? What are muscles? What is a gland? What is the use of the eye-glands? Are tears of any use to the eye? Show how. What organ sends the blood to every part of the body? What are arteries? What are veins? Is it more dangerous to cut an artery than a vein? Why? If an artery has been cut, how may the bleeding be stopped? What should we admire in the mechanism of our bodies?

MEMORIZE :—"It must be allowed that matter alone could no more have fashioned the human body for so many admirable purposes, than a beautiful discourse could be composed by a writer destitute of eloquence and skill."

eyeball	muscles	saliva
crystal	fibres	bile
iris	gland	structures
fluids	tendons	mechanism

DELAYS.

Robert Southwell, S. J., born 1560 ; martyred during the persecutions of Elizabeth's reign, in 1595. He was descended from an ancient family in Norfolk, educated on the Continent and received into the Jesuit Order at Rome. He was arrested, while on the English mission, in 1592, and thrown into prison, where he remained three years, during which term he was put on the rack on ten occasions. On the 21st of February, 1595, he was hanged, drawn and quartered at Tyburn. The bigotry which has pervaded English literature and history since the Reformation has prevented the recognition of Southwell's merits. And yet he is far ahead of his age in the vigor and energy of his diction, and is a better example of the progress of the English tongue of that period, towards its modern strength and fluency, than many quoted in the Rhetorics; while as regards the spirit of his writings, their noble moral elevation, beauty and pathos stand out in bright relief from the licentious literature of the Elizabethan era.

SHUN delays, they breed remorse,
   Take thy time, while time is lent thee ;

Creeping snails have weakest force—
Fly their faults, lest thou repent thee.
Good is best when soonest wrought,
Ling'ring labors come to naught.

Hoist thy sail while gale doth last,
Tide and wind stay no man's pleasure;
Seek not time, when time is past;
Sober speed is wisdom's leisure.
After-wits are dearly bought,
Let the fore-wit guide thy thought.

Time wears all his locks before,
Take then hold upon his forehead:
When he flies he turns no more,
And behind his scalp is naked.
Works adjourned have many stays,
Long demurs bring new delays.

Seek thy salve while young the wound,
Older sores ask deeper lancing;
After cures are seldom found,
Often sought, scarce ever chancing. .
In the rising, stifle ill,
Lest it grow against thy will.

Drops do pierce the stubborn flint,
Not by force, but often falling;
Custom kills with feeble dint,
More by use than strength prevailing.
Single sands have little weight,
Many make a drowning freight.

QUESTIONS AND COMPOSITION.

Why must delays be shunned? What is remorse? What are
"ling'ring labors?" Name some "ling'ring labors." When is good
"best?" Explain "lest thou repent thee." What dangers occur in
"hoisting sail?" Explain "sober speed is wisdom's leisure." What

are "after-wits?" Why must we seize time by the forehead? What are demurs? What is a "young wound?" Explain "ask deeper lancing." Put four substitutes for the word "ask." Copy last stanza and commit to memory. Write following lines in three ways:

> "Single sands have little weight,
> Many make a drowning freight."

| breed. | wits. | scalp. | salve. | flint. |
| Lingering | locks. | demurs | stifle. | dint. |

THE EAGLE.

THIS magnificent bird is found over a large portion of the world — in America, and in various parts of Europe, Asia, Africa. It is a splendid bird in point of size, for a full-grown female measures about three feet six inches in length, and the expanse of her wings is about nine feet. The male, less by about six inches.

The nest of the eagle is almost always made upon some elevated spot, generally upon a ledge of a rock, and is constructed of sticks, which are thrown apparently at random, and rudely arranged for the purpose of containing the eggs and the young. A neighboring ledge its generally reserved for a larder, where the parent eagles store up the food, which they bring from the plains below. The contents of this larder consist of hares, partridges and game of all kinds, lambs, rabbits, young pigs, fish, and other similar articles of food.

In hunting for their prey, the eagle and his mate mutually assist each other. As the rabbits and hares are generally under cover during the day, the eagle is forced to drive them from their place of concealment, and manages the matter in a very clever manner. One of the eagles conceals itself near the cover which is to be beaten, and its companion then dashes among the bushes, screaming and making such a disturbance that the terrified inmates rush out in hopes of escape, and are immediately pounced upon by the watchful confederate.

The prey is at once taken to the nest, and distributed to the young, if there should be any eaglets in the lofty cradle. Eagles always feed their young by tearing the prey in pieces, and giving it to them in morsels.

When in pursuit of its prey, it is a most daring bird, having been seen to carry off a hare from before the noses of the hounds. It is a keen fisher, catching and securing salmon and various sea-fish with singular skill. Sometimes it has met with more than its match, and has seized upon a fish that was too heavy for its powers, thus falling a victim to its sporting propensities. Several instances are known where eagles have been drowned by pouncing upon large pike, which carried their assailants under water.

It is a fierce fighter when wounded or attacked. An eagle was at one time captured in County Meath, in Ireland, by a gamekeeper, who, surprising the bird sleeping after a surfeit on a dead sheep, conceived the idea of taking him alive; and for that purpose approached the bird noiselessly, and clasped him in his arms. The eagle recovering, and unable to use his wings, clutched with his talons, one of which entered the man's chest, the hind claw meeting the others underneath the flesh. The man, unable to disengage the claw, strangled the bird; but the talons were yet too firmly clutched to open. Taking out his knife, he severed the leg from the body, and walked with the penetrating member to the village dispensary to have it removed.

A golden eagle had been captured in Scotland, and, being very tame, always accompanied the family to which it belonged in all their journeys. For some time it lived in the south-west of England, where it passed its existence fastened to a post by a tolerably long chain that allowed it a reasonable freedom of motion. Like other tame eagles, it would persist in killing cats, if they came within reach, although its ordinary food was fowl, rabbits, and other similar articles of diet. On one occasion a sickly, pining chicken, which seemed in a very bad state of health, was given to the eagle. The royal bird, however, refused to eat it; but seemed to be struck with pity at its miserable state, and took it under his protection. He even made it sit under his wing, which he extended as a shield; and once when a man endeavored to take it away, the eagle attacked him fiercely, injuring his leg severely, and drove him fairly off his premises.

The eagle is supposed to be a long-lived bird, and is thought to live a hundred years when at liberty and unrestrained in its native haunts. Even in captivity it has been known to attain a good old age, one of these birds, which lived at Vienna, being over one hundred years old when it died.

COMPOSITION.

(a) The plain below ; (b) this larder consists ; (c) the eagle and his mate mutually assist each other ; (d) are generally under cover ; (e) near the cover which is to be beaten; (f) a splendid bird in point of size.

magnificent	disturbance	existence
various	propensities	reasonable
measures	confederate	diet
elevated	conceived	premises
constructed	dispensary	unrestrained

THE GEYSERS.

A FTER fifteen hours of weary jogging, we found ourselves in the presence of the steaming geysers.
Naturally enough, our first impulse on dismounting was
to scamper off at once to the Great Geyser. As it lay at
the furthest end of the congeries of hot-springs, in order
to reach it we had to run the gauntlet of all the pools
of boiling water and scalding quagmires of soft clay that
intervened. A smooth, silicious basin, seventy-two feet
in diameter and four feet deep, with a hole at the bottom,
as in a washing-basin on board a steamer, stood before us
brimful of water just upon the simmer; while up into the
air, above our heads, rose a great column of vapor. The
ground about the brim was composed of layers of
incrusted silica, like the outside of an oyster, sloping
gently down on all sides from the edge of the basin.

It was one o'clock in the morning when we suddenly
heard a tremendous noise, and experienced a sensation
as if beneath our very feet a quantity of subterranean
cannon were going off. The whole earth shook, and the
guide, starting to his feet, flew off, full speed, toward the
great basin. By the time we reached its brim, however,
the noise had ceased, and all we could see was a slight
movement in the centre, as if an angel had passed by
and troubled the water.

As our principal object in coming so far was to see an
eruption of the Great Geyser, it was of course necessary
we should wait his pleasure; in fact, our movements
entirely depended upon his. For the next two or three
days, therefore, like pilgrims round some ancient shrine,
we patiently kept watch; but he scarcely deigned to
vouchsafe us the slighest manifestation of his latent
energies. Two or three times the cannonading we had

heard immediately after our arrival recommenced; and once an eruption to the height of ten feet occurred; but so brief was its duration, that by the time we were on the spot, although the tent was not eighty yards distant, all was over. As, after every effort of the fountain, the water in the basin mysteriously ebbs back into the funnel, this performance, though unsatisfactory in itself, gave us an opportunity of approaching the mouth of the pipe, and looking down into its scalded gullet. In an hour afterwards, the basin was brimful as ever.

We had been keeping watch for three days over the geyser, in languid expectation of the eruption which was to set us free, when, on the morning of the fourth day, a cry from the guides made us start to our feet, and with one common impulse rush to the basin. The usual subterranean thunder had already commenced; a violent agitation was disturbing the centre of the pool. Suddenly a dome of water lifted itself up to the height of eight or ten feet, then burst and fell; immediately after which, a shining liquid column, or rather a sheaf of columns, wreathed in robes of vapor, sprang into the air, and in a succession of jerking leaps, each higher than the last, flung their silver crests against the sky. For a few minutes the fountain held its own; then, all at once, appeared to lose its ascending energy. The unstable waters faltered, drooped, fell, "like a broken purpose," back upon themselves, and were immediately sucked down into the recesses of their pipe.

The spectacle was certainly magnificent; but no description can give any idea of its most striking features. The enormous wealth of water, its vitality, its hidden power; the illimitable breadth of sun-lit vapor, rolling out in exhaustless profusion,—all combined to make one feel the stupendous energy of nature's slightest movement.

And yet I do not believe the exhibition was so fine as some that have been seen; from the first burst upwards, to the moment the last jet retreated into the pipe, was no more than a space of seven or eight minutes, and at no moment did the crown of the column reach higher than sixty or seventy feet above the surface of the basin. Now, early travellers talk of 300 feet, which must, of course, be fabulous; but many trustworthy persons, have judged the eruptions at 200 feet; while well-authenticated accounts, when the elevation of the jet has been actually measured, make it to have attained a height of upwards of 100 feet.

With regard to the internal machinery by which these water-works are set in motion, I will only say, that the most generally received theory seems to be that which supposes the existence of a chamber in the heated earth, almost, but not quite, filled with water, and communicating with the upper air by means of a pipe, whose lower orifice, instead of being in the roof, is at the side of the cavern, and near the surface of the subterranean pond. The water, kept by the surrounding furnaces at boiling-point, generates, of course, a continuous supply of steam, for which some vent must be obtained; as it cannot escape by the funnel, the lower mouth of which is under water, it squeezes itself up within the arching roof, until at last, compressed beyond all endurance, it strains against the rock, and pushing down the intervening waters, with its broad, strong back, forces them below the level of the funnel, and dispersing part, and driving part before it, rushes forth in triumph to the upper air. The fountains, therefore, that we see mounting to the sky during an eruption are nothing but the superincumbent mass of waters in the pipe, driven into confusion before the steam at the moment it obtains its liberation.

COMPOSITION.

Describe the ra██over the ground dotted with small, boiling wells. Also the appearance of the border of the largest geyser. Show how this resembled the outside of an oyster shell. The effects noticed when the██uption was about to occur. Mention the account in the New Testament to which reference is made. What was done to while away ██me till next eruption. Mention some games that may have been introduced (*in that country*). Describe the spectacle *same order* as the book, but in your own words.

squagmire	fabulous	sheaf
simmer.	theory	exhaustless
sensation	orifice	generates
subterranean	gauntlet	intervening
eruption	silicious	congeries
languid	silica	superincumbent

RING OUT, WILD BELLS.

Alfred Tennyson, born in 1809, present Poet Laureate of England. The remarkable purity of contemporary English poetry, as compared with that of former periods, is largely owing to the influence of his writings, which are singularly chaste and noble. He is unsurpassed in descriptive power and in felicity of expression. In his hands the rugged English tongue becomes an instrument of most delicate harmony, capable of expressing with the utmost nicety the finest shades of thought and sentiment. Like all great bards, he is most truly poet when most truly Catholic. This is notably the case in some of the "Idylls," and in portions of "In Memoriam," which are his greatest poems. It is therefore to be regretted that in one of his later efforts, "Queen Mary," he has allowed the shade of bigotry to dim the brightness of his muse.

RING out, wild bells, to the wild sky,
  The flying cloud, the frosty light;
  The year is dying in the night:
Ring out, wild bells, and let him die.

Ring out the old, ring in the new,
  Ring, happy bells, across the snow;

The year is going — let him go:
Ring out the false, ring in the true.

Ring out the grief that saps the mind,
　　For those that here we see no more;
　　Ring out the feud of rich and poor,
Ring in redress to all mankind.

Ring out a slowly dying cause,
　　And ancient forms of party strife;
　　Ring in the nobler modes of life,
With sweeter manners, purer laws.

Ring out the want, the care, the sin,
　　The faithless coldness of the times;
　　Ring out, ring out my mournful rhymes,
But ring the fuller minstrel in.

Ring out false pride in place and blood,
　　The civic slander and the spite;
　　Ring in the love of truth and right,
Ring in the common love of good.

Ring out old shapes of foul disease,
　　Ring out the narrowing lust of gold;
　　Ring out the thousand wars of old,
Ring in the thousand years of peace.

Ring in the valiant man and free,
　　The larger heart, the kindlier hand;
　　Ring out the darkness of the land,
Ring in the Christ that is to be.

Questions :--Who wrote this? What is meant by Poet Laureate?
What is the influence of Tennyson's writings on English poetry at the
present day? What kind of composition do you call this? What year
is dying? Explain first two lines of third stanza. Explain "The
faithless coldness of the times." "The narrowing lust of gold."

saps　　feud　　redress　　minstrel　　civic　　lust　　rhymes

BUTTERED ON BOTH SIDES.

ONE winter evening, a country store-keeper in the Green Mountain State was about closing his doors for the night, when, while standing in the snow outside, putting up his window shutters, he saw through the glass a worthless fellow within, take half-a-pound of fresh butter from the shelf, and hastily conceal it in his hat.

The act was no sooner seen than the revenge was hit upon, and a very few moments found the Green Mountain store-keeper, at once indulging his appetite for fun to the fullest extent, and paying off the thief with a sort of torture for which he might have gained a premium.

"Stay, Seth!" said the storekeeper, coming in, and closing the door after him, slapping his hands over his shoulders, and stamping the snow off his shoes.

Seth had his hand on the door, and his hat upon his head, and the roll of butter in his hat, anxious to make his exit as soon as possible.

"Seth, we'll have something warm," said the Green Mountain grocer, as he opened the stove door and stuffed in as many sticks as the space would admit. "Without it you'd freeze going home such a night as this."

Seth felt very uncertain; he had the butter, and was exceedingly anxious to be off, but the temptation of "something warm" sadly interfered with his resolution to go. This hesitation, however, was soon settled by the right owner of the butter taking Seth by the shoulders and planting him in a seat close to the stove, where he was in such a manner cornered in by barrels and boxes that, while the country grocer sat before him, there was no possibility of his getting out, and right in this very place, sure enough, the storekeeper sat down.

Seth already felt the butter settling down closer to his hair, and he declared he must go.

"Not till you have something warm, Seth: come I've got a story to tell you, Seth: sit down now;" and Seth was again pushed into his seat by his cunning tormentor.

"Oh! it's too hot here," said the petty thief, again attempting to rise.

"I say, Seth, sit down; I reckon now, on such a night as this, a little something warm wouldn't hurt a fellow; come, sit down."

"Sit down — don't be in such a plaguy hurry," repeated the grocer, pushing him back in his chair.

"But I've got the cows to fodder, and some wood to split, and I must be off," continued the persecuted pilferer.

"But you mustn't tear yourself away, Seth, in this manner. Sit down; let the cows take care of themselves, and keep yourself cool; you appear to be fidgety," said the roguish grocer, with a wicked leer.

The next thing was the production of two smoking glasses of hot rum toddy, the very sight of which in Seth's present situation would have made the hair erect upon his head, had it not been oiled and kept down by the butter.

"Seth, I'll give you a toast now, and you can *butter* it yourself," said the grocer, yet with an air of such consummate simplicity, that poor Seth still believed himself unsuspected. "Seth, here's — here's Christmas goose, well roasted and basted, eh? I tell you, Seth, it's the greatest eating in creation. And, Seth, don't you use hog's fat or common cooking butter to baste a goose with. Come, take your butter — I mean, Seth, take your toddy."

Poor Seth now began to *smoke* as well as to *melt*, and his mouth was as hermetically sealed up as though he had been born dumb. Streak after streak of the butter came pouring from under his hat, and his handkerchief was already soaked with the greasy overflow. Talking away as if nothing was the matter, the grocer kept stuffing the wood into the stove, while poor Seth sat bolt upright, with his back against the counter, and his knees almost touching the red-hot furnace before him.

"Very cold night this," said the grocer; "why Seth, you seem to perspire as if you were warm! Why don't you take your hat off? Here, let me put your hat away."

"No!" exclaimed poor Seth at last, with a spasmodic effort to get his tongue loose, and clapping both hands upon his hat, "No!—I must go—let me out—I ain't well—let me go!" A greasy cataract was now pouring down the poor fellow's face and neck, and soaking into his clothes, and trickling down his body into his very boots, so that he was literally in a perfect bath of oil.

"Well, good night, Seth," said the humorous Vermonter, "if you *will* go;" adding, as Seth got out into the road, "Neighbor, I reckon the fun I've had out of you is worth ten cents, so I shall not charge you for that half-pound of butter."

COMPOSITION.

Describe the grocer's store, naming as many articles as possible, with the position of each. Give a particular account of the stove and its location. Tell why stoves give so much heat; and why is the heat soon lost.

•

Questions: — Which is the Green Mountain State? Why so called?

anxious	greasy	spasmodic
lounging	consummate	bolt
facetious	plaguy	hermetically
detected	fidgety	literally
exit	leer	humorous

ERIN'S FLAG.

Rev. Abram J. Ryan unites the characters of priest, poet and orator. The poet's spirit pervades and beautifies his eloquent sermons ; the orator's fire flashes through his poems, and religion in the character of the priest gives dignity and inspiration to both. His poems need not be read twice to convince one that they are the true offspring of the muse. Patriotism, sufferings of the "Lost Cause," to which he was devotedly attached ; and the sorrows, hopes and resignation of the christian life are the chief subjects of his muse. There is a tinge of romantic sadness in all his reflective verses. Life is a real "vale of tears," and the Christian's longing for heaven is that of a real exile after a once-enjoyed home.

UNROLL Erin's flag ! fling its folds to the breeze,
   Let it float o'er the land, let it flash o'er the seas,
Lift it out of the dust, let it wave as of yore,
When its chiefs with their clans stood around it and swore
That never ! no ! never, while God gave them life,
And they had an arm and a sword for the strife,
   That never ! no ! never, that banner should yield
   As long as the heart of a Celt was its shield ;
   While the hand of a Celt had a weapon to wield,
   And his last drop of blood was unshed on the field.

Lift it up ! wave it high ! 'tis as bright as of old !
Not a stain on its green, nor a blot on its gold
Though the woes and the wrongs of three hundred long years
Have drenched Erin's Sunburst with blood and with tears !
Though the clouds of oppression enshroud it in gloom,
And around it the thunders of tyranny boom,
   Look aloft ! look aloft ! lo ! the cloud's drifting by,
   There's a gleam through the gloom, there's a light in the sky,
   'Tis the Sunburst resplendent — far, flashing on high,
   Erin's dark night is waning ; her day-dawn is nigh.

Lift it up ! lift it up ! the old banner of green !
The blood of its sons has but brightened its sheen ;
What ! though the tyrant has trampled it down,

2

Are its folds not emblazoned with deeds of renown?
What! though for ages it droops in the dust,
Shall it droop thus forever? No! no! God is just!
　Take it up! take it up! from the tyrant's foul tread,
　Let him tear the Green Flag, we will snatch its last shred,
　And beneath it we'll bleed as our forefathers bled.
　And we'll vow by the dust in the graves of our dead,

And we'll swear by the blood which the Briton has shed,
And we'll vow by the wrecks which through Erin he spread,
And we'll swear by the thousands who, famished, unfed,
Died down in the ditches — wild — howling for bread,
And we'll vow by our heroes whose spirits have fled,
And we'll swear by the bones in each coffinless bed,
That we'll battle the Briton through danger and dread!
　That we'll cling to the cause which we glory to wed,
　Till the gleam of our steel and the shock of our lead
　Shall prove to our foe that we meant what we said—
　That we'll lift up the Green, and we'll tear down the Red!

Lift up the Green Flag! oh! it wants to go home;
Full long has its lot been to wander and roam;
It has followed the fate of its sons o'er the world,
But its folds, like their hopes, are not faded nor furled.
Like a weary-winged bird, to the East and the West
It has flitted and fled; but it never shall rest,
　Till, pluming its pinions, it sweeps o'er the main,
　And speeds to the shores of its old home again,
　When its fetterless folds o'er each mountain and plain
　Shall wave with a glory that never shall wane.

Take it up! take it up! bear it back from afar,
That Banner must blaze 'mid the lightnings of war;
Lay your hands on its folds, lift your gaze to the sky,
And swear that you'll bear it triumphant or die,
And shout to the clans scattered over the earth,
To join in the march to the land of their birth;

And wherever the Exiles, 'neath heaven's broad dome,
Have been fated to suffer, to sorrow and roam,
They'll bound on the sea, and away o'er the foam
They'll sail to the music of "Home, Sweet Home!"

folds	tyranny	weary-winged
yore	waning	pluming
Celt	shred	pinions
wield	wrecks	sword
enshroud	emblazoned	resplendent

Questions:—What names are used instead of Erin? What are clans? Name some Irish clans. Who are the Celts? When did they thus swear around their flag? Give another name for "Erin's Sunburst." What is the meaning of "a gleam through the gloom"? What is a banner's sheen? Mention some deeds of renown that emblazon Erin's banner. What is the meaning of "tyrant's foul tread"? What is a shred? When is a banner in shreds? What is the period called in which people die in "ditches — wild — howling for bread"? How does the bird plume its pinions? What exiles are meant in the last stanza? Where are these exiles found?

———o———

GEORGE STEPHENSON.

GEORGE Stephenson and James Watt are the two men to whom we owe much of the spread and comfort of railway travelling. James Watt, a Scotchman, devoted himself to the perfection of the steam-engine; and George Stephenson, the son of a poor engine-tender, succeeded in adapting the steam-engine for locomotion. George was born in 1781, at a mining village called Wylam, on the banks of the Tyne, about eight miles from Newcastle. When George was about eight years old his father removed to another coal mine at Dewley Burn, where George was sent to herd cows, for which he was paid five cents a day. And here we see him, a strong, bare-legged herd-boy, driving his cows or chasing butterflies, or amusing himself by making water-mills, ·or even going so far as to model small steam-engines in clay.

In these pursuits we have a glimpse of his genius for mechanics. Often we see that boys take a bent towards what first excites their fancy. Brought up among coal-pits and pumps, and wheels and engines, it was not surprising that his mind should be full of them. He pried into every mechanical contrivance that he came near, and acquired a knack of making things with no other help than an old knife. Leaving farm work, he got employment at Dewley Burn to drive a horse, by which change he had another rise of five cents a day, his wages being now sixty cents a week.

In a short time he went to act as an assistant-fireman to his father at Dewley. While at this occupation he developed a steady character — that was a great point gained. The world is always looking about for steady men, and sometimes it is not easy to get hold of them. George was rigorously sober, and was never so happy as when he was at work; though he took pleasure also, after work-hours, in wrestling, throwing the stone, and other feats of muscular skill. A general favorite for his good-nature and skill at games, George likewise gave satisfaction to his employers, and, being a clever, handy young man, was promoted to the situation of engineman at Newburn. It was an important post, and not without trouble. If the pumps went wrong, he had to go down into the pit, and do his best to set them right by plugging — that is, stuffing any hole or crevice to make them draw; and, if the defect was beyond his power to mend, his duty was to report to the chief engineer.

When the engine was going in excellent trim, and nothing was wrong with the pumps, there was little to do, and there was often time to spare. By way of occupying these idle minutes and hours, George began to model miniature steam-engines in clay, in which he had already some experience. It was a mere amusement, but it helped to fix shapes and proportions in his memory. While so engaged, he was told of engines of a form and character he had never seen. They were not within reach, but were described in books. If he read these, he would learn all about them. But George, though now eighteen years of age, was still ignorant of the alphabet. He clearly saw that unless he learned to read he must certainly stick where he was. So, having made up his mind that he would go to school, cost what it might, he found out a teacher who agreed to give him lessons in the evening, for which Stephenson was to pay him seven cents a week, and by the time he was nineteen he was able to write his name. As there was not much time for arithmetical study during his short school-hours, George got sums set on his slate, which next day he worked out while attending to his engine. And this was all the school education he ever got.

In 1810 an opportunity occurred for George Stephenson to signalize himself. A badly-constructed steam-engine at Killingworth High Pit could not do its work; one engineer after another tried to set it to rights, but all failed; and at last in despair they were glad to let "Georgie" try his hand, though, even with his reputation for cleverness, they did not expect him to succeed. To their mortification and astonishment, he was perfectly successful. He took the engine to pieces, re-arranged it skilfully, and set it to work in the most effectual manner. Besides receiving a present of $50 for this useful service, he was placed on the footing of a regular engineer, and was afterwards consulted in cases when the pumps were not working well.

Slowly, inch by inch, he fought his way against poverty and every other discouragement, until, in 1815, the invention of a safety-lamp brought his name before the public.

It was at Killingworth that Stephenson constructed his first locomotive. He was next employed to make a railway between Liverpool and Manchester. That he proposed to work the line with an engine which was to go at the rate of twelve miles an hour was a fact sufficient in itself, people thought, to show how wild and absurd the scheme was. "Twelve miles an hour!" said the *Quarterly Review* — "as well trust one's-self to be fired off on a Congreve rocket!" When the line was completed, the directors offered a prize of $2,500 for the best locomotive that could be brought forward to compete in running on a certain day. Stephenson won the prize, and his engine was not only remarkable for its speed, but also for the contrivances by which the speed was attained. This was in the year 1829.

And now the tide of fortune, for which Stephenson had worked so hard and waited so long, flowed in abundantly. In 1836, two hundred and fourteen miles of railway, involving a capital of twenty-five millions, were put under his direction; but, in the midst of his immense labors, his heart remained as youthful as ever. In spring he would snatch a day for bird-nesting or gardening, or in autumn to go nutting; and we find him even at this time writing a touching account to his son of a pair of robins. In the autumn of 1845 he visited Spain and Belgium to plan new railways, and on his way home he caught a severe cold, from which he never thoroughly recovered. He died at his country-seat of Tapton, in 1848, leaving in his life a noble instance of honest purpose and steady determination.

COMPOSITION.

Write a short sketch of Stephenson's life from this

SUMMARY:

James Watt and George Stephenson are the two great improvers of the steam-engine. George Stephenson was born near Newcastle in 1781. His first employment was herding cows at five cents a day. He was always very fond of examining mechanical contrivances, and of making models of them. At the age of thirteen he rose to be assistant-fireman to his father, with the wages of twenty-five cents a day. He was always perfectly steady and rigorously sober. He is promoted to be engineman at Newburn. In his spare time he models miniature steam-engines in clay. He learns to read, and to work sums in arithmetic at the age of eighteen. In 1810 he reconstructs an engine which all other engineers had failed to repair. In 1815 he invents a safety-'amp. In 1821 he constructs his first locomotive. In 1829 he wins a prize of $2,500 for the best locomotive. He is manager of 214 miles of railway in 1836. He dies in 1848.

pursuits	muscular	effectual
mechanical	trim	contrivances
contrivance	miniature	attained
acquired	described	involving
knack	opportunity	thoroughly
rigorously	signalize	purpose

———o———

"MY FATHER'S GROWING OLD."

MY father's growing old; his eye
　Looks dimly on the page;
The locks that round his forehead lie
　Are silver'd o'er by age;
My heart has learn'd too well the tale

Which other lips have told,
His years and strength begin to fail —
"My father's growing old."

They tell me, in my youthful years
    He led me by his side,
And strove to calm my childish fears,
    My erring steps to guide.
But years, with all their scenes of change,
    Above us both have roll'd,
I now must guide *his* faltering steps —
    "My father's growing old."

When sunset's rosy glow departs,
    With voices full of mirth,
Our household band with joyous hearts
    Will gather round the hearth.
They look upon his trembling form,
    His pallid face behold,
And turn away with chasten'd tones —
    "My father's growing old."

And when each tuneful voice we raise,
    In songs of "long ago,"
His voice which mingles in our lays
    Is tremulous and low.
It used to seem a clarion's tone,
    So musical and bold,
But weaker, fainter has it grown —
    "My father's growing old."

The same fond smile he used to wear
    Still wreathes his pale lips now,
But Time with lines of age and care
    Has traced his placid brow.
But yet amid the lapse of years
    His *heart* has not grown cold,

Though voice and footsteps plainly tell —
"My father's growing old."

My father! thou did'st strive to share
   My joys and calm my fears,
And now thy child, with grateful care,
   In thy declining years
Shall smooth thy path, and brighter scenes
   By faith and hope unfold;
And love thee with a holier love
   Since thou art "growing old."

Questions:— What is the meaning of: — "his eye looks dimly on the page"? "His locks are silvered o'er by age"? Give the last four lines of first stanza, in your own words. What did father do for me in my youth? What must I do now? What is "sunset's rosy glow"? When does it depart? Whither do the family then retire? What are "chasten'd tones"? What is said in this whisper? What are "songs of long ago"? "Lays"? "Clarion tones"? What is the meaning of "wreathes his pale lips"? How do father's voice and footsteps tell he's "growing old"? Give last stanza in your own words.

locks   glow   pallid   tremulous   wreathes
erring   hearth   chasten'd   fainter   declining

THE SHEPHERD AND THE PRINCE.

NOT far from Germany lies Switzerland, a small country, but well known in the history of nations. High are the hills there, and they seem to wish to conceal the eternal spring of Italy from the rest of Europe. But, notwithstanding this threatening look, and in spite of the cover of snow which, year after year, clothes them in a wintry dress, there are delightful valleys in their bosom. In one of these hidden valleys there stood, in olden times, an ancient castle on rocky ground, near a lake.

A shepherd-boy, who belonged to the neighboring district, had chosen the declivity that ran opposite the castle down to the lake, as a pasture-ground for his flock. Day after day, during the fine season, he sat on a rock that projected over the water, and made baskets, mats, and cages; often he played sweet airs upon his flute, while his lambs enjoyed the juicy herbs of the Alps. When the sounds of the shepherd's flute resounded so sweetly along the lonely shore, and the silence carried them to the opposite bank, a little window in the old castle was opened every day, and a pale but pleasant face looked out towards the shepherd-boy until twilight came, and the little musician drove his flock homeward. "Who can that poor boy be?" thought the good young shepherd; "why can they have locked him into that ugly castle, for he must be locked in, or he would come out to see me in the open air?"

With these thoughts in his mind, he wandered along the shore towards the castle, and he nodded to the boy with the black curls at the window. But beautiful as the songs were, kind words though he gave, and though he beckoned with all his heart, everything was in vain. The inhabitant of the castle shook his head sadly, and shrugged his shoulders, but he would not come.

"I must see what it is," cried Joseph — that was the shepherd's name — and he wandered on to the castle. He whistled to his faithful dog, and desired him to guard the sheep carefully until his return. He wagged his tail obediently, for he understood every word of his master's, and collected the flock to drive them back to their grazing place.

Joseph soon reached the gate of the castle; but what was his astonishment when he found armed men, with long beards and threatening swords, holding watch there.

ferrified, he was going to creep away; but it was too late. One of the soldiers had noticed him, and laid hold of him. They all began to question him — who he was? whence he came? what he wanted here? The boy was half-dead with terror, but as a good conscience never allows people to be disgraced, he soon recovered himself, and he told them openly what had brought him there.

"How?" cried the one who had caught him—"how? You wished to steal to the prisoner? You shall pay dearly for that; we will put you into a little chamber, where you will lose your curiosity soon enough."

Saying these words, the soldiers dragged Joseph into the courtyard, and he was just about to be thrown into a dark dungeon, when a gentle voice was heard from an upper window.

"Leave him alone, pray — the poor boy!" cried the little prisoner; "even if you wish to prevent him from coming up to me to lessen my sorrow a little, do not, please, harm him."

The men were moved to pity — they held a council together: and at last they led Joseph up to his unknown friend, who received him in a splendid room. The golden walls, the marble floor, the many splendors which Joseph saw here for the first time, made him silent, so that he scarcely returned the friendliness of the inhabitant of the castle.

"Don't be afraid," said he, "and give me your hand; your songs have given me much pleasure already, and I have great need of more."

"You cannot be in want of pleasure," replied Joseph courageously, "for here it is really too beautiful. But who are you?"

"I am an unhappy prince, who has been robbed of his

inheritance by a wicked man. That I might not be able to harm him, he has sent me hither, far, far from my native land. Ah, my fatherland! It lies opposite those high ice mountains, and is called Naples. There, it is never winter, and here I am often so cold! But I have said enough about myself. Come, my new young friend. I will now give you as much for your pleasant music as I can."

The prince took Joseph by the hand, and led him up and down through a row of rooms. One was still more splendid than the other. They were glittering with gold and silver; purple hangings, gay carpets, silken couches, and crystal candlesticks; everything was to be found here. Joseph clasped his hands together with wonder, and thought to himself in secret: "How delightful it would be to live in this castle!" A hundred times he wished himself in the place of the prince, and he could not understand how he could feel sorrowful, when nothing was wanting in this splendid abundance.

With jests and play the hours passed by quickly and unnoticed, till late evening approached, and the prince, although unwillingly, had to remind his friend that they must part. With aching heart Joseph prepared to leave the charming place and his delightful playfellow, after promising many times to return. The sentinels saved him the trouble, and told him when he reached the gate, that he must now stay with the prince, and would never be allowed to leave the castle again.

Who was better pleased than Joseph? who more delighted than the prince, who now had a companion, who seemed willing to share his lot with pleasure, and forget flock, home, and former friends, for this new mode of life? Games, stories, songs, and the sweet melodies of the flute shortened the days, and many of them had passed before discontent and sadness came into Joseph's heart. The boy, who had always been so lively before, sat now for hours in a corner, while the prince sat in another to lament the sorrow of his friend. A nameless longing had taken possession of the shepherd boy—homesickness—a desire for freedom robbed him of his rest. In vain he rolled about on his silken couches; in vain he tried to be pleased with the glittering toys. Sleep fled from his bed; the toys became disgusting in his sight; the food in the golden dishes made him sick, as well as the wine in the crystal cup. The song of the birds was tiresome; the funny chattering of the parrots he thought absurd; even his flute he would no longer touch, and when he went to the window, looked out into the blue sky, and his glance fell upon the sunny fields or the green surface of the lake, tears came into his eyes. Weeping, he fled from the room; but the noise of arms at the gate reminded him that he was a prisoner in the fortress. The prince consoled him as well as he could, but he could not silence the longing for home.

It happened that the prince fell asleep one afternoon on his couch, and Joseph went to the winwdo once more to cry. Behold! he fancied he saw his flocks grazing on the other side of the lake, his faithful dog seeming to look at him, with tail wagging, as if wishing to call his master over to him. It went to the boy's heart, and some voice within him cried: "Flee, flee quickly! This is the moment, or never!" He yielded to the feeling, and hastened to the door of the room. Then he thought of his young friend: to leave him so was hard. He would see him once more. He went over to his couch. The prince seemed sound asleep; but Joseph, bending down to listen to his breathing, became terrified, for the heart was no longer beating, no breath heaved his breast; a sweet death had delivered him gently from his sorrows. Joseph rushed into the passage to cry for help, but the court was empty, the gate of the castle was open, and the sentinels had fallen asleep from the sultry heat. The moment was favorable. One more farewell to the departed friend, a short prayer to his Father in heaven, and the shepherd boy stole safely past the soldiers out of the castle.

With hasty steps he had soon reached the spot where the faithful dog watched the flock intrusted to his care, though his poor fare had made him lean. The lambs and their four-footed protector received their long wished for master with the greatest joy; and full of delight to have escaped the prison, Joseph commenced a merry mountain lay. But the prince no longer leaned from the window to listen, and fresh tears to his memory interrupted the shepherd's song. The fresh evening breeze, the murmuring of the lake, and the joyful advances of his flock gave him the purest delight.

His breast grew light as he breathed the fragrant flowers and the pure air; and as he from afar beheld the modest thatched roof of his father's cottage, he shouted aloud with joy; and driving his flock to quicker pace by the sound of his flute, he cried: "Welcome, my father's roof! welcome, valley of my home! How gladly I have left the costly palace to return to thee! Here I find no gold or silver, or precious stones; but free from bars, no longer threatened by the swords of cruel watchmen, I shall enjoy calm peace — I shall be poor but I shall be happy."

NOTES FOR COMPOSITION.

A Swiss shepherd boy used to tend his flocks on the slope of a valley, opposite an old castle. While so doing he often played upon his flute

A pale-faced boy in the castle window used to listen to him all day.
The shepherd wishing to find out who the boy was, wandered one day
toward the castle. The soldiers on guard there caught him. They
were prevented from harming him by the little boy, at whose request
Joseph was led up to his room. The boy was a young prince, im-
prisoned by his enemy. He showed Joseph his beautiful rooms.
Joseph, after playing all day wished to go home, but the soldiers would
not let him. Joseph gladly remained, but soon began to sigh for home.
One afternoon the prince died. Joseph, alarmed, went to call help, but
seeing the door open escaped to his flocks again. He was happy to
see his poor home and no longer wished for riches or splendor.

glittering   crystal   yielded   interrupted

---o---

LINES WRITTEN IN RICHMOND CHURCH-YARD.

METHINKS it is good to be here;
  If thou wilt, let us build — but for whom?
Nor Elias nor Moses appear;
But the shadows of eve that encompass the gloom,
The abode of the dead, and the place of the tomb.

  Shall we build to ambition? Ah, no!
Affrighted, he shrinketh away;
  For, see! they would pin him below
In a small, narrow cave, and, begirt with cold clay,
To the meanest of reptiles a peer and a prey.

  To beauty? Ah, no! she forgets
The charms which she wielded before;
  Nor knows the foul worm that he frets
The skin which but yesterday fools could adore
For the smoothness it held, or the tint which it wore.

  Shall we build to the purple of pride —
The trappings which dizzen the crowd?
  Alas! they are all laid aside;

And here's neither dress nor adornment allowed,
But the long winding-sheet, and the fringe of the shroud.

To riches? Alas! 'tis in vain;
Who hid, in their turn have been hid;
 The treasures are squandered again;
And here in the grave are all metals forbid,
But the tinsel that shines on the dark coffin lid.

To the pleasures which mirth can afford —
The revel, the laugh and the jeer?
 Ah! here is a plentiful board!
But the guests are all mute as their pitiful cheer,
And none but the worm is a reveller here.

Unto sorrow? The dead cannot grieve,
Not a sob, not a sigh meets mine ear,
 Which compassion itself could relieve!
Ah! sweetly they slumber, nor hope, love, nor fear —
Peace, peace is the watchword, the only one here!

Unto death, to whom monarchs must bow?
Ah, no! for his empire is known,
 And here there are trophies enow!
Beneath, the cold dead, and around, the dark stone,
Are the signs of a sceptre that none may disown!

The first tabernacle to hope we will build,
And look for the sleepers around us to rise;
 The second to faith, which ensures it fulfilled;
And the third to the Lamb of the great sacrifice,
Who bequeathed us them both when he rose to the skies.

methinks	peer	adornment	reveller
encompass	wielded	fringe	trophies
affrighted	frets	shroud	enow
shrinketh	trappings	squandered	tabernacle
begirt	dizzen	tinsel	bequeathed

Questions : — What is ambition? How does all ambition end? What is meant by "the purple of pride"? Relate the parable of the New Testament where "fine purple" is spoken of. Explain "who hid, in their turn have been hid." How is the worm "a reveller"? Why has death trophies enough? Who is "the Lamb of the great sacrifice"?

Memorize the last stanza, and give it in your own words.

———o———

USING THE EYES.

A CCIDENT does very little toward the production of any great result in life. Though what is called "a happy hit" may be made by a bold venture, the old and common highway of steady industry and application is the only safe road to travel. Sedulous attention and painstaking industry always mark the true worker.

The greatest men are not those who "despise the doing of small things," but those who improve them the most carefully. Michael Angelo was one day explaining to a visitor at his studio, what he had been doing to a statue since his previous visit. "I have retouched this part, polished that, softened this feature, brought out that muscle, given some expression to this lip, and more energy to that limb." "But these are trifles," remarked the visitor. "It may be so," replied the sculptor, "but recollect that trifles make perfection, and perfection is no trifle." So it was said of Nicholas Poussin, the painter, that the rule of his conduct was, "whatever is worth doing at all, is worth doing well;" and when asked, later in life, by a friend, by what means he had gained so high a reputation among the painters of Italy, he emphatically answered: "Because I have neglected nothing."

Although there are discoveries which are said to

have been made by accident, if carefully inquired into it will be found that there has really been very little that was accidental about them. For the most part, these so-called accidents have only been opportunities carefully improved by genius.

The fall of the apple at Newton's feet has often been quoted in proof of the accidental character of some discoveries. But Newton's whole mind had already been devoted for years to the laborious and patient investigation of the subject of gravitation; and the circumstance of the apple falling before his eye was suddenly apprehended only as genius could apprehend it, and served to flash upon him the brilliant discovery then bursting on his sight.

The difference between men consists, in a great measure, in the intelligence of their observation. The Russian proverb says of the non-observant man: "He goes through the forest and sees no firewood." "The wise man's eyes are in his head," says Solomon; "but the fool walketh in darkness."

"Sir," said Johnson, on one occasion, to a fine gentleman, just returned from Italy, "some men will learn more in the Hampstead stage than others in the tour of Europe." It is the mind that sees as well as the eye.

Many, before Galileo, had seen a suspended weight swing before their eyes with a measured beat; but he was the first to detect the value of the fact. One of the vergers, in the cathedral at Pisa, after replenishing with oil a lamp which hung from the roof, left it swinging to and fro; and Galileo, then a youth of only eighteen, noting it attentively, conceived the idea of applying it to the measurement of time.

Fifty years of study and labor, however, elapsed before he completed the invention of his pendulum,—

an invention the importance of which, in the measurement of time, and in astronomical calculations, can scarcely be overvalued.

While Sir Samuel Brown was occupied in studying the construction of bridges, with the view of contriving one of a cheap description to be thrown across the Tweed, near which he lived, he was walking in his garden one dewy autumn morning, when he saw a tiny spider's net suspended across his path. The idea immediately occurred to him that a bridge of iron ropes or chains might be constructed in like manner, and the result was the invention of his Suspension Bridge.

So James Watt, when consulted about the mode of carrying water by pipes under the Clyde, along the unequal bed of the river, turned his attention, one day, to the shell of a lobster presented at table; and from that model he invented an iron tube, which, when laid down, was found effectually to answer the purpose.

Sir Isambard Brunel took his first lessons in forming the Thames Tunnel from the tiny ship-worm. He saw how the little creature perforated the wood with its well armed head, first in one direction and then in another, till the archway was complete, and then daubed over the roof and sides with a kind of varnish; and by copying this work exactly on a large scale, Brunel was at length enabled to accomplish his great engineering work.

So trifling a matter as the sight of sea-weed floating past his ship, enabled Columbus to quell the mutiny which arose amongst the sailors at not discovering land, and to assure them that the eagerly sought New World was not far off.

It is the close observation of little things which is the secret of success in business, in art, in science, and in every pursuit in life. Though many of these facts and

observatious seemed in the first instance to have but
slight significance, they are all found to have their
eventual uses, and to fit into their proper places.

| sedulous | gravitation | observaut |
| investigation | genius | vergers |

COMPOSITION.

Write a short sketch of this lesson, and give any othe **ıwwıww** you
may know of.

---o---

THE PICKET OF THE POTOMAC.

" ALL quiet along the Potomac," they say,
    "Except now and then a stray picket
Is shot as he walks on his beat to and fro,
    By a rifleman hid in the thicket."
'Tis nothing — a private or two now and then
    Will not count in the tale of the battle;
Not an officer lost — only one of the men
    Breathing out all alone the death rattle.

All quiet along the Potomac to-night,
    Where the soldiers lie peacefully dreaming,
Their tents in the ray of the clear autumn moon,
    And the light of the watch fires gleaming.
A tremulous sigh from the gentle night wind
    Through the forest leaves slowly is creeping,
While the stars up above, with their glittering eyes,
    Keep watch while the army is sleeping.

There's only the sound of the lone sentry's tread,
    As he tramps from the rock to the fountain,
And thinks of the two in the low trundle-bed
    Far away in the hut on the mountain.

His musket falls slack ; his face, dark and grim,
  Grows gentle with memories tender,
As he mutters a prayer for the children asleep,
  For their mother, — may heaven defend her !

The moon seems to shine as serenely as then,
  That night when the love, yet unspoken,
Lingered long on his lips, and when low murmured vows
  Were pledged, never more to be broken.
Then, drawing his sleeve roughly over his eyes,
  He dashes the tears that are welling,
And gathers his gun closer up to its place,
  As if to keep down the heart-swelling.

He passes the fountain, the blasted pine tree
  The footstep is lagging and weary;
Yet onward he glides through the broad belt of light,
  Towards the shade of a forest so dreary.
Hark ! Was it the night wind that rustled the leaves ?
  Is it moonlight so suddenly flashing?
It looked like a rifle — "Ha! Mary, good night!"
  His life-blood is ebbing and dashing.

All quiet along the Potomac to-night,
  No sound save the rush of the river;
But the dew falls unseen on the face of the dead —
  The picket's off duty for ever.

COMPOSITION.

Write an account of the death of a picket, from the following
summary : War is declared; the regular troops go to the front but
are insufficient; volunteers are called for, but still the enemy's advance
is not checked. A draft is ordered. (What is a draft? describe it).
A father of a family is drawn; having no substitute he is compelled to
serve. He is put on picket duty; tell what the duty of a picket is.
One moonlight night while pacing his rounds he thinks of his family;
he forgets himself, and steps within the enemy's range. Suddenly he

recollects himself, but too late; a hostile sentry has seen him and fired; he falls, breathing the names of his loved ones. Tell some of the sufferings caused by war.

rifleman	picket	serenely	lagging
Potomac	beat	roughly	glides
gleaming	glittering	welling	rustled
tremulous	trundle-bed	blasted	flashing

———o———

THE UNKNOWN PAINTER.

MURILLO, the celebrated artist of Seville, often found on the canvas of his pupils unfinished sketches bearing marks of rare genius. They were executed during the night, and he was utterly unable to conjecture the author.

One morning the pupils had arrived at the studio before him, and were grouped before an easel, uttering exclamations of surprise, when Murillo entered. His astonishment was equal to theirs on finding an unfinished head of the Blessed Virgin, of exquisite outline, with many touches of surpassing beauty. He appealed first to one and then to another of the young gentlemen, to see if any one of them would lay claim to it; but each returned a sorrowful negative. "He who has left this tracery will one day be master of us all," cried they.

"Sebastian," said Murillo to a youthful slave that stood trembling by, "who occupies this studio at night?" "No one but myself, senior." "Well, take your station here to-night; and if you do not inform me of the mysterious visitant to this room, thirty lashes shall be your reward on the morrow." The slave bowed in quiet submission, and retired.

That night he threw his mattress before the easel, and

slept soundly until the clock struck three. He then sprang from his couch and exclaimed: "Three hours are my own, the rest are my master's!" He seized a palette and took his seat at the frame, to erase the work of the preceding night. With brush in hand he paused before making the fatal stroke. "I cannot, oh, I cannot, erase it!" said he; "rather let me finish it!"

He went to work: a little coloring here, a touch there, a soft shade there; and thus three hours rolled unheeded by. A slight noise caused him to look up. Murillo with his pupils stood around! The sunshine was peering brightly through the casement, while yet the taper burned.

Again he was a slave. His eyes fell beneath the students' eager gaze.

"Who is your master, Sebastian?" "You, senior."— "Your drawing-master, I mean!" "You, senior."—"I have never given you lessons." "No, but you gave them to these young gentlemen, and I heard them."—"Yes, you have done better; you have profited by them.— Does this boy deserve punishment, or reward, my dear pupils?" "Reward, senior," was the quick response.— "What shall it be?"

One suggested a suit of clothes, another a sum of money; but no chord was touched in the captive's bosom. One said, "The master feels kindly to-day; ask your freedom, Sebastian." He sank on his knees, and lifting his eyes to his master's face, said: "The freedom of my father!"

Murillo was touched, and said: "Your pencil shows that you have talent; your request, that you have heart. *You* are no longer a slave; *your father* is a free man. Happy Murillo! I have not only painted — I have made a painter."

There may still be seen in classic Italy, in its convents and its churches, many beautiful specimens from the pencils of Murillo and Sebastian.

COMPOSITION.

Give all the questions and answers found in this lesson.

Describe the scene between the son and father when youug Murillo announced freedom to his beloved parent.

What Church is the true patroness of painting?

Do you know of any painters the Church has encouraged?

genius	grouped	appealed	palette
conjecture	exquisite	mysterious	chord

———o———

THE KNIGHT'S TOAST.

THE feast is o'er!   Now brimming wine
In lordly cup is seen to shine
Before each eager guest;
And silence fills the crowded hall,
As deep as when the herald's call
Thrills in the loyal breast.

Then up arose the noble host,
And smiling cried : "A toast! a toast!
To all our ladies fair!
Here, before all, I pledge the name
Of Staunton's proud and beauteous dame,—
The Lady Gundamere!"

Then to his feet each gallant sprang,
And joyous was the shout that rang,
As Stanley gave the word;
And every cup was raised on high,
Nor ceased the loud and gladsome cry,
Till Stanley's voice was heard.

"Enough, enough," he smiling said,
And lowly bent his haughty head;
  "That all may have their due,
Now each, in turn, must play his part,
And pledge the lady of his heart,
  Like gallant knight and true!"

Then, one by one, each guest sprang up,
Each drained in turn the brimming cup,
  And named the loved one's name;
And each, as hand on high he raised,
His lady's grace or beauty praised,
  Her constancy and fame.

'Tis now St. Leon's turn to rise;
On him are fixed those countless eyes;—
  A gallant knight is he;
Envied by some, admired by all,
Far famed in lady's bower and hall,—
  The flower of chivalry.

St. Leon raised his kindling eye,
Lifted the sparkling cup on high:
  "I drink to *one*," he said,
"Whose image never may depart,
Deep graven on this grateful heart,
  Till memory be dead;

"To one whose love for me shall last
When lighter passions long have passed,
  So holy 'tis and true;
To one whose love hath longer dwelt,
More deeply fixed, more keenly felt,
  Than any pledged by you."

Each guest up started at the word,
And laid a hand upon his sword,

With fury flashing eye ;
And Stanley said : "We crave the name,
Proud knight, of this most peerless dame,
  Whose love you count so high."

St. Leon paused, as if he would
Not breathe her name in careless mood,
  Thus lightly to another ;
Then bent his noble head, as though
To give that word the reverence due,
  And gently said —"My Mother !"

brimming	gallant	crave	reverence
loyal	constancy	peerless	mood

COMPOSITION.

A large, spacious hall. Tables beautifully decorated. Silver goblets with flashing wine before each guest. The host proposes "to the health of the fair ladies." Each knight in turn speaks the praises of his love, without hurting his neighbors' feelings. At length the finest looking of the knights stands to propose a toast. He says so many grand things of the lady he loves that the other knights become jealous. "Who can deserve such praise?" say they all. The noble knight continues his praises, and finally says :

"For you brave knights, go, love another ;
  My fondest, truest love's for 'Mother.'"

———o———

THE RISING TIDE.

HOPE and Cross remained some time quite absorbed in examining the form of the rock and the creatures within it. Hope was in the act of breaking off some small bits to carry home with him, when Cross suddenly gave a loud shout, calling out : "The Lord have mercy on us ! I forgot the tide, and here it comes !"

Hope turned towards the sea, and saw a stream of

water running at a rapid pace, and covering the sandy creek, where the eels had been found. Not aware of the danger, he said very quietly: "Oh, so it does; I suppose we had better be off!"

"If we can," said Cross. "By passing the rock, we may yet be in time." He looked rather pale as he spoke; and Hope, seeing his alarm, hastened to follow him. For the moment, Cross ceased speaking; he scrambled up the rocks, and began walking as rapidly as he could across them, towards the nearest shore; but the pace was necessarily slow, for the roughness in some parts, and the slipperiness in others, obliged them to pick their steps. The numberless chasms, which had been a source of amusement an hour before, now served still further to retard their progress, for they were forced to make many a detour to get past them. At last they reached the highest point, and could see before them.

"Thank God!" said Cross, "the land is not yet covered! But we must run for it."

The sand was, in fact, still visible; but small lines of blue water could be seen marking and breaking the surface.

They hastened on, Hope looking at these lines, which seemed rapidly to increase in breadth; but he was soon obliged to keep his eyes on the ground, for, in looking up, he had placed his foot on a bunch of weed, slipped, fell, and got a severe shake, besides cutting his hands.

In three minutes more, however, they were at the edge of the sand; but when they reached it they saw that the it was now in stripes, the water in sheets.

"We shall do yet," said Cross, "for here is a girl before us." He began to run rapidly, and Hope followed. They proceeded thus for about two hundred yards.

when they saw coming hastily towards them the little girl, who turned out to be the same from whom Hope had bought the crabs. She reached them before they had advanced many more paces; and as she ran she called out something, which they could not at first understand, for she was so much out of breath.

When she was close to them, they could distinguish that she said: "The wave! the wave! it is coming! Turn! turn and run or we are lost!"

They did turn; and they saw, far out to sea, a large wave rolling towards the shore. Tired as they were, they yet increased their speed as they retraced their steps towards the rocks they had just left.

The little girl passed them, and led the way; the two friends strained every nerve to keep pace with her, for, as they neared the rock, the wave still rolled on: the sand became gradually covered, and during their last ten steps they were up to their knees in water, but they were on the rock.

"Quick! quick!" said the girl; "there is the passage to cross; and if the second wave comes, we shall be too late."

She ran on for a hundred yards, till she came to a crack in the rock, six or seven feet wide, along which the water was rushing like a mill sluice.

"We are lost!" said the girl. "I cannot cross it; it will carry me away!"

"Is it deep?" asked Cross.

"Not very," she said; "but it is too strong!"

Cross lifted the girl in his arms, for he was a strong, big man, and plunged into the stream, which was up to his waist. With a few strides he was across, and set the girl down. He then held on by the rock, and stretched out his hand to Hope, who was following like an experienced wader, taking very short steps, and with his legs well stretched out, to prevent his being swept away by the force of the water. Hope grasped the hand thus held out to him, and in another second the two friends were standing by the girl.

"That is tremendous!" said Hope. "If I had not seen it, I never would have believed it!"

"It is indeed," said Cross; "and in winter, or in stormy weather, the tide-wave comes in with far greater force than the one we have just seen."

"Come on! come on!" cried the girl, as she again led the way to the higher point of light-colored rock, which Hope had remarked in the morning. When they had reached it she said: "We are safe now!" and kneeling down, she returned thanks to God for their deliverance.

After a few minutes thus spent, the girl smilingly looked up to Cross. "Thank you," said she, "for lifting me over! I could not have crossed alone. And," she continued, "the second wave has come, and it is all water now!"

The friends looked; all around them was the wide sea. They were on an island, which each moment became less; and this island was three quarters of a mile from the shore.

"I am afraid, sir, you will be cold!" said the little girl. "We are quite safe here, for this point is always above water, except in a storm; but we shall have to remain here three or four hours before we can go to the shore."

"Cold or hot," said Cross, "we may be thankful we are here! But what made you forget the tide, for you must know the coast so well?"

"I did not forget it," she said; "but I feared you would be drowned, as you are strangers, and I thought I should be in time to tell you; but I was too late, and the wave came!"

"And did you risk your own life to save ours?" said Hope, the tears starting into his eyes.

"I thought that at any rate I should get here," she replied. "As you are strangers, I knew you would not know that it is always dry here; and on the strand you would be lost: so I came to help you; for the gentleman was kind, and gave me a good price for my crabs. So I hoped I should be in time to warn you, but I was very nearly too late!"

Hope took the little girl in his arms, and kissed her. "We owe you our lives, brave little girl!" he said. "I thank you in the meantime, and hope to do more for you hereafter! I wonder what she would most like in the world?"

"Ask her," said Cross. Hope did so.

"To have a dress," she said, "just like the one Angela's sister had on last Sunday."

*　　　*　　　*　　　*

"You must bring Angela to see us to-morrow, and she will help us to get the dress we have promised."

"Oh, happy, happy day!" she said. "Angela will be so pleased."

"If ever we get ashore," said Hope; for a wave at that moment rolled past, and the waters began to run along the little platform they were sitting on. They all rose, and mounted on the rocky points, where they clustered, supporting one another. Another wave came: it appeared only like a ripple; but when they looked down, the water was a foot deep where they had previously been seated. There was silence for awhile. Another wave came: the water was within six inches of their feet

"It is a terribly high tide," said the girl; "but if we hold together we shall not be washed away."

Hope's face was towards the shore. "There are a great many people on the point," he said. "It is always a comfort to know that our fellow-beings take an interest in us; and I suppose those people are watching us."

The little girl turned to look. The faint sound of a cheer was heard, and they could see the people on shore wave their hats and handkerchiefs.

"They think the tide has turned," she said; "and they are shouting to cheer us."

She was right; the tide had turned. Another wave came and wet their feet: but when it had passed, the water had fallen, and in five minutes more the platform was again dry.

It was dark before the tide had receded far enough to admit of their wading across the sands to the shore.

NOTES FOR COMPOSITION.

Hope and Cross while examining the rocks on the sea-side are caught by the tide. They turn to go inland, but the frequent chasms impede their progress. While crossing the sands they meet a little girl. She points out a big wave rushing in. They run back to the high rocks. Cross has to lift the child and wade through the tide. They are now surrounded by water. The girl tells why she followed them. They see a great many people gathering on the shore. The tide at last turns and they escape at dark.

Memorize :—

> Lead, kindly light, amid th' encircling gloom,
> Lead thou me on !
> The night is dark, and I am far from home:
> Lead thou me on !
> Keep thou my feet; I do not ask to see
> The distant way: one step's enough for me.

absorbed	chasms	stretched	clustered
scrambled	stripes	tremendous	previously

AN APRIL DAY.

Geoffrey Chaucer (1328–1400) is called the Father of English Poetry.
He is the first great author in our literature whose diction approaches
the genius of our language. The Anglo-Saxon element in his
speech takes a more modern form ; the grammatical construction
is vastly ahead of even the prose of his time in its likeness to
later English ; rhyme and metre are introduced and wonderfully
perfected ; so that a modern reader, by a little attention to the final
accented *e*, and *ed* of verbs, will find that his verse reads with great
smoothness and harmony. His greatest poem, "Canterbury Tales," a
series of narratives by a company of pilgrims to Canterbury, is a
picture-gallery of the manners of the 14th century.

ALL day the low-hung clouds have dropt
  Their garnered fulness down ;
All day that soft gray mist hath wrapt
  Hill, valley, grove, and town.
There has not been a sound to-day
  To break the calm of nature ;
Nor motion, I might almost say,
  Of life, or living creature :
Of waving bough, or warbling bird,
  Or cattle faintly lowing ; —
I could have half believed I heard
  The leaves and blossoms growing.
I stood to hear — I love it well,
  The rain's continuous sound :
Small drops, but thick and fast they fell,
  Down straight into the ground ;
For leafy thickness is not yet
  Earth's naked breast to screen,
Though every dripping branch is set
  With shoots of tender green.
Sure, since I looked at early morn,
  Those honeysuckle buds
Have swelled to double growth ; that thorn
  Hath put forth larger studs ;

That lilac's cleaving cones have burst,
  The milk-white flowers revealing;
E'en now, upon my senses first·
  Methinks their sweets are stealing.
The very earth, the steamy air
  Are all with fragrance rife;
And grace and beauty everywhere
  Are flushing into life.
Down, down they come — those fruitful stores;
  Those earth-rejoicing drops!
A momentary deluge pours,
  Then thins, decreases, stops,
And ere the dimples on the stream
  Have circled out of sight,
Lo! from the West a parting gleam
  Breaks forth, of amber light.
But yet behold — abrupt and loud
  Comes down the glittering rain:
The farewell of a passing cloud,
  The fringes of her train.

garnered	honeysuckle	ere	abrupt
continuous	cleaving	amber	fringes

Questions:— What is the "garnered fulness" of the clouds? What has been wrapt by the mist? What kind of day has it been? Name various sounds unheard. What cattle low? What might one have *almost* believed? Why did you stand? To hear what? How did the rain fall? When is earth screened by leaves? How have the honeysuckle buds grown in a single day? What are "shoots of tender green"? What are "cleaving cones"? Show me the shape of a cone. Make a cone with a slip of paper. How are the "milk-white flowers revealed"? Through what sense does the odor of flowers steal upon us? When does the air appear steamy? Explain the term "rife." Use it in three or four sentences. Name six creatures rejoiced by rain falling. What is a "momentary deluge"? What are dimples? What are dimples on baby's face? To what does Chaucer compare "glitter·ing rain"? What is a train? How is rain like the fringes of a train? Name four places in sacred history where rain is mentioned.

NOBLE REVENGE.

A YOUNG officer had so far forgotten himself, in a moment of irritation, as to strike a private soldier, full of personal dignity, and distinguished for his courage. The inexorable laws of military discipline forbade the injured soldier any practical redress. In a tumult of indignation, the soldier said to the officer that he would make him repent it.

Some weeks after this a partial action took place. The armies are facing each other. But it is no more than a skirmish which is going on; in the course of which, however, an occasion suddenly arises for a desperate service. A redoubt, which has fallen into the enemy's hands, must be recaptured at any price. A strong party has volunteered for the service; there is a cry for somebody to head them; you see a soldier step out from the ranks to assume this dangerous leadership; the party moves rapidly forward; in a few minutes it is swallowed up from your eyes in clouds of smoke; for one half-hour from behind those clouds you receive hieroglyphic reports of bloody strife, fierce, repeating signals, flashes from the guns, rolling musketry and exulting hurrahs, advancing or receding, slackening or redoubling.

All is over: the redoubt has been recaptured. Crimsoned with glorious gore, the wreck of the conquering party is relieved, and at liberty to return. From the river you see it ascending. The plume-crested officer in command rushes forward, with his left hand raising his hat in homage to the blackened fragments of what once was a flag; whilst with his right hand he seizes that of the leader. They pause! This soldier, this officer, who are they? Reader, once before they stood face to face — once again they meet. As one who recovers a brother whom he has accounted dead, the officer springs forward, throws his arms round the neck of the soldier and kisses him, as if he were some martyr glorified by that shadow of death from which he was returning: while on *his* part, the soldier, stepping back, and carrying his open hand through the beautiful motion of the military salute to a superior, makes this immortal answer — an answer which effaced for ever the memory of the indignity offered to him, even whilst for the last time alluding to it: "Sir," said he, "I told you before that I would *make you repent it.*"

Questions :— What led to the ill feeling between the young officer and the soldier? How was the soldier prevented from retaliating? What did he say to the officer? What occasion soon arose for a display of courage on the part of the soldier? What is a *redoubt?* What did the soldier volunteer to do? What is meant by "hieroglyphic report"? What success attended the enterprise? How did the officer welcome back the conquering party? What took place when the officer and soldier again faced each other? How long did this hesitation last? How did the officer show his appreciation of the soldier's bravery? How did the soldier return this acknowledgment? How may we best *make one repent* of any indignity he may have offered us?

COMPOSITION.

Write an account of the incident related above, in your own words, from the following outline : A young officer strikes a private soldier. The soldier, prevented by discipline from retaliating, says he will make his superior repent it. A short time after the army is attacked ; a redoubt has to be recaptured ; a soldier steps forward to lead those who volunteer ; they charge, capture and hold ; when relieved and returning they meet an officer who salutes the victors. Suddenly he stops, he recognizes in the leader the soldier whom ho had struck ; the latter advances and accepts the hand offered him, saying, "I told you I would make you repent it." Give the Scriptural text in which the doctrine of forgiveness of injuries is inculcated.

irritation	redoubt	inexorable
redress	fragments	action

ANALYSIS.

"Pay close attention to the emotions or feelings the selection suggests."

"Give due attention to the vocal tones called for by the selection." What are the chief emotions suggested by "Noble Revenge"?

a) INTEREST, by the narration of fact contained in the sentence: "A young officer had so far forgotten himself, in a moment of irritation, as to strike a private soldier, FULL OF PERSONAL DIGNITY, AND DISTINGUISHED FOR HIS COURAGE."

The capitalized words add to the sense of injustice committed, and must therefore have special stress placed upon them.

(b) SELF-COMMAND, as required by the fact that "The inexorable laws of military discipline forbade the injured soldier any practical redress."

This entire sentence should be read in a half subdued, but equally sustained tone throughout.

(c) In a louder, but equally sustained tone, increased in strength towards the end, proceed:

"In a tumult of indignation, the soldier said to his officer that HE WOULD MAKE HIM REPENT IT."

The next few lines being a mere connection to the narrative, may be read in a monotone.

(d) A renewal of interest is created in the next paragraph, where it is related that:

"Some weeks after this a partial action took place. THE ARMIES ARE FACING EACH OTHER. But it is no more than a skirmish which is going on; in the course of which, however, an occasion suddenly arises for A DESPERATE SERVICE. A redoubt, which has fallen into the enemy's hands, MUST BE RECAPTURED AT ANY PRICE. A strong party has volunteered for the service; there is a cry for somebody to head them; you see a soldier step out from the ranks to assume THIS DANGEROUS LEADERSHIP; the party moves rapidly forward; IN A FEW MINUTES IT IS SWALLOWED UP IN CLOUDS OF SMOKE; for one half-hour from behind those clouds you receive hieroglyphic reports of BLOODY STRIFE, *fierce, repeating signals, flashes from the guns, rolling musketry and exulting hurrahs, advancing or receding, slackening or redoubling.*"

In the paragraph given above, the first sentence is read in a conversational tone. The second, capitalized, should be read slowly, very distinctly, and a prolonged pause follow before proceeding:

"But it is no more than a skirmish which is going on;" which should be spoken in a free, easy tone, to be followed in the tone by:

"In the course of which, however," followed by, uttered rapidly:

"An occasion suddenly arises;" and in an emphatic tone, and considerable force:

"for A DESPERATE SERVICE."

Continuing in an interesting, talkative tone, proceed to:

"MUST BE RECAPTURED AT ANY PRICE," to be read as the previous phrase.

The same holds true of capitalized phrases following.

The description of the signals, *italicized*, should be given rapidly, with some slight pause between each signal.

Thus we realize other rules suggested for EXPRESSIVE READING, viz.:

"Lay special stress on those points that are to attract the attention of an audience."

"The reading should be accelerated or retarded, the volume of voice increased or diminished, to express the progress of thought or sentiment, or to conform to the requirements of imitative harmony."

THE FOUNTAIN.

INTO the sunshine,
　Full of light,
Leaping and flashing
　From morn till night;

Into the moonlight,
　Whiter than snow,
Waving so flower like
　When the winds blow;

Into the starlight,
　Rushing in spray,
Happy at midnight,
　Happy by day;

Ever in motion,
　　Blithesome and cheery,
Still climbing heavenward,
　　Never aweary;

Glad of all weathers,
　　Still seeming best;
Upward or downward,
　　Motion, thy rest;

Full of a nature
　　Nothing can tame,
Changed every moment —
　　Ever the same;

Ceaseless aspiring,
　　Ceaseless content,
Darkness or sunshine
　　Thy element.

Glorious fountain,
　　Let my heart be
Fresh, changeful, constant,
　　Upward, like thee!

COMPOSITION.

Paraphrase "The Fountain," after the following:

The fountain gushes from morn till eve in the clear sunshine. Its waters, when shone upon by the moon's borrowed light, seem whiter than snow, and while the winds blow, the expanded waters look like outspread branches. All through the hours our fountain is happy and gay; its spray has a pretty glare, and being ever in motion, the fountain never seems weary or fatigued. All weather suits it, and its very motion affords it rest. Nothing can keep down the fountain, and though its waters are ever changing, the spring remains the same. We, like the fountain, must do our duty, unchangingly, and like the spring too, we must ever move upward, onward, and do good to all men.

spray   blithesome   aweary   element

THE MIDNIGHT SUN.

WHEN I went on deck, on the morning after our departure, we were in the narrow strait between the islands of Mageroe — the northern extremity of which forms the North Cape — and the mainland. On either side, the shores of bare, bleak rock, spotted with patches of moss and stunted grass, rose precipitously from the water, the snow filling up their ravines from the summit to the sea. Not a tree, nor a shrub, nor a sign of human habitation was visible; there was no fisher's sail on the lonely waters, and only the cries of some sea-gulls, wheeling about the cliffs, broke the silence.

The sea and fiords are alive with fish, which are not only a means of existence, but of profit to the Laplanders, while the wonderful Gulf Stream, which crosses five thousand miles of the Atlantic to die upon this Ultima Thule in a last struggle with the Polar Sea, casts up the spoils of tropical forests to feed their fires. Think of Arctic fishers burning upon their hearths the palms of Hayti, the mahogany of Honduras, and the precious woods of the Amazon and the Orinoco.

On issuing from the strait, we turned southward into the great fiord which stretches nearly a hundred miles into the heart of Lapland. Its shores are high and mountainous hills, half covered with snow, and barren of vegetation except patches of grass and moss. If once wooded, the trees have long since disappeared, and now nothing can be more bleak and desolate. Running along under the eastern shore, we exchanged the dreadful monotony through which we had been sailing, for more rugged and picturesque scenery.

Before us rose a wall of dark cliff, from five to six hundred feet in height, gaping here and there with sharp clefts or gashes, as if it had cracked in cooling, after the primeval fires. As we approached the end of the promontory which divides the fiords, the rocks became more abrupt and violently shattered. Huge masses, fallen from the summit, lined the base of the precipice, which was hollowed into cavernous arches, the home of myriads of sea-gulls.

Far to the North the sun lay in a bed of saffron light, over the clear horizon of the Arctic Ocean. A few bars of dazzling orange cloud floated above him; and, still higher in the sky, where the saffron melted through delicate rose color into blue, hung light wreaths of vapor, touched with pearly, opaline flushes of pink and golden gray. The sea was a web of pale slate color, shot through and through with threads of orange and saffron, from the dancing of a myriad of shifting and twinkling ripples.

The air was filled and permeated with the soft, mysterious glow, and even the very azure of the southern sky seemed to shine through a net of golden gauze. The headlands of this deeply indented coast lay around us, in different degrees of distance, but all with foreheads touched with supernatural glory. Far to the North-east was the most northern point of the mainland of Europe, gleaming rosy and faint in the full beams of the sun, and, just as our watches denoted midnight, the North Cape appeared to the westward — a long line of purple bluff, presenting a vertical cone of nine hundred feet in height to the Polar Sea.

Midway between these two magnificent headlands stood the MIDNIGHT SUN, shining on us with subdued fires, and with the gorgeous coloring of an hour, for which we have no name, since it is neither sunset nor sunrise, but the blended loveliness of both — but shining, at the same moment, in the heat and splendor of noonday, on the Pacific Isles. This was the Midnight Sun as I had dreamed it — as I had hoped to see it.

We ran out under the northern headland, which again charmed us with a glory peculiarly its own. Here the colors were a part of the substance of the rock, and the sun but heightened and harmonized their tones. The huge projecting masses of pale yellow had a mellow gleam, like golden chalk; behind them were cliffs, violet in shadow; broad strata of soft red, tipped on the edges with vermilion; thinner layers, which shot up vertically to the height of four or five hundred feet, and striped the splendid sea-wall with lines of bronze, orange, brown, and dark red, while great rents and breaks interrupted these marvellous frescos with their dashes of uncertain gloom.

I have seen many wonderful aspects of nature, in many lands, but rock painting such as this I never beheld. A part of its effects may have been owing to atmospheric conditions, which must be rare, even in the North; but, without such embellishments, I think the sight of this coast will nobly repay any one for continuing his voyage beyond Hammerfest. We lingered on deck, as point after point revealed some change in the dazzling diorama, uncertain which was finest, and whether something still grander might not be in store. But the North-east wind blew keenly across the Arctic Ocean, and we were both satisfied and fatigued enough to go to bed. It was the most northern point of our voyage, about 71° 20′, which is further north than I ever was before, or wish to be again.

Questions:— Point out the Straits of Magellan. Tell me anything you know about the Gulf Stream. What is meant by the "Ultima

Thule"?   Mention some fiord.   What sort of a country is Lapland?
What is meant by rock painting?   Where is Hammerfest?   Point out
71° 20´ N. on the map.

precipitously	saffron	blended	atmospheric
issuing	opaline	harmonized	embellishments
vegetation	ripples	strata	lingered
bleak	permeated	vermilion	diorama
primeval	azure	layers	gorgeous
abrupt	subdued	marvellous	dazzling

---o---

ANTONY CANOVA, THE SCULPTOR.

IT was in the little village of Possagno, in the Vene-
tian territory, that Canova first saw the light of day.
Falieri, the senator, was lord of this village.   One day he
gave a great dinner, and there was served up to his
guests the image of a lion beautifully formed in butter.
This unexpected dish gave as much surprise to the
senator as to his numerous guests.   He ordered his
cook to come upstairs, that he might congratulate him
in presence of the party, so much pleased was he with
the marvellous work of art.   The cook was introduced
into the banqueting hall, and was so overwhelmed with
congratulations that the tears came into his eyes.

"You weep for joy?" said his master to him.

"No, my lord," he replied; "it is through despair at
not having executed the work of art which is the object
of so much admiration."

"I should like to make the artist's acquaintance,"
said the senator.

The cook withdrew, assuring his master that his wish
would be gratified; and in a few minutes returned, leading the artist.   He was a little peasant boy, about ten

years old, meanly clad, for his parents were poor.   Needy
as they were, however, these worthy people had exposed
themselves to great straits, rather than deny to their son
lessons in the art of sculpture, which a professor had
undertaken to give for a very moderate fee.

Antony Canova had early exhibited a strong faculty
for statuary.   He modelled clay when he could get it,
and, with the help of his knife, carved little figures out
of all the chips of wood he could lay his hands on.   His
parents were acquainted with Senator Falieri's cook,
who, on the morning of the great dinner, told them of
the difficulty he had in giving a graceful finish to the
table.   He had exhausted all the resources of his skill
and imagination; but he still wanted one of those effective
dishes, capable of producing a great sensation, which
rear on a solid basis the reputation of the cook of a
great house.   The little Canova thought for a minute,
and then said: "Do not trouble yourself; I will soon
come to you.   Leave it to me, and I will answer for it
that your table will be complete."   The boy went as he
had promised to the senator's house, showed the cook
the design of the figure which he intended to execute,
answered for the success of the trial, and cut the block
of butter, with that purity of imagination and perfect
taste which he afterwards displayed in cutting blocks of
marble.   Surprised as the guests had been by the work,
they were much more so when they beheld the workman.   He was loaded with attentions, and from this
time forth, Falieri was the patron of young Canova.

The happy issue of the first attempt of the little
peasant boy suddenly made his name famous, and
opened up for him the road to permanent success.
Falieri placed him as a pupil in the studio of old Torretti,
the best sculptor of the time.   Two years after — that

is to say, when Canova was only twelve years of age—he sent his patron a gift of two marble fruit baskets of his own workmanship, which still adorn the Falieri palace at Venice.

You will learn elsewhere the claims of this great artist to the admiration of posterity. All the Academies of Europe solicited the honor of enrolling him among their members. Kings, even vied with one another in enriching their national museums with the beautiful products of his genius. He was elected Prince-perpetual of the Academy of St. Luke at Rome—a title conferred on no other artist since his death. The funeral ceremony with which his remains were honored was the grandest which had ever occurred in connection with the fine arts since the death of Raphael.

NOTES FOR COMPOSITION.

Falieri was lord of the village in which Canova was born. One day his guests were surprised at dinner by the skilful carving of a lion in butter. The cook was questioned, and brought in the artist, who was a poor peasant boy only ten years old. He used to practise cutting in wood and clay. Falieri's cook wanted a centre piece for the dinner. Canova offered to provide one, and so cut the lion in butter. This made his fortune. Falieri placed him at school. Canova was honored by all the Academies of Europe. (What is an Academy?) He had the grandest funeral since the death of Raphael.

Memorize:—"The more those ages which reared our monuments were distinguished for piety and faith, the more striking are those monuments for grandeur and elevation of character."

guests	gratified	imagination
congratulate	congratulations	surprised
acquaintance	admiration	sensation
banqueting	straits	permanent
overwhelming	modelled	museums

OLD TIMES.

Gerald Griffin, a distinguished novelist and dramatist of the present century, was born in the city of Limerick, in 1803. At an early age, when his talents were winning him fame and popularity in London, whither he had repaired, as he pleasantly expresses it in one of his letters, "with the modest desire of rivalling Scott and throwing Shakespeare into the shade," he suddenly withdrew from the path of literature, and became a devoted Brother of the Christian Schools, in which sphere of usefulness he died, in 1840, at the early age of 37. Some of Griffin's novels, and especially "The Collegians," "Suil Dhu," "Tracy's Ambition," and "Tales of the Five Senses," are equal to any thing of the kind in our language. His great historical novel of "The Invasion" contains a mine of antiquarian research. His tragedy of "Gisippus" holds one of the first places in the modern drama. As a poet Griffin was also eminently successful.

OLD times! old times! the gay old times!
　　When I was young and free,
And heard the merry Easter chimes,
　　Under the sally tree ;
My Sunday palm beside me placed,
　　My cross upon my hand,
A heart at rest within my breast,
　　And sunshine on the land!
　　　　　　Old times! old times!

It is not that my fortunes flee,
　　Nor that my cheek is pale,
I mourn whene'er I think of thee,
　　My darling native vale!
A wiser head I have, I know,
　　Than when I loiter'd there ;
But in my wisdom there is woe,
　　And in my knowledge care,
　　　　　　Old times! old times!

I've lived to know my share of joy,
　　To feel my share of pain,

To learn that friendship's self can cloy,
  To love, and love in vain ;
To feel a pang and wear a smile,
  To tire of other climes,
To like my own unhappy isle,
  And sing the gay old times !
      Old times ! old times !

And sure the land is nothing changed,
  The birds are singing still ;
The flowers are springing where we ranged,
  There's sunshine on the hill ;
The sally waving o'er my head
  Still sweetly shades my frame,
But ah, those happy days are fled,
  And I am not the same !
      Old times ! old times !

Oh, come again, ye merry times
  Sweet, sunny, fresh, and calm ;
And let me hear those Easter chimes,
  And wear my Sunday palm.
If I could cry away mine eyes
  My tears would flow in vain ;
If I could waste my heart in sighs
  They'd never come again !
      Old times ! old times !

COMPOSITION.

In the old times I was free from care; I sat under the sally tree to hear the church bells; my heart was at rest. My fortune has been fairly good, but my cheek is paled ; whenever I think of the valley in which I lived, I feel sad. I am wiser now than then, but I have learned through bitter experience. I have felt joy as well as pain; that friendship often fails; that those I love may abandon me. I have travelled, but find no place like home. I return, to find the land the same: birds still singing, flowers still budding, and my old sally tree still there to welcome me,—nothing has changed save myself. 'Tis vain trying to recall those days ; weeping is of no avail, and sighing useless.

Questions :--Where is the city of Limerick ? What is it celebrated for? What is a treaty ?

sally	pang	frame
loiter'd	ranged	chimes

----o----

ST. ELIZABETH OF HUNGARY.

Montalembert, Charles Forbes René de, born 1810, died in 1870 : French statesman, historian, and essayist. He belonged to the period called the "Catholic Revival" in France, of which himself, Chateaubriand, Lacordaire, Ozanam, Dupanloup, Auguste Nicolas, and the unfortunate Lamennais were the most prominent exponents. His best known works are the "Life of St. Elizabeth of Hungary," and the "Monks of the West." The former is the most perfect work of its kind that has ever been written ; the latter is a monument of patient research, and of devotion to the faith of the Middle Ages ; both are Catholic classics.

GENEROSITY to the poor, particularly that exercised by princes, was one of the most remarkable features of the age in which she lived ; but we perceive that in her charity did not proceed from rank, still less from the desire of obtaining praise or purely human gratitude, but from an interior and heavenly inspiration. From her cradle she could not bear the sight of a poor person without feeling her heart pierced with grief, and now that her husband had granted her full liberty in all that concerned the honor of God and the good of her neighbor, she unreservedly abandoned herself to her natural inclinations to solace the suffering members of Christ. Notwithstanding the resources which the charity of her husband placed at her disposal, she gave away so quickly all that she possessed, that it often happened that she would despoil herself of her clothes, in order to have the means of assisting the unfortunate.

But it was not alone by presents or with money that the young princess testified her love for the poor of Christ; it was still more by personal devotion, by those tender and patient cares which are assuredly, in the sight both of God and of the sufferers, the most holy and most precious alms.

And then, no distance, no roughness of road, could keep her from them. She knew that nothing strengthens feelings of charity more, than to penetrate into all that is positive and material in human misery. She sought out the huts most distant from her castle, which were often repulsive, through filth and bad air, yet she entered these haunts of poverty in a manner at once full of devotion and familiarity. She carried, herself, what she thought would be necessary for their miserable inhabitants. She consoled them, far less by her generous gifts than by her sweet and affectionate words. When she found them in debt and unable to pay, she engaged to discharge their obligations from her private purse.

One day, when accompanied by one of her favorite maidens, as she descended by a rude little path — still pointed out — and carried under her mantle bread, meat, eggs and other food to distribute to the poor, she suddenly encountered her husband, who was returning from hunting. Astonished to see her thus toiling on under the weight of her burthen, he said to her, "Let us see what you carry," — and at the same time drew open the mantle which she held closely clasped to her bosom; but beneath it were only red and white roses, the most beautiful he had ever seen; and as it was no longer the season of flowers this astonished him.

Seeing that Elizabeth was troubled, he sought to console her by his caresses, but he ceased suddenly, on seeing over her head a luminous appearance in the form of a crucifix. He then desired her to continue her route without being disturbed by him, and he returned to Wartburg, meditating on what God did for her, and carrying with him one of those wonderful roses, which he preserved all his life. At the spot where this meeting took place he erected a pillar, surmounted by a cross, to consecrate for ever the remembrance of that which he had seen hovering over the head of his wife.

Amongst the unfortunate who particularly attracted her compassion, those who occupied the chief place in her heart were the lepers; the mysterious and special character of their affliction rendered them, throughout the Middle Ages, objects of solicitude and affection mingled with fear.

Living thus with the poor and for them, it is not astonishing that God should have inspired her with that holy love of poverty which has rendered souls richest in His grace illustrious. Whilst from amongst the people, Francis of Assisi appeared to the world as a new sanctuary, whereto rushed all those who were eager for self-denial and sacrifice, God raised in the midst of the chivalry of Germany this king's daughter, who at the age of fifteen years already felt her heart burn with the love of evangelical poverty, and who confounded the pride and pomp of her person by a sovereign contempt of earthly grandeur.

We freely confess that in the life of this Saint, which we have studied with so much love, nothing appears to us more touching, more worthy of admiration — nay, almost even of envy, than this child-like simplicity, which may possibly bring to some lips the smile of dis-

4

dain. To our eyes, this force yielding to all impressions, these frequent smiles and tears, the girlish joys and sorrows, these innocent sports of her whose soul rested in the bosom of her heavenly Father — all these, mingled with such painful sacrifices, such grave thoughts, such fervent piety, such active, devoted, and ardent charity, offer the sweetest and most powerful charm.

It is beyond all, in times like our own, when flowers wither and no fruits ripen — when simplicity is dead in most hearts, in private life as well as in public society, that a Christian cannot study without emotion this development manifested in the soul of Elizabeth, whose short life was but a lengthened and heavenly infancy — a perpetual obedience to the words spoken by our Saviour, when, taking a little child and setting him in the midst of his disciples, he said to them : "Amen I say unto you, if you become not like unto little children, you shall not enter into the kingdom of heaven."

Questions :— What is meant by "solace the suffering members of Christ"? Why are the poor called "members of Christ"? Give texts from the New Testament in which our Lord shows his affection for the poor.

Explain the sentence, "She knew that nothing strengthens. . . position and material in human misery." Give it in your own words. In what virtue besides love of poverty does St. Elizabeth resemble St. Francis? (Simplicity.)

Write in your own words an account of the charities of St. Elizabeth, and the miraculous manner in which her sanctity was made known to her husband.

strengthens	repulsive	consecrate
discharge	descended	illustrious
mysterious	special	admiration
sacrifice	grandeur	emotion
simplicity	familiarity	development

LOVE OF COUNTRY.

Walter Scott (1771—1832), poet and novelist of the Romantic period
in English literature. His greatest poems, the "Lay of the Last Minstrel," "Marmion" and the "Lady of the Lake," appeared between 1805
and 1814. The popularity of his verse then declining, he entered
upon a new career, that of romancist, in which he has never been surpassed. "Waverly," "Ivanhoe," "Old Mortality," "Kenilworth," "Guy
Mannering," "Heart of Midlothian" and "Bride of Lammermoor" are
the most powerful of his tales. The chivalry of the Middle Ages, the
legends of Scottish history, the civil wars of the 16th and 17th centuries,
were the themes of which he sang and wrote. From the multitude
and individuality of his creations he has been styled the Shakespeare
of romance. His style is easy and animated, and the moral tone of his
works pure, manly and elevated. Yet he was not above an occasional
bigoted fling at Catholicism, and his tales are too often disfigured by
false statements or unkind insinuations against Catholic personages
or customs.

BREATHES there the man with soul so dead,
Who never to himself hath said
This is my own, my native land?
Whose heart hath ne'er within him burned,
As home his footsteps he hath turned,
From wandering on a foreign strand?
If such there breathe, go mark him well,
For him no minstrel raptures swell!
High though his titles, proud his name,
Boundless his wealth as wish can claim
Despite those titles, power, and pelf,
The wretch, concentred all in self,
Living, shall forfeit fair renown,
And doubly dying, shall go down
To the vile dust, from whence he sprung,
Unwept, unhonored, and unsung.

Questions:— What questions are asked in the first six lines? What
answer is to be given to such a person? Give another expression for
each of the following: native land, foreign strand, mark him well.

" boundless his wealth as wish can claim," "concentred all in self
" doubly dying."

native	foreign	minstrel
raptures	despite	titles
concentred	forfeit	renown

————o————

THE INTREPID YOUTH.

IT was a calm, sunny day in the year 1750 ; the scene
a piece of forest land in the North of Virginia, near
a noble stream of water. Implements for surveying were
lying about, and several men reclining under the trees
betokened, by their dress and appearance, that they
composed a party engaged in laying out the wild lands
of the country.

These persons had apparently just finished their
dinner. Apart from the group walked a young man of
a tall and compact frame, who moved with the elastic
tread of one accustomed to constant exercise in the open
air. His countenance wore a look of decision and man-
liness not usually found in one so young, for he was
apparently little over eighteen years of age. His hat
had been cast off, as if for comfort, and he had paused,
with one foot advanced, in a graceful and natural
attitude.

Suddenly there was a shriek, then another, and several
in rapid succession. The voice was that of a woman,
and seemed to proceed from the other side of a dense
thicket. At the first scream, the youth turned his head
in the direction of the sound ; but when it was repeated,
he pushed aside the undergrowth which separated
him from it, and, quickening his footsteps, as the cries

succeeded each other in alarming rapidity, he soon dashed into an open space on the banks of the stream, where stood a rude log cabin.

It was but the work of a moment for the young man to make his way through the crowd and confront the woman. The instant her eye fell on him, she exclaimed: "Oh! sir, you will do something for me. Make them release me, for the love of God! *My boy, my poor boy is drowning, and they will not let me go!*" "It would be madness; she will jump into the river," said one, "and the rapids would dash her to pieces in a moment!"

The youth scarcely waited for these words, for he recollected the child, a fine little boy of four years old, whose beautiful blue eyes and flaxen ringlets made him a favorite with all who knew him. He had been accustomed to play in the little inclosure before the cabin, but the gate having been left open, he had stolen incautiously out, reached the edge of the bank, and was in the act of looking over, when his mother saw him.

The shriek she uttered only hastened the catastrophe she feared; for the child, frightened at the cry of its mother, lost its balance, and fell into the stream, which here went foaming and roaring along amid innumerable rocks, constituting the most dangerous rapids known in that section of the country. Scream now followed scream in rapid succession, as the agonized mother rushed to the bank.

The party we left reclining in the shade within a few steps of the accident were immediately on the spot. Fortunate it was that they were so near, else the mother would have jumped in after her child, and both been lost. Several of the men approached the brink, and were on the point of springing in after the child, when the sight of the sharp rocks crowding the channel, the rush and whirl of the waters, and the want of any knowledge where to look for the boy, deterred them, and they gave up the hazardous enterprise.

Not so with the noble youth. His first work was to throw off his coat; next to run to the edge of the bank. Here he stood for a moment, running his eyes rapidly over the scene below, taking in with a glance the different currents and the most dangerous of the rocks, in order to shape his course when in the stream. He had scarcely formed his conclusion, when he saw in the water a white object, which he knew to be the boy's dress, and he plunged into the wild and roaring rapids.

" *Thank God, he will save my child,*" cried the mother; "*there he is!—oh! my boy, my darling boy, how could I leave you!*" Every one had rushed to the brink of the precipice, following with eager eyes the progress of the youth, like a feather in the embrace of the hurricane. Now it seemed as if he would be dashed against a jutting rock, over which the water threw its foam, and now a whirlpool would drag him in, from whose grasp escape would appear impossible.

At times the current bore him under, and he would be lost to sight; then, just as the spectators gave him up, he would appear, though far from where he vanished, still buffeting amid the vortex. Oh! how that mother's straining eyes followed him in his perilous career; how her heart sank when he went under; and with what a gush of joy she saw him emerge again from the waters, and, flinging the waves aside with his athletic arms, struggle on in pursuit of her boy!

But it seemed as if his generous efforts were not to avail; for, though the current was bearing off the boy before his eyes, scarcely ten feet distant, he could not, despite his gigantic efforts, overtake the drowning child.

On went the youth and child; and it was miraculous how each escaped being dashed to pieces against the rocks. Twice the boy went out of sight, and a suppressed shriek escaped the mother's lips; but twice he re-appeared, and then, with hands wrung wildly together, and breathless anxiety, she followed his progress, as his unresisting form was hurried onward with the current.

The youth now appeared to redouble his exertions, for they were approaching the most dangerous part of the river, where the rapids, contracting between the narrow shores, shot almost perpendicularly down a declivity of fifteen feet. The rush of the waters at this spot was tremendous, and no one ventured to approach its vicinity, even in a canoe, lest he should be dashed in pieces. What, then, would be the youth's fate, unless he soon overtook the child? He seemed fully sensible of the increasing peril, and now urged his way through the foaming current with desperate strength.

Three times he was on the point of grasping the child, when the waters whirled the prize from him. The third effort was made just as they were entering within the influence of the current above the fall; and when it failed, the mother's heart sank within her and she groaned, fully expecting the youth to give up his task. But no; he only pressed forward the more eagerly; and, as they breathlessly watched amid the boiling waters, they saw the form of the brave youth following close after that of the boy.

And now, like an arrow from the bow, pursuer and pursued shot to the brink of the precipice. An instant they hung there, distinctly visible amid the foaming waters. Every brain grew dizzy at the sight. But a shout of involuntary exultation burst from the spectators, when they saw the boy held aloft by the right arm

of the youth, — a shout that was suddenly checked wit
horror, when they both vanished into the abyss below

A moment elapsed before a word was spoken, or
breath drawn. The mother ran forward, and then stoo
gazing with fixed eyes at the foot of the cataract, as i
her all depended upon what the next moment shoul
reveal. Suddenly she gave the glad cry, " *There they are
See! they are safe!* — Great God, I thank thee!" And
sure enough, there was the youth still unharmed, anc
still buffeting the waters. He had just emerged fron
the boiling vortex below the cataract. With one hanc
he held aloft the child, and with the other he wa
making for the shore.

They ran, they shouted, they scarcely knew what they
did, until they reached his side, just as he was struggling to the bank. They drew him out almost exhausted
The boy was senseless; but his mother declared that he
still lived, as she pressed him frantically to her bosom.
The youth could scarcely stand, so faint was he from
his exertions.

Who can describe the scene that followed, — the
mother's calmness while she strove to resuscitate her
boy, and her wild gratitude to his preserver, when the
child was out of danger, and sweetly sleeping in her
arms? The pen shrinks at the task. But her words,
pronounced then, were remembered afterwards by more
than one who heard them.

" *God will reward you*," said she, "as *I* can not. He
will do great things for you in return for this day's work,
and the blessings of thousands besides mine will attend
you." And so it was; for, to the hero of that hour were
subsequently confided the destinies of a mighty nation.
But, throughout his long career, what tended to make
him more honored and respected than all other men, was

not the skill and daring which he exhibited in military
tactics, nor yet the brilliant victories he achieved, but
the *self-sacrificing spirit* which, in the rescue of that
mother's child, as in the more august events of his life,
characterized GEORGE WASHINGTON.

Memorize : — "It would have been nothing to him (Washington) that
his partisans or his favorites out-numbered, or out-looked, or out-
managed, or out-clamored those of other leaders. He had no favorites,
rejected all partisanship; and, acting honestly for the universal good,
he deserved, what he had so richly enjoyed, the universal love."

implements	betokened	compact	flaxen
ringlets	incautiously	catastrophe	reclining
attitude	graceful	release	tactics

———o———

PAUL REVERE'S RIDE.

Henry Wadsworth Longfellow, born in 1807, was educated at Bow-
doin, and studied for several years in Europe. He is a most accomplished linguist, and his poems show the influence of his philological
studies in their wonderful nicety of epithet and elaborate finish, and
when translations, in their fidelity to the matter and spirit of the
originals. Of all non-Catholic poets he is the most liberal, and
thoroughly imbued with the Catholic spirit when singing on religious
themes. This is evident in "Evangeline," "Robert of Sicily," "The
Vision Beautiful" and many other of his poems. "Tales of a Way-side
Inn," "The Skeleton in Armor," "Evangeline," "The Launching
of the Ship," "The Village Blacksmith," "Excelsior" and "Paul
Revere's Ride" are his most widely read poems.

L ISTEN, my children, and you shall hear
    Of the midnight ride of Paul Revere,
On the eighteenth of April, in seventy-five ;—
Hardly a man is now alive
Who remembers that famous day and year.

He said to his friend, "If the British march
By land or sea from the town to-night,

Hang a lantern aloft in the belfry arch
Of the North Church tower as a signal light,
One, if by land, and two, if by sea;
And I on the opposite shore will be,
Ready to ride and spread the alarm
Through every Middlesex village and farm,
For the country folk to be up and to arm."

Then said he, " good-night!" and with muffled oar
Silently rowed to the Charlestown shore,
Just as the moon rose over the bay,
Where swinging wide at her moorings lay
The Somerset, British man-of-war:
A phantom ship, with each mast and spar
Across the moon like a prison bar,
And a huge black hulk that was magnified
By its own reflection in the tide.

Meanwhile, his friend, through alley and street,
Wanders and watches with eager ears,
Till in the silence around him he hears
The muster of men at the barrack door,
The sound of arms and the tramp of feet,
And the measured tread of the grenadiers,
Marching down to their boats on the shore.

Then he climbed to the tower of the church,
Up the wooden stairs, with stealthy tread,
To the belfry chamber overhead,
And startled the pigeons from their perch
On the sombre rafters, that round him made
Masses and moving shapes of shade, —
Up the trembling ladder, steep and tall,
To the highest window in the wall,
Where he paused to listen, and look down
A moment on the roofs of the town,
And the moonlight flowing over all.

Beneath, in the church-yard, lay the dead,
In their night encampment on the hill,
Wrapped in silence so deep and still
That he could hear, like a sentinel's tread,
The watchful night wind, as it went
Creeping along from tent to tent,

And seeming to whisper, "*All is well!*"
A moment only he feels the spell
Of the place and the hour, and the secret dread
Of the lonely belfry and the dead ;
For suddenly all his thoughts are bent
On a shadowy something far away,
Where the river widens to meet the bay,
A line of black that bends and floats
On the rising tide, like a bridge of boats.
Meanwhile, impatient to mount and ride,
Booted and spurred, with a heavy stride
On the opposite shore walked Paul Revere

Now he patted his horse's side,
Now gazed at the landscape, far and near,
Then, impetuous, stamped the earth,
And turned and tightened his saddle-girth ;
But mostly he watched with eager search
The belfry tower of the Old North Church,
As it rose above the graves on the hill,
Lonely and spectral and sombre and still ;

And lo! as he looks on the belfry's height,
A glimmer, and then a gleam of light!
He springs to the saddle, the bridle he turns,
But lingers and gazes, till full on his sight
A second lamp in the belfry burns!

A hurry of hoofs in a village street,
A shape in the moonlight, a bulk in the dark,

And beneath, from the pebbles, in passing, a spark,
Struck out by a steed flying fearless and fleet:
That was all! And yet through the gloom and the light,
The fate of a nation was riding that night;
And the spark struck out by that steed in his flight
Kindled the land into flame with its heat.

He has left the village, and mounted the steep,
And beneath him, tranquil and broad and deep,
Is the Mystic, meeting the ocean tides;
And under the alders that skirt its edge,
Now soft on the sand, now loud on the ledge,
Is heard the tramp of his steed as he rides.

It was twelve by the village clock
When he crossed the bridge into Medford town.
He heard the crowing of the cock,
And the barking of the farmer's dog,
And felt the damp of the river fog,
That rises after the sun goes down.

It was one by the village clock
When he galloped into Lexington.
He saw the gilded weathercock
Swim in the moonlight as he passed,
And the meeting-house windows, blank and bare,
Gaze at him with a spectral glare,
As if they already stood aghast
At the bloody work they would look upon.

It was two by the village clock
When he came to the bridge in Concord town.
He heard the bleating of the flock,
And the twitter of birds among the trees,
And felt the breath of the morning breeze
Blowing over the meadows brown.
And one was safe and asleep in his bed

Who at the bridge would be first to fall,
Who that day would be lying dead,
Pierced by a British musket ball.

You know the rest. In the books you have read
How the British regulars fired and fled,—
How the farmers gave them ball for ball,
From behind each fence and farm-yard wall,
Chasing the redcoats down the lane,
Then crossing the fields to emerge again
Under the trees at the turn of the road,
And only pausing to fire and load.

So through the night rode Paul Revere ;
And so through the night went his cry of alarm
To every Middlesex village and farm,—
A cry of defiance, and not of fear,
A voice in the darkness, a knock at the door,
And a word that shall echo forevermore!
For, borne on the night wind of the Past,
Through all our history, to the last,
In the hour of darkness and peril and need,
The people will waken and listen to hear
The hurrying hoof beats of that steed,
And the midnight message of Paul Revere.

Questions:—When did the events here narrated take place? Where
did they take place? Why did Paul Revere want to rouse the
colonists to arms? Where is Charlestown? Explain the phrase,
"moonlight flowing over all." What does "creeping along from tent
tent" mean? What is the "shadowy something in the bay" which
he watches? What is meant by "the fate of a nation was riding
that night"? Where is Lexington? Concord? What was the
"bloody work" that Paul thought the windows looked aghast at?

COMPOSITION.

Give in your own words an account of Paul Revere's ride, from the
following summary, and foregoing questions:

Paul Revere tells his friend to show a light from the Old Church tower, if the British should leave town by night. He rows to the Charlestown shore and gets on his horse, ready to spread the alarm in the country. He passes the British man-of-war. His friend mounts to the Church tower and watches the British fleet and army. He sees the fleet move and gives the signal. Paul Revere sees the signal, mounts his steed, dashes down the village street. At twelve o'clock he reaches Medford; at one, Lexington; at two, Concord. The result of his warning was to prepare the colonists so that they were able to resist the advance of the British on the following day.

Middlesex	encampment	Medford
magnified	sombre	Lexington
muffled	impetuous	glare
Charlestown	spectral	Concord
Somerset	glimmer	bleating
man-of-war	fleet	twitter
spar	alders	regulars
grenadiers	ledge	midnight

————o————

THE REVOLUTIONARY ALARM.

George Bancroft was born in Worcester, Mass., in 1800. He graduated at Harvard, and studied for two years in German universities. He entered actively into political life at an early age, and held several high offices under the general government, including that of Minister to England. The first volume of the History of the United States appeared in 1834, and has been followed at intervals by others to the number of nine. This great work is remarkable for "patient industry, eloquent style, and a capacity to array the theme in a garb of philosophy." In the opinion of Dr. Brownson, "Bancroft has written the only work that deserves the title of History of the United States. From a Catholic point of view some objections can be made to the first volumes, but on the whole it is a noble monument of the genius of the author and the genius of his country."

DARKNESS closed upon the country and upon the town, but it was no night for sleep. Heralds on swift relays of horses transmitted the war message from hand

to hand, till village repeated it to village; the sea to the
backwoods; the plains to the highlands; and it was
never suffered to droop, till it had been borne North,
and South, and East, and West, throughout the land.

It spread over the bays that receive the Saco and the
Penobscot. Its loud reveille broke the rest of the trap-
pers of New Hampshire, and ringing like bugle notes
from peak to peak, overleapt the Green Mountains,
swept onward to Montreal, and descended the ocean
river, till the responses were echoed from the cliffs
of Quebec. The hills along the Hudson told to one
another the tale.

As the summons hurried to the South, it was one day
at New York; in one more at Philadelphia; the next it
lighted a watch fire at Baltimore; thence it waked an
answer at Annapolis. Crossing the Potomac near Mount
Vernon, it was sent forward without a halt to Williams-
burg. It traversed the Dismal Swamp to Nansemond,
along the route of the first emigrants to North Carolina.
It moved onwards and still onwards, through boundless
groves of evergreen, to Newbern and to Wilmington.

"For God's sake, forward it by night and by day,"
wrote Cornelius Harnett, by the express which sped for
Brunswick. Patriots of South Carolina caught up its
tones at the border and despatched it to Charleston,
and through pines and palmettos and moss-clad live-
oaks, further to the South, till it resounded among the
New England settlements beyond the Savannah.

The Blue Ridge took up the voice, and made it heard
from one end to the other of the valley of Virginia. The
Alleghanies, as they listened, opened their barriers
that the "loud call" might pass through to the hardy
riflemen on the Holston, the Watauga and the French
Broad. Ever renewing its strength, powerful enough

even to create a commonwealth, it breathed its inspiring word to the first settlers of Kentucky ; so that hunters who made their halt in the matchless valley of the Elkhorn commemorated the 19th day of April, 1776, by naming their encampment *Lexington*.

With one impulse the colonists sprang to arms ; with one spirit they pledged themselves to each other " to be ready for the extreme event." With one heart the continent cried, " LIBERTY OR DEATH."

Questions :--Explain " Darkness closed . . . . sleep." Mention three occasions on which a " reveille " is used. Tell anything historical you know about "the cliffs of Quebec " and " Revolution." Show the different places named in this lesson. Where are palmettos found ? What is a commonwealth ? Name some ''extreme events '' in history.

Memorize :—

"For freedom's battle once begun,
Bequeathed by bleeding sire to son,
Though baffled oft, is ever won."

relays	trappers	palmettos	impulse
Saco	responses	barriers	continent
Penobscot	patriots	commonwealth	pledged
reveille	despatched	commemorated	event

THE DYING CHRISTIAN TO HIS SOUL.

Alexander Pope was born in London, of Catholic parents, in 1668 ; died in 1744. His name marks an era in English poetry, that of the correct, classical school of Queen Anne's reign. His principal poems are a translation of the " Iliad " of Homer ; " The Dunciad," a bitter satire upon rival poets of his time ; a mock-heroic, entitled the " Rape of the Lock; " the "Imitations from Horace," the "Essay on Criticism," and the " Essay on Man." They are characterized by wit, brilliancy, and clearness, if not depth of thought, and by vigor and conciseness of expression. His verse is highly polished and harmonious, and

e language of poetry. It is to be regretted that a number of his
ntiments offend against religion and morals.

VITAL spark of heavenly flame,
    Quit, O quit this mortal frame!
Trembling, hoping, lingering, flying,
O, the pain, the bliss of dying!
Cease, fond nature, cease thy strife,
And let me languish into life.

Hark!—they whisper; angels say:—
"Sister spirit, come away!"
What is this absorbs me quite?
Steals my senses, shuts my sight,
Drowns my spirit, draws my breath?
Tell me, my soul, can this be death?

The world recedes; it disappears;
Heaven opens on my eyes; my ears
With sounds seraphic ring:—
Lend, lend your wings! I mount! I fly!
"O Grave, where is thy victory?
O Death, where is thy sting?"

Questions:—When is anything "vital"? Why is the soul called a
"vital spark"? What is "the mortal frame"? Why is man "trembling, hoping, lingering, flying"? How is death a pain, yet a bliss?
What does "languish into life" mean? Who is told to hearken?
Whose is the "sister spirit"? How does death "absorb us quite"?
"Steal our senses, shut our sight, drown our spirit"? What recedes
and disappears? What happens to my ears? Who are asked to lend
their wings? When are we victorious over death? When do we escape
its sting? What is said in Holy Writ of the just man's death? Name
some very good deaths you know, or have read of.

| lingering | absorbs | recedes |
| language | senses | seraphic |

INSUFFICIENCY OF NATURAL RELIGION.

IF Natural Religion is a sufficient revelation, and no other is necessary, it has been written with a sunbeam upon all lands, — it has been inscribed from the beginning of the creation upon the face of the glorious orb of day. But what is the result? What has Natural Religion effected, in any, in every age? — in any, in every country? "The heavens shew forth the glory of God, and the firmament declareth the work of his hands." But "the world by wisdom knew not God;" they "worshipped and served the creature rather than the Creator;" they fell down to the hosts of heaven; or "changed the glory of the incorruptible God into the likeness of the image of a corruptible man, and of birds, and of four-footed beasts, and of creeping things."

Now call for Natural Religion, and she shall answer you from the depths of the forest and the summits of the mountains; from the sea, and from the shore; from the crowded city, and the uncultivated desert; from the hut of the savage, and the dome of the monarch; — everywhere her altars are planted, and her worship maintained. Her influence and her footsteps may be traced on the face of the whole earth, in barbarous rites, revolting superstitions, and disgusting obscenities; in all the forms of idolatry, from the feathered gods of the South Sea Islands, to the misshapen logs of Africa, up to the three hundred and thirty-three thousand deities of philosophic India.

Would you see her in her own person? Bid her come forth, — she appears "in garments rolled in blood;" "the battle of the warrior with confused noise" rages around her; her children drop into the fires kindled to her honor; human victims are slaughtered on the altars raised to her praise, or crushed beneath the ponderous car upon which she sits enthroned. Around her, dying cries and agonizing shrieks mingle with loud acclamations and frantic songs; her look withers the country and depopulates the city.

This is Natural Religion, and not as she came from the hands of God, the witness of his eternal power and Godhead; but as she is deformed by the passions of men, and debased by their corruptions; not as "the image of the invisible Creator," but as the idol of the fallen and depraved creature. Yes, this is Natural Religion, stained with gore, and foul with crimes; not depicted by fancy, but demonstrated by facts, — by facts drawn from all climes and from all generations.

But *Reason* was to have rectified these errors; Reason was to sit supreme, enshrined in the light of Natural Religion, the arbitress of human destinies. To her was intrusted the key of knowledge, to unlock and dispense the riches of the universe. She was to be the architect, rearing a structure of happiness and of virtue, under which man should repose, and a temple of religion, in which he should worship. She was to be the polar star, upon which fixing a steady eye, he might safely sail over the stormy sea of life, and find a port of rest at last. But the light of the star is obscured; the plans of the architect are marred; the key of knowledge is mislaid; the arbitress of man's fate is dethroned.

How is it she has lost her high prerogative, and suffered her authority to be overthrown? How is it that she has fallen from her pinnacle of glory? She was beguiled by sense. "The invisible things of Him, from the creation of the world, are clearly seen, being understood by the things that are made: His eternal power also and Divinity." But when men became vain in their imaginations, — their foolish heart was darkened , and professing themselves to be wise, they became fools.

But *Philosophy* is to restore the reign of Natural Religion, of reason, of conscience, and of virtue. Were Greece and Rome, then, barbarians? Were they ignorant of philosophy? or was the experiment not made? It was not in a desert, surrounded by savages, but in the centre of Athens, encircled by philosophers, that Paul stood amidst the monuments and upon a mount of idolatry, — although a court, and the highest court of justice, evincing how closely allied the civil government was with their debasing superstitions, — and pointed to an altar inscribed : — *"To the unknown God."*

Such is the true character of every altar which reason and philosophy, and Natural Religion, unaided by revelation, have raised, although all do not bear the same inscription. These are the altars which the missionary of the Gospel is hastening to overthrow, to plant the cross in their place, and to proclaim to the poor idolater : — "What, therefore, you worship, without knowing it, that I preach to you."

And is it not to men like these, the mighty minds of departed ages, who sought after truth, but missed it, because they lacked the guiding ray of revelation, — is it not to men like these that infidels of the present day appeal, acknowledging them as masters, and adopting their systems, — men who, if they now lived, would be ashamed of their professed scholars? If, among such men, Natural Religion, and reason, and conscience, and philosophy, all proved an unequal guard against the passions of a corrupt nature, and a guide, absolutely insufficient through the mazes of ignorance, to the throne of God, — if, in such hands, the grand experiment altogether failed, what further pretensions have modern philosophers, the opposers of revelation, to advance?

They will not dare to tell you that it has been denied either time or space; it has been made nearly six thousand years, from the fall of man to the present time, — it has been made by the intellectual giants of the olden time. They will not dare to tell you that the results have ever been different from those which we have stated. They will not dare to deny, that such is, at this moment, the aggregate of the experiment now trying, among all states, whether savage or civilized, which revelation has not reached.

I disdain to contrast the intellectual and moral influence of Christianity, wherever it extends, with the scenes of horror and degradation to which I have alluded; but I demand of infidel opponents to explain, if they can, by what fatality, or by what chance, it occurs, that their efforts to elevate the moral condition of man have never succeeded, and that those of Christianity have never failed.

COMPOSITION.

Copy third and fourth paragraphs. Then answer the following questions: *(a)* How does Natural Religion treat children? *(b)* Tell the part of the New Testament where St. Paul speaks of the altar "to the unknown God." *(c)* Name six "intellectual giants" of the olden time.

Memorize: —

"Let us ask these martyrs,* then, these monarchs of the East,
Who are sitting now in heaven at their Saviour's endless feast,
To get us faith from Jesus, and, hereafter, faith's bright home,
And day and night to thank him for the glorious faith of Rome."

orb	obscenities	rectified	acknowledging
handiwork	depopulates	enshrined	pretensions
incorruptible	debased	experiment	alluded

* The three kings.

LINES ON A SKELETON.

BEHOLD this ruin! 'Twas a skull,
  Once of ethereal spirit full.
This narrow cell was Life's retreat,
This space was Thought's mysterious seat
What beauteous visions filled this spot,
What dreams of pleasure long forgot.
Nor Hope, nor Love, nor Joy, nor Fear,
Have left one trace of record here

Beneath this mouldering canopy
Once shone the bright and busy eye;
But, start not at the dismal void —
If social Love that eye employed,
If with no lawless fire it gleamed,
But through the dews of kindness beamed
That eye shall be forever bright
When stars and suns are sunk in night.

Within this hollow cavern hung
The ready, swift, and tuneful tongue.
If Falsehood's honey it disdained,
And where it could not praise, was chained;
If bold in Virtue's cause it spoke,
Yet gentle Concord never broke,.
This silent tongue shall plead for thee
When Time unveils Eternity.

Say, did these fingers delve the mine?
Or with its envied rubies shine?
To hew the rock, or wear the gem,
Can little now avail to them.
But if the page of Truth they sought,
Or comfort to the mourner brought,
These hands a richer meed shall claim
Than all that wait on Wealth or Fame.

Avails it whether bare or shod,
These feet the paths of duty trod?
If from the bowers of Ease they fled,
To seek Affliction's humble shed,
If Grandeur's guilty bribe they spurned,
And home to Virtue's cot returned,
These feet with angels' wings shall vie,
And tread the palace of the sky.

Questions:—What is a ruin? Why is the skull a ruin? What are found in ruins? What was once in this skull? Mention some ethereal things. What is a retreat? Name some favored American retreats. What kind of visions fill youthful heads, and older ones? Are any left? Where are canopies seen? Name some you have seen. What shone from out this canopy? What use must *we* make of our eyes? What will then be our reward? Where is the cavern? What use should we make of our tongue? What good things say? What evil avoid? What will be the result? How can "fingers shine with envied rubies"? What is all the same to those fingers now? How can our hands "comfort the mourner"? What society in the Catholic Church does this? What are "bowers of Ease"? How may we seek "Affliction's humble shed"? What is meant by "Grandeur's guilty bribe"? How will the feet of the just vie with angels' wings?

ethereal	rubies	mouldering
meed	canopy	shod
tuneful	bowers	unveils
spurned	delve	vie

A TERRIBLE FIFTY MINUTES.

IN August, 1859, I arrived at Chamounix with one of my friends, a traveller like myself. For about five weeks we had been exploring Switzerland, so that we had plenty of time to get used to snow and glaciers. We had made several ascents, one of 14,000 feet.

We had ascended the Brévent, and we now had only the Mer de Glace and the Jardin to visit. We slept

at the Montanvert in the solitary little inn at the foot
of the glacier. Next morning we were up at dawn.
Furnished with provisions and two bottles of wine, we
started with our guides. It was a splendid morning,
and augured well for our excursion. For half an hour
we followed a rough path which skirted the Mer de
Glace, which displayed below us its surface, riven with
crevasses and covered with rocks and fragments. Our
road ended at the glacier, upon which we now began to
descend, and to traverse in zig-zags in the midst of
numerous fissures. The Mer de Glace is not considered
dangerous, and it is quite the exception to take axes and
ropes, when crossing it. Alert and cheerful we hastened
on, without taking notice of the guide, who, some way
behind, cried out to us several times to be cautious and
wait for him. We were obliged at last to halt before a
vast crevasse which barred up our passage. It opened
with a length of some sixty yards, and ended upon our
left in a slope of ice, somewhat steep, but which I thought
I could easily mount. Using the iron spike of my
alpenstock as a hatchet, I began to cut holes in the ice,
large enough to put my feet in. At this moment our
guide rejoined us. He looked at the slope and at the
yawning crevasse below it, and said in a grave tone, "It
is dangerous; let us go round it."

With the help of my alpenstock I had already got
half-way up this icy hillock, and was now quite convinced
that it was too steep and slippery to be crossed without
an axe. The guide's warning confirmed my opinion. I
resolved to retrace my steps. I was cautiously lowering my right leg, seeking for the hole that I had made
in the ice; my foot passed it; I felt that I was sliding
down; there was nothing rough to stop me, not the
least projection by which I could hold myself in. The

declivity became perpendicular, and I fell into the gulf.

I heard the cries of despair of my companion and my guide. My own sensation cannot be described. I was giddy and half stunned, sent backwards and forwards rom one wall of ice to the other; I felt myself descend-ng to a great depth, condemned to be dashed to pieces, o die a horrible death. Suddenly something stopped ne, I felt myself suspended. I took breath again, and ould cry out, "A rope! a rope!"

By God's mercy I had fallen upon a narrow ledge of ce, which formed a sort of bridge across the crevasse. This frail support, as far as I could judge, was about our inches broad and eighteen thick. My head hung rom one side of it, my feet from the other. Instinc-ively, by what means I know not, I raised myself up nd stood upright on this projection, where there was a iollow just large enough for me to plant one foot.

My position was a terrible one, the thin ledge of ice ieing so narrow that I could not place both feet on it. I ould only support myself on one leg, half resting against ine of the ice walls, and pressing the other with my iand. The ice was smooth as a mirror, there was iothing to grasp. A stream of ice-water flowed down ipon my shoulders, piercing me to the very bones; above ny head I saw the long and narrow streak of the sky, iround which the mouth of the crevasse formed a frame.

The ice, which was of darkest blue color, encircling ne on all sides, looked threatening and gloomy. The iwo walls seemed as if they were about to meet in order io crush me, rather than to release their prey. Numer-ous watercourses streamed down their sides, but in this extent of more than sixty yards I could not see any other projection or obstacle, except this ledge on which I had so miraculously fallen.

I risked looking, for one second only, down into the terrible abyss above which I was suspended. At the spot where I was, the crevasse was not more than two feet wide, lower down it narrowed rapidly, and a hundred yards below the two sides appeared to touch each other. It was impossible to change my position without the risk of losing my balance. The cold of the wall of ice against which I was resting more and more benumbed me, the water continued to fall, and I dared not stir.

I called my companion; no one replied. I called again. Nothing! Nothing! Not a human being within reach of my voice. I was seized with giddiness as a thought crossed my brain.

"He has gone to see if the help is coming, and he cannot find the crevasse again. There are hundreds such — I am lost!"

I commended my soul to God. My strength was quite exhausted. I had never yet given up all hope. I was tempted to let myself fall, and thus put an end to this agony.

At this critical moment I heard myself called. My friend had run to look for the guide, but when he wished to return he was horror stricken on perceiving that the surface of the glacier was rent by countless crevasses, all so similar that there was not a single sign by which he could recognize the abyss where I was buried alive. In this cruel perplexity God led him to see a little knapsack which the guide had left at the edge of the gulf.

I felt that I could hold on but very little longer. The frail support on which my safety alone depended might yield at any moment and break beneath me. I remembered that I had a strong knife in my pocket, and I resolved to make use of it to draw myself out. I informed my companion of this project; he implored me to do nothing of the kind; but my situation had become intolerable. I made a notch in the ice, high enough for me to reach it, and large enough for me to insert my · hand in it; then about two feet above the little bridge I dug out a hole sufficiently large for me to place my foot in it. I succeeded, and grasping these two points of support, my back resting with all my strength against the opposite wall, I was able to raise myself and keep myself firm in this new position. I descended again upon the bridge, and began another notch above the first. I flattered myself that I should thus be able to escape from my prison, but a single slip, a false step, would precipitate me into the abyss.

I was working diligently at my second step when I heard a joyous cry above me: "Here they are! Three men with ropes — they are running as fast as their legs can carry them."

I steadied myself as firmly as possible upon the narrow and slippery bridge, so as to be able to seize the rope they were about to lower, and tie it around me. I saw the end of it swinging about two yards above my head. "May God have mercy upon me! it is too short!"

"We have another," cried they, to my delight.

That was fastened to the first, and let down. I seized the end of it. I bound it strongly around my waist, and grasping the rope with both hands I gave the signal for them to pull up.

They began — I was saved. A minute afterwards I was standing upon the glacier. I had passed fifty minutes in the crevasse, during which time I had happily lost neither my confidence in God nor my presence of mind.

fissures	augured	crevasses	zig-zags
alpenstock	exception	alert	cautious
sensation	yawning	hillock	retrace
instinctively	projection	declivity	perpendicular
· benumbed	stunned	suspended	frail
intolerable	streak	encircling	threatening
steadied	exhausted	perplexity	notch

Questions : — Where is Switzerland? What is a glacier? What does "augured well" mean? What is an alpenstock? What is a crevasse? Name other dangers of the Alps. What is an avalanche? What has been done to protect travellers? Tell all you know about the monks of St. Bernard. In what poem is death by the avalanche described? ("Excelsior.") What recent change has removed the necessity of riding over the mountain?

COMPOSITION.

Write an account of an imaginary adventure in the Alpine glaciers. A party of tourists stop at Mount St. Bernard. The monks warn them not to attempt to climb the mountain. They do not heed the advice · they procure guides and ropes. Descending the side they come to an ice-field traversed by a crevasse. Attempting to go around the opening, one of the number slips, fails to recover his footing and falls into the abyss. A ledge of ice stops his descent. His thoughts and movements there. His companions lower a rope ; it is too short. They run to the convent for another. Meanwhile he is about to succumb to the frost and to weakness. The rescuers cannot find their way back: at last they see a knapsack on the brink and recognize the spot. This time the rope is long enough and the man is lifted out.

Memorize : —

"Eternal Providence, exceeding thought,
Where none appears can make herself a way."

————o————

THE INQUIRY.

TELL me, ye winged winds,
That round my pathway roar,

Do ye not know some spot
  Where mortals weep no more? —
Some lone and pleasant dell,
  Some valley in the West,
Where, free from toil and pain,
  The weary soul may rest?,
The loud wind dwindled to a whisper low,
And sighed for pity as it answered, — "No."

Tell me, thou mighty deep,
  Whose billows round me play,
Know'st thou some favored spot,
  Some island far away,
Where weary man may find
  The bliss for which he sighs, —
Where sorrow never lives,
  And friendship never dies?
The loud waves, rolling in perpetual flow,
  Stopped for a while, and sighed to answer, — "No."

And thou, serenest moon,
  That, with such lovely face,
Dost look upon the earth,
  Asleep in night's embrace;
Tell me, in all thy round,
  Hast thou not seen some spot,
Where miserable man
  Might find a happier lot?
Behind a cloud the moon withdrew in woe,
And a voice, sweet, but sad, responded, — "No

Tell me, my secret soul,
  O! tell me, Hope and Faith,
Is there no resting-place
  From sorrow, sin, and death?
Is there no happy spot,

Where mortals may be blessed,
Where grief may find a balm,
And weariness a rest?
Faith, Hope, and Love, best boons to mortals given,
Waved their bright wings, and whispered,—" YES, IN HEAVEN!

Questions :— What question is asked in the first four lines ? How i
this spot described in the next four lines? Why did the wind sigh
What are the billows doing? What kind of a spot is "the favore
island"? For what does weary man sigh? What always lives an
what never dies in this isle? By what is the earth embraced a
night? What question is asked the moon? Why did the moon with
draw? What virtues are questioned in the last stanza? What ques
tion is asked them? What may grief find there? What are the bes
boons to mortal given? What did Faith and Hope answer?

| mortals | billows | serenest | responded |
| dwindled | perpetual | embrace | boons |

RULES OF BEHAVIOR.

EVERY action in company ought to be done with
some sign of respect to those present.

In presence of others, sing not to yourself with a
humming noise, nor drum with your fingers or feet.

Sleep not when others speak; sit not when others
stand; speak not when you should hold your peace;
walk not when others stop.

Turn not your back to others, especially in speaking,
jog not the table or desk on which another reads or
writes; lean not on any one.

Be no flatterer; neither play with any one that delights
not to be played with.

Read no letters, books, or papers, in company; but
when there is a necessity for doing it, you must ask
leave. Come not near the books or writings of any one

as to read them, unless desired, nor give your opinion
them unasked; also, look not nigh when another is
writing a letter.

When another speaks, be attentive yourself, and disturb not the audience. If any hesitate in his words,
help him not, nor prompt him, without being desired;
interrupt him not, nor answer him till his speech is ended.

Be not curious to know the affairs of others, neither
approach to those that speak in private.

Make no show of taking great delight in your
victuals; feed not with greediness; lean not on the
table; neither find fault with what you eat.

Let your discourse with men of business be short and
comprehensive.

In visiting the sick, do not presently play the physician, if you be not knowing therein.

Undertake not to teach your equal in the art he himself
professes; it savors of arrogancy.

Be not immoderate in urging your friend to discover
a secret.

If two contend together, take not the part of either
unconstrained, and be not obstinate in your own opinion; in things indifferent, be of the major side.

Speak not in an unknown tongue in company, but in
your own language, and as those of quality do, and not
as the vulgar; sublime matters treat seriously.

In dispute, be not so desirous to overcome, as [you
are] to give liberty to each one to deliver his opinion;
and submit to the judgment of the major part, especially
if they are judges of the dispute.

Be not angry at table, whatever happens, and if you
have reason to be so, show it not; put on a cheerful
countenance, especially if there be strangers present, for
good humor makes one dish of meat a feast.

When you meet with one of greater quality than yourself, stop and retire, especially if it be at a door or any strait place, to give way to him to pass.

They that are in dignity, or in office, have in all places precedency; but, while they are young, they ought to respect those who are their equals in birth, or other qualities, though they have no public charge.

It is good manners to prefer them, to whom we are to speak, before ourselves, especially if they be above us with whom in no sort we ought to begin.

In writing or speaking, give to every peson his due title, according to his degree and the custom of the place.

Strive not with your superiors in argument, but always submit your judgment to others with modesty.

Be not forward, but friendly and courteous; the first to salute, hear, and answer; and be not pensive when it is time to converse.

When your superiors talk to anybody, hearken not neither speak, nor laugh.

When you speak of God or of his attributes, let it be seriously, in reverence. Honor and obey your natural parents, although they be poor.

In your apparel be modest, and endeavor to accommodate nature, rather than to procure admiration; keep to the fashion of your equals, such as are civil and orderly with respect to times and places.

Play not the peacock, looking everywhere about you to see if you be well decked, if your shoes fit well, if your stockings set neatly, and clothes handsomely.

Think before you speak; pronounce not imperfectly, nor bring out your words too hastily, but orderly and distinctly.

Undertake not what you cannot perform, but be careful to keep your promise.

When you deliver a matter, do it without passion, and with discretion, however mean the person may be you do it to.

Be not tedious in discourse; make not many digressions, nor repeat often the same manner of discourse.

Use no reproachful language against any one, neither curse, nor revile.

Let your countenance be pleasant, but in all serious matters somewhat grave.

Being to advise or reprehend any one, consider whether it ought to be in public or private, presently or at some other time, in what terms to do it; and, in reproving, show no signs of choler, but do it with sweetness and mildness.

Mock not nor jest at anything of importance; break no jests that are sharp biting; and if you deliver anything witty and pleasant, abstain from laughing thereat yourself.

Associate yourself with men of good quality, if you esteem your own reputation; for it is better to be alone than in bad company.

Utter not base and frivolous things among grave and learned men; nor very difficult questions or subjects among the ignorant; nor things hard to be believed.

Break not a jest where none takes pleasure in mirth; laugh not aloud, nor at all without occasion. Deride no man's misfortune, though there seems to be some cause.

Go not thither where you know not whether you shall be welcome or not. Give not advice without being asked; and when desired, do it briefly.

Treat with men at fit times about business, and whisper not in the company of others.

Be not hasty to believe flying reports to the disparagement of any.

Speak not injurious words, neither in jest nor earnest, scoff at none, although they give occasion.

Detract not from others, neither be excessive in com mending.

Be not apt to relate news, if you know not the truth thereof. In discoursing of things you have heard, name not your author always. A secret discover not.

Show not yourself glad at the misfortune of another, though he were your enemy.

When a man does all he can, though he succeeds not well, blame not him that did it.

Let your conversation be without malice or envy, for it is a sign of tractable and commendable nature ; and, in all causes of passion, admit reason to govern.

Gaze not on the marks or blemishes of others, and ask not how they came. What you speak in secret to your friend, deliver not before others.

COMPOSITION.

Give first two advices in your own words.

hesitate	speak	digressions
comprehensive	precedency	intimate
savors	orderly	tractable
arrogancy	discretion	blemishes

EUROPEAN CIVILIZATION.

Abbé J. Balmez, born in Catalonia, Spain, in 1810 ; died in 1848. He is the intellectual phenomenon of the century. In lofty eloquence, keen historical insight, profound philosophy and solid learning he stands unrivalled amongst the writers of the age. The "Civilization of Europe" is a masterpiece. It should be read by every one who aspires to a true knowledge of the work of the Church in the advancement of mankind. "Fundamental Philosophy," translated by Henry F. Brownson, is the best work on Christian Philosophy which English

aders can consult. The "Criterion," translated by another author,
an admirably practical guide to the formation of sound habits of
udy, thought and action. It should be a text-book in the hands of
very young student.

IT is a fact now generally acknowledged, and openly
confessed, that Christianity has exercised a very
mportant and salutary influence on the development
f European civilization. If this fact has not yet had
iven to it the importance which it deserves, it is
ecause it has not been sufficiently appreciated. With
espect to civilization, a distinction is sometimes made
etween the influence of Christianity and that of Catho-
icity : its merits are lavished on the former, and stinted
o the latter, by those who forget that, with respect to
European civilization, Catholicity can always claim the
principal share ; and, for many centuries, an exclusive
ne ; since during a very long period she worked alone
it the great work. People have not been willing to
see that when Protestantism appeared in Europe the
work was bordering on completion ; with an injustice
and ingratitude which I cannot describe, they have
reproached Catholicity with the spirit of barbarism,
ignorance and oppression, while they were making an
ostentatious display of the rich civilization, knowledge
and liberty for which they were principally indebted
to her.

If they did not wish to fathom the intimate connection between Catholicity and European civilization,— if
they had not the patience necessary for the long inves-
tigations into which this examination would lead them,
at least it would have been proper to take a glance at
the condition of countries where the Catholic religion
has not exerted all her influence during centuries of
trouble, and compare them with those in which she has

been preaominant. The East and the West, both subject to great revolutions, both professing Christianity,
but in such a way that the Catholic principle was weak
and vacillating in the East, while it was energetic and
deeply rooted in the West; these, we say, would have
afforded two very good points of comparison to estimate
the value of Christianity without Catholicity, when the
civilization and the existence of nations were at stake.

In the West, the revolutions were multiplied and
fearful; the chaos was at its height; and, nevertheless,
out of chaos came light and life. Neither the barbarism
of the nations who inundated those countries, and
established themselves there, nor the furious assaults
of Islamism, even in the days of its greatest power and
enthusiasm, could succeed in destroying the germs of a
rich and fertile civilization. In the East, on the contrary, all tended to old age and decay; nothing revived;
and, under the blows of the power which was ineffectual
against us, all was shaken to pieces. The spiritual
power of Rome, and its influence on temporal affairs,
have certainly borne fruits very different from those
produced under the same circumstances by its violent
opponents.

If Europe were destined one day again to undergo a
general and fearful revolution, either by a universal
spread of revolutionary ideas, or by a violent invasion
of social and proprietary rights by pauperism; if the
Colossus of the North, seated on its throne of eternal
snows, with knowledge in its head, and blind force in
its hands, possessing at once the means of civilization
and unceasingly turning towards the East, the South,
and the West that covetous and crafty look which
in history is the characteristic march of all invading
empires; if, availing itself of a favorable moment, it

rere to make an attempt on the independence of Europe,
hen we should perhaps have a proof of the value of
he Catholic principle in a great extremity; then we
hould feel the power of the unity which is proclaimed
nd supported by Catholicity, and while calling to mind
he Middle Ages, we should come to acknowledge one of
he causes of the weakness of the East and the strength
f the West.

Then would be remembered a fact, which, though
ut of yesterday, is falling into oblivion, viz.: that the
ation whose heroic courage broke the power of
Tapoleon was proverbially Catholic; and who knows
rhether, in the attempts which the Vicar of Jesus
Christ has deplored in such touching language, — who
nows whether it be not the secret influence of a pre-
entment, perhaps even a foresight, of the necessity of
reakening that sublime power, which has been in all
ges, when the cause of humanity was in question, the
entre of great attempts? But let us return.

It cannot be denied that, since the sixteenth century,
European civilization has shown life and brilliancy; but
t is a mistake to attribute this phenomenon to Protest-
ntism. In order to examine the extent and influence
f a fact, we ought not to be content with the events
rhich have followed it; it is also necessary to consider
rhether these events were already prepared; whether
hey are any thing more than the necessary result of
nterior facts. Without Protestanism, and before it,
European civilization was already very much advanced,
hanks to the labors and influence of the Catholic
eligion; that greatness and splendor which it subsequently displayed were not owing to Protestantism, but
rose in spite of it.

COMPOSITION

State what is said about the identity of Christianity and Catholicity previous to the Protestant Reformation. Mention the mistake made by Protestant writers.

Continue by mentioning the degree to which civilization had arrived before the Reformation.

Show from the life of some saint, say St. Boniface or St. Augustine, how the Church civilized her first converts.

Still further elucidate this by referring to the history of early American missions among the Indians.

Memorize :—"The Church aims, not at making a show, but at doing a work. She regards this world, and all that is in it, as a mere show, as dust and ashes, compared with the value of one single soul."

development	ostentatious	vacillating	proprietary
stinted	predominant	Islamism	anterior

———o———

TACT AND TALENT

TALENT is something, but *tact** is everything. *Talent* is serious, sober, grave and respectable : *tact* is all that, and more too. It is not a sixth sense, but it is the life of all the five. It is the open eye, the quick ear, the judging taste, the keen smell, and the lively touch; it is the interpreter of all riddles, the ·surmounter of all difficulties, the remover of all obstacles. It is useful in all places, and at all times; it is useful in solitude, for it shows a man his way *into* the world; it is useful in society for it shows him his way *through* the world.

Talent is power, *tact* is skill; *talent* is weight, *tact* is momentum; *talent* knows *what* to do, *tact* knows *how* to do it; talent makes a man respectable, tact will make him respected; talent is wealth, tact is ready money.

---

* The expression "tact" is here used in the sense of "skilful prudence in action."

For all the practical purposes of life, tact carries it against talent, ten to one. Take them to the theatre, and put them against each other on the stage, and talent shall produce you a tragedy that will scarcely live long enough to be condemned, while tact keeps the house in a roar, night after night, with its successful farces. There is no want of dramatic talent, there is no want of dramatic tact; but they are seldom together: so we have successful pieces which are not respectable, and respectable pieces which are not successful.

Take them to the bar, and let them shake their learned curls at each other in legal rivalry; talent sees its way clearly, but tact is first at its journey's end. Talent has many a compliment from the bench, but tact touches fees from clients. Talent speaks learnedly and logically, tact triumphantly. Talent makes the world wonder that it gets on no faster, tact excites astonishment that it gets on so fast. And the secret is, that it has no weight to carry; it makes no false steps; it hits the right nail on the head; it loses no time; it takes all hints. Take them into the church. Talent has always something worth hearing, tact is sure of abundance of hearers; talent may obtain a living, tact will make one; talent gets a good name, tact a great one; talent convinces, tact converts; talent is an honor *to* the profession, tact gains honor *from* the profession.

Take them to court. Talent feels its weight, tact finds its way; talent commands, tact is obeyed; talent is honored with approbation, and tact is blessed by preferment. Place them in the senate. Talent has the ear of the house, but tact wins its heart, and has its votes; talent is fit for employment, but tact is fitted for it. Tact has a knack of slipping into place with a sweet silence and glibness of movement, as a billiard ball insinuates itself into the pocket. It seems to know every thing, without learning any thing. It has served an invisible and extemporary apprenticeship; it wants no drilling; it never ranks in the awkward squad; it has no left hand, no deaf ear, no blind side. It put son no looks of wondrous wisdom, it has no air of profundity, but plays with the details of place as dexterously as a well taught hand flourishes over the keys of the piano-forte. It has all the air of commonplace, and all the force and power of genius:

COMPOSITION.

Give six expressions in reference to tact. Explain the following sentences: *(a)* Take them to the bar, and let them shake their curls at each other in legal rivalry: talent sees its way clearly, but tact is first at its journey's end. *(b)* Tact has served an invisible and extemporary apprenticeship; it wants no drilling; it never ranks in the awkward squad; it has no left hand, no deaf ear, no blind side. *(c)* Tact seems to know everything without learning anything.

talent	tragedy	glibness
tact	rivalry	extemporary
interpreter	compliment	details
momentum	fees	dexterously

THE SHIP.

HER giant form
  O'er wrathful surge, through blackening storm,
Majestically calm would go
'Mid the deep darkness, white as snow!
But gently now the small waves glide,
Like playful lambs o'er a mountain's side
So stately her bearing, so proud her array,
The main she will traverse for ever and aye.

Many ports will exult at the gleam of her mast —
Hush! hush! thou vain dreamer: this hour is her last.

Five hundred souls in one instant of dread
    Are hurried o'er the deck;
And fast the miserable ship
    Becomes a lifeless wreck!
Her keel had struck on a hidden rock,
    Her planks are torn asunder,
And down come her masts with a reeling shock
    And a hideous crash like thunder.
Her sails are draggled in the brine
    That gladdened late the skies;
And her pennant, that kissed the fair moonshine
    Down many a fathom lies.
Her beauteous sides, whose rainbow hues
    Gleamed softly from below,
And flung a warm and sunny flush
    O'er the wreaths of murmuring snow,
To the coral rocks are hurrying down,
To sleep amid colors as bright as their own.

Oh! many a dream was in the ship
    An hour before her death;
And sights of home, with sighs disturb'd
    The sleepers' long-drawn breath.
Instead of the murmur of the sea,
The sailor heard the humming tree,
    Alive through all its leaves;
The hum of the spreading sycamore,
That grows before his cottage door,
    And the swallow's song in the eaves.
His arms enclose a blooming boy,
Who listen'd with tears of sorrow and joy
    To the dangers his father had pass'd;
And his wife — by turns she wept and smiled,

As sne look'd on the father of her child—
   Returned to her heart at last.
—He wakes at the vessel's sudden roll,
And the rush of the waters is in his soul.

Astounded, the reeling deck he paces,
'Mid hurrying forms and ghastly faces;—
   The whole ship's crew are there!
Wailing around and overhead—
Brave spirits stupefied or dead,
   With madness and despair.

Now is the ocean's bosom bare,
Unbroken as the floating air.
The ship hath melted quite away,
Like a struggling dream at break of day.
No image meets my wandering eye
But the new-risen sun and the sunny sky.
Though the nightshades are gone, yet a vapor dull
Bedims the waves so beautiful;
While a low and melancholy moan
Mourns for the glory that hath flown.

COMPOSITION

Describe a shipwreck from this
SUMMARY:

The ship is sailing proudly on the calm waters. A cloud is seen
the horizon. It grows bigger and blacker, the wind tosses
white caps on the waves. The captain gives orders to furl the sai
Suddenly the storm strikes the ship. The wind whistles through
rigging. The waves toss the ship about; she springs a leak; the m
are ordered to the pumps; the sea gains on them and the passeng
are called to assist. The masts go over; the life-boat is lowered, so
get in, others fall into the waves; some wait till the ship goes down a
cling to spars and rafts. Some may be afterwards picked up, wh
many are lost. Try to bring in quotations from above poem.

surge	array	pennant	sycamore	ghastly
majestically	draggled	fathom	eaves	bedims

ON THE SYMBOLISM - OF CHRISTIANITY.

Cardinal Wiseman (1802 – 1865) was born of Irish parents at Seville, Spain; ordained priest in 1825, and for several years was Rector of e English College at Rome. On the re-establishment, in 1850, of the nglish Catholic Hierarchy, he was appointed by Pius IX. Archbishop the new See of Westminster, and raised to the dignity of Cardinal. was a beneficent Providence which selected such a man for the vival of the Church in England. To the essentials of the priestly aracter he united the most profound and varied learning, the most eral and pleasing culture. In languages, in philology, in oriental- m, in theology, in literary criticism, in natural science, in contro- rsy, even in fiction — he has left the records of his versatile genius, d has shed lustre not only upon his Church but upon English erature. His "Lectures on Revealed Religion" are a complete swer to modern infidelity. His best known work is "Fabiola," a storical work of fiction.

WILL suppose, if you please, an ancient Roman revisiting the Pantheon : the first thing which would rike him would be the sign of salvation — the image Christ crucified, raised upon every altar, and most nspicuously upon the principal and central one. On e right, the picture of one whom men are stoning, hile he, with eyes uplifted, prays for their conversion, ould rivet his attention : and on the left, the modest atue of a virgin, with an infant in her arms, would vite him to inquiry. Then he would see monuments men, whose clasped or crossed hands express how ey expired in the prayer of hope ; the inscription, on e side, would tell him how the immortal Raphael had illed that no ornament should deck his tomb but that ry statue of God's mother which he had given to that urch ; another informs you that the illustrious states- an (Gonsalvi), after bequeathing the fortune he had ade in the service of the public, without reserve, to e propagation of Christianity among distant nations, ould have no tomb ; but that his friends had, as it were by stealth, erected to him that modest memorial.

Around him he would see, at whatever hour of the day he might enter, solitary worshippers, who gently come in through the ever-unclosed brazen portals, to keep watch, like the lamp which sheds its mild light upon them, before the altar of God. And I fancy it would be no difficult task, with these objects before us, to expound and fully develop to him the Christian faith : the life of our Redeemer, beginning with his birth from a virgin, to his death upon a cross; the testimony to his doctrine, and the power which accompanied it, exhibited in the triumph of the first among his martyrs : the humble and modest virtue his teaching inspired to his followers, their contempt of worldly praise, and the fixing of their hopes upon a better world; the constant and daily influence his religion exercises amongst its believers, whom it sweetly invites and draws to breathe a solitary prayer, amidst the turmoils of a busy life. And methinks this ancient heathen would have an idea of a religion immensely different from that which he had professed — the religion of the meek and of the humble, of the persecuted and the modest, of the devout and the chaste. I believe, too, that by seeing the substitution of symbol for symbol — of the cross, for the badge of ignominy; with its unresisting Victim, for the haughty thunderer; of the chastest of virgins, for the lascivious Venus; of the forgiving Stephen for the avenging god of war — he would thereby conceive a livelier idea of the overthrow of his idolatry by the mildest of doctrines; of the substitution of Christianity for heathenism, than if the temple had been merely stripped, and left a naked hall, or a tottering ruin.

For I think that the ark of God, standing in the very temple of Dagon, with the idol at its side, broken and so maimed that it might no longer be made to stand upon its pedestal, would convey a stronger and prouder demonstration of the superiority of the Law to the religion of Syria, than when concealed in silence behind the curtain of the sanctuary.

Pantheon	memorial	substitution
conspicuously	expound	haughty
rivet	solitary	lascivious
bequeathing	turmoils	pedestal

Questions:— Define "symbolism," "solitary worshippers;" and then resume second paragraph, showing how a Catholic church recalls the chief events in the life of our divine Lord. Or, write the death scene of "forgiving Stephen," and name an Apostle there converted through St. Stephen's prayer. What did St. Ambrose say to Monica about the fruit her prayer would bear for her hesitating son Augustine?

——o——

SPEECH OF LORD CHATHAM ON THE AMERCAN WAR.

I CANNOT, my lords, I will not, join in congratulation on misfortune and disgrace. This, my lords, is a perilous and tremendous moment. It is not a time for adulation: the smoothness of flattery cannot save us in this rugged and awful crisis. It is now necessary to instruct the throne in the language of truth. We must, if possible, dispel the delusion and darkness which envelop it, and display, in its full danger and genuine colors, the ruin which is brought to our doors. Can ministers still presume to expect support in their infatuation? Can Parliament be so dead to its dignity and duty, as to give its support to measures thus obtruded and forced upon it? Measures, my lords, which have reduced this late flourishing empire to scorn and

contempt! "But yesterday, and Britain might hav
stood against the world; now, none so poor as to do he
reverence." The people, whom we at first despised a
rebels, but whom we now acknowledge as enemies, ar
abetted against us, supplied with every military store
have their interest consulted, and their ambassador
entertained, by our inveterate enemy, — and ministers d
not, and dare not, interpose with dignity or effect. The
desperate state of our army abroad is in part known
No man more highly esteems and honors the Britisl
troops than I do; I know their virtues and their valor
I know they can achieve anything but impossibilities
and I know that the conquest of British America is a
utter impossibility. You cannot, my lords, you canno
conquer America. What is your present situation there'
We do not know the worst; but we know that in three
campaigns we have done nothing, and suffered much
You may swell every expense, accumulate every assist
ance, and extend your traffic to the shambles of every
German despot: your attempts will be for ever vain and
impotent — doubly so, indeed, from this mercenary aid
on which you rely; for it irritates, to an incurable
resentment, the minds of your adversaries, to overrun
them with mercenary sons of rapine and plunder, devoting
them and their possessions to the rapacity of hireling
cruelty. If I were an American, as I am an Englishman, while a foreign troop was landed in my country,
I never would lay down my arms — never, — never, —
never!

But, my lords, who is the man that, in addition to the
disgraces and mischiefs of war, has dared to authorize
and associate to our arms the tomahawk and scalping-
knife of the savage? — to call into civilized alliance,
the wild and inhuman inhabitant of the woods? — to

delegate to the merciless Indian the defence of disputed rights, and to wage the horrors of his barbarous war against our brethren? My lords, these enormities cry aloud for redress and punishment. But, my lords, this barbarous measure has been defended, not only on the principles of policy and necessity, but also on those of morality; "for it is perfectly allowable," says Lord Suffolk, "to use all the means which God and nature have put into our hands." I am astonished, I am shocked, to hear such principles confessed; to hear them avowed in this house, or in this country. My lords, I did not intend to encroach so much on your attention, but I cannot repress my indignation — I feel myself impelled to speak. My lords, we are called upon as members of this house, as men, as Christians, to protest against such horrible barbarity! "That God and nature have put into our hands!" What ideas of God and nature that noble lord may entertain, I know not; but I know, that such detestable principles are equally abhorrent to religion and humanity. What! to attribute the sacred sanction of God and nature to the massacres of the Indian scalping-knife! to the cannibal savage, torturing, murdering, devouring, drinking the blood of his mangled victims! Such notions shock every precept of morality, every feeling of humanity, every sentiment of honor. These abominable principles, and this more abominable avowal of them, demand the most decisive indignation.

I call upon the spirit and humanity of my country, to vindicate the national character. I invoke the genius of the Constitution. To send forth the merciless cannibal, thirsting for blood! against whom? Our brethren! To lay waste their country, to desolate their dwellings, and extirpate their race and name by the instrumentality of these horrible hounds of war! I solemnly call upon your lordships and upon every order of men in the state, to stamp upon this infamous procedure the indelible stigma of public abhorrence.

Questions : — What is it to join in congratulation? What is meant by "instructing the throne"? Name three prophets who thus instructed the throne. What is here meant by ministers? When are ministers of state infatuated? Name three ministers or kings who shared such infatuation and suffered for it. When is a parliament "dead to duty?' Name some parliament that was dead to duty in England, France or America. What body in the United States corresponds with the English Parliament? What is a foreign troop? Write the following sentence in four ways :

"If I were an American, as I am an Englishman, while a foreign troop was landed in my country, I would never lay down my arms — never, — never, — never!"

crisis	rapine	delusion	obtruded
vindicate	abetted	procedure	achieve
stigma	accumulate	abhorrence	mercenary

———o———

THE MEETING OF THE WATERS.

Thomas Moore (1779–1852) was a native of Dublin. The "Irish Melodies," undoubtedly his best production, have made the traditions, the trials, the patriotism, the hopes and the beauty of his native land famous the world over. In melody and neatness of versification, in clear and apt diction, in vigor and sprightliness, they have seldom been surpassed. "Lalla Rookh," his most ambitious work, is an Oriental love-tale, marked by great splendor of imagination, luxuriance of description and voluptuousness of sentiment. The decline in Moore's once great popularity is owing to lack of real poetic depth of sentiment, and to the evidence that his verse comes oftener from the head and the wit, than from the heart.

THERE is not in the wide world a valley so sweet
   As that vale in whose bosom the bright waters meet.
O, the last rays of feeling and life must depart,
Ere the bloom of that valley shall fade from my heart.

Yet it was not that Nature had shed o'er the scene
Her purest of crystal and brightest of green;
'Twas not her soft magic of streamlet or rill;
O, no ; it was something more exquisite still.

'Twas that friends, the beloved of my bosom, were near,
Who made every dear scene of enchantment more dear,
And who felt how the best charms of nature improve,
When we see them reflected from looks that we love.

Sweet Vale of Avoca! how calm could I rest
In thy bosom of shade with the friends I love best,
When the storms that we feel in this cold world shall cease
And our hearts, like thy waters, be mingled in peace!

crystal	exquisite	reflected
streamlet	enchantment	mingled

---o---

JOAN OF ARC.

Thomas De Quincey, (1785-1859) one of the greatest masters of
English prose, superior even to Macaulay in the extraordinary compass
of his diction, which, says an able critic, "accommodates itself without
efforts to the highest flights of imagination, to the minutest subtleties
of reasoning, and to the gayest vagaries of humor." He has written
many essays and literary criticisms; but it is rather to his unique style,
which will always be studied as a marvel of our literature, than to the
intrinsic value of his works, that his fame is to be attributed.

WHAT is to be thought of her? What is to be
thought of the poor shepherd girl from the hills
and forests of Lorraine, that, like the Hebrew shepherd
boy from the hills and forests of Judea, rose suddenly
out of the quiet, out of the safety, out of the religious
inspiration, rooted in deep pastoral solitudes, to a station
in the van of armies, and to the more perilous station at

6

the right hand of kings? The Hebrew boy inaugurated his patriotic mission by an *act*, by a victorious act, such as no man could deny. But so did the girl of Lorraine, if we read her story as it was read by those who saw her nearest. Adverse armies bore witness to the boy as no pretender; but so they did to the gentle girl. Judged by the voices of all who saw them *from a station of good-will*, both were found true and loyal to any promises involved in their first act. Enemies it was that made the difference between their subsequent fortunes. The boy rose to a splendor and a noonday prosperity, both personal and public, that rang through the records of his people, and became a byword amongst his posterity for a thousand years, until the sceptre was departing from Judea. The poor, forsaken girl, on the contrary, drank not herself from that cup of rest which she had secured for France. She never sang the songs that rose in her native Domremy, as echoes to the departing steps of invaders. She mingled not in the festal dances of Vaucouleurs, which celebrated in rapture the redemption of France. No! for her voice was then silent. No! for her feet were dust.

Pure, innocent, noble-hearted girl! whom from earliest youth ever I believed in, as full of truth and self-sacrifice, this was amongst the strongest pledges for *thy* side, that never once — no, not for a moment of weakness — didst thou revel in the vision of coronets and honor from man. Coronets for thee? Oh, no! Honors, if they come when all is over, are for those that share thy blood. Daughter of Domremy, when the gratitude of thy king shall awaken, thou wilt be sleeping the sleep of the dead. Call her, king of France, but she will not hear thee! Cite her by thy apparitors to come and receive a robe of honor, but she will be found *in contempt*. When the thunders of universal France, as even yet may happen, shall proclaim the grandeur of the poor shepherd girl that gave up all for her country, thy ear, young shepherd girl, will have been deaf for five centuries.

To suffer and to do, that was thy portion in this life: to *do* — never for thyself, always for others; to *suffer* — never in the persons of generous champions, always in thy own; that was thy destiny, and not for a moment was it hidden from thyself. "Life," thou saidst, "is short, and the sleep which is in the grave is long. Let me use that life, so transitory, for the glory of those heavenly dreams destined to comfort the sleep which is so long."

Pure from every suspicion of even a visionary self-interest, even as she was pure in senses more obvious, never once did this holy child, as regarded herself, relax from her belief in the darkness that was travelling to meet her. She might not prefigure the very manner of her death; she saw not in vision, perhaps, the aerial altitude of the fiery scaffold, the spectators without end, on every road, pouring into Rouen as to a coronation, the surging smoke, the volleying flames, the hostile faces all around, the pitying eye that lurked but here and there, until nature and imperishable truth broke loose from artificial restraints — these might not be apparent through the mists of the hurrying future; but the voice that called her to death, *that* she heard for ever.

Great was the throne of France, even in those days, and great was he that sat upon it; but well Joan knew that not the throne, nor he that sat upon it, was for *her;* but, on the contrary, that she was for *them:* not she by them, but they by her, should rise from the dust. Gorgeous were the lilies of France, and for centuries had they been spreading their beauty over land and sea.

until, in another century, the wrath of God and man combined to wither them; but well Joan knew — early at Domremy she had read that bitter truth — that the lilies of France would decorate no garland for *her.* Flower nor bud, bell nor blossom, would ever bloom for her.

Having placed the king on his throne, it was her fortune thenceforward to be thwarted. More than one military plan was entered upon which she did not approve. Too well she felt the end to be nigh at hand. Still she continued to jeopard her person in battle as before; severe wounds had not taught her caution; and at length she was made prisoner by the Burgundians, and finally given up to the English. The object now was to vitiate the coronation of Charles the Seventh as the work of a witch, and for this end Joan was tried for sorcery. She resolutely defended herself from this absurd accusation.

Never from the foundations of the earth was there such a trial as this, if it were laid open in all its beauty of defence and all its malignity of attack. O child of France! shepherdess, peasant girl! trodden under foot by all around thee, I honor thy flashing intellect, quick as the lightning and as true to its mark, that ran before France and laggard Europe by many a century, confounding the malice of the ensnarer, and making dumb the oracles of falsehood! "Would you examine me as a witness against myself?" was the question by which many times she defied their arts. The result of this trial was the condemnation of Joan to be burnt alive. Never was a fairer victim doomed to death by baser means.

Woman, sister! there are some things which you do not execute as well as your brother, man — no, nor ever will. Yet, sister, woman, cheerfully and with the love that burns in depths of admiration, I acknowledge that you can do one thing as well as the best of men — you can die grandly! On the 20th of May, 1431, being then about nineteen years of age, Joan of Arc underwent her martyrdom. She was taken, before midday, guarded by eight hundred spearmen, to a platform of prodigious height, constructed of wooden billets, supported by occasional walls of lath and plaster, and traversed by hollow spaces in every direction for the creation of air currents.

With an undaunted soul, but a meek and saintly demeanor, the maiden encountered her terrible fate. Upon her head was placed a mitre bearing the inscription, "*Relapsed heretic, apostate, idolatress.*" Her piety displayed itself in the most touching manner to the last, and her angelic forgetfulness of self was manifested in a remarkable degree. The executioner had been directed to apply his torch from below. He did so. The fiery smoke rose upward in billowing volumes. A monk was then standing at Joan's side. Wrapt up in his sublime office, he saw not the danger, but still persisted in his prayers. Even then, when the last enemy was racing up the fiery stairs to seize her, even at that moment did this noblest of girls think only for *him* — the one friend that would not forsake her — and not for herself, bidding nim with her last breath to care for his own preservation, but to leave *her* to God.

"Go down," she said, "lift up the cross before me, that I may see it in dying, and speak to me pious words to the end." Then, protesting her innocence and recommending her soul to heaven, she continued to pray as the flames leaped and walled her in. Her last audible word was the name of Jesus. Sustained by faith in him in her last fight upon the scaffold, she had triumphed gloriously; victoriously she had tasted death. A soldier who had sworn to throw a fagot on the pile, turned away, a penitent for life, on hearing her last prayer to her Saviour. He had seen, he said, a white dove soar to heaven from the ashes where the brave girl had stood.

Illustrious to-day, through the efforts of her country-man, Monseigneur Dupanloup, Joan's memory is to be held up to still greater fame. Through the sunlit windows of a great Cathedral, the gift of the noble of Joan's sex, her legend as told in the tinted glass will cause men to give glory to Him who was her strength. The name that fire could not tarnish will, through the cheery reflections of summer sun and autumn glow, through the gladdening gleams of spring's fair mornings, be reflected in the house of her Creator. The chills of the winter of historical falsehood have passed, Joan lives in the windows of holy Church; the glory of her sisters' land.

COMPOSITION.

Give a short sketch of Joan's execution. Name three or four noble ladies who also met with tragic deaths for their country or for God's sake.

volleying	thwarted	sorcery	laggard
restraints	jeopard	malignity	oracles

---o---

THERE'S NOTHING TRUE BUT HEAVEN.

THIS world is all a fleeting show,
 For man's illusion given;
The smiles of joy, the tears of woe,
Deceitful shine, deceitful flow—
 There's nothing *true* but Heaven.

And false the light on glory's plume,
   As fading hues of even ;
And love, and hope, and beauty's bloom
Are blossoms gathered for the tomb —
   There's nothing *bright* but Heaven.

Poor wanderers of a stormy day,
   From wave to wave we're driven ;
And fancy's flash, and reason's ray,
Serve but to light the troubled way —
   There's nothing *calm* but Heaven.

COMPOSITION.

Write the first stanza of each selection. Change all the nouns, adjectives and verbs in last two stanzas. Mention six circumstances in which we see "the smiles of joy ;" six on which we notice "the tears of woe." Explain "fancy's flash," "reason's ray."

illusion   deceitful   plume   fancy's

THE LION.

THE lion is often erroneously styled lord of the forest ; nevertheless, the forest is not his haunt; he lives in desert, arid plains, lightly covered with shrubby vegetation, or interspersed with tracts of low brushwood; or, in India, he frequents the borders of rivers, and makes his lair in the jungles. The lion slumbers during the day in his retreat, and as night falls he prowls abroad in search of prey. He loves the nocturnal tempests of wind and rain so common in Southern Africa; his voice mingles with the thunder, and adds to the terror of the timid animals, on whom he then boldly advances. He usually, however, waits in ambush, or creeps insidiously towards his victim, which he dashes to the earth, with a bound and a rush.

In South Africa the lion is seldom seen, unless surprised asleep in his lair of thicket. Except in darkness or during violent storms, which excite the fiercer carnivora, he is a timid animal, much less feared by the people than the angry and agile leopard. When encountered in the daytime, he stands a second or two gazing; then turns slowly round, and walks as slowly away for a dozen paces, looking over his shoulder; he then begins to trot, and when he thinks himself out of sight, bounds like a greyhound.

If attacked, however, he will show fight, as the following experience, not likely to be often repeated, will testify:—"Being about thirty yards off the foe," says Dr. Livingstone, "I took a good aim at his body, through the bush, and fired both barrels into it. The men then called out, 'He is shot! he is shot!' others cried, 'He has been shot by another man, too; let us go to him!' I did not see any one else shoot at him; but I saw the lion's tail erected in anger behind the bush, and, turning to the peeple, said, 'Stop a little, till I load again! When in the act of ramming down the bullets I heard a shout. Starting, and looking half round, I saw the lion just in the act of springing upon me. I was upon a little height. He caught my shoulder as he sprang, and we both came to the ground below together. Growling horribly close to my ear, he shook me as a terrier dog does a rat. The shock produced a stupor similar to that which seems to be felt by a mouse after the first shake of the cat. It caused a sort of dreaminess, in which there was no sense of pain or feeling of terror. It was like what patients partially under the influence of chloroform describe, who see all the operation, but feel not the knife. This singular condition was not the result of any mental process. The shake annihilated fear, and allowed no sense of horror in looking round at the beast. This peculiar state is probably produced in all animals killed by the carnivora; and, if so, is a merciful provision by our beneficent Creator for lessening the pain of death. Turning round to relieve myself of the weight, as he had one paw on the back of my head, I saw his eyes directed to Mebalwe, who was trying to shoot him at the distance of fifteen yards. His gun, a flint one, missed fire in both barrels. The lion immediately left me, and, attacking Mebalwe, bit his thigh. Another man, whose life I had saved before, after he had been tossed by a buffalo, attempted to spear the lion while he was biting Mebalwe. He left Mebalwe and caught this man by the shoulder, but at that moment the bullets he had received had taken effect, and he fell down dead. The whole was the work of a few moments, and must have been his paroxysm of dying rage. Besides crunching the bone into splinters, he left eleven teeth wounds in the upper part of my arm."

Dr. Livingstone contradicts the generally received stories about the majestic roar of the lion. "The silly ostrich," says he, "makes a noise as loud, yet it was never feared by man."

On my mentioning this fact some years ago the assertion was doubted; so I have been careful ever since to inquire the opinion of Europeans who have heard both, if they could detect any difference between the roar of a lion and that of an ostrich. The invariable answer was that they could not when the animal was at a distance. The natives assert that they can detect a variation at the commencement of the noise of each. There is, it must be admitted, a considerable difference between the singing noise of a lion when full, and his deep, gruff voice when hungry. In general, the lion's voice seems to come deeper from the chest than that of an ostrich: but to this day I can distinguish between them with certainty only by knowing that the ostrich roars by day, and the lion by night.

Attempts to deprive the lion of its prey are of frequent occurrence in the interior of Africa. Indeed, it is no unusual thing to find a number of natives residing near such pools of water as are frequented by antelopes, other wild animals, and their constant attendant, the lion, subsisting almost altogether in this way, or on carcasses which the lion has not had time to devour before the return of day, when it is his habit to return to his lair.

Questions: — Why should not the lion be termed the "lord of the forest"? Where does he usually live? When does he hunt his prey? What seasons are specially agreeable to him? What is his usual way of hunting his prey? What are the "carnivora"? What is his ordinary character? What animal do the natives of Africa dread more than the lion? How does the animal act when encountered in the daytime? Who was Dr. Livingstone? Give an account of his adventure with a lion. What effect had the shock upon him? What does he suppose was the cause of this state? What wise purpose may be seen in this? What is its great use? Does Dr. Livingstone believe in the "majestic ' roar of the lion? Whose cry does its roar resemble at other times? How was Dr. Livingstone able to distinguish between the cry of the ostrich and that of the lion? How does the lion contribute to the support of many of the natives of Africa?

COMPOSITION.

Write a short account of the lion's roar. Tell how it may be distinguished from the ostrich's cry. Describe the manner in which lions furnish some of the natives with food.

erroneously	insidiously	stupor	crunching
lair	carnivora	annihilated	subsisting

WHAT IS TIME?

I ASKED an aged man, a man of cares,
Wrinkled and curved, and white with hoary hairs:
"Time is the warp of life," he said. "Oh, tell
The young, the fair, the gay, to weave it well!"
I asked the ancient venerable dead,
Sages who wrote, and warriors who bled:
From the cold grave a hollow murmur flowed,
"Time sowed the seed we reap in this abode!"
I asked a dying sinner, ere the tide
Of life had left his veins: "Time!" he replied,
"I've lost it! ah, the treasure!" and he died.
I asked the golden sun, and silver spheres,
Those bright chronometers of days and years:
They answered, "Time is but a meteor glare!"
And bade us for eternity prepare.
I asked a spirit lost; but oh, the shriek
That pierced my soul! I shudder while I speak
It cried, "A particle! a speck! a mite
Of endless years, duration infinite!"
Of things inanimate, my dial I
Consulted, and it made me this reply:
"Time is the season fair of living well,
The path of glory, or the path of hell."
I asked old father Time himself, at last,
But in a moment he flew swiftly past;
His chariot was a cloud, the viewless wind
His noiseless steeds, which left no trace behind.
I asked the mighty angel, who shall stand,
One foot on sea, and one on solid land;
"By heavens," he cried, "I swear the mystery's o'er;
Time was, time is, but time shall be no more!"

Questions:—What persons were questioned? What is meant by.
'A man of cares"? "The warp of life"? "Tide of life"? "Silver

spheres"? Bright chronometers of days and years"? Give the words
of the dying sinner and of the spirit lost, in three ways.

———o———

DEATH OF MARY, QUEEN OF SCOTS.

John Lingard, D. D., was born in England in 1771 ; died in 1851.
His "History of England," complete in ten volumes, is the only
impartial history of that nation. The splendid styles of Hume and
Macaulay can never make amends for their false, unjust, or careless
treatment of Catholic questions. Lingard's style is pure, dignified
and classical ; but it is in the higher requisites of history, it is in fair-
ness, in accuracy and completeness of details, in diligent research, in
clear and methodical arrangement, that his work vindicates its claim
to be considered the standard book of reference on all disputed points
of English history.

IN the midst of the great hall of the castle had been
raised a scaffold, covered with black serge, and
surrounded with a low railing.   About seven, the doors
were thrown open; the gentlemen of the country entered
with their attendants ; and Paulet's * guard augmented
the number to between one hundred and fifty and two
hundred spectators.   Before eight, a message was sent
to the queen, who replied that she would be ready in
half an hour.

At that time, Andrews, the sheriff, entered the oratory,
and Mary arose, taking the crucifix from the altar in her
right, and carrying her prayer-book in her left hand.
Her servants were forbidden to follow; they insisted;
but the queen bade them be content, and turning,
gave them her blessing.   They received it on their

---

* This was Sir Amias Paulet, the appointed custodian of the
unfortunate queen. How unflinchingly he performed his office may be
inferred from a letter of Queen Elizabeth to him, in which she says:
"Amias, my most faithful and careful servant, God Almighty reward
thee treblefold for thy most troublesome charge so well discharged."

knees, some kissing her hands, others her mantle. The door closed; and the burst of lamentation from those within resounded through the hall.

Mary was now joined by the earl and her keepers, and descending the staircase, found at the foot Melville, the steward of her household, who, for several weeks, had been excluded from her presence. This old and faithful servant threw himself on his knees, and wringing his hands, exclaimed, — "Ah, madam, unhappy me! was ever a man on earth the bearer of such sorrow as I shall be, when I report that my good and gracious queen and mistress was beheaded in England!"

Here his grief impeded his utterance; and Mary replied: "Good Melville, cease to lament; thou hast rather cause to joy than mourn; for thou shalt see the end of Mary Stuart's troubles. Know that this world is but vanity, subject to more sorrow than an ocean of tears can bewail. But, I pray thee, report that I die a true woman to my religion, to Scotland, and to France. May God forgive them that have long thirsted for my blood, as the hart doth for the brooks of water. O God, thou art the author of truth, and truth itself. Thou knowest the inward chambers of my thoughts, and that I always wished the union of England and Scotland. Commend me to my son, and tell him that I have done nothing prejudicial either to the dignity or independence of his crown, or favorable to the pretended superiority of our enemies." Then bursting into tears, she said, — "Good Melville, farewell;" and kissing him, "once again, good Melville, farewell. and pray for thy mistress and thy queen." It was remarked as something extraordinary, that this was the first time in her life that she had ever been known to address a person with the pronoun thou."

Drying up her tears, she turned from Melville and made her last request, that her servants might be present at her death.   But the Earl of Kent objected that they would be troublesome by their grief and lamentations, might practice some superstitious trumpery, perhaps might dip their handkerchiefs in her grace's blood. "My lords," said Mary, "I will give my word for them. They shall deserve no blame.   Certainly your mistress, being a maiden queen, will vouchsafe, in regard of womanhood, that I have some of my own women about me at my death."

Receiving no answer, she continued, — " You might, I think, grant me a far greater courtesy, were I a woman of lesser calling than the Queen of Scots." Still they were silent; when she asked with vehemence, — "Am I not the cousin to your queen, a descendant of the blood royal of King Henry VII., and the anointed Queen of Scotland?"   At these words the fanaticism of the Earl of Kent began to yield; and it was resolved to admit four of her men and two of her women servants. She selected her steward, physician, apothecary, and surgeon, with her maids Kennedy and Curle.

The procession now set forward. It was headed by the sheriff and his officers; next followed Paulet and Drury, and the Earls of Shrewsbury and Kent; and lastly came the Scottish queen, with Melville bearing her train. She wore the richest of her dresses, — that which was appropriate to the rank of a queen dowager. Her step was firm, and her countenance cheerful. She bore without shrinking the gaze of the spectators, and the sight of the scaffold, the block, and the executioner, and advanced into the hall with that grace and majesty which she had so often displayed in her happier days, when in the palace of her fathers. To aid her as she mounted the scaffold, Paulet offered his arm. "I thank you, sir," said Mary; "it is the last trouble I shall give you, and the most acceptable service you have ever rendered me."

The queen seated herself on a stool which had been prepared for her. On her right stood the two earls; on the left the sheriff and Beal, clerk of the council; in front, the executioner from the Tower, in a suit of black velvet with his assistant, also clad in black. The warrant was read, and Mary, in an audible voice, addressed the assembly. She would have them recollect, also, that she was a sovereign princess, not subject to the Parliament of England, but brought there to suffer by injustice and violence. She, however, thanked her God that he had given her this opportunity of publicly professing her religion, and of declaring, as she had often before declared, that she had never imagined, nor compassed, nor consented to, the death of the English queen, nor ever sought the least harm to her person. After her death, many things, which were then buried in darkness, would come to light. But she pardoned from her heart all her enemies, nor should her tongue utter that which might turn to their prejudice.

Here she was interrupted by Dr. Fletcher, dean of Peterborough, who, having caught her eye, began to preach, and under cover — perhaps through motives of zeal — contrived to insult the feelings of the unfortunate sufferer. Mary repeatedly desired him not to trouble himself and her. He persisted; she turned aside. He made the circuit of the scaffold, and again addressed her in front. An end was put to this extraordinary scene by the Earl of Shrewsbury, who ordered him to pray. His prayer was the echo of his sermon; but Mary heard him not. She was employed at the time in her devotions, repeating with a loud voice, and in the Latin language, passages from the book of Psalms; and, after the dean was reduced to silence, a prayer in French, in which she begged of God to pardon her sins, declared that she forgave her enemies, and protested that she was innocent of ever consenting in wish or deed to the death of her English sister. She then prayed in English for Christ's afflicted Church, for her son James, and for Queen Elizabeth, and in conclusion, holding up the crucifix, exclaimed:— "As thy arms, O God, were stretched out upon the cross, so receive me into the arms of thy mercy, and forgive my sins."

When her maids, bathed in tears, began to disrobe their mistress, the executioners, fearing the loss of their usual perquisites, hastily interfered. The queen remonstrated, but instantly submitted to their rudeness, observing to the earls with a smile, that she was not accustomed to employ such grooms, or to undress in the presence of so numerous a company.

Her servants, at the sight of their sovereign in this lamentable state, could not suppress their feelings; but Mary, putting her finger to her lips, commanded silence, gave them her blessing, and solicited their prayers. She then seated herself again. Kennedy, taking from her a handkerchief edged with gold, pinned it over her eyes; the executioners, holding her by the arms, led her to the block; and the queen, kneeling down, said repeatedly with a firm voice, — "Into thy hands, O Lord I commend my spirit."

But the sobs and cries of the spectators disconcerted the headsman. He trembled, missed his aim, inflicted a deep wound in the lower part of the skull. The queen remained motionless; and, at the third stroke, her head was severed from her body. When the executioner held it up, the muscles of the face were so convulsed that the features could not be recognized. He cried as usual, — "God save Queen Elizabeth!"

"So perish all her enemies!" subjoined the dean of Peterborough.

"So perish all the enemies of the gospel!" exclaimed, in a still louder tone, the fanatical Earl of Kent.

Not a voice was heard to cry amen. Party feeling was absorbed in admiration and pity.

Questions: — Show three ways in which Mary proved her courage as a woman. Two, her independence as a Queen. Three, her devotedness as a Catholic.

serge	lamentation	impeded	utterance
trumpery	fanaticism	dowager	audible
compassed	prejudice	persisted	dean
protested	perquisites	remonstrated	lamentable
convulsed	recognized	fanatical	absorbed

——o——

A NAME IN THE SAND.

ALONE I walked the ocean strand;
　A pearly shell was in my hand;
I stooped and wrote upon the sand
　　My name, — the year, — the day.
As onward from the spot I passed,
One ling'ring look behind I cast;
　A wave came rolling high and fast,
　　And washed my lines away.

And so, methought, 'twill shortly be
With every mark on earth for me;
A wave of dark oblivion's sea
　　Will sweep across the place

Where I have trod the sandy shore
Of time, and be to me no more, —
Of me, — my day, — the name I bore,
　　To leave no track nor trace.

And yet with Him who counts the sands,
And holds the water in his hands,
I know a lasting record stands,
　　Inscribed against my name, —
Of all this mortal part has wrought;
Of all this thinking soul has thought;
And, from these fleeting moments caught,
　　For glory or for shame.

Questions: — What did you do with the shell? What washed the
lines away? What thought struck the author? Show difference
between track and trace. What is a lasting record? What will
be found in this book? What is your mortal part? What is the
immortal? Commit closing stanza to memory.

| strand | methought | trod | inscribed |
| ling'ring | oblivion's | record | wrought |

---o---

FUNERAL ORATION OF THE PRINCE OF CONDE.

COME now, you people; or rather, come, princes and
lords; and you, who judge the earth; and you, who
open to men the gates of heaven; and you, more than
all, princes and princesses, noble progeny of so many
kings, lights of France, but to-day obscured, and covered
with your grief as with a cloud; come and see the
little that remains to us of so august a birth, of so much
greatness, of so much glory. Cast your eyes on all
sides: behold all that magnificence and piety could do,
to honor a hero; titles, inscriptions, vain marks of that
which is no more; figures which seem to weep around

a tomb, and frail images of a grief which time bears away, along with all the rest; columns which seem as if they would raise to heaven the magnificent testimony of our nothingness; and nought, in fine, is wanted, amid all these honors, but he to whom they are given. Weep, then, over these feeble remains of human life; weep over that sad immortality which we give to heroes.

But approach, in particular, O you who run with so much ardor in the career of glory; warlike and intrepid souls! Who was more worthy to command you? yet in whom have you found authority more gentle? Weep, then, for this great captain, and say, with sighs,— Behold him who was our leader in dangers; under him have been formed so many renowned captains, whom his examples have raised to the first honors of war; his shade could still gain victories; and behold, now, in his silence, his very name animates, and at the same time warns us, that to find at death some rest from our labors, and not to arrive unprovided at our eternal dwelling, with the earthly king we must likewise serve the King of heaven. Serve, then, that King, immortal and so full of mercy, who will value a sigh and a glass of water given in his name, more than all others will ever do the effusion of all your blood; and begin to date the time of your useful services from the day on which you shall have given yourself to a master so beneficent.

For me, if it be allowed me, after all others, to come to render the last duties at this tomb, O prince, worthy subject of our eulogies and of our regrets, you shall live eternally in memory; your image shall there be traced, not with the boldness which promised victory; no, I will see nothing in you of that which is effaced by death. You shall have this image immortal lineaments; I shall there behold you such as you were at that last day under the hand of God, when his glory seemed already to appear to you. There I shall behold you more triumphant than at Fribourg and Rocroy; and, ravished by a triumph so splendid, I shall repeat, with thanksgiving, these beautiful words of the beloved disciple: "*And this is the victory which overcometh the world, our faith.*" Enjoy, prince, this victory; enjoy it eternally by the immortal virtue of this sacrifice. Accept these last efforts of a voice which was known to you. You. shall put an end to all these discourses. Instead of deploring the death of others, great prince, henceforward I will learn of you to render my own holy. Happy, if, warned by these white hairs of the account which I am to render of my ministry, I reserve for the flock which I ought to nourish with the word of life, the remains of a faltering voice and of an ardor which will soon be extinguished.

progeny	unprovided	Fribourg
august	effusion	Rocroy
nothingness	beneficent	ravished
intrepid	eulogies	deploring
animates	lineaments	faltering

COMPOSITION.

Copy the last seven lines, "Instead of deploring," etc., and write sentences in which *one* of the following words will occur in each:
Deploring, henceforward, account, ministry, nourish.

———o———

SMALL BEGINNINGS.

A TRAVELLER through a dusty road,
　　Strewed acorns on the lea;
And one took root, and sprouted up,

And grew into a tree;
Love sought its shade at evening time
   To breath its early vows ;
And age was pleased, in heat of noon,
   To bask beneath its boughs.
The dormouse loved its dangling twigs,
   The birds sweet music bore ·
It stood a glory in its place —
   A blessing evermore.

A little spring had lost its way,
   Amid the grass and fern;
A passing stranger scooped a well
   . Where weary men might turn.
He walled it in, and hung with care
   A ladle at the brink.
He thought not of the deed he did,
   But judged that toil might drink.
He passed again, and lo! the well,
   By summers never dried,
Had cooled ten thousand parching tongues
   And saved a life beside.

A dreamer dropped a random thought,
   'Twas old, and yet 'twas new —
A simple fancy of the brain,
   But strong in being true ;
It shone upon a genial mind,
   And lo! its light became
A lamp of life — a beacon ray —
   A monitory flame.
The thought was small, its issue great —
   A watch fire on the hill,
It sheds its radiance far adown,
   And cheers the valley still.

A nameless man, amid a crowd
   That thronged the daily mart,
Let fall a word of hope and love,
   Unstudied, from the heart—
A whisper on the tumult thrown,
   A transitory breath,
It raised a brother from the dust,
   It saved a soul from death.
O germ! O fount! O word of love!
   O thought at random cast!
Ye were but *little at the first,*
   But mighty at the last.

COMPOSITION.

Relate the circumstances mentioned in this poem. In connection with this narration give some idea contained in Tennyson's "Brook."

lea	scooped	beacon	thronged
bask	ladle	monitory	tumult
dormouse	parching	issue	transitory
dangling	genial	valley	fount

THE CHURCH PROGRESSIVE.

THE Church unquestionably stands at the head of the influences that have civilized mankind. If Guizot's definition of civilization, "The reform and elevation of society through the reform and elevation of the individual," is true, and that it is true the Protestant schools of history admit, then the Church must be regarded as the civilizer by excellence. Home, with its manifold influences, is deemed a powerful agency in the formation of individual perfection, and to the Church, under Christ, the modern world owes all expressed by those tender words, "home," and the "family circle."

Heathenism made the family, with all its relations, subject to the supreme arbitrament of the State. Deformed children were destroyed as prospectively unfit for military service. Infanticide was one of the most prevalent crimes of heathendom. It was the Babe of Bethlehem that saved his infant companions. The stability of the family is based on the indissolubility of the marital tie. This the Church has ever upheld and preserved. By insisting on it, the Church forms society into families and kin, throwing about them defences and safeguards of liberty and happiness, and out of the Christian family the civilized state, such as we have it, arose. Here is the first step in that march of progress in which the Church leads humanity. We often hear the axioms, proved by a thousand years' experience, that the family is the social unit. It was the Church that taught and realized the axioms which all statesmanship and political science accept as fundamental science.

After reforming the family, she reformed the State. Heathen statesmanship proceeded on the assumption that the governed were created for the governors. The pyramids overshadowed a multitude of toiling slaves, who were taught to regard their sovereign as God, the Supreme Disposer of their lives and fortunes. Republican Greece and Rome were never republican in the Christian sense. The Church, on the downfall of the Roman Empire, took the barbarians in hand, shaped their wild tribes into stable forms of government, and gave to their disunited clans an organic form. Guizot admits that the Church originated the idea of election, personal freedom, the right of the people to rebel against despotism, municipal independence, and the abolition of slavery. Here, then, is the Church fashioning the two elements of all progress, the family and the free state. Without these subsisting in the relations established by her, all progress is impossible. To her, as to source and fountain, all modern progress and civilization can, therefore, be traced.

deemed	stability	fundamental	municipal
arbitrament	indissolubility	originated	subsisting
prospectively	axioms	despotism	traced

QUESTIONS AND COMPOSITION.

Change first sentence. How is civilization effected? How was the family treated by heathenism? How were children treated? What is the marital tie? At what sacrifice were the pyramids erected? Show from Guizot's admission that the Catholic Church is favorable to Republics. What did Pius IX. say about his independence in the United States? Write four sentences, in defence of Catholicity, including the following expressions:

˙. . . . . . the Church had made slaves free.

By teaching princes their duty, the Church . . . . . . people their rights.

The Church which raised men from degradation brought about by tyranny must be able. . . . . . the right use of liberty.

In our own country. . . . . . the leaders of Catholic thought contributed no small share to liberty, which by its extent has become Catholic in character.

---◊---

DEATH'S FINAJ CONQUEST.

THE glories of our birth and state
    Are shadows, not substantial things
There is no armor against fate :
    Death lays his icy hands on kings ;
        Sceptre and crown
        Must humble down,
And in the dust must be equal made .
With the poor, crooked scythe and spade.

Some men with swords may reap the field,
　And plant fresh laurels where they kill;
But their strong nerves at last must yield,
　They tame but one another still;
　　　Early or late
　　　They stoop to fate,
And must give up their murmuring breath,
When they, pale captives, creep to death.

The garland withers on your brow,
　Then boast no more your mighty deeds!
Upon death's purple altar now
　See where the victor, victim bleeds;
　　　All heads must come
　　　To the cold tomb;
Only the actions of the just
Smell sweet and blossom in the dust.

COMPOSITION.

Write sentences with the words "substantial" and "shadows" in each. A sentence in which "humble" will qualify "crown." A sentence in which "sword" will be nominative to "kill." A sentence in which "tame" will be an adjective, "still" a noun, "laurels" a verb, and "sweet" an adverb.

substantial　　　armor　　　fate　　　blossom

WAGES.

WAGES are a compensation given to the laborer for the exertion of his physical powers, or of his skill and ingenuity. They must, therefore, vary according to the severity of the labor to be performed, or to the degree of skill and ingenuity required. A jeweller or engraver, for example, must be paid a higher rate of wages than a servant or laborer. A long course of training is necessary to instruct a man in the business of jewelling and engraving, and if the cost of his training were not made up to him in a higher rate of wages, he would, instead of learning so difficult an art, betake himself to such employments as hardly require any instruction.

The following are the chief circumstances which cause the rates of wages in some employments to rise above or fall below the general average:.

The pleasant or unpleasant nature of the employ ment. The *pleasantness* of an employment may arise from the lightness of the labor to be performed, its healthiness or cleanliness, and the degree of esteem in which it is held. The *unpleasantness* of any employment will arise from the opposite circumstances, — from the severity of the labor to be performed, its unhealthiness or dirtiness, and the degree of odium attached to it. Now it is not in the nature of things likely that any one will be so blind to his own interests as to engage in any occupation which is considered mean, or where the labor is severe, if he obtain only the same wages as are obtained by those engaged in employments that are held in higher esteem, and where the labor is light. The labor of the ploughman is not unhealthy, nor is it either irksome or disagreeable ; but being more *severe* than that of the shepherd, it is uniformly better paid. Miners, gilders, smiths, distillers, and all who carry on an unhealthy, disagreeable, and dangerous business, always obtain higher wages than those who are engaged in more agreeable employments.

The wages of labor, in particular employments, vary according to the comparative ease with which it be learned. There are many kinds of labor which a man may perform without any previous instruction whatever, and in which he will gain a certain rate of wages from the moment he is employed. But there are also many kinds of labor which can be carried on only by those who have been regularly instructed in them. Now, it is evident that the wages of the latter class of laborers must be greater than those of the first class, in order to make up to them the time lost, and the expense they have incurred in their education. A skilled mason, who has served a long apprenticeship to his trade, will always obtain higher wages than a common laborer, who has simply to use his mere bodily strength. Were it not so, there would be nothing to induce the mason to spend many years in learning a trade at which he could earn nc higher wages than the man who was simply qualified to carry lime in a hod, or to roll a wheelbarrow.

The wages of labor, in different employments, vary with the constancy and inconstancy of employment. Employment is much more constant in some trades than in others. Many trades can be carried on only in particular states of the weather, and seasons of the year; and if the workmen who are employed in these cannot easily find employment in others during the time they are thrown out of work, their wages must be proportionally raised. A journeyman weaver, shoemaker, or tailor may reckon, unless trade is dull, upon obtaining constant employment; but masons, bricklayers, pavers, and, in general, all those workmen who carry on their business in the open air, are liable to constant interruptions. Their wages, accordingly, must be sufficient to maintain them while they are employed, and also when they are *necessarily* idle. This principle shows how foolish is the opinion generally entertained respecting the great earnings of porters, cabmen, coachmen, painters and all workmen employed only for short periods, and on particular occasions. Such persons frequently make as much in an hour or two as a regularly employed workman makes in a day. But this greater hire scarcely ever compensates for the labor they perform, and the time they are necessarily idle. Such persons are almost always poorer than those who are employed in more constant occupations.

The wages of labor vary according to the small or great trust which must be reposed in the workmen. The wages of goldsmiths and jewellers are everywhere greater than those of many other workmen, not only of equal but of much superior ingenuity, on account of the precious materials with which they are intrusted. We trust our health to the physician; our fortune, and sometimes our life and character, to the lawyer. Their reward must be such, therefore, as may give them that rank in society which so important a trust requires.

The wages of labor in different employments vary according to the chances of success in them. If a young man is bound apprentice to a shoemaker or a tailor, there is hardly any doubt but he will attain to an ordinary degree of skill in his business, and that he will be able to live by it. But if he is bound apprentice to a lawyer, a musician, a sculptor, or a player, there are ten chances to one that he never attains such a degree of skill in any of these callings as will enable him to live on his earnings. But where many fail for one who succeeds, the fortunate one ought not only to gain such a rate of wages as will make up for the expense incurred in his education, but also for all that has been incurred in the education of his unsuccessful competitors. If we add together what is likely to be annually gained, and what

is likely to be annually spent, by all the different workmen in any common trade, such as that of shoemakers
or of weavers, we shall find that the sum gained will
usually be greater than the sum spent. But if we add
together the sums gained by all the students of law and
all the lawyers in the world, and then add the sums
spent by the same, we shall find that the annual gains
bear but a small proportion to the annual expense.
Why, then, is such a profession as the law so much run
after? The love of that wealth, power, and respect,
which most commonly attend superior excellence in any
of the liberal professions, and the confidence placed by
each individual in his own good fortune, are sufficient
to overbalance the drawbacks that attend them; and
never fail to crowd their ranks with all the most liberal
and generous minds.

From the preceding observations it is evident that
those who receive the highest wages are not, when the
cost of their education, the chances of their success, and
the various disadvantages incident to their professions
are taken into account, really better paid than those
who receive the lowest. The wages earned by the
different classes of workmen are *equal*, not when each
individual earns the *same* number of dollars in a given
space of time, but when each is paid in proportion to the
severity of the labor he has to perform, to the degree of
previous education and skill it requires, and to the other
causes of variation already mentioned. So long as each
individual is allowed to employ himself as he pleases,
we may be assured that the rate of wages in different
employments will be comparatively equal.

COMPOSITION.

Define the term "wages," in your own words. Show what causes difference in wages between jeweller and farm hand; the lawyer and the blacksmith. Is it wages alone that induce so many to embrace the practice of law? Is this difference in wages just? Illustrate this by a paraphrase of the third paragraph. (What is a paragraph?) Name some trades that call for higher wages, owing to the seasons in which work is suspended. Name some not given in the lesson. Go over the sixth paragraph, and carefully resume the last ten lines.

Memorize: —

> If little labor, little are our gains;
> Man's fortunes are according to his pains.

ingenuity	comparative	employments	compensates
odium	induce	vary	preceding

————o————

THE BRAVE MAN.

LOUD let the Brave Man's praises swell
  As organ blast or clang of bell.
Of lofty soul and spirit strong,
He asks not gold — he asks but song!
Then glory to God, by whose gift I raise
The tribute of song to the Brave Man's praise!

  The thaw wind came from the southern sea,
  Dewy and dark o'er Italy;
  The scattered clouds fled far aloof,
  As flies the flock before the wolf;
It swept o'er the plain, and it strewed the wood,
And it burst the ice bonds on river and flood.

  The snow-drifts melt, till the mountain calls,
  With the voice of a thousand waterfalls;
  The waters are over both field and dell —
  Still doth the land flood wax and swell;
And high roll its billows, as in their track
They hurry the ice crags, a floating wrack.

On pillars stout, and arches wide,
A bridge of granite stems the tide;
And midway o'er the foaming flood,
Upon the bridge the toll-house stood;
There dwelleth the gate-man, with babes and wife;
Oh, seest thou the water? quick! flee for thy life.

Near and more near the wild waves urge;
Loud howls the wind, loud roars the surge;
The gate-man sprang on the roof in fright,
And he gazed on the waves in their gathering might:
"All-merciful God! to our sins be good!
We are lost! we are lost! The flood! the flood!"

High rolled the waves! In headlong track
Hither and thither dashed the wrack!
On either bank uprose the flood;
Scarce on their base the arches stood!
The gate-man, trembling for house and life,
Out-screams the storm with his babes and wife.

High heaves the flood's wrack: block on block.
The sturdy pillars feel the shock;
On either arch the surges break,
On either side the arches shake:
They totter! they sink 'neath the 'whelming wave!
All-merciful heaven, have pity and save!

Upon the river's further strand
A trembling crowd of gazers stand;
In wild despair their hands they wring,
Yet none may aid or succor bring;
And the hapless gate-man, with babes and wife,
Is screaming for help through the stormy strife.

When shall the Brave Man's praises swell
As organ blast or clang of bell?

Ah! name him *now*, he tarries long;
Name him at last, my glorious song!
O! speed, for the terrible death draws near;
O Brave Man! O Brave Man! arise, appear!

Quick gallops up, with headlong speed,
A noble Count on noble steed!
And lo! on high his fingers hold
A purse well stored with shining gold.
"Two hundred pistoles for the man who shall save
Yon perishing wretch from the yawning wave!"

Who is the Brave Man? Say, my song,
Shall to the Count thy meed belong?
Though, heaven be praised, right brave he be,
I know a braver still than he.
O Brave Man! O Brave Man! arise, appear!
Oh, speed! for the terrible death draws near!

And ever higher swell the waves,
And louder still the storm-wind raves,
And lower sink their hearts in fear —
O Brave Man! Brave Man! haste, appear!.
Buttress and pillar, they groan and strain,
And the rocking arches are rent in twain!

Again, again, before their eyes,
High holds the Count the glittering prize;
All see, but all the danger shun —
Of all the thousand stirs *not one.*
And the gate-man in vain, through the tumult wild,
Out-screams the tempest, with wife and child.

But who amid the crowd is seen,
In peasant garb, with simple mien,
Firm, leaning on a trusty stave,.
In form and feature tall and grave?

He hears the Count, and the scream of fear;
He sees that the moment of death draws near!

    Into a skiff he boldly sprang;
    He braved the storm that round him rang;
    He called aloud on God's great name —·
    And back he a deliverer came.
But the fisher's skiff seems all too small,
From the raging waters to save them all.

    The river round him boiled and surged;
    Thrice through the waves his skiff he urged,
    And back, through wind and waters' roar,
    He bore them safely to the shore:
So fierce rolled the river, that scarce the last
In the fisher's skiff through the danger passed.

    Who is the Brave Man?   Say, my song,
    To whom shall that high name belong?
    Bravely the peasant ventured in,
    But 'twas, perchance, the prize to win.
If the generous Count had proffered no gold,
The peasant, methinks, had not been so bold.

    Out spake the Count: "Right boldly done!
    Here, take thy purse; 'twas nobly won."
    A generous act, in truth, was this,
    And truly the Count right noble is;
But loftier still was the soul displayed
By him in the peasant garb arrayed.

    "Poor though I be, thy hand withhold;
    I barter not my life for gold!
    Yon hapless man is ruined now;
    Great Count, on *him* thy gift bestow."
He spake from his heart in his honest pride,
And he turned on his heel and strode aside,

Then loudly let his praises swell,
As organ blast, or clang of bell;
Of lofty soul and spirit strong,
He asks not gold — he asks but song !
Then glory to God, by whose gift I raise
The tribute of song to the Brave Man's praise !

DIRECTIONS AND CAUTIONS FOR READING.

Verse 1. — Line 1: Avoid the verse accent on *let*, and hasten on to *brave* and *swell.* **Verse 2.** — Line 4 : No accent on *doth;* the emphatic word is *still.* Line 5 : Avoid the verse accent on *in.* Line 10 : Do not place any accent on *upon,* but read *upon-the-bridge* as one word. **Verse 3.** — Line 1: Read *and-more-near* as one word. Line 2 : *Loud* is the emphatic word. **Verse 4.** — Line 7 : No accent on *upon,* but hasten on to *further strand.* **Verse 5.** — Line 1: The word with the greatest weight of emphasis is *when,* and *shall* has none at all. **Verse 6.** — Line 1: The emphatic word is *who.* No emphasis at all on *is.* Line 2 : Hasten on to the emphatic word *Count.* **Verse 7.** — Line 2 : *High* is more emphatic than *holds.* Line 3 : *All* is emphatic ; not *see.* Line 4 : *Thousand* is the chief word; and then the two very emphatic words *not one.* **Verse 8.** — Line 8 : *Thrice* is emphatic, not *through.*

COMPOSITION.

Write the story of "The Brave Man" from the following headings: A flood in the north of Italy. The blocks of ice come down and strike a bridge. A large part of it is carried away. The bridge-keeper and his family are in danger. A gentleman offers a purse of gold to any one who will save them. A peasant jumps into a boat, and brings the family away in safety. The gentleman offers him the purse; but he says:—

"Poor though I be, thy hand withhold;
I barter not my life for gold !
Yon hapless man is ruined now;
Great Count, on *him* thy gift bestow."

lofty	wrack	whelming	yawning
aloof	stems	pistoles	meed
tumult	stave	arrayed	barter
mien	skiff	withhold	strode

EDUCATION.

WE are taught that we have three powers in our soul — memory, will, and understanding. These three powers are, as it were, shut up in the soul of every child when first it is born into the world. But something is necessary in order to *draw out* these powers and give them their proper direction, and this makes up what we call the work of education.

The word "education" is derived from a Latin term which means "to lead or draw forth," because the training of a man's soul is really the gradual bringing out of all his different powers. For we are not to suppose that education consists merely in the teaching which a child receives at school. Whatever influence, good or bad, calls out his faculties, and teaches him how to use them, is to him education. Thus all men are more or less educated; they cannot exist with eyes and ears, in a world full of varying objects, without receiving ideas and notions from what they see around them, and learning, by observation of other men, and a thousand means besides, how to use their natural powers.

But the education of rude nature is not sufficient to make man what his Creator designed that he should be. It acts very slowly and imperfectly, and only produces such results as are witnessed in wild and barbarous life. Savages are nature-educated men. They grow cunning and ingenious, and learn to catch animals that are suitable to serve them as food; they also make themselves canoes that can float them across rivers and seas, and fashion for themselves garments out of leaves and skins. But they are never able to compel the great physical powers of nature to work in their service and for their advantage;

neither can they control and direct their own impulses and passions.

Nations that are civilized are so precisely because they possess a higher kind of education. The ideas of other minds have been preserved among them, and have become their property ; they have been communicated from one individual to another, and have been written down, and kept in those registers of other men's thoughts which we call books. So that, as years roll on, the young start in the pursuit of knowledge and wisdom, furnished, with all that has been already gained and laid up for them, by the toil of those who have lived before ; and each age adds to the stores thus laid up for succeeding generations.

Education, properly so called, therefore, consists in the training of all the powers of the soul. In the popular way in which we use the term, it is very often made to express the particular training of the intellect or the memory. If a man learns to read or write, he is said to have some education ; if, in addition to this, he has been taught Greek, Latin, and mathematics, he is said to be *well* educated ; and yet, in spite of his learning, he may only be *half* educated, after all. His intellect may have been developed, but his other powers may never yet have been "drawn out;" nay, his very intellect may not have been properly directed, nor shown on what it may most worthily employ its strength ; and hence the man, with all his learning, may have less that will really serve his purpose than the nature-taught savage.

To understand the full meaning and real value of education, let us remember that everything in the world approaches perfection in proportion as it is adapted to its end. A knife that is made of gold and ornamented with jewels may be a handsome trinket, but it is not a good knife unless it cuts. And so a man's education must fit him for his end, or it would be simply good for nothing. It must call forth his powers of observation and reasoning, because in all the affairs of life he has need of good sense and sound judgment. It must strengthen his memory, and fill it with useful facts; and must aim at making him an intelligent being, with powers capable of being directed to the particular end which each man has to accomplish.

It is obvious, however, that every man does not stand in need of the same kind of education. A physician requires a different kind of teaching from a priest, and a soldier has to learn many things which would be quite useless to a ploughman, or a shoemaker. Of what use would it be to an artisan's wife if she thoroughly comprehended the whole solar system, and yet knew not how to make a shirt, or keep her husband's house in proper order? Or if her husband himself were to be learned in Greek and Latin, yet unable to cast accounts or spell his own language? There are some things, therefore, in which people do not all require the same kind of education, because all have not the same aim. But. again, in other respects they all *have* the same requirements, because in some things their end is the same. The real end of man is not to be a carpenter, or a physician, or a soldier; it is to know God, to love God, and to serve God in this world, and to be happy with him for ever in the next. Without recollecting this, we can never form any true idea of what constitutes education. For without this thought in our minds, how can we know in what direction our powers are to be "led out," on what objects they are to be employed, and to what purpose we shall use them? If things are perfect in proportion as they are fitted for their end, how can the powers of my soul reach perfection if they be not trained to do that for which God created them? Unless my *memory* shall have been taught to think of God, and my *will* to love him and serve him, by resisting what is evil and resolving on what is good, and unless my *understanding*, enlightened by faith, shall have been directed to distinguish truth from falsehood — my education is imperfect; for surely that would be a sorry education by which the intellect had only been nurtured in error. Never, therefore, let us fall into the common mistake of thinking a man well educated simply because he knows many things. Knowledge alone is not education, any more than it is wisdom. Knowledge is merely the information of the memory — a very useful part of education, provided always that the facts so communicated be good and true; for there may be a knowledge of evil.

Neither is a man well educated merely because he can think and reason. Here again we have a great power; but does he think and reason rightly? Steam is an enormous power also; but what would be the result if it were set in motion for some mischievous purpose? Instead of propelling a railway engine or working a cotton-mill, it might crush a hundred men, or blow up a dozen houses. And human reason needs control and direction quite as much as any steam-engine. The education of the understanding is not intended merely to make a man into a reasoning machine, but to lead him to form true conclusions, and to teach him how sometimes to use and sometimes to submit his judgment

And what shall we say of the will of man — that gigantic power which all are conscious of possessing, and on the use of which all our other powers depend for good or for evil? Shall not this also have its education?

hall we know how to work our intellects, and yet never
ive learned how to command our passions? Shall
ir heads be trained to a thousand difficult exercises,
id our hearts, from which are the issues of life and
iath, be still untamed, undisciplined, and savage?
It is evident that religion and religious influences are
quired in order to "lead out" all our powers, and
iape them to their true end, by training our whole
tellectual and spiritual nature "to the measure of the
ie of the fulness of Christ."

COMPOSITION.

Write the following in four ways:
"A knife that is made of gold . . . . unless it cuts."
"Never, therefore, let us fall into . . . . nurtured in error."

faculties	intellect	sorry
varying	developed	propelling
ingenious	obvious	issues
impulses	requirements	undisciplined

----o----

THE MESSIAH.

RAPT into future times, the bard began:
  A virgin shall conceive, a virgin bear a son!
From Jesse's root behold a branch arise,
Whose sacred flow'r with fragrance fills the skies:
The ethereal spirit o'er its leaves shall move,
And on its top descends the mystic dove.
Ye heavens! from high the dewy nectar pour,
And in soft silence shed the kindly show'r!
The sick and weak, the healing plant shall aid,
From storms a shelter, and from heat a shade.
All crimes shall cease, and ancient frauds shall fail;

Returning Justice lift aloft her scale·
Peace o'er the world her olive wand extend,
And white-robed Innocence from heaven descend.
Swift fly the years, and rise the expected morn;
Oh, spring to light, auspicious Babe; be born!
Hark! a glad voice the lonely desert cheers;
Prepare the way! a God, a God appears!
Lo! earth receives him from the bending skies;
Sink down, ye mountains, and ye valleys rise!
With heads reclined, ye cedars homage pay;
Be smooth, ye rocks; ye rapid floods give way!
The Saviour comes! by ancient bards foretold;
Hear him, ye deaf; and all ye blind, behold.
He from thick films shall purge the visual ray,
And on the sightless eyeball pour the day:
'Tis he the obstructed paths of sound shall clear,
And bid new music charm the unfolding ear;
The dumb shall sing, the lame his crutch forego,
And leap exulting, like the bounding roe.
No sigh, no murmur, the wide world shall hear;
From every face he wipes off every tear.
In adamantine chains shall Death be bound,
And hell's grim tyrant feel the eternal wound.
As the good shepherd tends his fleecy care,
Seeks freshest pasture, and the purest air;
Explores the lost, the wandering sheep directs,
By day o'ersees them, and by night protects;
The tender lambs he raises in his arms,
Feeds from his hand, and in in his bosom warms;
Thus shall mankind his guardian care engage,
The promised Father of the future age.
No more shall nation against nation rise,
Nor ardent warriors meet with hateful eyes,
Nor fields with gleaming steel be cover'd o'er,
The brazen trumpets kindle rage no more;

But useless lances into scythes shall bend,
And the broad falchion in a ploughshare end.
The lambs with wolves shall graze the verdant mead,
And boys in flow'ry bands the tiger lead.
The steer and lion at one crib shall meet,
And harmless serpents lick the pilgrim's feet.
The smiling infant in his hands shall take
The crested basilisk and speckled snake,
Pleased, the green lustre of the scales survey,
And with their forky tongue shall innocently play.
The seas shall waste, the skies in smoke decay,
Rocks fall to dust, and mountains melt away;
But fix'd his word, his saving power remains;
Thy realm forever lasts, thy own Messiah reigns!

Questions:—Explain "from Jesse's root;" "from high the dewy nectar pour;" "returning Justice lift aloft her scale;" "olive wand." What *auspicious Babe* is meant? Whose voice said "Prepare ye the way of the Lord"? Explain:

"But useless lances into scythes shall bend,
And the broad falchion in a ploughshare end."

What is peculiar about the basilisk's eye?

root	wand	roe	falchion
ethercal	bards	adamantine	graze
nectar	films	grim	crib
frauds	visual	explores	basilisk

---o---

LETTER TO THE MARQUIS WELLESLEY.

OUR creed, my lord, is short; all we believe is embodied in the profession of faith, published under the name of Pius IV., and found in many of our books of common prayer, and in all our rituals or liturgies: it is detailed and justified, and defined, in the decrees of the Council of Trent; and if your excellency should ever have cast your eye over it, you might not prefer it to that which you profess, but it is impossible that you would not respect it; it is quite impossible that your excellency would deem it a slavish superstition, or say that those who professed it were thereby rendered unfit for freedom.

It was the creed, my lord, of a Charlemagne, of a St. Louis, of an Alfred and an Edward, of the monarchs of the feudal times, as well as of the emperors of Greece and Rome; it was believed at Venice and at Genoa, in Lucca and the Helvetic nations, in the days of their freedom and greatness.: all the barons of the Middle Ages, all the free cities of latter times, professed the religion we now profess. You well know, my lord, that the charter of British freedom, and the common law of England, have their origin and source in Catholic times. Who framed the free constitution of the Spanish Goths? Who preserved science and literature during the long night of the Middle Ages? Who imported literature from Constantinople and opened for her an asylum at Rome, Florence, Padua, Paris, and Oxford? Who polished Europe by art, and refined her by legislation? Who discovered the New World, and opened a passage to another? Who were the masters of architecture, of painting, of music? Who invented the compass, and the art of printing? Who were the poets, the historians, the jurists, the men of deep research and profound literature? Who have exalted human nature, and made man appear little less than the angels? Were they not almost exclusively the professors of our creed? Were they who created and possessed freedom under every shape and form, unfit for her enjoyment? Were men, deemed even now the lights of the world, and the benefactors of the human race, the deluded victims of a slavish superstition?

But what is there in our creed, which renders us unfit for freedom? Is it the doctrine of passive obedience? No; for the obedience we yield to authority is not blind, but reasonable; our religion does not create despotism; it supports every established constitution, which is not opposed to the laws of nature, unless it be altered by those who have the right to change it. In Poland it supported an elective monarch; in France, an hereditary sovereign; in Spain, an absolute or constitutional king indifferently; in England, when the houses of York and Lancaster contended, it declared that he who was king *de facto*, was entitled to the obedience of the people. During the reign of the Tudors, there was a faithful adherence of the Catholics to their prince, under trials the most severe and galling, because the constitution required it: the same was exhibited by them to the ungrateful race of Stuart; but since the expulsion of James, (foolishly called an abdication,) have they not adopted with the nation at large, the doctrine of the revolution, "that the crown is held in trust for the benefit of the people; and that should the monarch violate his compact, the subject is freed from the bond of his allegiance?" Is there any obligation, either to a prince or to a constitution, which it does not enforce?

For nearly four centuries, whilst two nations struggled in the womb of Ireland, the one laboring to conquer, the other to defend, we find Religion always recommending an adjustment, and exhibiting to her infuriated children the olive-branch of peace: we find her in the person of O'Toole, the archbishop of Dublin, standing between the living and the dead, praying for the people, whilst the plague raged. Has she ever ceased to pour

the balm of consolation upon the wounds of the countrɔ
and to instil hope or resignation into her almost broke
heart? Yet this is the religion which is said to unf
us for freedom.

COMPOSITION.

Write out questions 1, 2, 3, 4, and answer in as few words ɑ
possible. Then, take question 5 :

"Who discovered the New World, and opened a passage to aɲ
other?" It may be answered thus :

"Columbus, aided by Catholic Isabella and Ferdinand of Spaiɲ
and also encouraged in his venture by Dominican friars, discovereɩ
the New World, and opened a passage to another.

rituals	Goths	passive
liturgies	architecture	hereditary
superstition	jurists	constitutionaɪ
Charlemagne	research	Tudors
Helvetic	exclusively	womb
framed	deluded	instil

————o————

THE INCHCAPE BELL

Robert Southey (1774-1843), one of the Lake School of poets. His
literary activity was wonderful. The list of his published writings
numbers 109 volumes, besides which he contributed 149 articles to the
reviews. His poetry is very much neglected, and most of it will soon
be quite forgotten. The "Metrical Tales," of which the following is a
specimen, are the best of his poems. As a prose writer he ranks high.
Of his prose works the best known is the Life of Nelson, written for
young readers.

NO stir in the air, no stir in the sea,
    The ship was as still as she could be;
Her sails from heaven received no motion,
Her keel was steady in the ocean.

Without either sign or sound of their shock,
The waves flowed over the Inchcape Rock;
So little they rose, so little they fell,
They did not move the Inchcape Bell.

The Abbot of Aberbrothok
Had placed that bell on the Inchcape Rock;
On a buoy in the storm it floated and swung,
And over the waves its warning rung.

When the rock was hid by the surge's swell,
The mariners heard the warning bell;
And then they knew the perilous rock,
And blessed the Abbot of Aberbrothok.

The sun in heaven was shining gay,
All things were joyful on that day;
The sea-birds screamed as they wheeled around,
And there was joyaunce in their sound.

The buoy of the Inchcape Bell was seen
A darker speck on the ocean green;
Sir Ralph the Rover walked his deck,
And he fixed his eye on the darker speck.

He felt the cheering power of spring,
It made him whistle, it made him sing;
His heart was mirthful to excess —
But the Rover's mirth was wickedness.

His eye was on the Inchcape float:
Quoth he, "My men, put out the boat,
And row me to the Inchcape Rock,
And I'll plague the Abbot of Aberbrothok

The boat is lowered, the boatmen row,
And to the Inchcape Rock they go;

Sir Ralph leant over from the boat,
And cut the bell from the Inchcape float.

Down sank the bell with a gurgling sound,
The bubbles rose and burst around;
Quoth Sir Ralph, "The next who comes to the rock
Won't bless the Abbot of Aberbrothok."

Sir Ralph the Rover sailed away,
He scoured the seas for many a day;
And now, grown rich with plundered store,
He steers his course for Scotland's shore.

So thick a haze o'erspreads the sky,
They cannot see the sun on high.
The wind hath blown a gale all day,
At evening it hath died away.

On the deck the Rover takes his stand,
So dark it is they see no land.
Quoth Sir Ralph, "It will be lighter soon,
For there is the dawn of the rising moon."

"Canst hear," said one, "the breakers' roar!
For, methinks, we should be near the shore.
Yet where we are I cannot tell,
I wish I could hear the Inchcape Bell."

They hear no sound, the swell is strong;
Though the wind hath fallen they drift along,
Till the vessel strikes with a shivering shock,—
"O Heavens! it is the Inchcape Rock!"

Sir Ralph the Rover tore his hair,
And beat his breast in his despair;
The waves rushed in on every side,
And the ship sank down beneath the tide.

Questions :--Give the first two stanzas in your own words. Change
he adjectives and verbs in third and fourth. What was Sir Ralph's
occupation ? How was he punished ? What conversation had taken
place previously ?

| Inchcape | buoy | joyaunce | float |
| Aberbrothok | surge's | excess | swell |

----o----

THE REAPER.

William Wordsworth (1770-1850) was the first great poet who turned
the current of English poetry into its present channel, that of *humanity*;
by which we mean those sentiments arising from the contemplation
of the threefold relations of God, man's soul, and nature. We say
the first *great* poet, because before his time such poets as Cowper, and
Goldsmith, and Burns, had really begun the re-action against roman-
ticism, and Wordsworth has been given the credit of originating a
movement of which he was but the instrument. The " Excursion "
is his greatest poem. It is philosophy in numbers. Many of Wordsworth's sonnets are the finest in the language. All his reflective
poems are marked by great loftiness of sentiment, and are better
appreciated as the mind grows older and lays aside the passions and
ardor of youth.

BEHOLD her, single in the field, you solitary Highland Lass ! reaping and singing by herself ; stop
here, or gently pass ! Alone she cuts and binds the
grain, and sings a melancholy strain ; Oh listen ! for the
vale profound is overflowing with the sound. No
nightingale did ever chaunt more welcome notes to
weary bands of travelers, in some shady haunt among
Arabian sands : no sweeter voice was ever heard in
spring-time from the cuckoo-bird, breaking the silence
of the seas among the farthest Hebrides. Will no one
tell me what she sings ? Perhaps the plaintive numbers
flow for old, unhappy, far-off things, and battles long
ago : or is it some more humble lay, familiar *matter of*

been, and may be again? Whate'er the theme, the maiden sang as if her song could have no ending; I saw her singing at her work, and o'er the sickle bending; I listened till I had my fill; and as I mounted up the hill, the music in my heart I bore long after it was heard no more.

COMPOSITION.

Re-write the above in verse form.

Highland　　　Lass　　　Hebrides　　　sickle

———o———

THE IDEA OF A SAINT.

John Henry, Cardinal Newman, was born in England in 1801. He was educated at Oxford. In 1845 he became a convert to the Catholic faith; in 1847 was ordained priest, and in 1848 established the Oratory of St. Philip Neri in England. He was the first rector of the Catholic University of Ireland, which office he held for several years. He is unquestionably one of the leading minds of the age. In his writings a profound and varied learning, a mind eminently philosophical and a keen analytic genius are displayed, through the medium of a style at once copious and compact, full of vigor and nervous energy, and yet of majestic and sustained harmony. He is the greatest living master of English prose. His best known works are "Grammar of Assent," "Apologia pro Vita Sua," "Discourse on University Education," "History of Arianism," "Loss and Gain" and "Callista," the two latter being works of fiction.

WORLDLY-MINDED men, however rich, if they are Catholics, cannot, till they utterly lose their faith, be the same as those who are external to the Church; they have an instinctive veneration for those who have the traces of heaven upon them, and they praise what they do not imitate.

Such men have an idea before them which a Protestant nation has not; they have the idea of a Saint

ey believe they realize the existence of those rare
servants of God, who rise up from time to time in the
Catholic Church like angels in disguise, and shed around
them a light as they walk on their way heavenward.
They may not in practice do what is right and good,
but they know what is true; they know what to think and
how to judge.   They have a standard for their principles
of conduct, and it is the image, the pattern of Saints
which forms it for them.   Very various are the Saints,
their variety being a token of God's workmanship; but
however various, and whatever was their special line of
duty, they have been heroes in it; they have attained
such noble self-command, they have so crucified the flesh,
they have so renounced the world; they are so meek,
so gentle, so tender-hearted, so merciful, so sweet, so
cheerful, so full of prayer, so diligent, so forgetful of
injuries; they have sustained such great and continued
pains, they have persevered in such vast labors, they
have made such valiant confessions, they have wrought
such abundant miracles, they have been blessed with
such strange successes, that they have set up a standard
before us of truth, of magnanimity, of holiness, of love.
They are not always our examples, and we are not
always bound to follow them; not more than we are bound
to obey literally some of our Lord's precepts, such as
turning the cheek or giving away the coat; not more than
we can follow the course of the sun, moon, or stars in
the heavens; but, though not always our examples, they
are always our standard of right and good; they are
raised up to be monuments and lessons, they remind us
of God, they introduce us into the unseen world, they
teach us what Christ loves, they track out for us the
way which leads heavenward.   They are to us who see
them, what wealth, notoriety, rank and name are to the

multitude of men who live in darkness, — objects o
veneration and of our homage.

Questions : — What feeling distinguishes even worldly-minded
olics, who have not lost their faith? What pattern do Catholic&
for their lives? What name is given the Saints here? Why were
heroes? Name their chief works. Why were the Saints raise&
Name six Saints whose lives you admire, and say why.

---o---

THE VIRGIN.

MOTHER! whose virgin bosom was uncross'd
  With the least shade of thought to sin allied,
Woman! above all women glorified,
Our tainted nature's solitary boast;
Purer than foam on central ocean tossed,
  Brighter than eastern skies at daybreak, strewn
  With fancied roses, than the unblemish'd moon
Before her vane begins on heaven's blue coast,
Thy image falls to earth. Yet some I ween,
  Not unforgiven, the suppliant knee might bend,
  As to a visible power, in which did blend
  All that was mix'd and reconciled in thee
  Of mother's love with maiden purity,
Of high with low, celestial with terrene.

It is this thought to-day that lifts
  My happy heart to heaven,
That for our sakes thy choicest gifts
  To thee, dear Queen, were given.
The glory that belongs to thee
  Seems rather mine than thine,
While all the cares that harass me
  Are rather thine than mine.

Ave Maria ! thou whose name
All but adoring love may claim,
   Yet may we reach thy shrine :
For he, thy Son and Saviour, vows
To crown all humble, lowly brows
   With love and joy like thine.

COMPOSITION.

ive the following in two ways.

> " Mother! whose virgin bosom was uncross'd
> With the least shade of thought to sin allied."

he first four lines of the second selection.   The first two lines of
third selection.

tainted   vane   terrene

TALK WITH YOUNG FOLKS.

OING ! Going ! Gone !
   The other day, as I was walking through a side
eet in one of our large cities, I heard these words
ging out from a room so crowded with people
at I could but just see the auctioneer's face and up-
ted hammer above the heads of the crowd.

" Going ! Going ! Go-ing ! Gone ! "   and down came
e hammer with a sharp rap.

I do not know how or why it was, but the words
ruck me with a new force and significance. I had
ard them hundreds of times before, with only a
nse of amusement. This time they sounded solemn.

" Going ! Going ! Gone ! "

" That is the way it is with life," I said to myself ;
·" with time." This world is a sort of auction-room ;
e do not know that we are buyers : we are, in fact,

more like beggars ; we have brought no money to exchange for precious minutes, hours, days, or years; they are given to us. There is no calling out of terms, no noisy auctioneer, no hammer ; but, nevertheless, the time is "going! going! gone!"

The more I thought of it, the more solemn did the words sound, and the more did they seem to me a good motto to remind one of the value of time.

When we are young we think old people are preaching and prosing when they say so much about it,—when they declare so often that days, weeks, even years, are short. I can remember when a holiday, a whole day long, appeared to me an almost inexhaustible play-spell : when one afternoon, even, seemed an endless round of pleasure, and the week that was to come seemed longer than does a whole year now.

One needs to live many years before one learns how little time there is in a year,—how little, indeed, there will be even in the longest possible life,—how many things one will still be obliged to leave undone.

But there is one thing, boys and girls, that you can realize if you will try—if you will stop and think about it a little ; and that is, how fast and how steadily the present time is slipping away. However long life may seem to you as you look forward to the whole of it, the present hour has only sixty minutes, and minute by minute, second by second, it is "going! going! gone!" If you gather nothing from it as it passes, it is "gone" forever. Nothing is so utterly, hopelessly lost as "lost time." It makes me unhappy when I look back and see how much time I have wasted : how much I might have learned and done if I had but understood how short is the longest hour.

All the men and women who have made the world

better, happier, or wiser for their having lived in it,
have done so by working diligently and persistently.
Yet, I am certain that not even one of these, when
"looking backward from his manhood's prime, saw
not the specter of his mis-spent time." Now, don't
suppose I am so foolish as to think that all the
preaching in the world can make anything look to
young eyes as it looks to old eyes ; not a bit of it.

But think about it a little ; don't let time slip away
by the minute, hour, day, without getting something
out of it ! Look at the clock now and then, and listen
to the pendulum, saying of every minute, as it flies,—
"Going ! going ! gone !"

A SCENE FROM TELL.

*Enter Sarnem with soldiers, bearing Gesler's cap upon
a pole, which he fixes in the ground, the people looking on
in silence and amazement ; the guards station themselves
near the pole.*

Sarnem.   Ye men of Altorf,
   Behold the emblem of your master's power
   And dignity.   This is the cap of Gesler,
   Your governor ; let all bow down to it
   Who owe him love and loyalty.   To such
   As shall refuse this lawful homage, or
   Accord it sullenly, he shows no grace,
   But dooms them to the penalty of bondage
   Till they're instructed ; 'tis no less their gain
   Than duty, to obey their master's mandate.
   Conduct the people hither, one by one,
   To bow to Gesler's cap.

Tell.   Have I my hearing?

   [*Peasants pass, taking off their hats, and bowing to Ge.
     ler's cap.*]

Verner.   Away! Away!

T. O sight! They do it, Verner!
   They do it!—Look—Ne'er call me man again!
   I'll herd with baser animals! *They* keep
   Their station.

V. Come away, before they mark us.

T. No! no! since I have tasted,
   I will e'en taste on; I begin, methinks, to like it
   [*Pierre passes the cap, smiles, and bows lightly.*]

S. What smiled you at?

Pierre. You saw I bowed as low as he did.

S. Nay, but you smiled. How dared you smile?

T. Good! good!

S. (*Striking*) Take that; remember, when you smile
   again,
   To do it in season.

V. (*Takes hold of Tell's arm.*) Come away.

T. Not yet—not yet.
   Why would you have me quit the feast? Me-
   thinks
   It grows richer and richer!

S. (*Striking another blow*) Bow lower, slave!

T. Do you feel
   That blow? My flesh doth tingle with it. Well
   done!
   How pleasantly the knave doth lay it on!
   Well done! well done! I would it had been I!

V. You tremble, William. Come, you must not stay.

T. Why not? What harm is there? I tell thee,
   Verner,
   I know no difference twixt enduring wrong

And living in the fear of it. I do not wear
The tyrant's fetters when it only wants
His nod to put them on, and bear his stripes.
When that I suffer, then he needs but hold
His finger up. Verner, you are not the man
To be content because a villain's mood
Forbears? You are right—you are right! Have
   with you, Verner.
[*Enter Michael through the crowd.*]

S. Bow, slave. (*Tell stops and turns.*)

Michael. For what? (*Laughs*)

S. Obey, and question then.

M. I'll question now, and perhaps not then obey.

T. A man! a man!

S. 'Tis Gesler's will that all bow to that cap.

M. Were it thy lady's cap, I'd courtesy to it.

S. Do you mock us, friend?

M. Not I; I will bow to Gesler, if you please,
   But not to his cap, nor cap of any there be
   In Christendom!

T. A man! I say, a man!

S. I see you love a jest; but jest not now;
   Else you may make a mirth, and pay for it, too.
   Bow to the cap; do you hear?

M. I do.

T. Well done! The lion thinks as much of cowering
   As he does!

S. Once for all, bow to that cap!

T. Verner, let go my arm!

S. Do you hear me, slave?

M. Slave?

T. Let me go!

V. He is not worth it, Tell;
   A wild and idle gallant of the town.

T. A man—I'll swear, a man! Don't hold me, Verner;
  Verner, let go my arm! Do you hear me, man?
  You must not hold me, Verner.

S. Villain, bow to Gesler's cap!

M. No! not to Gesler's cap.

T. (*Rushing forward*) Off, off, you base and hireling
  pack!
  Lay not your brutal touch upon the thing!
  God made it his own image. Crouch yourselves!
  'Tis your vocation, which you should not call
  On freeborn men to share with you, who stand
  Erect, except in presence of their God alone!

S. What! shrink you coward? Must I do your duty
  for you?

T. Let them but stir! I have scattered
  A flock of hungry wolves outnumbering them—
  For sport I did it, sport! I scattered them
  With but a staff not half as thick as this—
  [*Thrusts Sarnem's weapon from him ; Sarnem and
soldiers fly.*]
  What! Ha! Beset by hares! Ye men of Altorf,
  What fear ye? See what things you fear—the
  shows
  And surfaces of men! Why stand you wondering
  there?
  Why look you on a man that's like yourselves,
  And see him do the deeds yourselves might do,
  And act them not? Or know you not yourselves
  That ye are men?—that ye have hearts and
  thoughts
  To feel and think the deeds of men, and hands
  To do them? Fear you God, and fear you him
  Who fears *not* God, but in his sight defies him?
  You hunt the chamois and have seen him take

The precipice, before he'd yield the freedom
Which Heaven ne'er gave the little chamois ;
Why gaze you still with blanched cheeks upon me ?
Lost you the manhood even to look on,
And see the deeds achieved by other hands ?
Or doth that cap still hold you thralls to fear ?
Be free, then !   There !   Thus do I trample on
The cap of Gesler, as I would on him !   (*Throws
down the pole.*)

S. (*Suddenly entering with soldiers*)   Seize him !
[*All the people except Verner and Michael fly.*]

T. Ha !   Surrounded ?

M. Stand !   I'll back thee !

V. Madman !   Hence ! (*Forces Michael off.*)

S. Upon him, slaves.   Upon him all at once !
[*Tell, after a struggle, is secured and thrown to
the ground, where they proceed to chain him.*]

Questions :—Require the pupil—To answer historical allusions. Mention the characters in this scene. What is meant by a scene? Of what was Gesler's cap the emblem? Give in your own words the leading incidents of the scene.

———o———

THE HEROISM OF ST. MARTINA.

THE peerless soul of a virgin is the brightest spot on earth, and the most pleasing to God.   He has frequently chosen the meek and humble frame of girlhood for the most extraordinary manifestations of His power or His goodness.   He has sent from time to time beings who seemed to be angels clothed in human form, to attract us by the loveliness of virtue, and to show us the great mystery of love in which He unites

Himself to the human soul.   God has ever been wonderful in His saints.

'Martina was the only child of one of the consuls of the Roman Empire.   She lost her parents in her infancy and inherited an immense fortune.   Sentiments of piety and virtue had been early instilled into her young mind, so that she had learned the sublime lessons of the Christian school.

Knowing the danger of riches, and wishing to give herself entirely to God, one of her first acts was to distribute her wealth to the poor.   Domitian Ulpian, a wicked prefect, had for some time cast an evil eye on the orphan virgin, and finding he could not succeed in making her his wife, caused her to be brought to the temple to offer sacrifice to the gods, so that, if she should refuse, he would have her completely in his power.

Two lictors were sent to seize the Christian virgin and bring her before the prefect.   She refused to sacrifice to the idol, and Ulpian determined to force her to submit.   "Never," said she, "will you force me to offer incense to creatures of man's making, or to honor the odious ideas that paganism has exalted."

Her delicate and tender flesh was torn with whips, but Martina remained firm and steadfast.   She was then suspended from the yoke, and her flesh was torn with iron hooks and other instruments of torture; still she remained constant.   Then she was brought to the temple of Diana and Apollo, to offer sacrifice, when, behold! a fire descended from heaven and consumed the altars.

The tyrant prefect, hardened by vice and blinded by passion, ordered boiling oil and pitch to be poured over her lacerated body, but what was intended as a fresh punishment became a source of greater glory and triumph. They saw her surrounded by a halo of glory, a delicious odor issued from her wounds, and at times she was raised from the ground in an ecstasy of heavenly joy.

The prefect, filled with rage and confusion, determined to have her devoured by the wild beasts of the amphitheatre, and before the populace of Rome.

Next day, Martina was led into the arena. The white sand scarcely yields to her delicate tread. She steps over a pool of fresh blood—the life-stream of the last gladiator that had fallen.

But there bounds a captive lion into the arena. He looks around in surprise. His eyes are darting fire with hunger and rage. Suddenly he sees a figure in his own domain—'tis Martina, kneeling and wrapt in prayer. He prepares for a desperate spring. A death-like stillness reigns around; every head is stretched forward, every eye fixed on the arena, and an involuntary shudder passes through every frame.

But lo! what do the spectators see? The king of the forest crouching at the feet of the youthful maiden!

Thus did God, in whom she placed her trust, defend her. Thus did His almighty power confound her enemies.

Questions :—Use some other word instead of peerless. What did Martina inherit? Did she prefer wealth or poverty? Why did Martina refuse to sacrifice to the idols? When is a person filled with rage? Write a composition on Martina's heroism.

clothed	attract	odious	delicate
brightest	instilled	paganism	consumes
completely	distribute	involuntary	amphitheatre

HOME, SWEET HOME.

'Midst pleasures and palaces though we may roam,
Be it ever so humble, there's no place like home !
A charm from the skies seems to hallow all there
Which, seek through the world, is ne'er met with elsewhere.
　　　Home ! home ! sweet home !
　　　There's no place like home ɪ
An exile from home, splendor dazzles in vain :
Oh, give me my lowly thatched cottage again ;
The birds singing gaily that came at my call :
Give me these, and the peace of mind dearer than all.
　　　Home ! sweet, sweet home !
　　　There's no place like home !

Questions:—What are palaces ?　Give the definition of the word **roam.**
What is it makes home so pleasant ?　Write a composition on home.

———o———

IN THE LABORATORY WITH AGASSIZ.

IT is more than fifteen years ago that I entered the laboratory of Professor Agassiz and told him that I had enrolled my name in the Scientific School, as a student of natural history.　He asked me a few questions about my object in coming and my antecedents generally.

"When do you wish to begin?" he asked.

"Now," I replied.

This seemed to please him, and with an energetic "very well" he reached from a shelf a huge jar of specimens in alcohol.

"Take this fish," said he, "and look at it ; by-and-by I will ask you what you have seen."

With that he left me, but in a moment he returned

with explicit instructions as to the care of the object intrusted to me.

"No man is fit to be a naturalist," said he, "who does not know how to take care of his specimens."

I was to keep the fish before me in a tin tray, and occasionally moisten the surface with alcohol.

In ten minutes I had seen all that could be seen in that fish. I then started in search of the Professor, who had, however, left the museum.

I returned to my place and began to look again at my fish. Half an hour passed,—an hour,—another hour ; the fish then began to look loathsome. I was in despair. It was now time for luncheon, and with feelings of great relief I replaced the fish carefully in the jar, and for an hour I was free.

On my return I learned that the Professor had come back, but that he had left the museum and would not return for several hours. Slowly I drew forth that hideous fish, and with feelings of desperation again looked at it.

I was not allowed to use a magnifying glass ; the use of instruments of all kinds was forbidden. I began to count the scales in the different rows. Finally, a happy thought struck me. I concluded to draw the fish, and when I started I began to discover new features in the creature ; just then the Professor came in.

"That is right," said he, "a pencil is one of the best of eyes. I am glad to notice, too, that you keep your specimen wet, and your bottle corked."

With these encouraging words, he added :

"Well, what is it like."

He listened attentively to my brief rehearsal of the structure of the parts whose names were still unknown to me. When I had finished he waited, as if expecting more, and then, with an air of disappointment, said :

"You have not looked very carefully. Why," he continued more earnestly, "you haven't even seen one of the most conspicuous features of the fish, which is as plainly before your eyes as the fish itself; look again ; look again," and he left me to my misery.

I was piqued ; I was mortified. Still more of that wretched fish ! But now I set myself to my task with a will, and discovered one new feature after another, until I saw how just the Professor's criticisms had been. The afternoon passed quickly, and when, toward its close, the professor inquired :

"Do you see it yet ? "

"No," I replied, "I am certain I do not, but I see now how little I saw before."

"That is the next best," said he, earnestly, "but I won't hear you now ; put away your fish and go home ; perhaps you will be ready with a better answer in the morning. I will examine you before you look at the fish."

This was, indeed, discouraging. Not only must I think of my fish all night, but I must give an account of it the next day.

The cordial greeting from the Professor the next morning was reassuring ; here was a man who seemed to be quite as anxious as I that I should see for myself what he saw.

"Do you, perhaps, mean," I asked, "that the fish has symmetrical sides with paired organs ? "

His thoroughly pleased " of course, of course," was pleasant music to my ears.

After he had discoursed most happily and enthusiastically—as he always did—upon the importance of observation, I ventured to ask him what I should do next.

"Oh! look at your fish!" he said, and left me again to my own devices. In a little more than an hour he returned and heard my new catalogue.

"That is good, that is good!" he repeated; "but that is not all; go on; "and so for three days he placed that fish before my eyes, forbidding me to look at any thing else, or to use any artificial aid. "Look, look, look," was his repeated injunction.

This was the best lesson I ever had—a lesson whose influence has extended to the details of every subsequent study; a legacy the Professor has left to me, as he has left it to many others, of such inestimable value that it is the basis of much of our success.

Questions:—What is a laboratory? Mention some scientific school. What is a naturalist? Give the name of some celebrated museum. What are "encouraging words?" Give the name of some symmetrical object. How would you make a catalogue? What lesson did the Professor teach the students?

antecedent	enrolled	criticism	energetic
encouraging	catalogue	desperation	laboratory
enthusiastically	details	observation	injunction

THE ANNOUNCEMENT TO THE SHEPHERDS.

A MILE and a half, it may be two miles, southeast of Bethlehem, there is a plain separated from the town by an intervening swell of the mountain. Besides being well sheltered from the north wind, the vale was well covered with a growth of sycamore, dwarf-oak, and pine trees, while in the glens and ravines adjoining there were thickets of olive and mulberry; all at this season of the year invaluable for the support of sheep, goats, and cattle, of which the wandering flock consisted.

At the side farthest from the town, close under a bluff, there was an extensive sheep-cot, ages old. A number of shepherds, seeking fresh halts for their flocks, led them up to the plain, and when the sun went down, they led the way to the sheep-cot and by nightfall had everything safe in the field; then they kindled a fire down by the gate, partook of their humble supper, and sat down to rest and talk, leaving one on the watch.

The night, like most nights of the winter season in the hill country, was clear, crisp, and sparkling with stars. There was no wind. The stillness was more than silence. It was a holy hush. A warning that heaven was stooping low to whisper some good thing to the listening earth.

By the gate the watchman halted. At times he stopped, attracted by a stir among the sleeping herds or by a jackal's cry, off on the mountain side. The midnight was slow in coming to him; but it came at last. He moved towards the fire but paused. A light was burning round him, soft and white like the moon's. He waited breathlessly; the light deepened; things before invisible came into view. He looked up; the stars were gone; the light was dropping as from a window in the sky. As he looked, it became a splendor; then, in terror, he cried :—

"Awake, awake!"

Up sprang the dogs, and, howling, ran away.

The herd rushed together, bewildered.

The men clambered to their feet, weapons in hand.

"What is it?" they asked in one voice.

"See!" cried the watchman, "the sky is on fire!"

Suddenly, the light became intolerably bright, and they covered their eyes and dropped upon their knees; then, as their souls shrank with fear, they fell upon their faces, blind and fainting.

" Fear not ! "

And they listened.

" Fear not : for behold, I bring you good tidings of great joy, that shall be to all the people."

The voice, in sweetness and soothing more than human, penetrated their being and filled them with assurance. They rose upon their knees and, looking worshipfully, beheld in the centre of a great glory the appearance of a man clad in a robe intensely white. His hands were stretched towards them in blessing, and his face was serene and divinely beautiful.

Sweetly the angel continued :—

" For this day is born to you a Saviour, who is Christ the Lord, in the city of David."

. Again, there was a rest, while the words sank into their minds.

" And this shall be a sign unto you," the angel said. " You shall find the infant wrapped in swaddling clothes and laid in a manger."

The angel spoke not again. His good tidings were told ; yet he staid awhile. Suddenly, the light of which he seemed the centre turned roseate and began to tremble. Then, up, far as the men could see, there was flashing of white wings, and coming and going of radiant forms, and voices as of a multitude chanting in unison.

" Glory to God in the highest, and on earth, peace to men of good will." Not once but many times.

Then the angels departed. Long after they were gone, down from the sky fell the refrain in measure mellowed by distance. " Glory to God in the highest, and peace on earth, to men of good will."

Write a composition, giving in your own words the substance of the piece.

———o———

A STORM ON THE ATLANTIC.

THE gale came on about eleven o'clock at night, not violent at first, but increasing every moment. I slept soundly until after five in the morning, and then awoke with a confused recollection of much rolling and thumping. It was still quite dark, but four of the sails were already in ribbons; the winds were whistling through the cordage, the rain was dashing furiously and in torrents, and the noise and spray were scarcely less than I found them under the great sheet at Niagara.

We had encountered, as yet, however, only the commencement of the gale, whose terrors had been heightened by its suddenness, and by the darkness and confusion. For twenty-four hours it continued to blow furiously. The ship was driven madly through the raging waters; and when it was impossible to walk the deck without imminent risk of being lifted up and carried away by the winds, the poor sailors were kept aloft, tossing and swinging about the yards and in the tops, clinging to the spars with mysterious tenacity by their bodies, feet, and arms, while their hands were employed in taking in and securing sail.

The weather, especially along the surface of the sea, was so thick and hazy that you could not see more than a mile in any direction, but within that horizon the spectacle was one of majesty and power; within that circumference there were mountains and plains, the alternate rising and sinking of what seemed like the action of some volcanic power beneath. You saw immense masses of uplifted waters, emerging from the darkness on one side and rushing and tumbling across the valleys which remained after the passage of their predecessors, until, like them, they rolled away into similar darkness on the opposite side.

Both mountains and plains of the infuriated waters were covered with white foam, against which the winds first struck, and which, from high points, was lifted up into spray, but in all other places was hurled along with the intense rapidity of its own motion, until the whole prospect on the lee side of the ship seemed one field of drifting snow, dashed furiously along its dark borders by the howling storm.

In the meantime, our ship gathered herself up into the compactness and buoyancy of a duck, and except the feathers that had been plucked from her wings before she had time to fold her pinions, she rode out of the storm without damage and in triumph. True it is, she was made to whistle through her cordage, to creak and moan through all her timbers, even to her masts ; true it is, she was made to plunge and reel, and stagger ; still, she continued to scale each watery mountain and ride on its very summit, until, as it rolled onward from beneath her, she descended on her pathway, ready to triumph again and again over each succeeding wave.

Questions:—What is a gale? What caused the sails to be in ribbons? Give in your own words the substance of the first paragraph. Mention the name of some ship that was lost at sea. What is the lee side of a ship?

violent	imminent	mysterious
whistling	alternate	compactness
buoyancy	tenacity	predecessors
summit	infuriated	commencement

—— —o—— —

NOW.

RISE! for the day is passing,
   And you lie dreaming on ;
The others have buckled their armor
   And forth to the fight are gone.
A place in the ranks awaits you,
   Each man has some part to play ;
The Past and the Future are nothing
   In the face of the stern To-day.

Rise ! from your dreams of the Future—
   Of gaining some hard-fought field;
Of storming some airy fortress,
   Or bidding some giant yield.
Your future has deeds of glory,
   Of honor (God grant it may !)—
But your arm will never be stronger,
   Nor the need of you great as To-day.

Rise ! if the Past detains you,
   Her sunshine and storms forget ;
No chains so unworthy to hold you
   As those of a vain regret ;
Sad or bright, she is lifeless ever ;
   Cast her phantom arms away,
Nor look back, save to learn the lesson
   Of a nobler strife To-day.

Rise ! for the day is passing ;
   The sound that you scarcely hear

Is the enemy marching to battle :
Arise! for the foe is here!
Stay not to sharpen your weapons,
Or the hour will strike at last,
When, from dreams of a coming battle,
You may wake to find it past!

Questions:—Give in your own language the meaning of the first stanza. What are dreams of the future? Mention some deeds of glory. What enemy have we most to fear? Who is the author of this poem? Can you mention others written by her?

———o———

TRUST IN GOD.

ONCE, during a great war, the inhabitants of a house in a lonely neighborhood were thrown into great consternation. Just at nightfall, it was reported that the enemy was in the vincinity. Soon the reflection of great conflagrations made the sky appear red in different directions, and the rattle of musketry was frequently heard. It was winter, and the weather was very cold and stormy. The poor people feared that they would be plundered and driven from their home in the most severe season of the year.

The old grandmother alone remained calm, as she was accustomed to place her trust in God in all dangers. From her old prayer-book she read aloud to her children and grandchildren a prayer in which were the words : "Build up, O Lord! a strong wall to preserve this habitation from the enemy."

One of the grandchildren, who had listened attentively, said that it was too much to expect that God would build up a wall for them, and that such impossible things should not be prayed for. The grandmother answered : "These words are not to be taken literally. They only mean that God can protect us from the enemy, as safely as if a strong wall surrounded our house. Nevertheless, if God really wished to raise up a wall around us, do you think that even such a thing would be impossible to Him?"

In the meantime the night passed without a single hostile soldier having come near them. They were all astonished at this. When daylight appeared they ventured to the door, and behold! along the side of the house which faced the enemy's position the snow had drifted in such quantities as to form a high barrier, through which it would be almost impossible to penetrate.

They all praised and thanked God. The grandmother said : "You see that God actually did build a wall to keep the enemy away from our house. He is good and merciful, and can preserve us from danger in thousands of ways. We should, therefore, never despair, but place our entire trust in Him.

Questions:—What is the rattle of musketry? When is a person in great consternation? What did the grandmother read from the book? What made the old lady so calm? How did God reward her confidence?

different   vicinity   musketry   habitation

———o———

THOUGHT-PEARL.

Innocence is like incense from heaven. It is a full-blown flower among thorns and brambles ; it is the lily of the valley which refreshes and gladdens the sight, —The crown and glory of the soul.

A VISIT TO THE SHRINE OF ST. ALPHONSUS.

SALERNO! lovely spot—fit resting-place for the Evangelist St. Matthew, who lies buried in the marble vaults of the old Cathedral. How beautiful it looked on that midsummer Sunday, as it lay beneath the Italian sun, contrasting the dazzling whiteness of its houses with the soft blue of the Mediterranean. But we were to start for the Shrine of St. Alphonsus, to leave the sea behind us for a while, and to exchange the pleasures of scenery for the more devotional joys of a pilgrimage to the tomb of the holy Doctor. The pilgrimage would have been by rail, but we arrived too late at the station, in spite of all the energetic driving of our coachman. "How far is Pagani by road?" was the only question which suggested itself. "Nine miles," was the reply. "How much do you want?" we said.

"Thirteen francs," responded the driver, delighted at the prospect of a bargain.

Well, anything was better than putting off our expedition, and, in a few moments, we were on the dusty road that leads inland from Salerno.

The monastery at Pagani was one of the houses founded by St. Liguori himself; thither he retired to die after resigning his laborious bishopric. It is a large, solidly built house, with long corridors. The Superior was most affable to his English visitors, gave us relics of his great Patron, and had us conducted to the little apartment where St. Alphonsus breathed his last. What a small, silent room it was; poor, scantily furnished, and insignificant; left just as it appeared, on that first of August, 1787, when it witnessed the death of one of the greatest propagators of

Christianity that the world has seen since the days
of St. Paul. The bed was in the corner, the mattress
upon it, and at the foot of it, the linen carefully folded
and tied with ribbon. It reminded one of the Sepulchre, in which the linen was folded, but the Body was
gone ; and so, from this bed of suffering, the good servant had gone to his reward, leaving, nevertheless, innumerable souls to deplore his loss.

There still hangs the little picture of the Madonna
and Child on which the saint fixed his dying eyes, and
close to it, the candle which he held at death. We
took a small portion of the wax, a precious relic of
one who has taught so many thousands how to die.
It is interesting to recall the words with which St.
Liguori has apostrophized the death-candle. In his
sermon for the fifteenth Sunday after Pentecost he
says : " O Candle, O Candle, enlighten us while we are
still in life ; at our last hour thy light shall serve us
no more, save only to terrify and alarm us."

What awe we felt in that chamber of death! It
seemed as if the spirit of God's loving servant still
haunted the spot. Near us, in the anteroom, stood the
altar at which he had so often said Mass. From the
window, one saw the orange groves upon which, doubt-
less, he had so often gazed when composing those spiritual treatises which have proved the salvation of countless souls. It was with regret that we left so sacred a
spot. We next visited the church. Under a side
altar lie the bones of our Saint, dressed in full pontifi-
cals, and the head is incased in a plaster effigy.
Leaving the altar, we entered the sacristy ; here were
shown the cassock, collar, breviary, etc., just as the
holy Doctor left them at death. There is nothing
very noticeable in the central aisle of the church,

xcept, perhaps, the vast inscription over the High
ltar, " **QUIS UT DEUS.**" (" Who like God.")

The afternoon congregation had now assembled, and
he Superior was preaching a sermon quite in the
tyle of his predecessor ; but we were obliged to leave,
ad had no time to thank him for the cordial welcome
e had given us. In another moment we were hurry-
ag to the station. It was not till the train was fairly
ff that one had time to admire the greatness of a man
rho had abandoned the honors and comforts of life to
pend his days in teaching the way to truth, and in
roclaiming to the world the infinite love of its Re-
leemer.

uestions:—What is a cathedral? Explain the words dazzling white-
ess? What are the pleasures of scenery? What is the value of a franc?
Hive the name of some spiritual treatise. What is a predecessor?
Jse a sentence in which the word proclaiming occurs.

prospect	scenery	breathed	precious
exchange	energetic	furnished	assembled
contrasting	apartments	mattress	pontificals

—————o—————

NIGHT IN THE DESERT.

HOW beautiful is night !
　　A dewy freshness fills the silent air ;
No mist obscures, nor cloud, nor speck, nor stain
　　　　Breaks the serene of heaven :
In full-orbed glory yonder moon divine
Rolls through the dark blue depths :
　　　　Beneath her steady ray
　　　　The desert-circle spreads,
Like the round ocean, girdled with the sky.
　　　　How beautiful is night !

PAST AND PRESENT.

Thomas Hood (1799-1845), is one of the "poets" of Englis
Literature. The frolicsome disportings of his mirth and the dee
melancholy of his graver musings are almost childlike in their sudde
alternations, and win our hearts like the gleeful rompings and fitft
sorrows of a child. He was undoubtedly the greatest wit an
humorist of his time; but his wit is quite often far-fetched an
apparently "made to order." His reputation rests rather upo
pathos, upon his insight into the sorrows of humanity and his kee
sympathy for them. Consequently he is best known by those poem
in which that sympathy is expressed. Among these the principal are
"The Bridge of Sighs," "Eugene Aram," "The Song of the Shirt,
"The Death-Bed," and the one here quoted.

I REMEMBER, I remember
   The house where I was born,
The little window where the sun
   Came peeping in at morn:
He never came a wink too soon,
   Nor brought too long a day;
But now I often wish the night
   Exchanged for light of day.

I remember, I remember
   The roses red and white,
The violets and the lily-cups —
   Those flowers made of light;
The lilacs where the robin built,
   And where my brother set
The laburnum on his birthday —
   The tree is living yet.

I remember, I remember
   Where I was used to swing,
And thought the air must rush as fresh
   To swallows on the wing:
My spirit flew in feathers then,
   That is so heavy now,

And summer pools could hardly cool
    The fever on my brow.

I remember, I remember
    The fir-trees dark and high;
I used to think their slender tops
    Were close against the sky:
It was a childish ignorance
    But now 'tis little joy
To know I'm further off from heaven
    Than when I was a boy.

Questions: — What do you remember about sunrise? Name some of the flowers that grew around your birthplace, and their general appearance. Relate your play at "swing," and narrate an imaginary incident likely to have happened in this place. What thought makes one sad in the lines

> "But now 'tis little joy
>   To know I'm further off from heaven
>   Than when I was a boy?"

Memorize the following lines from "The God of my Childhood," and give them in your own words:

> "At school Thou wert a kindly face
>   Which I could almost see;
> But home and holiday appeared
>   Somehow more full of Thee."

laburnum   pools   fir-trees

———o———

PETER OF CORTONA.

A LITTLE shepherd boy twelve years old one day
    gave up the care of sheep he was tending, and
betook himself to Florence, where he knew no one but
a lad of his own age, nearly as poor as himself, and

who had lived in the same village, but who had gone to Florence to be scullion in the house of Cardinal Sachetti. It was for a good motive that little Peter desired to come to Florence: he wanted to be an artist, and he knew there was a school for artists there. When he had seen the town well, Peter stationed himself at the Cardinal's palace; and inhaling the odor of the cooking, he waited patiently till his Eminence was served, that he might speak to his old companion Thomas. He had to wait a long time; but at length Thomas appeared.

"You here, Peter! What have you come to Florence for?"

"I am come to learn painting."

"You had much better learn kitchen work to begin with; one is then sure not to die of hunger."

"You have as much to eat as you want here, then?" replied Peter.

"Indeed I have," said Thomas; "I might eat till I made myself ill every day, if I chose to do it."

"Then," said Peter, "I see we shall do very well. As you have too much and I not enough, I will bring my appetite, and you will bring the food; and we shall get on famously."

"Very well," said Thomas.

"Let us begin at once, then," said Peter; "for as I have eaten nothing to-day, I should like to try the plan directly."

Thomas then took little Peter into the garret where he slept, and bade him wait there till he brought him some fragments that he was freely permitted to take. The repast was a merry one, for Thomas was in high spirits, and little Peter had a famous appetite.

"Ah," cried Thomas, "here you are fed and lodged.

ow the question is, how are you going to study?"
"I shall study like all artists—with pencil and
aper."
"But then, Peter, have you money to buy the paper
nd pencils?"
"No, I have nothing; but I said to myself, 'Thomas,
ho is scullion at his lordship's, must have plenty of
noney!' As you are rich, it is just the same as if I was."
Thomas scratched his head and replied, that as to
roken victuals, he had plenty of them; but that he
rould have to wait three years before he should receive
rages. Peter did not mind. The garret walls were
rhite. Thomas could give him charcoal, and so he set
o draw on the walls with that; and after a little while
omebody gave Thomas a silver coin.
With joy he brought it to his friend. Pencils and
aper were bought. Early in the morning Peter went
ut studying the pictures in the galleries, the statues in
he streets, the landscapes in the neighborhood; and in
he evening, tired and hungry, but enchanted with what
ie had seen, he crept back into the garret, where he was
ilways sure to find his dinner hidden under the mattress
o *keep it warm*, as Thomas said. Very soon the first
harcoal drawings were rubbed off, and Peter drew his
est designs to ornament his friend's room.
One day Cardinal Sachetti, who was restoring his
)alace, came with the architect to the very top of the
iouse, and happened to enter the scullion's garret. The
:oom was empty; but both Cardinal and architect were
itruck with the genius of the drawings. They thought
they were executed by Thomas, and his Eminence sent
for him. When poor Thomas heard that the Cardinal
had been in the garret, and had seen what he called
Peter's daubs, he thought all was lost.

"You will no longer be a scullion," said the Cardina
to him; and Thomas, thinking this meant banishmen
and disgrace, fell on his knees, and cried, "Oh, my lor
what will become of poor Peter?"

The Cardinal made him tell his story.

"Bring him to me when he comes in to-night," sai
he, smiling.

But Peter did not return that night, nor the next, ti
at length a fortnight had passed without a sign of hin
At last came the news that the monks of a distant con
vent had received and kept with them a boy of fourtee
who had come to ask permission to copy a painting o
Raphael in the chapel of the convent. This boy wa
Peter. Finally, the Cardinal sent him as a pupil to on
of the first artists in Rome.

Fifty years afterwards there were two old men wh
lived as brothers in one of the most beautiful houses i
Florence. One said of the other, "He is the greates
painter of our age." The other said of the first, "He i
a model for evermore of a faithful friend."

COMPOSITION.

Write out the conversation between the two young friends, i
your own words, making the talk as natural as possible. Try to fin
four cases in history where monks helped poor young men to acquir
fame, and give a very short account of one of these instances of thei
encouragement.

tending	inhaling	famously	enchanted
scullion	Eminence	victuals	restoring

---o---

DEATH.

FROM death the strongest spirit shrinks,
For mystery veils the last dread strife·

None loves to die. And yet methinks
   We have been dying all our life.

When first thy Childhood sang its hymn
   Above the opening bud, that hour
Thine Infancy with eyelids dim
   Lay cold in death, a faded flower!

When Youth in turn its place had won,
   What whispered Childhood's ebbing breath?
Sad words it sighed o'er bright things gone,
   And that first sin, true Childhood's death.

And Youth was dead ere Manhood came:
   And wisdom's fruits of bitter taste
Were rooted in a soil of shame,
   Poor funeral fruits of Manhood's waste.

Oh Life, long-dying, wholly die,
   That Death not less may die at last:
And live, thou great Eternity
   That Present art at once and Past!

COMPOSITION.

Write a short composition from the following ideas, taken from above stanzas on death:

The strongest minds draw back from death, for men cannot tell what is then to happen. No one likes to die, and still we are dying every day.

Our infancy dies so soon as we enter childhood, and youth, even while continuing external life, dies the most deplorable death when the first grievous sin is committed.

Long before we become men we have, perhaps, thus died. From experience we have learned the bitterness of sin, and our strength has been wasted away in allowing evil habits to grow up in the soil of our soul.

To prevent the habit of sin and its consequences, we must remember that "in the midst of life we are in death:" that is, we may die at any moment. Also recall that the wages of sin is death, and that the death of the sinner is the beginning of a life without past o future, being an eternally miserable present.

Commit to memory the following stanza:

> Men drop so fast, ere life's mid stage we tread,
> Few know so many friends alive as dead.

shrinks   ebbing   **waste**

A STORY OF TOURS.

IN the latter part of the thirteenth century, there dwelt in the city of Tours, in France, a poor widow, who eked out a scanty living by letting a few rooms in her house to any strangers whom business or pleasure might attract to the ancient capital of Touraine.

Amongst her lodgers was one who, at the period of the occurrence we are about to relate, had already resided some months in her house. He was a young lawyer; his days, and even many of his nights, were spent in studying all the subtleties of the intricate science to which he had devoted himself; and already he had acquired a distinguished reputation.

But he was more than learned; he was truly pious, as his devout attention to his religious duties amply testified.

Soon the fame of his learning and piety spread abroad, and numbers of poor persons flocked to him in their necessities. Often he pleaded their causes gratuitously, and obtained justice for those whose poverty might otherwise have prevented them from getting a hearing. Thus he led the life of a saint, while pursuing a career which is usually supposed to offer greater temptations than almost any other.

During his stay the annual fair took place, and the

own was consequently crowded with merchants, traders,
and adventurers from all parts.

Two persons, belonging apparently to the former class,
ook up their abode in the house of the widow. They
appeared to be wealthy, and carried with them a large
eathern bag of money, which they seemed in great fear
of losing, as it might be supposed there were many
dishonest persons among the multitudes who filled the
town. In order, therefore, to avoid the risk of carrying
such a large sum constantly about with them, they
persuaded their hostess to take charge of it for them
until such time as they should require it.

They further stipulated that, in order to avoid any
possibility of fraud, she should only deliver up the bag
of money to the two friends together, not to either
separately.

A day or two passed away; her two lodgers made
themselves extremely agreeable, and the good woman
congratulated herself upon having such worthy people
in her house.

One morning they bade her "good day," as usual,
and were leaving the house together, when one of them
returned, saying he would be glad if she would give
them the bag of money, which they had only just
recollected they should that day require.

Quite unsuspectingly, she gave it to him, and he took
his departure.

In the course of the day, his companion returned, said
they had been making some purchases, and requested
to have the bag of money. The widow at once replied
that she had given it them that very morning.

He answered that she had given it to his companion
when he was not present; that she had done very wrong,
and had acted quite in opposition to the agreement.

She said that she had fully believed him to be stand
close to the door. He replied that such was not
case; and that she must make good the loss.

The poor woman assured him that she had acted
good faith, and that all she possessed would not m₂
up the sum which he declared the bag to contain.

He said that he would compel her to pay the sum d
to him according to agreement; and the next morni
he had her summoned to court.

When she received the summons, her heart at fi
sank within her; but, presently, calling to mind t
wisdom and learning of her young lodger, she went
him and made known her trouble. He at once perceiv₄
that it was a scheme devised by those two heartle
villains to ruin his poor hostess, and to defraud her ₄
her little possessions. He bade her, however, be ₄
good courage, for that he would be present on th
following day to plead her cause.

The next day the widow appeared before the judg
and told her tale, with a sincerity that was convincing.

Still the judge decided that as she had paid the money
only one of the owners being present, the other wa
fairly entitled to redress.

Then, up rose the young lawyer, and, assuring the
judge that he bowed to his most just decision, he
addressed his adversary, asking him if he were quite
certain that such was the agreement, that the money
should be paid in the presence of both parties.

"Such was one of the conditions of the agreement,"
he replied.

"Then," said the lawyer, "by what right do you
claim to have it paid to you, as your companion is not
present? Bring your friend into this court, and the
money shall be forthcoming immediately."

The rogue was thus caught in his own snare, and the lwyer, turning to the judge, requested that he might e detained while officers of justice were sent in search f his companion, who was discovered with the leathern ag in his possession, which, upon examination, was und to contain only pebbles.

The two heartless thieves suffered the punishment of heir crime. The lawyer afterwards entering the cclesiastical state, became a bishop, and was subsequently canonized; he has been ever since venerated as he patron of lawyers, under the name of St. Yves.

COMPOSITION.

Write the above story in your own language, from the following
SUMMARY:

A young lawyer boarding with a poor widow at Tours is noted for his learning and piety. During his stay the town fair is held. Merchants, travellers and adventurers attend it. Two men, apparently merchants, put up at the widow's inn. They ask her to keep their bag of money and to deliver it only in presence of both. After a few days one obtains the bag in the absence of the other, who shortly returns and demands his money. The widow, threatened with the law, appeals to the young lawyer. The judge deciding against her, the lawyer tells her prosecutor that as the money was to be paid to both together, he must bring his friend forward in order to receive the purse. The scheme thus laid bare, the judge sends men to capture the absent knave, and both are punished. The lawyer becomes a priest, and, under the name of St. Yves, is the patron of lawyers.

eked	gratuitous	unsuspectingly
ancient	temptations	departure
occurrence	adventurers	purchases
lawyer	apparently	summons
subtleties	dishonest	villains
intricate	hostess	defraud
reputation	congratulated	ecclesiastical
necessities	require	subsequently

THE NATIONAL BANNER.

A LL hail to our glorious ensign! Courage to the
heart and strength to the hand to which in all
times it shall be entrusted; may it ever wave in honor,
in unsullied glory and patriotic hope, on the dome of
the Capitol, on the Country's stronghold, on the tented
plain, on the wave-rocked topmast!

Wherever, on the earth's surface, the eye of the
American shall behold it, may he have reason to bless
it! On whatever spot it is planted, there may freedom
have a foothold, humanity a brave champion, and religion an altar! Though stained with blood in a
righteous cause, may it never in any cause be stained
with shame!

Alike, when its glorious folds shall wanton in lazy
holiday triumphs on the summer breeze, and its
tattered fragments be dimly seen through the clouds
of war, may it be the joy and pride of the American
heart! First raised in the cause of right and liberty,
in that cause alone may it forever spread out in streaming blazonry to the battle and the storm! Having
been borne victoriously across the continent, and on
every sea, may virtue and freedom and peace forever
follow where it leads the way.

Questions:—What is our ensign? How may our flag be stained with
shame?

surface   tattered   fragments

---o---

A WASTED LIFE.

O youth, fertile and inexhaustible source of beauty,
grace, force, and life! I cannot avoid following
and contemplating you, so fresh and pure from the

hand of God! You recall to me my noble origin; you cause me to remember that I, too, was once pure and innocent, and that I must soon return to Him from whom I came.

O youth, I love you, because you are so beautiful! I love you, and at the same time pity you, for your hour of suffering is not yet come. When my life is ended, then will yours begin; when I sleep beneath the waving grass, it will be your youth that will bear you through the burden of life. Such were the thoughts that filled the mind of a poor old man, as he sat on a bench in one of the parks of a large city, watching the innocent mirth of children at play.

This old man was known as a tramp—one of those outcasts of society, to whom the comforts of a home had been unknown for many a year. He led a vagrant life, spending the pleasant portion of the year in the country, and the winter in the city.

He was the only son of a wealthy merchant, on whom every care that affection and wealth could procure was lavished. He received a careful training at home, and when he reached his seventeenth year was sent to college, where he soon became a favorite with teachers and students.

His large dark eyes, the magnificent, black, curling hair, the beautiful proportion of the neck, the aristocratic manner in which he held his head, and the gracefulness and ease of every movement of his well-knit and handsome form, combined to produce a charming figure, while the keen, penetrating intellect, brilliant imagination, oratorical powers, and agility in sport, caused him to be admired.

For three years his college career was one of fun and enjoyment. But he always managed to keep the

letter of the college·rules. He was at the head of his
class, and many predicted a brilliant future for him.
In the beginning of his fourth year at college, he associated with three students whose bad conduct led to
their expulsion. He, too, would have been expelled,
but for his previous record and the intervention of his
father.

A few months later, his father's sudden death put
him in possession of a large fortune. His life henceforth was one of continued dissipation. In less than
ten years he had squandered his fortune and was
penniless. Each succeeding year found him poorer
and more degraded than the year before, until we find
him friendless and alone, sitting on the bench, thinking over his own childish days and the pleasure of the
children.

What will become of this man? He is too weak to
work, and the shadows of death are gathering round
him. If we would but follow him to the end, a pauper's
grave would meet our eyes.

Alas! such a history is painful to dwell upon, but
one is constrained to write it down in simple and
earnest truth, that all may learn that the life which is
not devoted to duty is thrown away ; that it is the path
of duty and not of inclination which leads to happiness
here, and to something which is more than earthly happiness in the better land, beyond the everlasting shores.

Questions:—Of what is youth the source? What is an outcast? Why
has the old man no home? What is agility in sport? Give an account of the games you like best.

avoid	mirth	college	predicted
burden	comforts	charming	penniless
watching	received	penetrating	inclination

TRUE HEROISM.

LET others write of battles fought,
　Of bloody, ghastly fields,
Where honor greets the man who wins,
　And death the man who yields ;
But I will write of him who fights
　And vanquishes his sins,
Who struggles on, through weary years,
　Against himself, and wins.

He is a hero staunch and brave
　Who fights an unseen foe,
And puts at last beneath his feet
　His passions base and low ;
Who stands erect in manhood's might,
　Undaunted, undismayed,
The bravest man who e'er drew sword
　In foray or in raid.

It calls for something more than brawn
　Or muscle, to o'ercome
An enemy who marcheth not
　With banner, plume, and drum ;
A foe forever lurking nigh,
　With silent stealthy tread,
Forever near your board by day,
　At night beside your bed.

All honor then to that brave heart !
　Though poor or rich he be,
Who struggles with his baser part,
　Who conquers and is free.
He may not wear a hero's crown
　Or fill a hero's grave,
But Truth will place his name among
　The bravest of the brave.

Questions : —In what does true heroism consist? Who is the her
staunch and true? To whom should honor be given? What is al
unseen foe?

fought	ghastly	vanquishes	undismayed
banner	staunch	lurking	conquers
forever	undaunted	stealthy	struggles

CHARITY.

IF I speak with the tongues of men and of angels, and
have not charity, I am become as sounding brass, or
a tinkling cymbal.

And if I should have prophecy, and should know all
mysteries, and all knowledge, and if I should have all
faith, so that I could remove mountains, and have not
charity, I am nothing.

And if I should distribute all my goods to feed the
poor, and if I should deliver my body to be burned,
and have not charity, it profiteth me nothing.

Charity is patient, is kind : charity envieth not, dealeth
not perversely : is not puffed up,

Is not ambitious, seeketh not her own, is not provoked
to anger, thinketh no evil,

Rejoiceth not in iniquity, but rejoiceth with the truth :

Beareth all things, believeth all things, hopeth all
things, endureth all things.

Charity never falleth away : whether prophecies shall
be made void, or tongues shall cease, or knowledge shall
be destroyed.

For we know in part, and we prophecy in part.

But when that which is perfect is come, that which
is in part shall be done away.

When I was a child, I spoke as a child, I understood as a child, I thought as a child. But when I became a man, I put away the things of a child.

We see now through a glass, in a dark manner: but then face to face. Now I know in part: but then I shall know even as I am known.

And now there remain, faith, hope, charity, these three: but the greatest of these is charity.

COMPOSITION.

Give, as tersely as possible, the substance of above quotation; or, write a short sketch of St. Paul's conversion.

tinkling	prophecy	envieth	perversely
cymbal	mysteries	dealeth	tongues

————o————

THE VISION OF THE MONK GABRIEL.

'Tis the soft twilight. Round the shining fender,
  Two at my feet and one upon my knee,
    Dreamy-eyed Elsie, bright lipped Isabel,
    And thou, my golden-headed Raphael,
  My fairy, small and slender,
    Listen to what befell
    Monk Gabriel,
  In the old ages ripe with mystery —
Listen, my darlings, to the legend, tender.

A bearded man with grave, but gentle look —
  His silence sweet with sounds
  With which the simple-hearted Spring abounds:
  Lowing of cattle from the abbey grounds,
Chirping of insect, and the building rook,
  Mingled like murmurs of a dreaming shell;
Quaint tracery of bird, and branch, and brook,

Flitting across the pages of his book,
Until the very words a freshness took.
　　Deep in his cell
　　Sat the Monk Gabriel.

In his book he read
The words the Master to His dear ones said:
　"A little while and ye
　Shall see,
　Shall gaze on Me;
A little while again,
Ye shall not see Me then."
　A little while !

The Monk looked up — a smile
　Making his visage brilliant, liquid-eyed:
"O Thou who gracious art
Unto the poor of heart,
　O blessed Christ!" he cried,
" Great is thy misery
Of mine iniquity;
But would *I* now might see,
Might feast on Thee!"

The blood with sudden start,
Nigh rent his veins apart —
　(O condescension of the crucified!)
In all the brilliancy
Of his humanity —
　The Christ stood by his side!

Pure as the early lily was His skin,
　His cheek outblushed the rose,
　His lips, the glows
　Of autumn sunset on eternal snows;
And His deep eyes within,

Such nameless beauties, wondrous glories dwelt,
The monk in speechless adoration knelt.

In each fair Hand, in each fair Foot there shone,
The peerless stars He took from Calvary:
Around His brows in tenderest lucency,
The thorn-marks lingered, like the flush of dawn;
And from the opening in His side there rilled
A light, so dazzling, that the room was filled
With heaven: and transfigured in his place,
His very breathing stilled,
The friar held his robe before his face,
And heard the angels singing!

'Twas but a moment — then upon the spell
Of this sweet Presence, lo! a something broke:
A something, trembling, in the belfry woke,
A shower of metal music flinging
O'er wold and moat, o'er park and lake and fell,
And thro' the open windows of the cell
In silver chimes came ringing.

It was the bell
Calling Monk Gabriel
Unto his daily task
To feed the paupers at the abbey gate.
No respite did he ask,
Nor for a second summons idly wait;
But rose up, saying in his humble way,
"Fain would I stay,
O Lord! and feast alway
Upon the honeyed sweetness of Thy beauty —
But 'tis *Thy* will, not mine, I must obey;
Help me to do my duty!"
The while the Vision smiled,
The monk went forth, light-hearted as a child.

An hour thence, his duty nobly done,
  Back to his cell he came.
Unasked, unsought, lo! his reward was won!
  Rafters and walls and floor were yet aflame
With all the matchless glory of the Sun,
And in the centre stood the Blessed One —
  (Praised be His holy Name!)
Who for our sakes our crosses made His own,
  And bore our weight of shame.

)own on the threshold fell
Monk Gabriel,
  His forehead pressed upon the floor of clay;
  And while in deep humility he lay
  (Tears raining from his happy eyes away),—
  "Whence is this favor, Lord?" he strove to say

The Vision only said,
Lifting Its shining head:
If *thou* hadst staid, O son! *I* must have fled!

COMPOSITION.

Write out the first three stanzas, in prose. Name six early monks
What is a monk? Tell how Gabriel was rewarded, and *why*.

fended	glows	rilled	moat
iniquity	peerless	belfry	fell
condescension	lucency	spell	rafters
outblushed	lingered	wold	threshold

———o———

CATHOLIC MISSIONS IN THE NORTHWEST.

RELIGIOUS zeal not less than commerical ambition
had influenced France to recover Canada; and
Champlain, its governor, whose imperishable name will

rival with posterity the fame of Smith and Hudson, ever disinterested and compassionate, full of honor and probity, of ardent devotion and burning zeal, esteemed "the salvation of a soul worth more than the conquest of an empire."

Thus it was neither commercial enterprise nor royal ambition which carried the power of France into the heart of our Continent; the motive was religion. Religious enthusiasm founded Montreal, made a conquest of the wilderness of the upper lakes, and explored the Mississippi. The Roman (Catholic) Church created for Canada its Altars, its Hospitals, and its Seminaries....The first permanent efforts of French enterprise in colonizing America preceded any permanent English settlement on the Potomac.

Years before the pilgrims landed in Cape Cod, the Roman (Catholic) Church had been planted, by missionaries from France, in the eastern moiety of Maine; and Le Caron, an unambitious Franciscan, had penetrated the land of the Mohawks, had passed to the North of the hunting-grounds of the Wyandots, and, bound by his vows to the life of a beggar, had, on foot, or paddling a bark canoe, gone onward, and still onward, taking alms of the savages, till he reached the rivers of Lake Huron.

While Quebec contained scarcely fifty inhabitants, priests of the Franciscan Order — Le Caron, Fiel Lagard — had labored for years as missionaries in Upper Canada, or made their way to the neutral Huron tribe that dwelt on the waters of the Niagara.

To confirm the missions, the first measure was the establishment of a College in New France, and the parents of the Marquis de Gamache, pleased with his pious importunity, assented to his entering the Order of the Jesuits, and added from their ample fortunes the means of endowing a Seminary for education at Quebec. Its foundation was laid, under happy auspices, in **1635**, just before Champlain passed from among the living; and two years before the emigration of John Harvard, and one year before the General Court of Massachusetts had made provisions for a College.

The fires of charity were at the same time enkindled. The Duchess D'Aguillon, aided by her uncle, the Cardinal Richelieu, endowed a public hospital dedicated to the Son of God, whose blood was shed in mercy for all mankind. Its doors were opened, not only to the sufferers among the emigrants, but to the maimed, the sick, and the blind of any of the numerous tribes between the Kennebec and Lake Superior; it relieved misfortune without asking its lineage. From the hospital nuns of Dieppe, three were selected, the youngest but twenty-two, to brave the famine and rigors of Canada in their patient mission of benevolence.

The same religious enthusiasm, inspiring Madame de la Peltier, a young and opulent window of Alençon, with the aid of a nun of Dieppe and two others from Tours, established the Ursuline Convent for girls. Is it wonderful that the natives were touched by a benevolence which their poverty and squalid misery could not appall? Their education was attempted; and the venerable ash-tree still lives beneath which Mary of the Incarnation, so famed for chastened piety, genius, and good judgment, toiled, though in vain, for the education of the Huron children.

The life of the missionary on Lake Huron was simple and uniform. The earliest hours, from four to eight, were absorbed in private prayer. The day was given to schools, visits, instructions in the catechism, and a service for proselytes. Sometimes, after the manner of

St. Francis Xavier, Brebeuf would walk through the village and its environs ringing a little bell, and inviting the Huron braves and counsellors to a conference. There, under the shady forest, the most solemn mysteries of the Catholic faith were subject to discussion.

Yet the efforts of the Jesuits were not limited to the Huron race. Within thirteen years, the remote wilderness was visited by forty-two missionaries, members of the Society of Jesus, besides eighteen others, who, if not initiated, were yet chosen men, ready to shed their blood for their faith. Twice or thrice a year they all assembled at St. Mary's; during the rest of the time they were scattered through the infidel tribes.

The first missionaries among the Hurons — Fathers De Brebeuf, Daniel, and Lallemand — all fell glorious martyrs to their devoted zeal. . . . . Father Reymbault soon after fell a victim to the climate, and died in Quebec (1642). His associate, Father Jogues, who with him had first planted the cross in Michigan, was reserved for a still more disastrous, though glorious, fate. He was taken prisoner by the fierce Mohawks, and was made to run the gauntlet at three different Mohawk villages.

For days and nights he was abandoned to hunger and every torment which petulant youth could contrive. But yet there was consolation, — an ear of Indian corn on the stalk was thrown to the good Father; and see, to the broad blade there clung little drops of dew, or of water — enough to baptize two captive neophytes. He had expected death; but the Mohawks, satisfied, perhaps, with his sufferings, or awed at his sanctity, spared his life, and his liberty was enlarged.

On a hill apart, he carved a long cross on a tree; and there, in the solitude, meditated the Imitation of Christ, and soothed his griefs by reflecting that he, alone in

that vast region, adored the true God of earth and
heaven. Roaming through the stately forests of the
Mohawk valley, he wrote the name of Jesus on the bark
of trees, engraved the cross, and entered into possession
of these countries in the name of God — often lifting up
his voice in a solitary chant. Thus did France bring its
banner and its faith to the confines of Albany. The
missionary himself was humanely ransomed from
captivity by the Dutch, and sailing for France, soon
returned to Canada.

Similar was the fate of Father Bressani. Taken
prisoner while on his way to the Hurons; beaten,
mangled, mutilated; driven barefoot over rough paths,
through briers and thickets; scourged by a whole
village; burned, tortured, wounded, and scarred; — he
was an eye-witness to the fate of one of his companions,
who was boiled and eaten. Yet some mysterious awe
protected his life, and he, too, was humanely rescued by
the Dutch.

In 1655, Fathers Chaumont and Dablon were sent on
a mission among the tribes of New York. They were
hospitably welcomed at Onondaga, the principal village
of that tribe. A general convention was held at their
desire; and before the multitudinous assembly of the
chiefs and the whole people, gathered under the open
sky, among the primeval forests, the presents were
delivered; and the Italian Jesuit, with much gesture,
after the Italian manner, discoursed so eloquently to the
crowd, that it seemed to Dablon as if the word of God
had been preached to all the nations of that land. On
the next day, the chiefs and others crowded round the
Jesuits with their songs of welcome.

"Happy land," they sang, "happy land, in which the
Jesuits are to dwell!" and the chief led the chorus,

" Glad tidings! glad tidings! It is well that we have spoken together; it is well that we have a heavenly message." At once a chapel sprung into existence, and by the zeal of the nation was finished in a day. "For marble and precious stones," writes Dablon, "we employed only bark; but the path to heaven is as open through a roof of bark as through arched ceilings of silver and gold." The savages showed themselves susceptible of the excitements of religious ecstasy; and there, in the heart of New York, the solemn services of the Roman (Catholic) Church were chanted as securely as in any part of Christendom.

The Cayugas also desired a missionary, and they received the fearless René Mesnard. In their village a chapel was erected, with mats for the tapestry; and there the pictures of our Saviour and of the Virgin Mother were unfolded to the admiring children of the wilderness. The Oneidas also listened to the missionary; and early in 1657, Chaumont reached the most fertile and densely peopled lands of the Senecas. The Jesuit priests published their faith from the Mohawk to the Genesee. The Missions stretched westward along Lake Superior to the waters of the Mississippi. Two young fur traders, having travelled to the West five hundred leagues, returned in 1656, attended by a number of savages from the Mississippi valley, who demanded missionaries for their country.

Their request was eagerly granted; and Gabriel Dreuillettes, the same who carried the cross through the forests of Maine, and Leonard Gareau, of old a missionary among the Hurons, were selected as the first religious envoys to a land of sacrifices, shadows and deaths. The canoes are launched; the tawny warriors embark; the oars flash, and words of triumph and joy mingle with their last adieus. But just below Montreal a band of Mohawks, enemies to the Ottawas, awaited the convoy: in the affray Gareau was mortally wounded, and the fleet dispersed.

But the Jesuits were still fired with zeal to carry the cross westward. "If the Five Nations," they said, "can penetrate these regions to satiate their passion for blood; if mercantile enterprise can bring furs from the plains of the Sioux, why cannot the cross be borne to their cabins!" The zeal of François de Laval, the Bishop of Quebec, kindled with a desire himself to enter on the mission; but the lot fell to René Mesnard. He was charged to visit Green Bay and Lake Superior, and on a convenient inlet to establish a residence as a common place of assembly for the surrounding nations.

His departure was immediate (A. D. 1660), and with few preparations; for he trusted — such are his words — "in the Providence which feeds the little birds of the desert, and clothes the wild flowers of the forests." Every personal motive seemed to retain him in Quebec; but powerful instincts impelled him to the enterprise. Obedient to his vows, the aged man entered on the path that was red with the blood of his predecessors, and made haste to scatter the seeds of truth through the wilderness, even though the sower cast his seed in weeping. "In three or four months," he wrote a friend, "you may add me to the *memento* of deaths."

His prediction was verified. Several months after, while his attendant was employed in transporting the canoe, Mesnard was lost in the forest, and never seen more. Long afterwards, his cassock and breviary were kept as amulets among the Sioux. Similar was the death of Father Marquette, the discoverer of the Mississippi. Joliet returned to Quebec to announce the discovery, but the unaspiring Marquette remained to preach the Gospel to the Miamis, who dwelt in the northern part of Illinois, around Chicago. Two years afterwards (A. D. 1675), sailing from Chicago to Mackinaw, he entered a little river in Michigan. Erecting an altar, he said Mass after the rites of the Catholic Church; then, begging the men who conducted his canoe to leave him alone for a half hour,

> "In the darkling wood,
> Amid the cool and silence, he knelt down
> And offered to the Mightiest solemn thanks
> And supplication."

At the end of half an hour they went to seek him, and he was no more. The good missionary, discoverer of a new world, had fallen asleep on the margin of the stream which bears his name. Near its mouth the canoe men dug his grave in the sand. Ever after, the forest rangers, if in danger on Lake Michigan, would invoke his name. The people of the West will build his monument.

COMPOSITION.

Make three columns. Put names of persons in *(a)*; places in *(b)*, in *(c)* put the affirmation as to persons and places in other columns. Thus:

(a) PERSON.	*(b)* PLACE.	*(c)* ASSERTION.
	France	sent Champlain to save the natives of Canada.
	Montreal	was founded through religious enthusiasm.
Smith and Hudson		were bold adventurers, who, however, had not the religious zeal of Catholic pioneers.
	Potomac	foundations were preceded by many years, through the efforts of Catholic explorers.
	Maine	foundations had been made by French missionaries long before the Pilgrim Fathers touched the shores of Cape Cod.

(a) PERSON.	(b) PLACE.	(c) ASSERTION.
Le Caron, ..	*Maine*, ..	a fearless Franciscan, travelled in a frail canoe amid many dangers, on treacherous waters, or trudged through still more threatening haunts of savage tribes, till he reached the borders of Lake Huron.

Divide the class into as many sections as there are paragraphs in the lesson, and let each section work up its paragraph in manner above indicated.—

This plan may be adopted with advantage in many of the historical or descriptive selections.

Let the principal words or phrases be taken in different ways, and treated, making the subject the object, and *vice versa.*

posterity	benevolence	humanely	mercantile
enthusiasm	squalid	mutilated	immediate
permanent	environs	hospitably	instincts
moiety	braves	convention	predecessors
importunity	disastrous	susceptible	breviary
endowing	petulant	launched	amulets

————o————

TO THE EVENING WIND.

William Cullen Bryant (1794–1878) is the most national of all our poets. He is the poet of nature, not of character or passion; and so deeply inspired with the spirit of American scenery is his free, lofty, and thoughtful muse, that, in the words of his most intelligent critic, "any reader on the other side of the ocean, gifted with a small degree of sensibility and imagination, may derive from his poems the very awe and delight with which the first view of one of our majestic forests would strike his mind." "Thanatopsis," "The Ages," "Green River," "The Prairies," "The Evening Wind," and the "Flood of Years," are among the most popular of Bryant's poems.

SPIRIT that breathest through my lattice, thou
　　That cool'st the twilight of the sultry day,
Gratefully flows thy freshness round my brow;
　　Thou hast been out upon the deep at play,

ding all day the wild, blue waves till now,
　Roughening their crests and scattering high the spray,
　　And swelling the white sail.   I welcome thee
　　To the scorched land, thou wanderer of the sea!

or I alone: a thousand bosoms round
　Inhale thee in the fulness of delight;
nd languid forms rise up, and pulses bound
　Livelier at the coming of the wind of night;
nd, languishing to hear thy grateful sound,
　Lies the vast inland stretched beyond the sight.
　　Go forth into the gathering shade, go forth,
　　God's blessing breathed upon the fainting earth!

o rock the little wood-bird in his nest,
　Curl the still waters, bright with stars, and rouse
he wide, old wood from his majestic rest,
　Summoning from the innumerable boughs
he strange, deep harmonies that haunt his breast:
　Pleasant shall be thy way where meekly bows
　　The shutting flower, and darkling waters pass;
　　And where the o'ershadowing branches sweep the grass

he faint, old man shall lean his silver head
　To feel thee; thou shalt kiss the child asleep,
nd dry the moistened curls that overspread
　His temples, while his breathing grows more deep;
nd they who stand about the sick man's bed
　Shall joy to listen to thy distant sweep,
　　And softly part his curtains to allow
　　Thy visit, grateful to burning brow.

o; but the circle of eternal change,
　Which is the life of nature shall restore,
Vith sounds and scents from all thy mighty range, ●
　Thee to thy birthplace f the deep once more;

Sweet odors in the sea-air, sweet and strange,
  Shall tell the homesick mariner of the shore,
    And, listening to thy murmur, he shall deem
    He hears the rustling leaf and running stream.

COMPOSITION AND QUESTIONS.

Write the following in two ways:

First three lines of first stanza, changing nouns and adjectives.

"I welcome thee to the scorched land, thou wanderer of the sea," changing verb, adjective, and nouns.

Last two lines of second stanza,

In the third stanza, what is the wind told to do? Who are relieved by the evening wind?

lattice	inhale	summoning	homesick
sultry	languid	haunt	deem
roughening	rouse	range	rustling

THE AFFECTION AND REVERENCE DUE A MOTHER.

WHAT an awful state of mind must a man have attained, when he can despise a mother's counsel! Her very name is identified with every idea that can subdue the sternest mind; that can suggest the most profound respect, the deepest and most heartfelt attachment, the most unlimited obedience. It brings to the mind the first human being that loved us, the first guardian that protected us, the first friend that cherished us; who watched with anxious care over infant life, whilst yet we were unconscious of our being; whose days and nights were rendered wearisome by her anxious cares for our welfare; whose eager eye followed us through every path we took; who gloried in our honor; who sickened in heart at our shame; who loved and mourned, when others reviled and scorned; and whose affection for us survives the wreck of every other feeling within. When her voice is raised to inculcate religion, or to reprehend irregularity, it possesses unnumbered claims to attention, respect and obedience. She fills the place of the eternal God; by her lips that God is speaking; in her counsels he is conveying the most solemn admonitions; and to disregard such counsel, to despise such interference, to sneer at the wisdom that addresses you, or the aged piety that seeks to reform you, is the surest and the shortest path which the devil himself could have opened for your perdition. I know no grace that can have effect; I know not any authority upon earth to which you will listen, when once you have brought yourself to reject such advice. Nothing but the arm of God, that opens the rock and splits the mountain, can open your heart to grace, or your understanding to correction.

COMPOSITION.

Give two examples in ancient history of reverence and affection shown a mother. Give three examples from the life of our Lord, showing his love and reverence for the Blessed Virgin.

Memorize:—

A mother's love, how sweet the name
What is a mother's love?
A noble, pure and tender flame,
Enkindled from above,
To bless a heart of earthly mould,
The warmest love that can grow cold,—
This is a mother's love.

identified	profound	unconscious	piety
sternest	cherished	sneer	reject

LOVE DUE TO THE CREATOR.

A ND ask ye why He claims our love?
    O answer, all ye winds of even!
O answer, all ye lights above,
    That watch in yonder darkening heaven!
Thou Earth, in vernal radiance gay
    As when His angels first arrayed thee,
And thou, O deep tongued Ocean, say
    Why man should love the Mind that made thee!

There's not a flower that decks the vale,
    There's not a beam that lights the mountain,
There's not a shrub that scents the gale,
    There's not a wind that stirs the fountain,
There's not a hue that paints the rose,
    There's not a leaf around us lying,
But in its use or beauty shows
    True love to us, and love undying.

There is an eye that never sleeps,
    Beneath the wing of night;
There is an ear that never shuts,
    When sink the beams of light.

There is an arm that never tires,
    When human strength gives way;
There is a love that never fails,
    When earthly loves decay.

That eye is fix'd on seraph throngs;
That ear is fill'd with angels' songs;
That arm upholds the world on high;
That love is throned beyond the sky.

But there's a power which man can wield,
    When mortal aid is vain,

That eye, that arm, that love to reach,
  That list'ning ear to gain.
That power is prayer, which soars on high,
And feeds on bliss beyond the sky!

Questions : — When is mortal aid vain? What is the greatest power
  man's possession? Name six instances in the Holy Bible, showing
e power of prayer. What are "seraph throngs"? Explain the difference
tween "throng" and "crowd." What spirits are higher than seraphs?
ive three texts of holy writ showing Christ's valuation of prayer.
hat is "the wing of night"? Give fourth stanza in your own words.

even	arrayed	shrub	wield
vernal	decks	seraph	vain

————o————

MAJESTY AND SUPREMACY OF THE SCRIPTURES.

CONFESSED BY A SCEPTIC.

[WILL confess that the majesty of the Scriptures
strikes me with admiration, as the purity of the
Gospel hath its influence on my heart. Peruse the
works of our philosophers with all their pomp of diction.
How mean, how contemptible are they, compared with
the Scriptures! Is it possible that a book, at once so
simple and sublime, should be merely the work of man?
Is it possible that the sacred personage, whose history
it contains, should be himself a mere man? Do we
find that he assumed the tone of an enthusiast or
ambitious sectary?

What sweetness, what purity in his manner! What
an affecting gracefulness in his delivery! What
sublimity in his maxims! What profound wisdom in
his discourses! What presence of mind, what subtlety,
what truth in his replies! How great the command
over his passions! Where is the man, where the

philosopher, who could so live, and so die, without weakness and without ostentation? When Plat described his imaginary good man, loaded with all the shame of guilt, yet meriting the highest rewards of virtue, he describes exactly the character of JESU CHRIST.

What prepossession, what blindness must it be, to compare the son of SOPHRONISCUS to the son of MARY What an infinite disproportion there is between them SOCRATES, dying without pain or ignominy, easily supported his character to the last; and if his death however easy, had not crowned his life, it might have been doubted whether SOCRATES, with all his wisdom was anything more than a vain sophist. He invented it is said, the theory of morals. Others, however, had before put them in practice; he had only to say, therefore what they had done, and reduce their examples to precepts.

ARISTIDES had been *just* before Socrates defined justice; LEONIDAS had given up his life for his country before Socrates declared patriotism to be a duty; the Spartans were a sober people, before Socrates recommended sobriety; before he had even defined virtue Greece abounded in virtuous men. But where did JESUS learn, among his competitors, that pure and sublime morality, of which he only hath given us both precept and example? The greatest wisdom was made known among the most bigoted fanaticism, and the simplicity of the most heroic virtues did honor to the vilest people on earth.

The death of Socrates, peaceably philosophizing with his friends, appears the most agreeable that could be wished for; that of JESUS, expiring in the midst of agonizing pains, abused, insulted, and accused by a 'hole nation, is the most horrible that could be feared. ocrates, in receiving the cup of poison, blessed indeed ıe weeping executioner who administered it; but ESUS, in the midst of excruciating torments, prayed ır his merciless tormentors. Yes, if the life and death [Socrates were those of a sage, the life and death of ESUS are those of a GOD.

Shall we suppose the evangelic history a mere fiction? ndeed, it bears not the marks of fiction; on the contrary, he history of Socrates, which nobody presumes to oubt, is not so well attested as that of JESUS CHRIST. Juch a supposition, in fact, only shifts the difficulty vithout obviating it;—it is more inconceivable that a number of persons should agree to write such a history, han that one only should furnish the subject of it. The Jewish authors were incapable of the diction, and strangers to the morality contained in the Gospel, the marks of whose truth are so striking and inimitable, that the inventor would be a more astonishing character than the hero.

COMPOSITION.

Copy the first paragraph, and write each of the following sentences in three ways:

(*a*) How mean, how contemptible are the works of our philosophers, when compared with the Scriptures. (*b*) Is it possible that a book (the Bible), at once so simple and sublime, should be merely the work of a man? (*c*) Yes, if the life and death of Socrates were those of a sage, the life and death of Jesus are those of a God.

majesty	sublimity	ignominy	competitors
peruse	maxims	Aristides	fanaticism
personage	subtlety	defined	excruciating
enthusiast	Plato	Leonidas	fiction
ambitious	imaginary	patriotism	supposition
sectary	Socrates	Spartans	obviating

POLONIUS' ADVICE TO HIS SON.

Shakespeare, "the myriad-minded," is said to have been born abo 1564. He died in 1616. Very little is known concerning his perso history. He is without doubt the greatest poet mankind has ever see His plays are a world in themselves; in his own words they "hold th mirror up to nature," and exhibit humanity in its countless phase Like humanity too, the good in them is mingled with the bad; th pure with the licentious; the noble and elevating with the degrading and vile. And as youth should be restrained from too early a intercourse with the mixed characters of the world, so should the acquaintance with these plays be deferred to maturer years. Some of the historical dramas, Roman and English, are free from the above mentioned defects, and, though sometimes false and inaccurate in fact, are useful to the student of history, as they serve to impress the characters of their time more vividly upon the mind.

G IVE thy thoughts no tongue,
   Nor any unproportioned thought his act.
Be thou familiar, but by no means vulgar.
The friends thou hast, and their adoption tried,
Grapple them to thy soul with hooks of steel;
But do not dull thy palm with entertainment
Of each new-hatched, unfledged comrade. Beware
Of entrance to a quarrel; but, being in,
Bear it, that the opposer may beware of thee.
Give every man thine ear, but few thy voice:
Take each man's censure, but reserve thy judgment.
Costly thy habit as thy purse can buy,
But not expressed in fancy; rich, not gaudy;
For the apparel oft proclaims the man;
And tney in France, of the best rank and station,
Are must select and generous, chief in that.
Neither a borrower nor a lender be;
For loan oft loses both itself and friend,
And borrowing dulls the edge of husbandry.
This above all, — to thine own self be true;
And it must follow, as the night the day,

Thou canst not then be false to any man.
Farewell! my blessing season this in thee.

Questions: — Explain the sentence "Give thy thoughts no tongue."
That is an "unproportioned" act? How can we dull our palm (hand)
ith unknown or too youthful (unfledged) comrades? How may we
give ear" to friends without giving them our voice? How does
hakespeare advise us to dress? What does the dress often indicate?
That do we often lose by lending? To whom must we above all be
ue? Will this prevent us from being false to others? Name some
ie in the New Testament who was very false to his best friend. One
ho was most faithful. What is meant by a blessing "seasoning"
dvice? How would you season meat? And fruit? Wine? A reading
sson? An instructive sermon?

unproportioned	censure	apparel
vulgar	judgment	husbandry
unfledged	gaudy	season

---o---

FAMILIAR QUOTATIONS.

THE FORCE OF PRAYER.

MORE things are wrought by prayer
  Than this world dreams of.   Wherefore let thy voice
Rise like a fountain for me night and day.
For what are men better than sheep and goats,
That nourish a blind life within the brain,
If, knowing God, they lift not hands of prayer,
Both for themselves and those who call them friends?
For so the whole round world is every way
Bound by gold chains about the feet of God.

He prayeth well, who loveth well
  Both man, and bird, and beast;
He prayeth best, who loveth best
  All things both great and small:

For the dear God who loveth us,
He made and loveth all.

In the morning, prayer is a golden key to open the
for God's service; and in the evening, it is an iron
guard the heart against sin. "He that loves his ne
fulfils the law."

TRUTH.

Dare to be true; nothing can need a lie,
The fault which needs it most, grows two thereby.

To thine own self be true;
And it must follow, as the night the day,
Thou canst not then be false to any man.

Errors, like straws, upon the surface float,
He who would seek for pearls, must dive below.

How many among us at this very hour,
Do forge a lifelong trouble for ourselves,
By taking true for false, or false for true;
Here through the feeble twilight of this world,
Groping, how blindly, until we pass and reach
That other, where we see as we are seen!

COMPOSITION.

Give the first quotation on "Truth" in your own words. (
the nouns, pronouns and verbs in the last.

----o----

WIT AND WISDOM.

THERE is an association in men's minds, bet
dulness and wisdom, amusement and folly, w
has a very powerful influence in decision upon chara

ıd is not overcome without considerable difficulty.
ıe reason is, that the *outward* signs of a dull man and
wise man are the same, and so are the outward signs
a frivolous man and a witty man; and we are not to
:cept that the majority will be disposed to look to
uch *more* than the outward sign. I believe the fact
be, that wit is very seldom the *only* eminent quality
hich resides in the mind of any man; it is commonly
:companied by many other talents of every description,
ıd ought to be considered as a strong evidence of
fertile and superior understanding. Almost all the
:eat poets, orators, and statesmen of all times have
een witty.

The meaning of an extraordinary man is, that he is
ght men, not one man; that he has as much wit as if
e had no sense, and as much sense as if he had no
it; that his conduct is as judicious as if he were the
ullest of human beings, and his imagination as brilliant
s if he were irretrievably ruined. But when wit is
ombined with sense and information; when it is softened
y benevolence, and restrained by strong principle;
'hen it is in the hands of a man who can use it and
espise it, who can be witty, and something much *better*
han witty, who loves honor, justice, decency, good-
ature, morality, and religion, ten thousand times better
han wit; — wit is *then* a beautiful and delightful part
f our nature. There is no more interesting spectacle
han to see the effects of wit upon the different
haracters of men, than to observe it expanding caution,
elaxing dignity, unfreezing coldness, — teaching age
nd care and pain to smile, — extorting reluctant
jleams of pleasure from melancholy, and charming even
he pangs of grief. It is pleasant to observe how it
ıenetrates through the coldness and awkwardness of

society, gradually bringing men nearer together, and like the combined force of wine and oil, giving every man a glad heart and a shining countenance. Genuine and innocent wit like this is surely the *flavor of the mind!* Man could direct his ways by plain reason, and support his life by tasteless food; but God has given us wit, and flavor, and laughter, and perfumes, to enliven the days of man's pilgrimage, and to "charm his painful steps over the burning marl.'

COMPOSITION.

Copy the first paragraph. Give sentences in which the following words will occur in the same sense as that in which they are used in this lesson:

Association, amusement, influence, difficulty, frivolous, eminent fertile.

association	irretrievably	extorting
influence	benevolence	reluctant
frivolous	restrained	pilgrimage
judicious	expanding	marl

---o---

CURIOSITIES OF WORDS.

TRIBULATION.—We all know in a general way that this word, which occurs not seldom in Scripture and in the liturgy, means affliction, sorrow, anguish; but it is quite worth our while to know *how* it means this, and to question the word a little closer. It is derived from the Latin *tribulum,* which was the threshing instrument or roller whereby the Roman husbandman separated the corn from the husks; and *tribulatio,* in its primary significance, was the act of this separation. But some Latin writer of the Christian Church appropriated the word and image for the setting forth of a

gher truth; and sorrow, distress, and adversity being
e appointed means for the separating in men of what-
ver in them was light, trivial, and poor from the solid
d the true, their chaff from their wheat, he therefore
lled these sorrows and trials "tribulations;" threshings,
at is, of the inner spiritual man, without which there
uld be no fitting him for the heavenly garner.

MISER.—Every one must, I think, acknowledge it as
remarkable fact, that men should agree to apply the
ord *miser* or *miserable* to the man eminently addicted
the vice of covetousness—to him who loves his
oney with his whole heart and soul. Here, too, the
oral instinct lying deep in all hearts has borne testimony
the tormenting nature of this vice, to the gnawing
ares with which even here it punishes him that
ntertains it—to the enmity which there is between it
nd all joy; and the man who enslaves himself to his
noney is proclaimed in our very language to be a
'miser" or miserable man.

PASSION.—There is much, too, that we may learn
from the word "passion." We sometimes think of the
"passionate" man as a man of strong will, and of real
though ungoverned energy. But this word declares to
us most plainly the contrary; for it, as a very solemn
use of it declares, means properly "suffering:" and a
passionate man is not a man doing something, but one
suffering something to be done to him. When, then, a
man or child is "in a passion," this is no coming out in
him of a strong will, of a real energy, but rather the
proof that, for the time at least, he has no will, no
energy; he is suffering, not doing—suffering his anger,
or what other evil temper it may be, to lord over him
without control. Let no one, then, think of passion as
a sign of strength. As reasonably might one assume

that it was a proof of a man being a strong man, that he was often well beaten; such a fact would be evidence that a strong man was putting forth his strength on him, but of anything rather than that he himself was strong.

HUSBAND and WIFE, and other words there are, having reference to the family and the relations of family life, which are not less full of teaching, while each may serve to remind of some duty. For example, "husband" is properly "houseband," the *band* and *bond* of the *house*, who shall bind and hold it together. Thus old Tusser, in his *Points of Husbandry :*

> The name of the husband, what is it to say?
> Of wife and of *house*hold the *band* and the stay.

So that the very name may put him in mind of his authority, and of that which he ought to be to all the members of the house. And the name "wife" has its lesson too, although not so deep a one as the equivalent word in some other tongues. It belongs to the same family of words as "weave," "woof," "web," and the German "weber." It is a title given to her who is engaged at the web and woof, these having been the most ordinary branches of female industry, of wifely employment, when the language was forming. So that in the word itself is wrapped up a hint of earnest, indoor, stay-at-home occupations as being the fittest for her who bears this name.

To the foreigner, however, the use of most ordinary words is not so apparent. Blaine illustrates this difficulty in an amusing way in his " *Wonders of the English Language,*" as follows :·

"The construction of the English language must seem most formidable to foreigners. One of them, looking at a picture of a number of vessels, said, 'See what a flock of ships!' He was told that a flock of ships is called a fleet, and that a fleet of sheep is called a flock. And it was added, for his guidance in mastering the intricacies of our language, that a flock of girls is called a bevy, that a bevy of wolves is called a pack, and a pack of thieves is called a gang, and a gang of angels is called a host, and a host of porpoises is called a shoal, and a shoal of buffaloes is called a herd, and a herd of children is called a troop, and a troop of partridges is called a covey, and a covey of beauties is called a galaxy, and a galaxy of ruffians is called a horde, and a horde of rubbish is called a heap, and a heap of oxen is called a drove, and a drove of blackguards is called a mob, and a mob of whales is called a school, and a school of worshippers is called a congregation, and a congregation of engineers is called a corps, and a corps of robbers is called a band, and a band of locusts is called a swarm, and a swarm of people is called a crowd."

COMPOSITION.

Take "Wonders of the English Language" as a model, and write something similar, starting with the expressions "a cluster of stars," "a bunch of flowers," etc.

significance	evidence	intricacies
garner	reference	bevy
addicted	formidable	horde

---o---

WATERLOO.

George Gordon, Lord Byron (1788-1824), for many years wielded an unparalleled influence upon English poetry. Fortunately for the purity and health of our literature, that influence has been dissipated by the more beneficent spirit of Wordsworth and Tennyson. No other poet has excelled Byron in intensity of feeling and in vividne of description; no other, alas, has shown a gloomier misanthropy more sarcastic contempt for religion and morality. And yet, in t midst of his most cynical and atheistical revilings will often be fou passages of wondrous pathos, beauty, and majesty of sentimen like flowers blooming in a charnel-house. But the reading of] poems by youth should be discouraged.

THERE was a sound of revelry by night,
And Belgium's capital had gathered then
Her beauty and her chivalry; and bright
The lamps shone o'er fair women and brave men;
A thousand hearts beat happily; and when
Music arose with its voluptuous swell,
Soft eyes look'd love to eyes which spake again,
And all went merry as a marriage bell;—
But hush! hark! a deep sound strikes like a rising knell.

Did ye not hear it? No; 'twas but the wind,
Or the car rattling o'er the stony street.
On with the dance! let joy be unconfined,
No sleep till morn, when youth and pleasure meet
To chase the glowing hours with flying feet;
But hark! that heavy sound breaks in once more,
As if the clouds its echo would repeat!
And nearer, clearer, deadlier than before!
Arm! arm! it is—it is—the cannon's opening roar!

Within a window'd niche of that high hall
Sate Brunswick's fated chieftain; he did hear
That sound the first amidst the festival,
And caught its tone with death's prophetic ear;
And when they smiled, because he deemed it near—
His heart more truly knew that peal too well,
Which stretched his father on a bloody bier,,
And roused the vengeance blood alone could quell—
He rush'd into the field, and, foremost fighting, fell!

Ah! then and there was hurrying to and fro,
And gathering tears, and tremblings of distress,
And cheeks all pale, which but an hour ago
Blush'd at the praise of their own loveliness;
And there were sudden partings, such as press
The life from out young hearts, and choking sighs
Which ne'er might be repeated: who could guess
If ever more should meet those mutual eyes,
Since upon night so sweet, such awful morn could rise.

And there was mounting in hot haste, the steed,
The mustering squadron, and the clattering car,
Went pouring forward with impetuous speed,
And swiftly forming in the ranks of war;
And the deep thunder, peal on peal afar,
And near, the beat of the alarming drum,
Roused up the soldier ere the morning star;
While throng'd the citizens with terror dumb,
Or whispering ·with white lips, "the foe! they come—the
    come!"

And wild and high the "Cameron's gathering" rose,
The war-note of Lochiel, which Albyn's hills
Have heard, and heard, too, have her Saxon foes
How in the noon of night that pibroch thrills,
Savage and shrill!   But with the breath which fills
Their mountain pipe, so filled the mountaineers
With the fierce native daring which instils
The stirring memory of a thousand years,
And Evan's, Donald's fame rings in each clansman's ears.

And Ardennes waves above them her green leaves,
Dewy with nature's tear drops, as they pass,
Grieving, if aught inanimate e'er grieves,
Over the unreturning brave,—alas!
Ere evening to be trodden down like grass.

Which now beneath them, but above shall grow
In its next verdure, when this fiery mass
Of living valor, rolling on the foe,
And burning with high hope, shall moulder cold and low.

Last noon beheld them full of lusty life,
Last eve in beauty's circle proudly gay;
The midnight brought the signal-sound of strife,
The morn the marshalling in arms, — the day
Battle's magnificently stern array!
The thunder-clouds close o'er it, which, when rent,
The earth is covered thick with other clay,
Which her own clay shall cover, heap'd and pent,
Rider and horse, — friend, foe, — in one red burial blent!

Questions : — What description is given in the first stanza? What
was heard, as described in second? Who was Brunswick's "fated
chieftain"? What scene followed the roar of cannon? How did the
officers mount? Tell who were the various parties named in the sixth
stanza. What is described in the last stanza? Write the last line in
your own words.

| voluptuous | fated | peal | squadron |
| niche | prophetic | partings | burial |

---o---

LOVE FOR THE DEAD.

THE sorrow for the dead is the only sorrow from which
we refuse to be divorced. Every other wound we
seek to heal — every other affliction to forget; but this
wound we consider it a duty to keep open — this affliction
we cherish and brood over in solitude. Where is the
mother who would willingly forget the infant that
perished like a blossom from her arms, though every
recollection is a pang? Where is the child that would
willingly forget the most tender of parents, though to

remember be but to lament? Who, even in the hour of agony, would forget the friend over whom he mourns? Who, even when the tomb is closing upon the remains of her he most loved — when he feels his heart, as it were, crushed in the closing of its portal — would accept of consolation that must be bought by forgetfulness?

No, the love which survives the tomb is one of the noblest attributes of the soul. If it has its woes, it has likewise its delights; and when the overwhelming burst of grief is calmed into the gentle tear of recollection — when the sudden anguish and the convulsive agony over the present ruins of all that we most loved, is softened away into pensive meditation on all that it was in the days of its loveliness — who would root out such a sorrow from the heart? Though it may sometimes throw a passing cloud over the bright hour of gayety, or spread a deeper sadness over the hour of gloom, yet who would exchange it, even for the song of pleasure or the burst of revelry? No, there is a voice from the tomb sweeter than song. There is a remembrance of the dead to which we turn even from the charms of the living. Oh, the grave! the grave! It buries every error — covers every defect — extinguishes every resentment. From its peaceful bosom spring none but fond regrets and tender recollections. Who can look down upon the grave even of an enemy, and not feel a compunctious throb, that he should ever have warred with the poor handful of earth that lies mouldering before him?

* * * * * *

Ay, go to the grave of buried love, and meditate! There settle the account with thy conscience for every past benefit unrequited — every past endearment unregarded, of that departed being who can never — never — never return to be soothed by thy contrition!

If thou art a child, and hast ever added a sorrow to the soul, or a furrow to the silvered brow of an affectionate parent; if thou art a husband, and hast ever caused the fond bosom that ventured its whole happiness in thy arms to doubt one moment of thy kindness or thy truth; if thou art a friend, and hast ever wronged, in thought, or word, or deed, the spirit that generously confided in thee; if thou art a lover, and hast ever given one unmerited pang to that true heart which now lies cold and still beneath thy feet — then be sure that every unkind look, every ungracious word, every ungentle action, will come thronging back upon thy memory, and knocking dolefully at thy soul; then be sure that thou wilt lie down sorrowing and repentant on the grave, and utter the unheard groan, and pour the unavailing tear — more deep, more bitter, because unheard and unavailing.

Then weave thy chaplet of flowers, and strew the beauties of nature about the grave; console thy broken spirit, if thou canst, with these tender yet futile tributes of regret; but take warning by the bitterness of this thy contrite affliction over the dead, and henceforth be more faithful and affectionate in the discharge of thy duties to the living.

QUESTIONS AND COMPOSITION.

What is an ordeal? What are precincts? Name the precincts of this school. What is a survivor? Give names of some survivors. What is it to "brood over"? When do boys brood over anything? What is the dying child compared to? Why is it like a blossom? What is it to "survive"? What is revelry? What is a resentment? Give some simple expression explaining "a compunctious throb." Explain "unrequited." How can you soothe pain? What is a "silvered brow"? What is an "ungracious word"? Explain "knocking dolefully." What is a "chaplet of flowers"? What are "futile tributes"? How may we repay our neglect of those now dead? Who are the living? What general name is applied to the living? Who is my neighbor?

Memorize: —

> There is no death ! What seems so is transition.
>   This life, its mortal breath,
> Is but a suburb of the life elysian,
>   Whose portals we call Death.

Paraphrase the above.

divorced	convulsive	unrequited	thronging
brood	pensive	endearment	dolefully
survives	gayety	pang	unavailing
attributes	resentment	ungracious	futile

ANALYSIS.

"Pay close attention to the emotions or feelings the selection suggests."

"Give due attention to the vocal tones called for by the selection."

"Lay special stress on those points that are to attract the attention of the audience."

What is the general sentiment suggested by "Love for the Dead"? One of subdued emotion, requiring sustained, quiet, soft, yet firm intonation. In the first sentence,

"The sorrow for the dead is the only sorrow from which we refuse to be divorced," the chief words requiring special attention are SORROW FOR THE DEAD, ONLY SORROW, REFUSE, DIVORCED; and among these: THE DEAD, ONLY, REFUSE, call for more particular emphasis. Thus,

"The SORROW for THE DEAD is the ONLY SORROW from which we REFUSE to be DIVORCED," would suggest a proper reading, the emphasis being in proportion to the capitalizing.

In the following sentence, the appositeness of the adjective clauses must be attended to. Thus,

"EVERY OTHER wound we seek to heal — EVERY OTHER affliction to forget; but THIS wound we consider it a DUTY to keep open — THIS affliction we cherish and brood over in solitude."

In the following series of interrogatory sentences, the climax must be indicated by the gradual increasing of the strength and earnestness of tone:

"Where is THE MOTHER who would WILLINGLY FORGET the INFANT that perished like a blossom from her arms, though EVERY RECOLLECTION is a pang?' "Where is THE CHILD that

would WILLINGLY FORGET the MOST TENDER OF PARENTS, thoug
to remember be but to lament? " etc.

In the first part of second paragraph we have a change of tone to the
of assertion of a noble principle, requiring strength of colo
ing and boldness of utterance :

'No, the love which SURVIVES THE TOMB is one of the NOBLES
attributes of the soul.   If it has its WOES, it has likewise it
DELIGHTS ; and when the OVERWHELMING BURST of grief i
calmed into the gentle tear of recollection, when the SUDDE
ANGUISH and the CONVULSIVE AGONY over the present ruins o
all that we most loved, *is softened away into pensive meditatio*
on all that it was in the days of its loveliness — who would roo
out such a sorrow from the heart?   Though it may SOME
TIMES throw a passing cloud over the bright hour of gayety,
or spread a DEEPER SADNESS over the hour of gloom, yet WHO
would exchange it, EVEN FOR THE SONG OF PLEASURE OR THE
BURST OF REVELRY?   No, THERE IS A VOICE FROM THE TOMB
SWEETER THAN SONG."

In the third stanza we have the expression of counsel, requiring
" grave and sustained tone. '

"AY, go to the grave of buried love, and THERE MEDITATE !
THERE settle the account with thy conscience, for EVERY
PAST BENEFIT UNREQUITED — EVERY PAST ENDEARMENT UNRE-
GARDED, of that departed being, who CAN NEVER—NEVER —
NEVER RETURN to be soothed by thy contrition !"

Continuing, we again have a climax, requiring same treatment as
previously indicated, etc., etc.

———o———

THE CARRIER-PIGEON.

CHANGED customs and the progress of science have
almost rendered extinct two features of the romantic
Middle Ages, — the use of the falcon and the carrier-dove.
The former no longer darts upon its timid prey from its
dainty perch on jewelled finger of maid or dame.   The
latter, once the poetic bearer of messages of love, or the
swift courier of thrones of state, has been superseded
by the prosy telegraph, and its performances, with one

exception, have in recent times been confined to contests of speed for the amusement of the amateur. The carrier-pigeon is a remarkable instance of what can be effected by the natural instinct of the animal kingdom, assisted by cultivation and training. Somewhat larger and heavier than the ordinary dove, it is still further distinguished by the great size of the muscles of the breast, which indicate its powers of flight, and by a bunch of naked skin which hangs across its bill like a hood or cowl.

The instinct which makes this bird so valuable is its strong love for home. The manner of training and developing this instinct, as adopted in Turkey, is as follows: As soon as the young birds are able to fly, they are taken in a covered basket to a distance of twenty or thirty yards from their cotes. They are then suddenly released. Those that find their way back are retained for further training. The distance is gradually increased from one mile to twenty or thirty miles. Birds that can find their way home from this distance can generally be trusted for any number of miles, limited only by their power of endurance. When first released from its receptacle, the carrier-pigeon flies upward in a spiral until it reaches a height from which it can descry some familiar landmark, by which it immediately directs its course. Should it fail to discover such a point, either by reason of fog or the distance of its home, it either returns, or, losing its way, is never again seen. The speed of the carrier-pigeon is marvellous. Thirty miles an hour is a very easy performance for a good bird, and well authenticated instances of forty, fifty and sixty miles an hour are on record. At the annual contest of the Fanciers' Association of Ghent in 1833 one of the pigeons flew from Rouen to

that city, a distance of one hundred miles, in one
and a half hours. Audubon, the naturalist, mentions
the fact of a bird being found near New York with its
crop full of rice, which could not have been obtained
nearer than the rice fields of Georgia or the Carolinas.
The digestive powers of the carrier-pigeon being very
strong and rapid, the inference is that the bird must
have flown that immense distance in a very few hours.

The use of the carrier-dove as a messenger dates
from remote times. Sir John Mandeville mentions
their use by the Chinese and the Romans. They were
employed during the crusade under St. Louis; and
Tasso, in his "Jerusalem Delivered," makes Godfrey
defend one of them from a falcon. The most remarked
instance of their use in modern times is afforded by the
siege of Paris. By their services on that memorable
occasion they proved not only their great utility, but
also their necessity in times of war, when the telegraph
lines and railroads are in possession of the enemy.
The pigeons used during the siege of Paris were sent
out of the city by means of balloons, and in due time
returned to their accustomed cotes.

The arrival of a pigeon was an event of great interest.
The letters which they carried were written in very
small characters and on very thin paper. The paper
was rolled up tightly and enclosed in a quill, and the
quill was fastened under the wing of the pigeon. In
this way important messages were safely conveyed to
the besieged city. Sometimes a whole newspaper was
photographed on a minute scale and delivered by the
aerial postman. When received it could be read only
with the aid of a powerful magnifying-glass. Sometimes
the besiegers tried to bring down the birds with their
rifles; but they seldom succeeded, so high and so swiftly

lo these birds fly. Once or twice, however, the little etter carrier arrived with its feathers ruffled and stained with its own blood. Thus, all through that terrible winter, often in the midst of blinding storms and over fields of carnage, was the gentle dove the bearer of messages of love and hope between anxious friends.

With this simple exception, the carrier-pigeon in modern times has figured only in racing trials. Breeding societies in Belgium have made the cultivation and speeding of pigeons a favorite amusement, and of late years the same sport has been introduced into the United States, where it bids fair to soon become very popular.

COMPOSITION.

Describe the arrival of a carrier-pigeon into the besieged city of Paris, from the following notes:

A snow storm prevails. Amid the white specks a very large one is seen. It is examined. Powerful glasses are brought to bear upon the fast moving object. A general cry is heard: — "The carrier-pigeon." The bird descends. Around its neck a string; under its wing a quill. In this quill "news from other lands." The bird is petted, fed, and delivered to its cote.

customs	muscles	receptacle	besieged
extinct	cowl	spiral	photographed
romantic	developing	authenticated	aerial
superseded	cotes	naturalist	besiegers
amateur	endurance	inference	carnage

———o———

AN UNKNOWN SISTER OF CHARITY.

UNKNOWN to fashion's tinsel throng,
  The soulless and the vain; ·
Unknown where ringeth folly's song,
  And pleasure's siren strain.

Unknown where fickle fame bestows
  Her evanescent crown,
While, for a fleeting instant, glows
  The light of earth's renown.
Unknown in life, unknown in death,
  Thus would she live and die —
She needed not the trumpet's breath
  To waft her deeds on high;
But where the plague, at noonday, trod
  O'er earth his fatal way,
And where, beneath his blighting rod,
  The stricken thousands lay;
Where fiercely burned the fever flame,
  And rung the dying groan,
Full well the Sister's holy name
  And gentle face were known.
And while life's latest murmur breath'd
  On her its blessings fond,
Her fadeless coronal was wreath'd
  The "jasper walls" beyond.
She saw, in every tortured one,
  Her anguish-laden Lord;
For him her holy work was done,
  From him it claimed reward.
What though no flaunting banners wave,
  Where mercy's martyr sleeps;
What though above her nameless grave
  No earthly mourner weeps;
When soared her soul, on eager wing,
  Beyond the gates of pain,
The white-robed legions of the King
  Were her triumphal train.
And where love wrote her blessed name
  Above his radiant throne,
In heaven's light of fadeless fame
  She lives, forever known.

COMPOSITION.

Take the short selection from "The Sister of Charity," and write
t in your own words, in two forms. Give three historical instances
f queens or other distinguished ladies who became nuns. Relate
ny circumstances you may know of where sisters have distinguished
hemselves on the battle field or in the sick room. Consult Long-
ellow's "Evangeline" for points.

insel	siren	evanescent	waft	coronal
ıoulless	fickle	renown	blighting	flaunting

———o———

TRUE AND FALSE SUCCESS.

IT should be remembered that success in life is to be
regarded as a means and not as an end; and that
therefore there is such a thing possible as *unsuccessful
success* — such a thing as gaining every end, while the
whole *life* has been a failure. "What doth it profit a
man, if he gain the whole world, and suffer the loss of
his soul?" This is the final test of the value of earthly
prosperity, and unless our lives be guided by the
spirit of these memorable words, we shall have lived
in vain. Viewed in the light of the Evangelist's words,
many a career that the world deems a brilliant success,
is a most miserable failure; and many a life that the
world considers commonplace and humble, is crowned
with an enduring triumph.

Why were you sent into this world? Better and
clearer than all the high-sounding phrases of philosophers comes the simple answer of the catechism —
"to know, love, and serve God in this world and be
happy with him forever in the next." To this end must
you make tend every action of your life; and whatever
success you may attain in your chosen calling, must be
looked upon as a God-given means of contributing to

his glory, to the good of your neighbor and to the happiness of your immortal soul.

This alone is true success, and it is attainable in the humblest as well as in the most exalted position; for in every station of life will you find the opportunity of loving God, of practising virtue and of edifying others. The meanest calling can be positively ennobled by cheerfully and honestly performing the duties which belong to it.

> "Honor and shame from no condition rise.
> Act well your part, there all the honor lies."

God has given every man a mission to perform in this world, for which his talents precisely fit him; and, having found what that mission is, he must throw into it all the energies of his soul, seeking its accomplishment, not his own pleasure.

As has been wisely said, "Man is not born to solve the problem of the universe, but to find out what he has to do, and to restrain himself within matters that he understands." Having found out what you have to do — whether to lead an army or to sweep a crossing, to harangue senates, or address juries, or prescribe medicines — do it with all your might, because it is your duty.

Are your intellectual endowments small, and are you despondent because your progress must be slow? Remember that if you have but one talent, you are responsible only for *its* wise use. If you cannot do all you wish, you can at least do your best; and, if there be one thing on earth which is truly admirable, it is to see God's wisdom blessing an inferiority of natural powers, when they have been honestly, truly and zealously cultivated. Remembering that the battle of life cannot be fought by proxy, be your own helper, be earnest, be watchful, be diligent; and if you do not obtain success, you will have done the next best thing —you will have deserved it.

Is your calling one which the world calls mean or humble? Show by the spirit that you carry into it, that, to one who has self-respect and an exalted soul, the most despised profession may be made honorable; that it is the heart, the inspiring motive, not the calling, that degrades; that the mechanic may be as high-minded as the poet, the day-laborer as noble as the artist.

Are you prosperous in business, honored by your fellow-men? If so, you must be doubly careful lest your temporal success so engross your attention as to blind you to your eternal interests. Too often the intoxicating fumes of success make hearts that once throbbed with generous emotions callous and insensible to every lofty inspiration.

The incense of admiration, of self glorification at one's success, seems to envelop men in a fog, through which they grope aimlessly on till suddenly death dispels the mist, and the vast, unseen expanse of eternity, for which they have made no preparation, bursts upon their terrified gaze. To keep the heart fresh and enthusiastic amid all the distractions of a busy life is a rare gift; but it is in every one's power to be mindful of his soul, and in the busiest as well as in the most tranquil pursuits to keep alive the ideal and the practice of a better life by prayer; and in particular, by the exercise of that greatest of virtues, — Charity.

COMPOSITION.

Give the substance of above lesson, from following hints:

Success in life is a means, not an end. We labor to become rich, not for the sake of riches, but that we may do good with wealth.

This is taught us by Christ, who says, "What doth it profit . . . . . . '
Lives that appear most brilliant are not always most admirable. Give
example. (Cæsar, Alexander, Napoleon, Dives, Crœsus.) The greatest
and truest success in life is to secure the end for which life is given
us. To act so as to attain this end is to choose the better part, the one
only thing necessary. What has been "wisely said"? We are not to
be discouraged because we have to move slowly. If we have but one
talent, an account of but one will be required. Refer to the "parable
of the talents." Next to securing success, the most consoling thing
is to deserve it. We will be rewarded, not according to our success,
but "according to our works."

mission	admirable	degrades
harangue	proxy	aimlessly
senates	inspiring	ideal

————o————

THE BELLS OF SHANDON.

WITH deep affection and recolloction,
    I often think of those Shandon bells,
Whose sound so wild would, in days of childhood
    Fling round my cradle their magic spells.
On this I ponder where'er I wander,
    And thus grow fonder, sweet Cork, of thee;
        With thy bells of Shandon,
        That sound so grand on
The pleasant waters of the River Lee.

I've heard bells chiming full many a clime in,
    Tolling sublime in cathedral shrine;
While at a glib rate brass tongues would vibrate
    But all their music spoke naught like thine;
For memory, dwelling on each proud swelling
    Of thy belfry, knelling its bold notes free,
        Made the bells of Shandon
        Sound far more grand on
The pleasant waters of the River Lee.

I've heard bells tolling old Adrian's Mole in,
  Their thunder rolling from the Vatican,
And cymbals glorious, swinging uproarious
  In the gorgeous turrets of Notre Dame:
But thy sounds were sweeter than the dome of Peter
  Flings o'er the Tiber, pealing solemnly.
      O! the bells of Shandon
      Sound far more grand on
  The pleasant waters of the River Lee.

There's a bell in Moscow; while on tower and kiosk, O!
  In St. Sophia the Turkman gets,
And loud in air calls men to prayer,
  From the tapering summits of tall minarets.
Such empty phantom I freely grant them;
  But there's an anthem more dear to me:
      'Tis the bells of Shandon,
      That sound so grand on
  The pleasant waters of the River Lee.

Questions:— Point out the several places named in this selection. What is meant by "Adrian's Mole"? "The Vatican"? What is meant by "pealing solemnly"? When do Catholic church bells peal solemnly and joyously? When solemnly and sadly? Mention some tapering points in or near your residence. Name some bells which the writer says are less sonorous than those of Shandon. Give the names of any very fine chimes of bells in America.

Shandon	belfry	gorgeous	tapering
clime	knelling	turrets	minarets
glib	Mole	Moscow	phantom
vibrate	Vatican	kiosk	anthem

ST. FRANCIS XAVIER.

A S the vessel in which the saint embarked for India
  floated down the Tagus and shook out her reefs to

the wind, many an eye was dimmed with unwonte
tears; for she bore a force of a thousand men to reinforc
the garrison of Goa; nor could the bravest of tha
gallant host gaze on the receding land, without forebod
ing that he might never see again those dark chestnu
forests and rich orange groves, with their peacefu
convents and loved homes reposing in their bosom
The countenance of Xavier alone beamed with delight.
He knew that he should never tread his native mountains
more; but he was not an exile. He was to depend for
food and raiment on the bounty of his fellow-passengers;
but no thought for the morrow troubled him. He was
going to convert nations, of which he knew not the
language nor even the names; but he felt no misgivings.
Worn by incessant sea-sickness, with the refuse food of
the lowest seamen for his diet, and the cordage of the
ship for his couch, he rendered to the diseased services
too revolting to be described; and lived among the dying
and the profligate, the unwearied minister of consolation
and of peace. In the midst of that floating throng, he
knew how to create for himself a sacred solitude, and how
to mix in all their pursuits in the free spirit of the man of
the world, a gentleman and a scholar. With the viceroy
and the officers he talked, as pleased them best, of war
or trade, of politics or navigation; and to restrain the
common soldiers from gambling, would invent for their
amusement less dangerous pastimes, or even hold the
stakes for which they played, that by his presence and
his gay discourse, he might at least check the excesses
which he could not prevent.

Five weary months (weary to all but him) brought
the ship to Mozambique, where an endemic fever
threatened a premature grave to the apostle of the
Indies. But his was not a spirit to be quenched or

allayed by the fiercest paroxysms of disease. At each remission of his malady, he crawled to the beds of his fellow-sufferers to soothe their terrors, or assuage their pains. To the eye of any casual observer the most wretched of mankind; in the esteem of his companions the happiest and the most holy, he reached Goa just thirteen months after his departure from Lisbon.

At Goa he was shocked, and, had fear been an element in his nature, would have been dismayed, by the almost universal depravity of the inhabitants. It exhibited itself in those offensive forms which characterize the crimes of civilized men, when settled among a feebler race, and released from even the conventional decencies of civilization. Swinging in his hand a large bell, he traversed the streets of the city, and implored the astonished crowd to send their children to him, to be taught the religion which they still at least professed. Though he had never been addressed by the soul-stirring name of father, he knew that in the hardest and most dissolute heart which had once felt the parental instinct, there is one chord which can never be wholly out of tune. A crowd of little ones was quickly placed under his charge. He lived among them as the most laborious of teachers, and the gentlest and the gayest of friends; and then returned them to their homes, that by their more hallowed example they might there impart, with all the unconscious eloquence of filial love, the lessons of wisdom and of piety they had been taught. No cry of human misery reached him in vain. He became an inmate of the hospitals, selecting that of the leprous as the object of his peculiar care. Even at the tables of the profligate he was to be seen, an honored and a welcome guest; delighting that most unmeet audience with the vivacity of his discourse, and sparing neither pungent jests to render vice ridiculous, nor sportive flatteries to allure the fallen back to the still distasteful paths of soberness and virtue. Strong in purity of purpose, and stronger still in one sacred remembrance, he was content to be called the friend of publicans and sinners. He had long since deserted the standard of prudence — the offspring of forethought, for the banners of wisdom — the child of love, and followed them through perils not to be hazarded under any less triumphant leader.

From the days of St. Paul to our own, the annals of mankind exhibit no other example of a soul borne onward so triumphantly through distress and danger, in all their most appalling aspects. He battled with hunger and thirst, and nakedness and assassination, and pursued his mission of love, with ever increasing ardor, amidst the wildest war of the contending elements. At the island of Moro (one of the group of the Moluccas), he took his stand at the foot of a volcano, and as the pillar of fire threw up its wreaths to heaven, and the earth tottered beneath him, and the firmament was rent by falling rocks and peals of unremitting thunder, he pointed to the fierce lightnings, and the river of molten lava, and called on the agitated crowd which clung to him for safety, to repent and to obey the truth; figuring to them, at the same time, that the sounds which racked their ears were as the groans of the infernal world, and the sights which blasted their eyes, as an outbreak from the atmosphere of the place of torment. Repairing for the celebration of Mass to some edifice which he had consecrated for the purpose, an earthquake shook the building to its base. The terrified worshippers fled; but Xavier, standing in meek composure before the rocking altar, deliberately completed that mysterious sacrifice, rejoicing, as he states in his description of the scene, to perceive that the demons of the island thus attested their flight before the archangel's sword, from the place where they had so long exercised their foul dominion. There is no schoolboy of our days who could not teach much, unsuspected by St. Francis Xavier, of the laws which govern the material and the spiritual worlds; but we have not many doctors who know as much as he did of the nature of Him by whom the worlds of matter and of spirit were created; for he studied in the school of protracted martyrdom and active philanthropy, where are divulged secrets unknown and unimagined by the wisest and the most learned of ordinary men. Imparting everywhere such knowledge as he possessed, he ranged over no small part of the Indian archipelago, and at length retraced his steps to Malacca, to see if even yet his exhortations and his prayers might avert her threatened doom.

COMPOSITION.

Write a short sketch of St. Francis Xavier, from the following points: Starts down the Tagus. Sorrow of friends. St. Francis Xavier, filled with delight, hopes for the reward promised to those who "leave father and mother, sister and brother," for Christ's sake. His labors and sufferings on board. He takes part in the sailors' and soldiers' games, to prevent sin. While suffering from fever he waits on his sick companions. His love of children. His labors in hospitals. Traits of resemblance between St. Paul and St. Francis Xavier. Both learned, both zealous, both afflicted for Christ's sake, both "all to all" to gain all to Christ. St. Paul calm in midst of storms and shipwreck. St. Francis serene amid earthquake and panic. St. Paul and St. Francis both "Apostles of nations."

reefs	endemic	unmeet	appalling
raiment	paroxysms	pungent	deliberately
misgivings	assuage	sportive	protracted
incessant	casual	allure	philanthropy
cordage	depravity	distasteful	archipelago

CŒUR DE LION AT THE BIER OF HIS FATHER.

TORCHES were blazing clear,
  Hymns pealing deep and low,
Where a king lay stately on his bier
  In the Church of Fontevrault.
Banners of battle o'er him hung,
  And warriors slept beneath,
And light as noon's broad light was flung
  On the settled face of death.

On the settled face of death
  A strong and ruddy glare,
Though dimmed at times by the censer's breath,
  Yet it fell still brightest there,
As if each deeply furrowed trace
  Of earthly years to show, —
Alas! that sceptred mortal's race
  Had surely closed in woe!

The marble floor was swept
  By many a long, dark stole,
As the kneeling priests, round him that slept,
  Sang Mass for the parted soul.
And solemn were the strains they pour'd
  Through the stillness of the night,
With the cross above, and the crown and sword,
  And the silent king in sight.

There was heard a heavy clang,
  As of steel-girt men the tread,
And the tombs and the hollow pavement rang
  With a sounding thrill of dread;
And the holy chant was hush'd awhile
  As, by the torch's flame,
A gleam of arms up the sweeping aisle,
  With a mail-clad leader came.

He came with a haughty look,
  An eagle glance and clear,
But his proud heart through its breastplate shook,
  When he stood beside the bier!
He stood there still with drooping brow,
  And clasp'd hands o'er it raised;
For his father lay before him low,—
  It was Cœur de Lion gazed!

And silently he strove
  With the workings of his breast,
But there's more in late repentant love
  Than steel may keep suppress'd!
And his tears brake forth, at last, like rain,
  Men held their breath in awe,
For his face was seen by his warrior train,
  And he reck'd not that they saw.

He looked upon the dead,
  And sorrow seemed to lie —
A weight of sorrow, e'en like lead —
  Pale on the fast shut eye.
He stoop'd and kiss'd the frozen cheek,
  And the heavy hand of clay,
Till bursting words — yet all too weak —
  Gave his soul's passion way.

"Oh, father! is it vain,
  This late remorse and deep?
Speak to me, father! once again,
  I weep — behold, I weep!
Alas! my guilty pride and ire!
  Were but this work undone,
I would give England's crown, my sire!
  To hear thee bless thy son.

"Speak to me! mighty grief
  Ere now the dust hath stirred!
Hear me, but hear me! — father, chief,
  My king! I *must* be heard! —
Hush'd, hush'd — how is it that I call,
  And that thou answerest not?
When was it thus, woe, woe for all
  The love my soul forgot!

"Thy silver hairs I see
  So still, so sadly bright!
And father, father! but for me,
  They had not been so white.
I bore thee down, high heart! at last
  No longer couldst thou strive;
Oh! for one moment of the past,
  To kneel and say — 'forgive!'

"Thou wert the noblest king,
  On royal throne e'er seen!
And thou didst wear in knightly ring,
  Of all, the stateliest mien;
And thou didst prove, where spears are proved,
  In war, the bravest heart, —
Oh, ever the renown'd and loved
  Thou wert, — and *there* thou art!

"Thou that my boyhood's guide
  Didst take fond joy to be!
The times I've sported at thy side,
  And climb'd thy parent knee!
And there before the blessed shrine,
  My sire, I see thee lie!
How will that sad, still face of thine
  Look on me till I die!"

Say what the priests were doing. What was next heard? Who was coming? How did he come? What struggle took place in his heart? Explain "He reck'd not that they saw." What words of sorrow and of self-reproach did Cœur de Lion speak? (Give your own words.) What is to pursue the youth through life?

stately	censers	girt	train
ruddy	sceptred	mail	reck'd

———◇———

NOVEL READING.

IT is argued in favor of novel reading, that works of fiction of the present day are, in their general character, so correct in principle, so unexceptionaƀle in narrative, sometimes even so high-toned in morality, and, in the case of some particular authors, so finished in style, and so rich in the varied beauties of good composition, that they may be read not only without injury, but actually, under some aspects, with positive advantage. As clever delineations of character, too, they are said to afford so deep an insight into human nature, and so profitable a knowledge of the world and its ways, as to be in those respects a useful study for the inexperienced.

There can be no doubt of the vast improvement of the present period in that description of literary production emphatically called light. We know by hearsay that the romances of former days were not calculated to promote the health either of mind or heart; and that they should have been superseded by fictitious works of a more refining tendency, and a more enlightened character, cannot but be deemed an advantage. Yet, according to all the merit they can possibly claim, and viewing them under their very best and mòst favorable aspects, they are in many ways, to say the least, very dangerous.

Novels are in general pictures, usually very highly wrought pictures, of human passions; and it has been remarked, that although the conclusion of the tale frequently awards signal punishment and degradation to some very gross offender, yet that in a far greater number of instances passion is represented as working out its ends successfully, and attaining its object even by the sacrifice of duty — an evil lesson for the heart yet unacquainted with vice, and uncontaminated by the world. It may indeed be safely questioned whether the knowledge of human nature thus acquired is of a profitable kind, and whether experience of life might not, for all practical purposes, be derived from other and purer sources than the teachings of romances.

Again, novels, as a class, present false views of life; and as it is the error of the young to mistake those for realities, they become the dupes of their own ardent and enthusiastic imaginations, which, instead of trying to control and regulate, they strengthen and nourish with the poisonous food of phantoms and chimeras.

When the thirst for novel reading has become insatiable, as with indulgence it is sure to do, they come at last to live in an unreal fairy-land, amid heroes and heroines of their own creation. The taste for serious reading and profitable occupation is destroyed — all relish for prayer is lost. In addition to their other disadvantages, many of these books unfortunately teem with maxims subversive of simple faith, and in cordial irreverence for the truths of religion; and so it too frequently happens, as the climax of evil, that faith suffers to a greater or lesser extent from their habitual, indiscriminate perusal.

As a recreation, light works may, of course, be occasionally resorted to; but so many and so great are their attendant dangers, that extreme care should be taken to neutralize their poison by infallible antidotes. The selection of such works should always be left to a religious parent, to a well-read teacher or a pious and intelligent friend. They should never be made an occupation, but merely serve as a pastime, and that occasionally. They should never be perused in the early part of the day, but only in the evening hour, specially set aside for relaxation. They should never be continued beyond the moderate length of time to which, under prudent and pious direction, you have limited yourself, and never resumed after night prayers.

They should not be allowed to engross the mind to the exclusion of all other thoughts; but more especially during their perusal should the sweet, refreshing, invigorating thought of God's presence be often recalled, and our aspirations ascend to his throne, that he who is the author of all the happiness we enjoy may bless and sanctify even our amusements.

The observance of these conditions no doubt requires some self-control; but if you cannot exercise that control, neither can you expect to peruse works of fiction without material, perhaps fatal injury to your precious soul. If you cannot exercise that control, you should never read novels. If there be one more than another of these conditions to which you are recommended strict fidelity, it is to the first. By referring, for directions in your reading, to a pious, experienced guide, you will be secured against making selections among that class of fictitious works impregnated with the venom of anti-Catholic maxims.

And, as the spirit of impiety and infidelity so prevalent

in the literary world, seeks a medium for its venom no
less in works of science than in works of fiction, you wil
find the advantage of applying the foregoing rule in the
one case as in the other, never reading a suspected author
without having ascertained how far your doubts are
well founded.

COMPOSITION.

Take the fourth paragraph. Write the portion, "When the thirst
for novel reading .... all relish for prayer is lost." Relate what you
remember about light reading as seen in lives of SS. Augustin, Theresa,
Ignatius-Loyola. Name some of the good books you have read and
give a detailed account of one such book or a portion of it. What has
his Holiness, Pius IX., said about the power of the Press (newspaper)?
Consult the reading lesson on "Studies," and show how you may
realize the instructions given as to the manner of reading. Is it
advisable for young people to visit public libraries? Give your
reasons as fully as possible. What does Rodriguez say in "Christian
Perfection" about a "good book"?

unexceptionable	dupes	neutralize
delineations	phantoms	antidotes
emphatically	chimeras	relaxation
fictitious	insatiable	impregnated
uncontaminated	subversive	suspected
romances	indiscriminate	ascertained

———o———

TO A CANARY BIRD.

WHILE all the noisy raving town
    Is drown'd in recreation,
With thee, my bird, I'll sit me down,
    In sober meditation.

This world, for all it knows, my bird,
    Is oft to pity blinded,

And sorrow's cry is seldom heard
  But where 'tis little minded.

But thine's a friendly little heart,
  And when my own is aching,
Thy mirth can make its griefs depart,
  E'en though 'twere almost breaking

While thoughts of home and fervent friends
  Are all I've left to cheer me,
Fain wouldst thou make some faint amends
  By piping wildly near me.

That moral has no charm for me
  That's wreath'd in blinding letter:
I'll find in musing here with thee
  One easier learn'd and better.

At eve, high perch'd, with rounded breast
  And wing wrapp'd in so fairly,
Thou seem'st to bid me seek my rest
  While yet the night is early.

When through my window morn hath flung
  Its first uncertain gleaming,
Notes startling high and loud and long
  Dispel my idle dreaming.

If thoughts of care my mind engage,
  Thy song reminds me daily,
That e'en within a captive's cage
  The heart can flutter gaily.

And if thy time goes all for naught,
  And some would thoughtless blame thee,
We know that life, whence thou wert brought
  Had nothing that could shame thee.

Thus by thy simple life we see
   What lessons men have near them,
From things all reasonless like thee,
   If they would stoop to hear them.

Our human guides, their counsel, all
   Abound in precepts ample,
But oh! how short of thee they fall,
   For thine is all example.

COMPOSITION.

Give in your own words the first stanza, in two ways. Also:

    "Fain wouldst thou make some faint amends
    By piping wildly near me."

Also fifth stanza. Then:

    "Notes startling high and loud and long
    Dispel my idle dreaming."

Also tenth stanza (especially).

amends	perch'd	réasonless
piping	gleaming	ample

THE CRADLE OF RELIGIOUS LIBERTY.

THE foundation of the colony of Maryland was peacefully and happily laid. Within six months it had advanced more than Virginia had done in as many years. The proprietary continued with great liberality to provide everything that was necessary for its comfort and protection, and spared no cost to promote its interests. Under the mild institutions and munificence of Lord Baltimore, the dreary wilderness soon bloomed with the swarming life and activity of prosperous settlements; the Roman Catholics, who were oppressed by the laws of England, were sure to find a peaceful asylum in the quiet harbors of the Chesapeake; and there, too, Protestants were sheltered against Protestant intolerance. Such were the beautiful auspices under which the province of Maryland started into being. Its history is the history of benevolence, gratitude, and toleration.

In April, 1649, as if with a foresight of impending danger, and an earnest desire to stay its approach, the Roman Catholics of Maryland, with the earnest concurrence of their governor and of the proprietary, determined to place upon their statute book an act for the religious freedom which had ever been sacred on their soil. "And whereas the enforcing of the conscience · in matters of religion,"—such was the sublime tenor of a part of the statute—"hath frequently fallen out to be of dangerous consequence in those commonwealths where it has been practised; and for the more quiet and peaceable government of this province, and the better to preserve mutual love and amity among the inhabitants, no person within this province shall be in any ways troubled, molested, or discountenanced for his or her religion, or in the free exercise thereof."

Thus did the early star of religious freedom appear as the harbinger of day, though, as it first gleamed above the horizon, its light was colored and obscured by the mists and exhalations of morning. The greatest of English poets, when he represents the ground teeming with living things at the word of the Creator, paints the moment when the forms, so soon to be instinct with perfect life and beauty, are yet emerging from the inanimate earth, and when but

Half appeared
The tawny lion pawing to get free;

―――― then springs, as broke from bonds,
And rampant shakes his brinded mane.

So it was with the freedom of religion in the United States.

The clause for liberty in Maryland extended only to Christians, and was introduced by the proviso that "whatsoever person shall blaspheme God, or shall deny or reproach the Holy Trinity, or any of the three persons thereof, shall be punished with death." But the design of the law of Maryland was undoubtedly to protect freedom of conscience; and some years after it had been confirmed, the apologists of Lord Baltimore could assert that his government, in conformity with his strict and repeated injunctions, had never given disturbance to any person in Maryland for matters of religion; that the colonists enjoyed freedom of conscience, not less than freedom of person and estate, as amply as ever any people in any place of the world. The disfranchised friends of liberty from Virginia, and their imitators from Massachusetts, were welcomed to equal liberty of conscience and political rights in the Roman Catholic province of Maryland.

Questions:— What is meant by "proprietary"? To what does the historian refer when he says "*there, too, Protestants were sheltered from Protestant intolerance*"? What is meant by "hath fallen out to be of dangerous consequence"? Express this phrase in modern style. What is meant by "disfranchised friends of liberty"? What other colony established religious toleration? Give first paragraph in your own words. Retain construction of sentences but substitute synonymes where possible.

proprietary	benevolence	harbinger
liberality	concurrence	exhalations
prosperous	conscience	undoubtedly
intolerance	commonwealths	injunctions
auspices	discountenanced	disfranchised

ELEGY IN A COUNTRY CHURCH-YARD.

Thomas Gray (1716–1771), one of the greatest of England's lyric poets, His productions are very few, but excellent. His finest compositions are those entitled "The Bard," the "Progress of Poetry," the ode to "Adversity," and the famous "Elegy in a Country Church-yard," by which he is best known. Indeed it is more frequently called "Gray's Elegy" than by its proper title. In the exquisite finish of his verse, Gray surpassed all his predecessors.

THE curfew tolls the knell of parting day,
   The lowing herd winds slowly o'er the lea,
The plowman homeward plods his weary way,
   And leaves the world to darkness and to me.

Now fades the glimmering landscape on the sight,
   And all the air a solemn stillness holds,
Save where the beetle wheels his droning flight,
   And drowsy tinklings lull the distant folds;

Save that from yonder ivy-mantled tower
   The moping owl does to the moon complain
Of such as, wandering near her secret bower,
   Molest her ancient solitary reign.

Beneath those rugged elms, that yew-tree's shade,
   Where heaves the turf in many a mouldering heap,
Each in his narrow cell forever laid,
   The rude forefathers of the hamlet sleep.

The breezy call of incense-breathing morn,
   The swallow twittering from the straw-built shed,
The cock's shrill clarion, or the echoing horn,
   No more shall rouse them from their lowly bed.

For them no more the blazing hearth shall burn,
   Or busy housewife ply her evening care;
No children run to lisp their sire's return,
   Or climb his knees the envied kiss to share.

Oft did the harvest to their sickle yield,
　Their furrow oft the stubborn glebe has broke:
How jocund did they drive their team afield!
　How bowed the woods beneath their sturdy stroke.

Let not Ambition mock their useful toil,
　Their homely joys, and destiny obscure;
Nor Grandeur hear, with a disdainful smile,
　The short and simple annals of the poor.

The boast of heraldry, the pomp of power,
　And all that beauty, all that wealth e'er gave,
Await alike th' inevitable hour:
　The paths of glory lead but to the grave.

Nor you, ye proud, impute to these the fault,
　If Memory o'er their tomb no trophies raise,
Where through the long-drawn aisle and fretted vault
　The pealing anthem swells the note of praise.

Can storied urn, or animated bust,
　Back to its mansion call the fleeting breath?
Can Honor's voice provoke the silent dust,
　Or Flattery soothe the dull, cold ear of death?

Perhaps in this neglected spot is laid
　Some heart once pregnant with celestial fire;
Hands that the rod of empire might have swayed,
　Or waked to ecstasy the living lyre;

But Knowledge to their eyes her ample page,
　Rich with the spoils of time, did ne'er unroll;
Chill Penury repressed their noble rage,
　And froze the genial current of the soul.

Full many a gem, of purest ray serene,
　The dark, unfathomed caves of ocean bear;

Full many a flower is born to blush unseen,
 And waste its sweetness on the desert air.

Some village Hampden, that with dauntless breast
 The little tyrant of his fields withstood;
Some mute, inglorious Milton here may rest;
 Some Cromwell, guiltless of his country's blood.

Th' applause of listening senates to command,
 The threats of pain and ruin to despise,
To scatter plenty o'er a smiling land,
 And read their history in a nation's eyes,

Their lot forbade, nor circumscribed alone
 Their growing virtues, but their crimes confined;
Forbade to wade through slaughter to a throne,
 And shut the gates of mercy on mankind,

The struggling pangs of conscious truth to hide,
 To quench the blushes of ingenuous shame,
Or heap the shrine of luxury and pride
 With incense kindled at the Muse's flame.

Far from the maddening crowd's ignoble strife,
 Their sober wishes never learned to stray.
Along the cool, sequestered vale of life
 They kept the noiseless tenor of their way.

Yet e'en these bones from insult to protect,
 Some frail memorial still erected nigh,
With uncouth rhymes and shapeless sculpture decked,
 Implores the passing tribute of a sigh.

Their names, their years, spelt by th' unlettered Muse
 The place of fame and elegy supply;
And many a holy text around she strews,
 That teach the rustic moralist to die.

For who, to dumb forgetfulness a prey,
　This pleasing, anxious being e'er resigned,
Left the warm precincts of the cheerful day,
　Nor cast one longing, lingering look behind?

On some fond breast the parting soul relies,
　Some pious drops the closing eye requires;
E'en from the tomb the voice of nature cries,
　E'en in our ashes live their wonted fires.

For thee, who, mindful of th' unhonored dead,
　Dost in these lines their artless tale relate,
If chance, by lonely contemplation led,
　Some kindred spirit shall inquire thy fate, —

Haply some hoary-headed swain may say,
　"Oft have we seen him at the peep of dawn,
Brushing with hasty steps the dews away,
　To meet the sun upon the upland lawn.

"There, at the foot of yonder nodding beech,
　That wreathes its old fantastic roots so high,
His listless length at noontide would he stretch,
　And pore upon the brook that babbles by.

"Hard by yon wood, now smiling as in scorn,
　Muttering his wayward fancies, would he rove,
Now drooping, woful wan, like one forlorn,
　Or crazed with care, or crossed in hopeless love.

"One morn I missed him on the customed hill,
　Along the heath, and near his favorite tree:
Another came, — nor yet beside the rill,
　Nor up the lawn, nor at the wood was he:

"The next, with dirges due, in sad array,
　Slow through the church-way path we saw him borne

Approach and read (for thou canst read) the lay
Graved on the stone beneath yon aged thorn."

THE EPITAPH.

HERE RESTS HIS HEAD UPON THE LAP OF EARTH,
A YOUTH TO FORTUNE AND TO FAME UNKNOWN:
FAIR SCIENCE FROWNED NOT ON HIS HUMBLE BIRTH,
AND MELANCHOLY MARKED HIM FOR HER OWN.

LARGE WAS HIS BOUNTY, AND HIS SOUL SINCERE,
HEAVEN DID A RECOMPENSE AS LARGELY SEND:
HE GAVE TO MISERY — ALL HE HAD — A TEAR,
HE GAINED FROM HEAVEN ('TWAS ALL HE WISHED) A FRIEND

NO FURTHER SEEK HIS MERITS TO DISCLOSE,
OR DRAW HIS FRAILTIES FROM THEIR DREAD ABODE
(THERE THEY ALIKE IN TREMBLING HOPE REPOSE),
THE BOSOM OF HIS FATHER AND HIS GOD.

Questions:—Explain: "And leaves the world to darkness and to
me." "And drowsy tinklings lull the distant folds." "Yonder ivy-
mantled tower." "Heaves the turf in many a mouldering heap."
"Forefathers of the hamlet." "The stubborn glebe." "The boast
of heraldry." "Th' inevitable hour." "Storied urn." "Pregnant
with celestial fire." What is "the living lyre"? Was Cromwell
"guiltless of his country's blood"? Continue the analysis of balance
in same way.

tolls	afield	elegy
lowing	sturdy	kindred
droning	heraldry	haply
lull	impute	fantastic
rugged	urn	woful
clarion	pregnant	dirges
ply	penury	melancholy
sire's	Hampden	merits
glebe	ingenuous	frailties
jocund	uncouth	bosom

THE CONVERSATION OF AN EDUCATED MAN.

WHAT is that which first strikes us, and strikes us at once, in an educated man; and which, among men of education, so instantly distinguishes the man of superior mind, that (as was observed with eminent propriety of the late Edmund Burke) "we cannot stand under the same archway during a shower of rain without finding him out"?

Not the weight or novelty of his remarks; not any unusual interest of facts communicated by him; for we may suppose both the one and the other precluded by the shortness of our intercourse and the triviality of the subjects. The difference will be impressed and felt, though the conversation should be confined to the state of the weather or the pavement.

Still less will it arise from any peculiarity in his words and phrases. For, if he be, as we now assume, a well-educated man, as well as a man of superior powers, he will not fail to follow the golden rule of Julius Cæsar, "Avoid an unusual word as you would a rock," unless where new things necessitate new terms. It must have been among the earliest lessons of his youth that the breach of this precept, at all times hazardous, becomes ridiculous in the topics of ordinary conversation.

There remains but one other point of distinction possible; and this must be, and in fact is, the cause of the impression made on us. It is the unpremeditated and evidently habitual arrangement of his words, grounded on the habit of foreseeing, in each integral part, or, more plainly, in every sentence, the whole that he then intends to communicate. However irregular and desultory his talk, there is method in the fragments

Listen, on the other hand, to an ignorant man, though perhaps shrewd and able in his particular calling, whether he be describing or relating. We immediately perceive that his memory alone is called into action; and that the objects and events recur in the narration in the same order, and with the same accompaniments, however accidental or impertinent, as they had first occurred to the narrator.

The necessity of taking breath, the efforts of recollection, and the rectification of its failures, produce all his pauses; and with exception of the " and then," the " and there," and the still less significant " and so," they constitute likewise all his connections.

Questions:—What is said of Edmund Burke? What is it to "preclude"? What is meant by "a man of superior powers"? Name six men who had superior powers. What is an integral part? Name some integral parts of this school. Of this Reader. Of the church we go to for holy Mass. What is "desultory talk"? Show from a familiar example how I could use my memory and throw aside my judgment. How may we rectify failures? How should a child rectify failures in duty to parents or teachers?

educated	necessitate	desultory	narrator
propriety	hazardous	shrewd	rectification
precluded	topics	narration	constitute
triviality	premeditated	order	likewise

———o———

MOTHER SETON.

L O! the hosts of valiant women!
   Lo! the legions, brave and strong,
That have "come up from the desert"
   In a grand, immortal throng;
That have fought, with hearts undaunted,
   'Gainst a fierce and hydra foe,

Till, within the dust degrading,
    They have brought his standard low!
But they seek no vain applauses,
    And they court no gazing crowd,
And they stand not in the forum,
    Lifting clamor shrill and loud.
No! the true strong-minded follow
    Where a calmer guidance leads,
And the lowly path of duty
    Is their field for lofty deeds.
Ay, they tread, with steady footsteps,
    In *her* still, secluded way,
Who was stronger in her meekness,
    Than a host in war array;
Who, in Nazareth's cottage lowly,
    Bore her blest, yet hidden part,
While she kept her Saviour's sayings
    Fondly treasured in her heart.
And amid those silent toilers
    Is a wonder-working band,
Who have brought the boons of heaven.
    As they pass from land to land;
Who have braved the ocean tempest
    And the desert's burning ray,
From the Northland to the Tropics,
    From Columbia to Cathay.
Noble daughters of Saint Vincent!
    Where the hosts to match with ye
Legions of the Lord of pity!
    Valiant band of charity!
Who hath won your angel presence,
    Who hath brought your labors blest
To the mighty land of freedom,
    To the empire of the West?
"In a sunny southern valley
    Is an Eden, calm and sweet,

Where we gird our toiling armies
  For 'the burden and the heat;'
And that vale of blest Saint Joseph
  Hath a dear and sacred trust,
For it shrineth *one* whose life-deeds
  Blossom, fragrant, in the dust.
Oh, a rare and matchless treasure
  Is that angel-guarded grave,
Though no pompous tomb is o'er it,
  And no stately banners wave;
For the mortal shrine reposing
  Till the resurrection there,
Held a stainless spirit flower,
  In its casket, sweet and fair.
O our loved and saintly mother!
  O our foundress, true and brave!
Deathless are the links that bind us
  To thy dear and sacred grave.
And where'er our feet may wander,
  And whate'er our labors be,
While we serve our lowly Master,
  In his cause of charity;
While we keep our silent vigils
  By the weary couch of pain,
While we stanch the flowing life-stream
  On the ghastly battle plain;
As we soothe the orphan's wailing,
  And assuage the mourner's woe,
As we turn the sinner's glances
  Where the beams of mercy glow;
In the streets of crowded cities,
  On the wide and lonely sea,
Still we shrine our saintly foundress,
  In our tend'rest memory."
O ye hearts that bless the Sisters
  For the conquests they have wrought,

For the reaped and garnered harvest,
　　With its rich abundance fraught!
Hail the noble hand that founded,
　　That hath sown the magic seed,
That hath sought the earliest workers
　　In the time of direst need.
Oh, on earth, sweet Mother Seton,
　　Thou hast won a deathless name,
And the seraph hosts of heaven
　　Shall for ever sing thy fame

Questions : — Explain:

"Till within the dust degrading,
　　They have brought his standard low!"
"And the lowly path of duty
　　Is their field for lofty deeds."

Name the part of New Testament whence the words ' fondly treasured in her heart" are taken. What is "the flowing life-stream"? Who shrine their "saintly foundress" in their "tend'rest memory"?

valiant	hydra	toilers	pompous
throng	forum	Cathay	couch
undaunted	shrill	fragrant	assuage

————o————

THE SKY.

John Ruskin, LL. D., born in 1819, artist and art critic of great productiveness and originality. No other author of the time has been the recipient of more exaggerated praise or more indiscriminate censure. Yet not one fair observer can over-estimate his services to the cause of Art. Though often dogmatic, arrogant, conceited and absurd, he has discovered and applied valuable principles in art criticism, and may be said to have founded a new literature. the literature of Art.* His style is rich and clear, powerful and eloquent. His descriptions are in reality *word paintings*, as vivid and

---

* He teaches that fitness is the element of beauty, and that true art should seek to study and reproduce nature.

strongly colored as his friend Turner's canvas. His two best known works are: "The Modern Painters Superior to the Ancients in Landscape Painting," and the "Stones of Venice."

IT is a strange thing how little in general people know about the sky. It is the part of creation in which Nature has done more for the sake of pleasing man, more for the sole and evident purpose of talking to him and teaching him, than in any other of her works, and it is just the part in which we least attend to her.

There are not many of her other works in which some more material or essential purpose than the mere pleasing of man is not answered by every part of their organization; but every essential purpose of the sky might, so far as we know, be answered, if once in three days, or thereabouts, a great, ugly, black rain cloud were brought up over the blue, and everything well watered, and so all left blue again till next time, with, perhaps, a film of morning and evening mist for dew

And, instead of this, there is not a moment of any day of our lives, when Nature is not producing scene after scene, picture after picture, glory after glory, and working still upon such exquisite and constant principles of the most perfect beauty, that it is quite certain it is all done for us, and intended for our perpetual pleasure. And every man, wherever placed, however far from other sources of interest or of beauty, has this doing for him constantly.

The noblest scenes of earth can be seen and known but by few: it is not intended that man should live always in the midst of them; he injures them by his presence; he ceases to feel them, if he be always with them; but the sky is for *all*; bright as it is, it is not "too bright, nor good, for human nature's daily food;" it is fitted in all its functions for the perpetual comfort and exalting of the heart, for the soothing it and purifying it from its dross and dust.

Sometimes gentle, sometimes capricious, sometimes awful, never the same for two moments together; almost human in its passions, almost spiritual in its tenderness, almost divine in its infinity, its appeal to what is immortal in us is as distinct, as its ministry of chastisement or of blessing to what is mortal is essential.

And yet we never attend to it, we never make it a subject of thought, but as it has to do with our animal sensations; we look upon all by which it speaks to us more clearly than to brutes—upon all which bears witness to the intention of the Supreme, that we are to receive more from the covering vault than the light and the dew which we share with the weed and the worm— only as a succession of meaningless and monotonous accidents, too common and too vain to be worthy of a moment of watchfulness, or a glance of admiration.

If, in our moments of utter idleness and insipidity, we turn to the sky as a last resource, which of its phenomena do we speak of? One says it has been wet, and another it has been windy, and another it has been warm. Who, among the whole chattering crowd, can tell me of the forms and the precipices of the chain of tall, white mountains that girded the horizon at noon yesterday? Who saw the narrow sunbeam that came out of the South and smote upon their summits until they melted and mouldered away in a dust of blue rain? Who saw the dance of the clouds when the sunlight left them last night, and the wind blew them before it like withered leaves?

All has passed, unregretted as unseen; or, if the apathy be ever shaken off, even for an instant, it is only by what is gross or what is extraordinary; and yet it is not in the fierce manifestations of the elemental energies, not in the clash of the hail, nor the drift of the whirlwind, that the highest characters of the sublime are developed. God is not in the earthquake, nor in the fire, but in the still, small voice. They are but the blunt and lost faculties of our nature, which can only be addressed through lamp-black and lightning.

It is in quiet and subdued passages of unobtrusive majesty, the deep, and the calm, and the perpetual, — that which must be sought ere it is seen, and loved ere it is understood; things which the angels work out for us daily, and yet vary eternally, which are never wanting, and never repeated, which are to be found always, yet each found but once, — it is through these that the lesson of devotion is chiefly taught, and the blessing of beauty given.

It seems to me that in the midst of the material nearness of the heavens, God means us to acknowledge his own immediate presence as visiting, judging, and blessing us. "The earth was moved, and the heavens dropped, at the presence of the God of Sina!" "He will set his bow in the cloud," and thus renew, in the sound of every dropping swathe of rain, his promises of everlasting love. "He hath set his *tabernacle* in the sun," whose burning ball, which, without the firmament, would be seen as an intolerable and scorching circle in the blackness of vacuity, is by that firmament surrounded with gorgeous service, and tempered by mediatorial ministries; by the firmament of clouds the golden pavement is spread for his chariot wheels at morning; by the firmament of clouds the temple is built for his presence to fill with light at noon; by the firmament of clouds the purple veil is closed at evening round the sanctuary of his rest; by the mists of the firmament his implacable light is divided, and its separated fierceness appeased into the soft blue that fills the depth of distance with its bloom, and the flush with which the mountains burn as they drink the overflowing of the day-spring.

And, in this tabernacling of the unendurable sun with men, through the shadows of the firmament, God would seem to set forth the stooping of his own majesty to men, upon the *throne* of the firmament. As the creator of all the worlds, and the inhabiter of eternity, we can not behold him; but as the judge of the earth and the preserver of men, those heavens are, indeed, his dwelling-place. "Swear not at all, neither by heaven, for it is the throne of God; nor by the earth, for it is his footstool." And all those passings to and fro of fruitful shower and grateful shade, and all those visions of silver palaces built about the horizon, and voices of moaning winds and threatening thunders, and glories of colored robe and cloven ray, are but to deepen in our hearts the acceptance, and distinctness, and dearness of the simple words, — "*Our Father who art in Heaven!*"

QUESTIONS AND COMPOSITION.

What portion of the creation offers most to man's temptation? What does the author say the sky *might be, for all essential purposes?* What occurs in the sky at every moment? What are the ordinary expressions used about the sky? What questions are asked in latter portion of seventh paragraph? What is meant by saying that the faculties of our nature can only be addressed through "lamp-black and lightning"? What texts of Scripture are given in last paragraph? (In your own words).

Divide fifth paragraph into four sentences. Give the idea, but change nouns and adjectives.

evident	capricious	unobtrusive
organization	sensations	vary
film	insipidity	mediatorial

THE OLD SONGS.

WHEN through life unblest we rove,
 Losing all that life made dear,
Should some notes we used to love
 In days of boyhood meet our ear;
Oh! how welcome breathes the strain,
 Wakening thoughts that long have slept,
Kindling former smiles again
 In faded eyes that long have wept.

Like the gale that sighs along
 Beds of oriental flowers
Is the grateful breath of song,
 That once was heard in happier hours.
Filled with balm the gale sighs on,
 Though the flowers have sunk in death;
So, when pleasure's dream is gone,
 Its memory lives in Music's breath.

Music! — oh! how faint, how weak,
 Language fades before thy spell!
Why should feeling ever speak,
 When thou canst breathe her soul so well?
Friendship's balmy words may feign,
 Love's are e'en more false than they
Oh! 'tis only Music's strain
 Can sweetly soothe, and not betray!

Questions:—When do we rove through life unblest? How may notes meet our ear? What causes eyes to fade? What Apostle's eyes thus faded? What does the sound of old tunes do for the eye? How is the sound of old songs like a soft gale? Is language as powerful and universal as music? What does the sound of music do while refusing to betray? Name some songs that always touch our hearts. Can you recite any lines from old songs?

  strain   oriental   spell   feign

INFLUENCE OF THE CRUSADES.

THE Crusades exercised a marked influence over the manners of the age, specially by imparting a more religious spirit to the feudal and military institutions already existing. In those rude times, when almost every man was a soldier, the Church, extending her gentle influence over the fierce nobles of Western Europe, had directed them to use their strength and valor to protect the weak and succor the distressed She transformed the half savage warrior into the Christian knight, and taught him to raise his sword in defence of truth and justice, to be merciful in the hour of victory, and to keep faith with God and man. Hence grew up the laws and customs of *chivalry,* and the religious enthusiasm which was fostered by the Crusades gave to knighthood an almost sacred character.

When a young noble was about to be admitted to the order of knighthood, care was taken to impress him with a deep sense of its obligations. Clothed in white robes — the tokens of a spotless life — he passed the night keeping watch beside his arms, which were placed in the church; when morning came, he confessed and communicated, and after Mass his arms were blessed by the priest. Then, kneeling before some elder knight, he pronounced the solemn vows of chivalry. He swore to fight only in a righteous cause, to be the champion of the weak, never to stain his knightly honor by a lie, to be loyal to God and his sovereign lord, and to give his life in defence of his brethren. He then received his arms; his gilded spurs were clasped on his feet, and his sword buckled by his side; and lastly, the knight who received his vows struck him on the shoulder with a sword, and bade him arise, in the name of God, St. Michael and St. George.

The benefits which chivalry produced on society can scarcely be overrated. It inspired men with a reverence for lofty and generous virtues; for the true knight was to be courteous to friend and foe, and was taught never to make war for selfish interests or the mere hope of gain. And though in this respect the laws of chivalry were often enough violated, and offered but a weak restraint to the passions of lawless men, yet, on the other hand, we have many instances where the true knightly character appears in all its splendor. Thus, when some Norman knights had delivered the kingdom of Salerno from the hands of the Saracens, the king offered them a splendid recompense if they would remain with him and protect his dominions. But the brave knights refused to accept the proffered gifts; they could not, they said, be paid in money for services they had rendered out of their pure love of God. Even amid the fury of battle, the laws of knighthood laid a check upon the cruelty and bloodshed of the victors.

COMPOSITION.

Answer the following questions, briefly, but clearly as possible:

How did the Crusades exercise a *marked influence* upon the manners of the age? What gave rise to the laws and customs of chivalry? Give the pith of the knight's oath at his initiation. What advantage did society receive from the carrying out of the knight's oath, and from chivalry, so long as the latter remained true to the mission given it by the Church? Give the knights' answer to the King of Salerno. State the influence of chivalry on the knights engaged in battle

institutions	fostered	lofty
faith	order	courteous
chivalry	righteous	violated
enthusiasm	overrated	lawless

THE HEAVENS DECLARE THE GLORY OF GOD.

THE spacious firmament on high,
With all the blue, ethereal sky,
And spangled heavens, a shining frame
Their great Original proclaim;
Th' unwearied SUN, from day to day,
Does his Creator's power display,
And publishes to every land
The work of an Almighty hand.

Soon as the evening shades prevail,
The MOON takes up the wondrous tale,
And nightly to the listening earth,
Repeats the story of her birth;
While all the stars that round her burn,
And all the planets in their turn,
Confirm the tidings as they roll,
And spread the truth from pole to pole.

What though, in solemn silence, all
Move round the dark terrestrial ball?
What though no *real* voice or sound
Amid their radiant orbs be found?
In *Reason's* ear they all rejoice,
And utter forth a glorious voice,
Forever singing as they shine,
" *The Hand that made us is divine!* "

COMPOSITION.

Write a paraphrase of the first stanza, in which tell what it is that
proclaims the power of God. Take special care to bring out the
ideas contained in the expressions, "spacious firmament," "blue,
ethereal sky," "spangled heavens," "shining frame." Elaborate
ideas of "th' unwearied Sun," "Almighty hand."

prevail   tidings   terrestrial   radiant

A PEN PICTURE FROM FATHER DALGAIRNS.

I WAS sitting in an old castle on the banks of the Frith of Clyde, on a beautiful morning in September. It was the eve of Our Lady's Nativity, and all nature seemed to have put on its best to prepare to celebrate Mary's birth-day. The castle was built on a high terrace, separated only by a green meadow from the waters of the noble estuary. The wind was swaying to and fro the boughs of the still leafy trees in the noble woods of beech and oak around the house ; its sound was inexpressibly soothing to ears accustomed to the roar of London, and to nerves still painfully twittering with the irritating roll of cabs and omnibuses. The breeze could just break the surface of the water without lashing it into waves, and convert the burnished mirror into a glittering and sparkling sheet of fretted silver. The little wavelets seemed to leap with joy under the bright, shining sun. The sky was by no means spotless ; heavy, white clouds hung on the horizon, but islands of blue sky were left here and there, and high overhead the sun lorded it in a clear heaven, and beautifully lit up the fleecy masses, till they were absolutely dazzling and saturated with light. Guarding the entrance of the Ganloch from the waters of the Frith lies the wooded promontory of Roseneath. It is said that there had been of old a convent there, and a fitter spot could not have been chosen. Even the restless waters lay still, deep, and black along its winding shores. The massive trees, which, robed in every tint of green, grew down to the water's edge, threw motionless shadows over the mossy turf which appeared at intervals between their huge trunks. A more peaceful scene could not be conceived : even the humming of the bees around the pale flowers of the jessamine, which, mingled with myrtle, tapestried the walls of the castle with its matted shoots, and embowered my window, only contributed to make the stillness more soothing.

Amidst all this tranquil beauty, there was one object alone which pained and excited me. On the opposite side of the Frith, in a strange proximity to rock, wood, and mountain, at the foot of a long range of highlands, purpled here and there with heather, green with pastures, and yellow with corn-fields, lay the busy, populous town of Greenock. It looked peaceful enough ; the huge line-of-battle ship, with its little fleet of gun-boats, lay perfectly still on the bosom of the deep estuary. The innumerable masts of the merchant-ships in the harbor were too far off to be distinctly seen, especially as the smoke issuing from several tall chimneys hung like a pall over the town, and the hum of its busy streets was perfectly inaudible. Still, it was impossible to look at it without thinking of what marred the peacefulness of the scene. It probably was not worse than other sea-ports, yet some thousands of human beings could not be collected together without bringing with them sorrow, passion, and sin in their train. There were thousands of passionate human hearts in all their varieties—loving, hating, fiery and icy-cold, happy and miserable, restless and weary hearts. Nor was it possible to forget one dear inmate there, one inhabitant of Greenock. In a little back street, under a most lonely roof, tended only by a few faithful ones, lay Jesus in the tabernacle, with His little lamp burning before Him. There was consolation enough to heal the most broken-hearted ; peace to still the wildest

tempest of the soul ; love, more than enough, to fill
the most craving void of the meanest heart. Yet all
these treasures are unknown, unexpected, or derided.

Who can help thinking of all this? I could not
help saying to myself : Oh! for the time when every
man, woman, and child, from John O'Groat's house to
Solway Frith, and on to the Land's End of Cornwall,
was naturally, by birth-right and without effort, a be-
liever in the Blessed Sacrament! Is this state of
things forever past? God alone knows ; but meanwhile, there is only one thing which we can do to
alleviate, if not to remedy, this mighty evil ; we can
surround our dear Lord with redoubled love, to make
up to Him for the souls which He loses. Let each of
us do his little best to make Him better known; for, if
He is better known He must be better loved.

Questions:—What thoughts did the writer of this selection have ?
What was it that pained him ? What is an estuary ? Write a composition, describing in your own words the thoughts of the writer.

terrace	painfully	horizon	heather
estuary	absolutely	motionless	distinctly
irritating	accustomed	promontory	innumerable

THE STAR SPANGLED BANNER.

Oh ! say, can you see by the dawn's early light,
    What so proudly we hailed at the twilight's last gleaming ?
Whose broad stripes and bright stars, through the perilous
        fight,
    O'er the ramparts we watched were so gallantly streaming ;
And the rockets' red glare, the bombs bursting in air,
Gave proof through the night that our flag was still there ;

Oh! say, does that star-spangled banner yet wave
O'er the land of the free and the home of the brave?

On the shore, dimly seen through the mists of the deep,
 Where the foe's haughty host in dread silence reposes,
What is that which the breeze, o'er the towering steep,
 As it fitfully blows, half conceals, half discloses?
Now it catches the gleam of the morning's first beam,
In full glory reflected now shines on the stream;
'Tis the star-spangled banner! Oh, long may it wave
O'er the land of the free and the home of the brave!

And where is that band, who so vauntingly swore
 That the havoc of war and the battle's confusion
A home and a country should leave us no more?
 Their blood has washed out their foul footsteps' pollution;
No refuge could save the hireling and slave
From the terror of death and the gloom of the grave;
And the star-spangled banner in triumph shall wave
O'er the land of the free and the home of the brave!

Oh! thus be it ever, when freemen shall stand
 Between their loved homes and the war's desolation;
Blessed with victory and peace, may the heaven-rescued land
 Praise the power that has made and preserved us a nation.
Then conquer we must, for our cause it is just,
And this be our motto, "In God is our trust."
And the star-spangled banner in triumph shall wave
O'er the land of the free and the home of the brave!

Questions:—Explain the dawn's early light; perilous fight; gallantly
streaming. What country is the land of the free and the home of the
brave? What is meant by the words "heaven-rescued nation"? Write
a short composition, containing at least twenty-five words taken from
the lesson. Give the history of the poem.

haughty	stripes	triumph	hireling
gleaming	silence	confusion	desolation
ramparts	reflected	vauntingly	pollution

CHARGE OF THE LIGHT BRIGADE.

HALF a league — half a league —
   Half a league onward,
All in the valley of Death,
   Rode the Six Hundred!

Into the valley of Death
   Rode the Six Hundred!
For up came an order which
   Some one had blundered:
" Forward, the Light Brigade!
Take the guns!" Nolan said.
   Into the valley of Death
   Rode the Six Hundred!

" Forward, the Light Brigade!"
No man was there dismayed —
Not though the soldiers knew
   Some one had blundered.
Theirs not to make reply;
Theirs not to reason why;
Theirs but to do and die!
   Into the valley of Death
   Rode the Six Hundred!

Cannon to right of them,
Cannon to left of them,
Cannon in front of them,
   Volleyed and thundered!

Stormed at with shot and shell,
Boldly they rode, and well;
Into the jaws of Death,
Into the mouth of hell,
   Rode the Six Hundred!

Flashed all their sabres bare,
Flashed all at once in air,
Sabring the gunners there,
    Charging an army, while
        All the world wondered.
Plunged in the battery smoke,
With many a desperate stroke
The Russian line they broke;
    Then they rode back, but not —.
        Not the Six Hundred!

Cannon to right of them,
Cannon to left of them,
Cannon behind them,
        Volleyed and thundered.

Stormed at with shot and shell,
While horse and hero fell,
Those that had fought so well
Came from the jaws of Death,
Back from the mouth of hell,
    All that was left of them —
        Left of Six Hundred!

When can their glory fade?
Oh, the wild charge they made!
    All the world wondered.
Honor the charge they made!
    Honor the Light Brigade —
        Noble Six Hundred!

COMPOSITION.

Say something about the importance of obedience, in all stations
and at all times in life. Give some examples furnished in the Bible
of how God appreciates and requires obedience, and how he abhors
and punishes disobedience. Then state that in our own day obedience
is equally necessary. Give a sketch of the obedience shown by the
Noble Six Hundred.

Go over the account given in the poem, arrange the information in your own mind, then try to give the same facts in your own words. Show how these six hundred were doubly brave, since they obeyed an order which was known to be a blunder. Show that life is one continual struggle, and that the obedient man alone "shall speak of victory." Quote some lines from lessons on: "The Flight into Egypt," "How they Brought the Good News from Ghent to Aix," "Noble Revenge," the story of Saul and Samuel, and others, to prove the importance of obedience.

dismayed   volleyed   sabres   sabring

ON STUDIES.

Francis, Lord Bacon (1561-1626), philosopher, jurist, politician and courtier of the reigns of Queen Elizabeth and James I. His fame rests upon the "Novum Organum," in which he expounds the laws of the inductive or experimental method as applied to natural science, sometimes called from him the "Baconian Philosophy." It was for a long time the fashion with the literary *claqueurs* of the "Reformation" and the materialistic school, to extol Bacon as if he were the creator of new intellectual faculties. The more temperate criticism of recent times has assigned him his true position, as the exponent and director of the spirit of investigation in natural science, which had been at work long before his time, and which, four centuries previous, had found its first disciple in the monk Roger Bacon, who not only formulated the same laws as his namesake, the courtier, but had far excelled the latter in the knowledge of natural phenomena and their causes.

STUDIES serve for delight, for ornament, and for ability. Their chief use for delight, is in privacy and retiring; for ornament, is in discourse; and for ability, is in the judgment and disposition of business. For expert men can execute, and perhaps judge of particulars, one by one; but the general counsels, and the plots, and marshalling of affairs, come best from those that are learned.

To spend too much time in studies, is sloth; to use

them too much for ornament, is affectation; to make judgment wholly by their rules, is the humor of a scholar.

They perfect nature, and are perfected by experience

For natural abilities are like natural plants, that need pruning by study; and studies themselves do give forth directions too much at large, except they be bounded in by experience.

Crafty men contemn studies; simple men admire them; and wise men use them: for they teach not their own use; but that is wisdom without them, and above them, won by observation.

Read not to contradict and confute; nor to believe and take for granted; nor to find talk and discourse; but to weigh and consider.

Some books are to be tasted, others to be swallowed, and some few to be chewed and digested: that is, some books are to be read only in parts; others to be read, but not curiously; and some few to be read wholly, and with diligence and attention. Some books also may be read by deputy, and extracts made of them by others: but that would be only in the less important arguments, and the meaner sort of books: else distilled books are, like common distilled waters, flashy things.

Reading maketh a full man, conference a ready man, and writing an exact man. And, therefore, if a man write little, he had need have a great memory; if he confer little, he had need have a present wit: and if he read little, he had need have much cunning, to seem to know that he doth not.

Histories make men wise; poets, witty; the mathematics, subtle; natural philosophy, deep; moral, grave; logic and rhetoric, able to contend. *Abeunt studia in mores.** Nay, there is no stond or impediment in the

---

* *Studies pass into manners* (form character). Ovid. *Her.* xv. 83.

wit but may be wrought out by fit studies : like as diseases of the body may have appropriate exercises, — shooting for the lungs and breast ; gentle walking for the stomach ; riding for the head ; and the like. So if a man's wit be wandering, let him study the mathematics ; if his wit be not apt to distinguish or find differences, let him study the schoolmen ; if he be not apt to beat over matters, and to call up one thing to prove and illustrate another, let him study the lawyers' cases.

COMPOSITION.

Write the sixth paragraph carefully. Insert, in brackets, synonymes or equivalents for every word you can change.

Put this same paragraph in three ways, using the first person in first alteration, second person in next, and third person in last. Thus :

I will not read that I may find fault with others, and prove them wrong in what they say ; but I will read that I may explain and defend my views. I will not believe everything I read in secular works or in merely pious works, but I will think over what I may read, and accept what I think right in secular questions. In religious works I will be guided by Holy Mother Church, and never question her decisions.

| expert | experience | witty | subtle |
| marshalling | distilled | deputy | schoolmen |

———o———

SONG OF THE MYSTIC.

I WALK down the Valley of Silence,
  Down the dim, voiceless valley alone!
And I hear not the fall of a footstep
  Around me, save God's and my own;
And the hush of my heart is as holy
  As hovers where angels have flown!

Long ago was I weary of voices
  Whose music my heart could not win;

Long ago I was weary of noises
   That fretted my soul with their din;
Long ago was I weary of places
   Where I met but the human — and sin.

I walked in the world with the worldly;
   I craved what the world never gave;
And I said: "In the world each Ideal,
   That shines like a star on life's wave,
Is wrecked on the shores of the Real,
   And sleeps like a dream in a grave."

And still did I pine for the Perfect,
   And still found the False with the True;
I sought mid the Human for Heaven,
   But caught a mere glimpse of its blue;
And I wept when the clouds of the Mortal
   Veiled even that glimpse from my view.

And I toiled on, heart-tired of the Human;
   And I moaned 'mid the mazes of men;
Till I knelt long ago at an altar
   And heard a voice call me; — since then
I walk down the Valley of Silence,
   That lies far beyond mortal ken.

Do you ask what I found in the Valley?
   'Tis my trysting-place with the Divine;
And I fell at the feet of the Holy,
   And above me a voice said "Be mine!"
And there arose from the depths of my spirit
   An echo — "My heart shall be thine."

Do you ask how I live in the Valley?
   I weep — and I dream — and I pray.
But my tears are as sweet as the dewdrops
   That fall on the roses in May;

And my prayer, like a perfume from censers,
  Ascendeth to God night and day.

In the hush of the Valley of Silence
  I dream all the songs that I sing;
And the music floats down the dim Valley
  Till each finds a word for a wing,
That to hearts, like the dove of the Deluge,
  A message of peace they may bring.

But far on the deep there are billows
  That never shall break on the beach;
And I have heard songs in the silence,
  That never shall float into speech;
And I have had dreams in the Valley
  Too lofty for language to reach.

And I have seen Thoughts in the Valley.
  Ah me! how my spirit they stirred!
And they wear holy veils on their faces, —
  Their footsteps can scarcely be heard:
They pass through the Valley like virgins,
  Too pure for the touch of a word!

Do you ask me the place of the Valley,
  Ye hearts that are harrowed by care?
It lieth afar between mountains,
  And God and his angels are there;
And one is the dark mount of Sorrow,
  And one, — the bright mountain of Prayer.

COMPOSITION.

Write sentences containing the following: "Where angels have
flown;" "craved what the world cannot give;" "glimpse of its blue;"
"knelt long ago at an altar;" "too pure for the touch of a word."
Give last stanza in your own words.

| dim | ideal | perfume |
| bovers | mazes | harrowed |

MARGARET OF NEW ORLEANS.

In 1872 I was in the city of New Orleans, and among my first visits to public places was my visit to the Infant Orphan Asylum. I was pleased with the lovely grounds and the fine building. I said to myself: How wonderfully God helps those who labor for Him! These dear Sisters of Charity see God in His poor, and therefore they become servants of the suffering." I was welcomed warmly, and invited to wait for a few moments in a large reception room.

In front of me, over the mantel of the fireplace, hung a portrait which attracted my attention. It represented a woman whose countenance was brightened by an extraordinary expression of benevolence and spirituality. Two small children stood by her side and leaned upon her lap. The longer I looked, the more I was interested.

" I see, Madam," said the Sister, as she entered the room, " you are studying our portrait."

" Yes," I answered ; " I am wondering who this lady can be."

" That is Margaret, to whom we owe so much. She was once a poor woman, and a stranger in the city, but with her help our house has risen from poverty and become prosperous beyond all anticipation. Oh ! you must see our Margaret, or you will leave New Orleans without seeing one of its most interesting women."

Shortly after leaving the asylum my carriage reached the bakery of the benefactress of the orphan asylum. I alighted from the carriage and went into the office on the first floor.

Not more than half an hour elapsed when, to my

surprise, a pretty carriage drove up, and from it stepped out a counterpart of the portrait.

She paused a moment to hear from the office boy that I was waiting for her, and then she walked forward with the step and air of a queen. She greeted me very kindly. I told her that her portrait in the asylum had attracted my attention and had led me to make her this visit. "And now, Margaret, may I, too, call you Margaret?" I asked.

"Oh, yes! I would not know any other name; call me Margaret."

"I would like to know how it was that you became such a patron of the orphan asylum, as they tell me you are."

She looked kindly into my face, laid her hand motherly on my arm, and drawing her chair nearer to mine, said :—

"I had from childhood a great love for infants, particularly infant orphans. Our Lord gave me this love and the desire to work and care for them." Here her countenance lighted with the subject. "Would you," she asked, "like to hear my story?"

"Yes, Margaret, and from a better motive, I hope, than idle curiosity."

"Well, dear," she began, "when I first came to New Orleans the asylum had not long been opened. I had come to New Orleans from Baltimore. The Sisters told me of their great poverty and their need of a responsible person to take the place of cook. After entering on my duties, they left me to do as I pleased. I discovered that the two cows they had would help me to give some nourishing food, besides supplying drink for the infants. But at that time hay was very dear, particularly cartage to the asylum. By going myself for the hay, I could save a considerable sum each month ; but in order to avoid contact in the street with boys inclined to jeer at such a sight, I went with my wheelbarrow after day-break, and wheeled home a bale whenever I needed it. Little by little my humble efforts were blessed, and I then began to sell milk and cream.

"The demand became so great that we had to get more cows and a wagon. Still, I delivered the milk in the wagon, and did all the work of the kitchen. But one day a Sister sent by the superior came to the kitchen and announced that a member of the community would henceforth fill my place. I felt sorry to leave the asylum ; I was very happy in being able to serve these good women and the dear orphans, but my leaving the asylum was the means of putting me in a position where I would be able to do a greater share of good. I enlarged the milk business and with the profits bought this bakery."

I remarked, "you have, notwithstanding your dismissal, continued your large charity to the orphans."

"Yes," she replied, "I am only working in God's field, and for him only, and He has given the increase."

I was pleased and edified by this visit, and when parting with her I expressed the hope that we might meet again. Several letters passed between us, but we never had the pleasure of meeting.

Before parting I asked her who painted her portrait.

"Several artists had asked me to sit for my portrait, but I refused. The city desired my picture, but I would not grant a sitting. Finally an artist came who wished to paint my portrait for the asylum ; a number of the patrons had asked for it. I said that if they would pay the artist and give to the asylum a handsome sum of money, I would sit for the picture. My offer was accepted."

The only monument ever erected in the United States to a woman has been raised in New Orleans, since her death, to Margaret, whom the people love to call the lady of the city.

building	answered	community
bakery	asylum	supplying
suffering	monument	nourishing

Questions:—What are public places? Whom does God particularly bless? How can persons become prosperous? When does a boy or girl become idly curious? Give the names of some patrons of celebrated works? What is it to be edified? When do we work in God's field?

Commit to memory the following:

"For as the light
Not only serves to show, but render us
Mutually profitable; so our lives,
In act exemplary, not only win
Ourselves good names, but do to others give
Matter for virtue's deeds, by which we live."

———o———

HOPE.

Thomas Campbell, born in Scotland in 1777; died in 1844. His principal poems are "The Pleasures of Hope" and "Gertrude of Wyoming;" but it is to his lyrics, which are among the finest in any language, that Campbell owes his fame. "The Exile of Erin," "Lochiel's Warning," "O'Connor's Child," "Hohenlinden," "Ye Mariners of England," and many others, are familiar wherever the English tongue is spoken. The best evidence of Campbell's popularity is the great number of quotations from his poems which have passed into aphorisms.

AT summer eve, when heaven's ethereal bow
Spans with bright arch the glittering hills below,

Why to yon mountain turns the musing eye,
Whose sun-bright summit mingles with the sky?
Why do those cliffs of shadowy tint appear
More sweet than all the landscape smiling near?—
'Tis distance lends enchantment to the view,
And robes the mountain in its azure hue.
Thus, with delight we linger to survey
The promised joys of life's unmeasured way;
Thus, from afar, each dim-discover'd scene
More pleasing seems than all the past has been,
And every form that fancy can repair
From dark oblivion, glows divinely there.

HOPE.

Oliver Goldsmith (1728 – 1774), presented in his life and character the strangest mixture of genius and vagabondism. Failing to pass at the University of Dublin, he became in turn poor teacher, literary hack, medical quack and wandering minstrel. He tramped through Europe, living by his flute, and the result of his sight-seeing he gave to the world in the "Traveller." This made him known to fame, but his shiftlessness, improvidence and generosity always kept him struggling with want. His next great work, that by which he will ever be remembered, was "The Vicar of Wakefield." "The Deserted Village" and the comedy, "She Stoops to Conquer," were the last of his most famous productions. Goldsmith is one of those authors that are always *read*, while more magnificent names are only *praised*. In everything that he wrote there is a cheerfulness, a purity of sentiment, a quaint, droll humor, that seems to permeate his very *words*, and cause the printed page to speak like the author's luring voice. He is probably the best example in English Literature of what is called the "natural style."

THE wretch condemn'd with life to part,
 Still, still on hope relies;
 And every pang that rends the heart,
Bids expectation rise.

Hope, like the glimm'ring taper's light,
 Adorns and cheers the way;

And still, as darker grows the night,
Emits a brighter ray.

| musing | robes | glimm'ring |
| tint | oblivion | emits |

COMPOSITION.

Change the first four lines by Campbell. Explain: "'tis distance lends enchantment to the view," "we linger to survey," "from dark oblivion, glows divinely there."

Change the first stanza from Goldsmith.

———o———

THE RELIGIOUS MISSION OF THE IRISH PEOPLE.

THE real importance of a man or a people cannot be estimated by their worldly position. There is no more fatal error than to imagine that the future belongs to those who possess the present. To be great, man must unite himself with a great cause. He must lose his life in something higher and holier than himself before he can find its fullest power; and thus we may by experiment verify the truth that they who abandon all find all; and hence those whom God destines to do a divine and immortal work are taught wisdom by suffering and privation. Whom he loves he chastens, and whom he would use to great ends, he sorely tries.

Now the one constant and abiding cause, amid the rise and fall of empires, is religion, by which alone man can hope to be redeemed from the perishing elements which everywhere surround him; and the one and only true religion is that of Christ, who has founded forever the worship of God in spirit and in truth; and Christ's religion is historically expressed and embodied in the Catholic Church. She is God's real, authentic kingdom in this world, and to be called to do a great work for her is to have a sublime and a heavenly mission.

Though guided and protected by the Holy Spirit, she, in her progress through time, is in many ways left to the care and devotion of her children. As she may be attacked by men, she may also be defended by them; and her defenders know that, though open to attack, yet is she invincible: a standing miracle, and the world-wide example of the immutability of God's decrees.

It is good to fight for a power which is holy and strong, which is able to wring victory from defeat, and which is immortal. To die in such a cause were a man's chief glory, and God's providence can prepare no higher destiny for a people than to make them the witnesses and apostles of the truth as revealed in Christ.

And this, as I take it, is the religious mission of the Irish people in the new era upon which the Catholic Church is now entering. Let us, before we direct our thoughts to the present and future, cast a glance at the past. She has seen and known cities of men, and manners, climates, councils, governments. She has known the worst, and therefore trusts her destiny, and proclaims without fear her heavenly mission. She is certain of herself. She has definite aims and fixed purposes. It is surely something to have come down the long centuries and still to have faith and hope and love; to have a venerable past, and yet not despair of the future. And since the Church has already proven that she is able to live in this democratic land, will not the fact that she has lived in all the centuries since Christ was born, and in many climes, and amongst many people, in deserts and in catacombs, in tents of savages and in palaces of kings, throw the mystery and splendor as of the setting sun over her new rising in this other world?

If, now, we turn to explain this rebirth of Catholicism among the English speaking peoples, we must at once admit that the Irish race is the providential instrument through which God has wrought this marvellous revival. As in another age men spoke of the *gesta Dei per Francos*, so may we now speak of the *gesta Dei per Hibernos*. Were it not for Ireland, Catholicism would to-day be feeble and non-progressive in England, America and Australia. Nor is the force of this affirmation weakened by the weight and significance which must be given to what the converts in England, and the Germans and the French in the United States, have done for the Church. The Irish have made the work of the converts possible and effective, and they have given to Catholicism in this country a vigor and cohesiveness which enable it to assimilate the most heterogeneous elements, and without which it is not at all certain that the vast majority of Catholics emigrating hither from other lands would not have been lost to the Church. No other people could have done for the Catholic faith in the United States what the Irish people have done. Their unalterable attachment to their priests; their deep Catholic instincts, which no combination of circumstances has ever been able to bring into conflict with their love of country; the unworldly and spiritual temper of the national character; their indifference to ridicule and contempt, and their unfailing generosity, all fitted them for the work which was to be done, and enabled them, in spite of the strong prejudices against their race, which Americans have inherited from England, to accomplish what could not have been accomplished by Italian, French or German Catholics.

At the **breaking** out of the war of independence there

were not more than twenty-five thousand Catholics in a population of three millions; and this handful of believers was sunk in a life of religious ignorance and indifference. They had not, like the Catholics of England and Ireland, a past history filled with glorious names and their hallowed memories. Great cathedrals reared by Catholic hands did not look down upon them to speak of the faith and charity of their fathers, and sad ruins did not plead with them to rebuild the desecrated sanctuary of God. They had lost sight of Europe, and found themselves in a new world with the old faith, and yet without visible evidence, or almost any knowledge of the mighty things which it had wrought in the past.

An observer who, a hundred years ago, should have considered the religious condition of this country, could have discovered no sign whatever that might have led him to suppose that the faith of this little body of Catholics was to have a future in the American Republic; whereas now there are many reasons for thinking that no other religion is so sure of a future here as the Catholic. The Church in the United States is no longer confined to three or four counties of a single State. It is co-extensive with the country, embracing North and South, East and West. It is a great and public fact which man cannot, if he would, ignore.

It is our only historic religion. Outside its fold there are views and opinions, but here is an organism which shoots its roots deep into the hidden strata of buried ages. None others had received the same providential training for this work; of no other people had God required such proofs of love.

Like the children of Israel, the Irish had borne the

yoke of bondage; had been rescued from the sea of blood and had wandered for weary years in the desert, without home, without country; cut off from all contact with other people, and saved from despair and death only by the presence of the pillar of fire which is God's Catholic Church.

Their very language had died away upon their lips, and they began to speak the tongue of the persecutor whom they were to evangelize. Nothing was left them but faith and virtue, that they might fully realize that these are the best gifts of God, and are enough. They found Christ's Church, which was to be their only hope, poor and lowly as the infant Saviour in the stable of Bethlehem; but kings and wise men brought no offerings of gold, incense, and myrrh. The heavenly bride was left alone with the priest and the people, despised, unthought of, like the divine Master on the cross, that so the poor might gather about her as in the early ages, and learn to know her·hidden beauty. There were no mystic ceremonies, no rich altar; there was no stately cathedral, no pomp and splendor of worship—none of all those things through which alone, it is thought, the Church holds sway over the multitude; and yet they knelt to her with hearts of purest love, nor cared to have either a home or a country, if she were not there!

Questions:—Give the first sentence in two ways. Who find all? Prove this from the New Testament. What is God's kingdom on Earth? To whose care and devotion is she in part left? What is the highest mission God can give a man? How was Catholicity situated in the early days of the United States? What characteristics fitted the Irish for their religious mission in America? Give the following passages in your own words:

"Outside its fold ... .. strata of buried ages." "There were no mystic........if she were not there."

experiment   significance   organism
chastens   cohesiveness   evangelize
elements   assimilate   comeliness
invincible   prejudices   splendor

KING ROBERT OF SICILY.

ROBERT of Sicily, brother of Pope Urbane
    And Valmond, emperor of Allemaine,
Apparell'd in magnificent attire,
With retinue of many a knight and squire,
On St. John's Eve, at Vespers, proudly sat
And heard the priests chant the Magnificat.
And as he listen'd, o'er and o'er again
Repeated, like a burden or refrain,
He caught the words, "*Deposuit potentes
De sede, et exaltavit humiles;*"
And slowly lifting up his kingly head,
He to a learned clerk beside him said,
"What mean these words?"   The clerk made answer meet

"He has put down the mighty from their seat,
And has exalted them of low degree."
Thereat King Robert mutter'd scornfully,
"'Tis well that such seditious words are sung
Only by priests, and in the Latin tongue;
For unto priests and people be it known,
There is no power can push me from my throne."
And leaning back, he yawn'd and fell asleep,
Lull'd by the chant monotonous and deep.

When he awoke, it was already night;
The church was empty, and there was no light,
Save where the lamps, that glimmer'd few and faint,
Lighted a little space before some saint.

He started from his seat and gazed around,
But saw no living thing and heard no sound.
He groped towards the door, but it was lock'd;
He cried aloud, and listen'd, and then knock'd,
And utter'd awful threatenings and complaints
And imprecations upon men and saints.   .
The sounds re-echo'd from the roof and walls
As if dead priests were laughing in their stalls.

At length the sexton, hearing from without
The tumult of the knocking and the shout,
And thinking thieves were in the house of prayer,
Came with his lantern, asking, "Who is there?"
Half choked with rage, King Robert fiercely said,
"Open — 'tis I, the king! Art thou afraid?"
The frighten'd sexton, muttering with a curse,
"This is some drunken vagabond, or worse,"
Turn'd the great key, and flung the portal wide;
A man rush'd by him at a single stride,
Haggard, half naked, without hat or cloak,
Who neither turn'd nor look'd at him, nor spoke,
But leap'd into the blackness of the night,
And vanish'd like a spectre from his sight.

Robert of Sicily, brother of Pope Urbane
And Valmond, emperor of Allemaine,
Despoil'd of his magnificent attire,
Bareheaded, breathless, and besprent with mire,
With sense of wrong and outrage desperate,
Strode on and thunder'd at the palace gate;
Rush'd through the court-yard, thrusting in his rage
To right and left each seneschal and page,
And hurried up the broad and sounding stair,
His white face ghastly in the torches' glare.
From hall to hall he pass'd with breathless speed;
Voices and cries he heard, but did not heed;

Until at last he reach'd the banquet room,
Blazing with light, and breathing with perfume.
There on the dais sat another king,
Wearing his robes, his crown, his signet ring;
King Robert's self in features, form and height,
But all transfigured with angelic light!
It was an angel, and his presence there
With a divine effulgence fill'd the air,
An exaltation, piercing the disguise,
Though none the hidden angel recognize.

A moment speechless, motionless, amazed,
The throneless monarch on the angel gazed,
Who met his looks of anger and surprise
With the divine compassion of his eyes;
Then said, "Who art thou? and why com'st thou here?"
To which King Robert answer'd with a sneer,
"I am the king, and come to claim my own
From an impostor, who usurps my throne!"
And suddenly, at these audacious words,
Up sprang the angry guests, and drew their swords.
The angel answer'd, with unruffled brow,
"Nay, not the king, but the king's jester; thou
Henceforth shalt wear the bells and scallop'd cape,
And for thy counsellor shalt lead an ape;
Thou shalt obey my servants when they call,
And wait upon my henchmen in the hall."

Deaf to King Robert's threats and cries and prayers,
They thrust him from the hall and down the stairs;
A group of tittering pages ran before,
And as they open'd wide the folding door
His heart fail'd; for he heard, with strange alarms,
The boisterous laughter of the men-at-arms,
And all the vaulted chamber roar and ring
With the mock plaudits of "Long live the king!"

Next morning, waking with the day's first beam,
He said within himself, "It was a dream!"
But the straw rustled as he turn'd his head;
There were the cap and bells beside his bed,
Around him rose the bare, discolor'd walls,
Close by the steeds were champing in their stalls,
And in the corner, a revolting shape,
Shivering and chattering, sat the wretched ape.
It was no dream; the world he loved so much
Had turn'd to dust and ashes at his touch!

Days came and went; and now return'd again
To Sicily the old Saturnian reign;
Under the angel's governance benign
The happy island danced with corn and wine,
And deep within the mountain's burning breast
Enceladus, the giant, was at rest.
Meanwhile King Robert yielded to his fate,
Sullen and silent and disconsolate.
Dress'd in the motley garb that jesters wear,
With looks bewilder'd and a vacant stare,
Close shaven above the ears, as monks are shorn,
By courtiers mock'd, by pages laughed to scorn,
His only friend the ape, his only food
What others left, --- he still was unsubdued.
And when the angel met him on his way,
And half in earnest, half in jest, would say —
Sternly, though tenderly, that he might feel
The velvet scabbard held a sword of steel —
"Art thou the king?" the passion of his woe
Burst from him in resistless overflow,
And, lifting high his forehead, he would fling
The haughty answer back, "I am, I am the king!"

Almost three years were ended, when there came
Ambassadors of great repute and name

From Valmond, emperor of Allemaine,
Unto King Robert, saying that Pope Urbane
By letter summon'd them forthwith to come
On Holy Thursday to his city of Rome.
The angel with great joy received his guests,
And gave them presents of embroidered vests,
And velvet mantles with rich ermine lined,
And rings and jewels of the rarest kind.
Then he departed with them o'er the sea
Into the lovely land of Italy,
Whose loveliness was more resplendent made
By the mere passing of that cavalcade,
With plumes, and cloaks, and housings, and the stir
Of jewell'd bridle and of golden spur.

And lo, among the menials, in mock state,
Upon a piebald steed, with shambling gait,
His cloak of fox-tails flapping in the wind,
The solemn ape demurely perch'd behind,
King Robert rode, making huge merriment
In all the country towns through which they went.

The Pope received them with great pomp, and blare
Of banner'd trumpets, in St. Peter's square,
Giving his benediction and embrace,
Fervent, and full of apostolic grace.
While with congratulations and with prayers
He entertain'd the angel unawares,
Robert, the jester, bursting through the crowd,
Into their presence rush'd, and cried aloud,
"I am the king!   Look, and behold in me
Robert, your brother, King of Sicily!
This man, who wears my semblance to your eyes,
Is an impostor in a king's disguise.
Do you not know me?   Does no voice within
Answer my cry, and say we are akin?"

The Pope, in silence, but with troubled mien,
Gazed at the angel's countenance serene;
The emperor, laughing, said, "It is strange sport
To keep a madman for thy ool at court!"
And the poor baffled jester in disgrace
Was hustled back among the populace.

In solemn state the Holy Week went by,
And Easter Sunday gleam'd upon the sky;
The presence of the angel, with its light,
Before the sun rose, made the city bright,
And with new fervor fill'd the hearts of men,
Who felt that Christ indeed had risen again.
Even the jester, on his bed of straw,
With haggard eyes th' unwonted splendor saw;
He felt within a power unfelt before,
And, kneeling humbly on his chamber floor,
He heard the rushing garments of the Lord
Sweep through the silent air, ascending heavenward.

And now the visit ending, and once more
Valmond returning to the Danube's shore,
Homeward the angel journey'd, and again
The land was made resplendent with his train,
Flashing along the towns of Italy
Unto Salerno, and from there by sea.
And when once more within Palermo's wall,
And seated on the throne in his great hall,
He heard the Angelus from convent towers,
As if the better world conversed with ours,
He beckon'd to King Robert to draw nigher,
And with a gesture bade the rest retire;
And when they were alone the angel said,
"Art thou the king?" Then, bowing down his head,
King Robert cross'd both hands upon his breast,
And meekly answer'd him: "Thou knowest best!

My sins as scarlet are; let me go hence,
And in some cloister's school of penitence,
Across those stones, that pave the way to heaven,
Walk barefoot till my guilty soul is shriven!"
The angel smiled, and from his radiant face
A holy light illumined all the place;
And through the open window, loud and clear,
They heard the monks chant in the chapel near,
Above the stir and tumult of the street:
"He has put down the mighty from their seat,
And has exalted them of low degree!"
And through the second melody
Rose like the throbbing of a single string:
"I am an angel, and thou art the king!"
King Robert, who was standing near the throne,
Lifted his eyes, and, lo, he was alone!
But all apparell'd as in days of old,
With ermined mantle and with cloth of gold;
And when his courtiers came, they found him there,
Kneeling upon the floor, absorb'd in silent prayer.—

COMPOSITION.

Select a text from the Holy Bible or some other good book, as an introduction to a sketch of Robert of Sicily. Tell something about Sicily, and describe the church in which the Vespers are being sung. Relate how Robert listened, and was annoyed at the saying: "He has put down the mighty from their seat." Give an idea of the great stillness after all had retired save Robert. Robert's conduct before darting into darkness. His mad course through the streets. How he resembled a spectre.

Take balance of lesson, and talk the matter over as a class, making each scholar give a portion of the description, in a consecutive way, that all the sayings, following in due order, may form a narrative verbally given.

apparell'd	despoil'd	bewildered
retinue	besprent	unsubdued
knight	seneschal	ambassadors

LITTLE WILFRID.

A N Angel's tears must be all joys. There is no unhappiness among the Angels.

Sorrow is not unhappiness. This is a great secret ;
indeed, it is the great secret of the world. All the
world is always nearly telling it, nearly, but not quite.
When the leaves rustle on the trees, they want to tell
it. When the stars twinkle, as if they had tears in
their eyes, they almost tell the secret by their looks.
When the sea beats with a hollow sound upon the
sand, it murmurs the great secret of the world, that
sorrow is not unhappiness.

You did not know little Wilfrid ; I saw him only
once myself. It was easy to see that he was a child
who had some great vocation from God. It is not
grown-up men only who have vocations. Children
make a little Catholic Church, where God is always
being loved and served in a particular way ; and in
this Child-Church there are wonderful things done.
It is very much mixed up with the kingdom of the
Angels. It also has sorrow of its own, and joys of
its own, beautiful, mysterious vocations sent by our
Heavenly Father.

Wilfrid had one of these vocations. You might
have been certain he would have to suffer, and that
he would have the grace to love suffering, because he
was so merry a child. His soul was full of brightness and gladness, even to overflowing. These are
the children out of whom strong men are made.
Strength comes out of brightness. Endurance depends on happiness.

Wilfrid was one of those children the very sight of
whom makes old people young again. Somehow,

even when he talked nonsense, he made you think of
God and heaven; and when he laughed, you felt a
wish to shed sweet tears. There are many children
who live more in the night than in the day. They
are wise and old in their dreams by night, even when
they are light and careless in their games and tasks
by day. This was the case with Wilfrid, and if you
had shut your eyes when he was telling one of his
dreams, you would have thought it was some grown-
up poet or artist who was describing things. His
descriptions were almost unnatural, they were so like
the descriptions of an educated man. But there he
was, with his black hair and with barely seven summers twinkling in his eyes.

One afternoon Wilfrid had a severe headache, and
he went to bed. He had been sleeping for an hour.
His mother kissed him, and it seemed as if the kiss
awoke him. He found he had turned his face on one
side, where a little, white crucifix was lying, and that
his forehead was pressing upon it, and that the pain
was greater than before. His mother dipped a handkerchief in vinegar to bind round his head, and as she
stooped over to tie it on, he put out his hand, and
taking the handkerchief, squeezed some of the vinegar
into his mouth and swallowed it.

"Why have you done that, my darling child?" said
his mother.

"Because I was thirsty, and I wished to be like
Jesus."

As he said this he smiled into his mother's face.
It was a wonderful smile; it was as if he had in his
sleep grown as old as the oldest saint, and as wise as
the wisest Doctor in the Church, and yet was as arch
and as playful and simple a child as ever. I am sure,

his mother will never forget that look as long as she lives.

Have you ever felt one of those summer afternoons, which are so beautiful that you do not even like to play, but prefer to sit still, and let yourself be happy, you do not know how or why? The quietness is so quiet that you can almost hear it breathing ; the flowers smell with an unusual sweetness ; the trees seem to have gone to sleep, and no birds are singing. Even the cows in the field lie down. The church clock trembles while it strikes, as if it were almost afraid of doing wrong in striking at such a peaceful time.

It was a calm like this while Wilfrid was sleeping. But there came a freshness towards evening, and an awakening of all nature. There was a sound of air in the tree-tops, like the murmur of a distant sea. The cattle rose and began to crop the grass, and the birds also began to sing. Wilfrid also awoke. He awoke that he might die. His vespers were to be sung in Heaven. The evening was to be to him an everlasting morning.

Outside the house the sun still shone very brightly, and it seemed in the silent rooms as if the birds had never sung so loud before. Wilfrid sank very quietly. Some children belong to God and to their mothers ; but some seem to belong to God only. These die soon, and they like to die. Yet they love their mothers better than other children do. They are happy mothers who have such children. We call them God's Early Blossoms. Most mothers have one such.

Before the sun went down Wilfrid was gone. There was one look in his eyes as if some new kind of pain startled him, and then a look of peace into his mother's face, a look which told her all was well. He was now part of God's pure glory, and his home was among the saints forever.

Questions :—What is meant by a vocation ? What are dreams? Have
children vocations as well as grown-up persons? Give the names of
some prominent artists. The name of one American poet. What is a
Doctor of the Church? Explain the sentence "But there came a
freshness towards evening." Write a description of Wilfrid, using
your own words.

rustle	mysterious	endurance	vocations
particular	twinkle	vespers	describing
swallowed	murmurs	dipped	handkerchief

———o———

WORDS OF STRENGTH.

THERE are three lessons I would write,
 Three words, as with a burning pen,
In tracings of eternal light,
 Upon the hearts of men.

Have hope!   Though clouds environ now,
 And gladness hides her face in scorn,
Put thou the shadow from thy brow,
 No night but hath its morn.

Have faith!   Where'er thy bark is driven—
 The calm's disport, the tempest's mirth ;—
Know this—God rules the hosts of heaven,
 The inhabitants of earth.

Have love!   Not love alone for one,
 But man as man thy brother call,
And scatter, like the circling seed,
 Thy charities on all.

Thus grave these lessons on thy soul—
 Hope, Faith, and Love—and thou shalt find
Strength, when life's surges rudest roll,
 Light, when thou else wert blind.

LIVING WELL.

He liveth long who liveth well!
All other life is short and vain;
He liveth longest who can tell
Of living most for heavenly gain.

———o———

TO A WATER-FOWL.

WHITHER, midst falling dew,
  While glow the heavens with the last steps of day,
Far through their rosy depths dost thou pursue
  Thy solitary way?

Vainly the fowler's eye
  Might mark thy distant flight to do thee wrong,
As, darkly painted on the crimson sky,
  Thy figure floats along.

Seek'st thou the plashy brink
  Of weedy lake, or marge of river wide,
Or where the rocking billows rise and sink
  On the chafed ocean side?

There is a power whose care
  Teaches thy way along that pathless coast,
The desert and illimitable air,
  Lone wandering, but not lost.

All day thy wings have fanned,
  At that far height, the cold, thin atmosphere,
Yet stoop not, weary, to the welcome land,
  Though the dark night is near.

And soon that toil shall end;
  So shalt thou find a summer home, and rest,

And scream among thy fellows; reeds shall bend
  Soon o'er thy shelter'd nest.

Thou'rt gone; the abyss of heaven
  Hath swallowed up thy form; yet on my heart
Deeply hath sunk the lesson thou hast given,
  And shall not soon depart.

He who from zone to zone
  Guides through the boundless sky thy certain flight,
In the long way that I must tread alone,
  Will lead my steps aright.

COMPOSITION.

Write first stanza in your own words. Write the question asked
in third stanza. Speak of the power meant in fourth and last stanzas.

crimson   plashy   illimitable   abyss   zone   tread

———o———

NECESSITY OF RELIGION.

SO far from wishing to proscribe religious instruction,
I maintain that it is more essential at this day than
ever. The more a man grows, the more he ought to
believe. As he draws nearer to God, the better ought
he to recognize his existence. It is the wretched
tendency of our times to base all calculations, all efforts,
on this life only; to crowd every thing into this narrow
span. In limiting man's end and aim to this terrestrial
and material existence, we aggravate all his miseries by
the terrible negation at its close. We add to the
burdens of the unfortunate the insupportable weight of
a hopeless hereafter. God's law of suffering we convert·
by our unbelief, into hell's law of despair. Hence these
deplorable social convulsions.

That I am one of those who desire — I will not say with sincerity merely, but with inexpressible ardor, and by all possible means — to ameliorate the material condition of the suffering classes in this life, no one in this assembly will doubt. But the first and greatest of amelioration is to impart hope. How do our finite miseries dwindle in the presence of an infinite hope! Our first duty, then, whether we be clergymen or laymen, bishops or legislators, priests or writers, is not merely to direct all our social energies to the abatement of physical misery, but, at the same time, to lift every drooping head towards heaven — to fix the attention and the faith of every human soul on that ulterior life, where justice shall preside, where justice shall be awarded! Let us proclaim it aloud to all: No one shall unjustly or needlessly suffer! Death is restitution. The law of the material world is gravitation: of the moral world, equity. At the end of all re-appears God. Let us not forget; let us everywhere teach it, — there would be no dignity in life, it would not be worth the holding, if in death we wholly perish. All that lightens labor and sanctifies toil — all that renders man brave, good, wise, patient, benevolent, just, humble, and, at the same time, great, worthy of intelligence, worthy of liberty — is to have perpetually before him the vision of a better world, darting its rays of celestial splendor through the dark shadows of this present life.

For myself, since chance will have it that words of such gravity should at this time fall from lips of such little authority, let me be permitted here to say, and to proclaim from the elevation of this tribune, that I believe, that I most profoundly and reverently believe, in that better world. It is to me more real, more substantial, more positive in its effects, than this evanescence which we cling to and call life. It is unceasingly before my eyes. I believe in it with all the strength of my convictions; and, after many struggles and much study and experience, it is the supreme certainty of my reason, as it is the supreme consolation of my soul!

I desire, therefore, most sincerely, strenuously and fervently, that there should be religious instruction but let it be an instruction of the Gospel, and have heaven, not earth, for its end!

proscribe	social	equity
essential	sincerity	perpetually
recognize	ameliorate	tribune
tendency	dwindle	reverently
calculations	ulterior	substantial
aggravate	restitution	evanescence
deplorable	gravitation	unceasingly

COMPOSITION.

Copy the third paragraph. Write the following sentences in two different ways:

(a) I most profoundly and reverently believe in a better world. (b) There would be no dignity in life, it would not be worth holding, if in death we wholly perish. (c) So far from wishing to proscribe religious instruction, I maintain that it is more essential at this day than ever. (d) Man should perpetually have before him the vision of a better world, darting its rays of celestial splendor through the dark shadows of this present life.

---o---

THE BLIND MEN AND THE ELEPHANT.

IT was six men of Indostan,
    To learning much inclined,
Who went to see the Elephant
    (Though all of them were blind),

That each by observation
  Might satisfy his mind.

The first approached the Elephant,
  And happening to fall
Against his broad and sturdy side,
  At once began to bawl:
" Why, bless me! — but the Elephant
  Is very like a wall! "

The second, feeling of the tusk,
  Cried, " Ho! — what have we here,
So very round and smooth and sharp?
  To me 'tis mighty clear,
This wonder of an Elephant
  Is very like a spear! "

The third approached the animal,
  And happening to take
The squirming trunk within his hands,
  Thus boldly up and spake:
" I see," quoth he, " the Elephant
  Is very like a snake! "

The fourth reached out his eager hand,
  And felt about the knee.
" What most this wondrous beast is like,
  Is very plain," quoth he;
" 'Tis clear enough, the Elephant
  Is very like a tree! "

The fifth, who chanced to touch the ear,
  Said, " E'en the blindest man
Can tell what this resembles most;
  Deny the fact who can,
This marvel of an Elephant
  Is very like a fan! "

The sixth no sooner had begun
  About the beast to grope,
Than, seizing on the swinging tail
  That fell within his scope,
"I see," quoth he, "the Elephant
  Is very like a rope!"

And so these men of Indostan
  Disputed loud and long,
Each in his own opinion
  Exceeding stiff and strong,
Though each was partly in the right,
  And all were in the wrong!

MORAL.

So, oft in philosophic wars,
  The disputants, I ween,
Rail on in utter ignorance
  Of what each other mean,
And prate about an Elephant
  Not one of them has seen!

COMPOSITION.

Go over the stanzas and give each blind man's saying, in your own words. Describe the action performed by each while speaking. Give the *moral* in three ways, — in the first, second and third persons.

observation	resembles	disputants
sturdy	marvel	ween
squirming	scope	rail
quoth	philosophic	prate

-----o-----

INTELLECTUAL EDUCATION.

IT has often been truly observed that, when the eyes of the infant are first opened upon the world, the **reflected** rays of light, which strike them from the myriad of surrounding objects, present to him no image, but a medley of colors and shadows.

They do not form into a whole; they do not rise into foregrounds and melt into distances; they do not divide into groups; they do not coalesce into unities; they do not combine into persons; but each particular hue and tint stands by itself, wedged in amid a thousand others upon the vast and flat mosaic, having no intelligence, and conveying no story, any more than the wrong side of some rich tapestry.

The little babe stretches out his arms and fingers, as if to grasp or to fathom the many-colored visions; and thus he gradually learns the connection of part with part, separates what moves from what is stationary, watches the coming and going of figures, masters the idea of shape and of perspective, calls in the information conveyed through the other senses to assist him in his mental process, and thus gradually converts a kaleidoscope into a picture.

The first view was the more splendid, the second the more real; the former more poetical, the latter more philosophical. Alas! what are we doing all through life, both as a necessity and as a duty, but unlearning the world's poetry, and attaining to its prose! This is our education, as boys and as men, in the action of life, and in the closet or library; in our affections, in our aims, in our hopes, and in our memories.

And in like manner it is the education of our intellect. I say that one main portion of intellectual education, of the labors of both school and university, is to remove the original dimness of the mind's eye; to strengthen and perfect its vision; to enable it to look out into the world right forward, steadily and truly; to give the mind clearness, accuracy, precision; to enable it to use words aright, to understand what it says, to conceive justly what it thinks about, to abstract, compare, analyze, divide, define, and reason correctly.

There is a particular science which takes these matters in hand, and it is called logic; but it is not by logic, certainly not by logic alone, that the faculty I speak of is acquired. The infant does not learn to spell and read the hues upon his retina by any scientific rule; nor does the student learn accuracy of thought by any manual or treatise. The instruction given him, of whatever kind, if it be really instruction, is mainly, or at least pre-eminently, this,—a discipline in accuracy of mind.

Questions:—What does Cardinal Newman mean by "the world's poetry" and "the world's prose"? Explain: "they do not coalesce into unities;" "the original dimness of the mind's eye." Name some "foregrounds" and some "distances" in the country surrounding the place in which you live. Mention six *stationary* things of importance in your parish. What are mental processes? Name four great libraries. Name four or five remarkable men converted about the same time as Cardinal Newman.

myriad	mosaic	kaleidoscope	analyze
coalesce	perspective	closet	retina

————o————

THE FEAST OF SS. PETER AND PAUL IN ROME.

TO know what Saint Peter is to Christendom one must come to Rome. We may talk about the feast of St. Philip Neri, or of Saint Aloysius, in Rome. They are very wonderful, certainly; but the feast of SS. Peter and Paul, as kept in the Basilica of Saint Peter, completely absorbs that of all other saints; stands above them all in the very same way in which

Saint Peter stands above them as the Prince of the Apostles. One comprehends on the 29th of June, in Rome, how Saint Paul could say: "I condescended not to flesh and blood. Neither went I to Jerusalem to the apostles who were before me; but I went to Arabia, and again I returned to Damascus. Then, after three years, I went to Jerusalem to see Peter," to see Peter as the head of that visible Church against which the " gates of hell should not prevail."

All these things had a new reality about them, as we drove towards Saint Peter's a little after five o'clock, on the afternoon of the 28th of June, to attend the first vespers of the feast of the morrow. There was something contagious, too, in the enthusiasm of this crowd setting steadily towards Ponte San Angelo, then growing denser and denser as it surged through the two narrow streets leading to San Pietro, until the crowd emerged on the great piazza.

Nowhere in the world can such a crowd be gathered as in this piazza and in this basilica. We stood to watch them. Crowds on foot, crowds in carriages, crowds in omnibuses; old and young, even infants in arms; rich and poor, literally from the prince to the beggar. Priests in Roman hat and soutane; Benedictine monks; every shade and variety of sandalled, bare-headed Franciscans in their brown or black habits, bearded as Capuchins, or closely shaven; Dominicans, in the white habit and black cloak of the preaching friars; Carmelites, in white cloaks; Passionists; Redemptorists; Brothers of the Christian Schools; Sisters of Charity, and Sisters in all sorts of white bonnets and black bonnets, quilled-frills and veils; long lines of Seminarians in red, purple, black; and all these divisions divided and subdivided by sashes and stripes of red or blue braid to distinguish their several college:

As we lifted the heavy curtains at the door, w
heard the pulsations of the organs in the prelude fc
vespers and were in time to catch, not the first cras
of a chorus of a hundred voices, but the clear swee
ness of one voice in the antiphon. To this antipho
succeeded the psalm, its verses sung by alternat
choirs, in the high wonderful harmony of voices givin,
forth celestial canticles ; voices which seem to hav
been fed on an "ampler ether, a diviner air," thai
those of other mortals. No matter how high thos
voices might soar, they were sure to float in thos
upper regions, nor did they ever lose the sweetness o
their natural warble.

But where were the thousands on thousands whc
had entered Saint Peter's while we stood to watch
them ? They were all within, and so were the thousands they found there before them ; but there was no
jostling, no crowding, no hurry. There were no seats
within ; and just as great a variety as we had seen enter, might be seen perched on the bases of the great
columns or on the steps of Altars and Confessionals,
or, in numbers not to be counted, standing patiently
for hours, between the two choirs and before the sanctuary in front of Saint Peter's choir, where were the
Cardinal, with his readers and cantors, and all the
canons of the Basilica. Hundreds, too, were kneeling
around the confession of SS. Peter and Paul, adorned
as it was with immense bouquets, and garlands of nat-
urals flowers, and tall wax candles, towering above the
lamps. On the floor of the confession was laid one of
those tapestry carpets, on which the arms of Pope
Sixtus V. are to be seen. Then another multitude
gathered around Saint Peter as he sat in his chair,

dressed in his mitre and cope, in all the glory of the chief Bishop; while on the hand raised in blessing was the ring of his high office. Another multitude could be seen before the Chapel of the Blessed Sacrament, where the music of the choirs was to be heard, perhaps, finer than anywhere else, softened as it was by distance, and changed from a mortal song into one which angels might have sung.

But it was not for this reason that this multitude lingered where they were. Absorbed in adoration, the music was only a part of the inspiration which urged them to send up their whole souls in prayer to God, while something akin to this was to be seen all along, down the grand nave and in the side-chapels, until we came to the chapel of the Mother of Dolors, to see before that most sorrowful image a few heads bent to the ground in supplication.

Questions:—For what is St. Peter's Church in Rome renowned? Give the meaning of the word contagious? When are people enthusiastic? What are Seminarians, Passionists, Dominicans? Who founded the Passionists? Write a composition describing the music.

comprehends　　　Capuchins　　　antiphon

————o————

AUDUBON AT NIAGARA.

AFTER wandering on some of our great lakes for many months, I bent my course toward the celebrated Falls of Niagara, being desirous of taking a sketch of them. This was not my first visit to them, and I hoped it would not be the last. Returning, as I thus was, from a tedious journey, and possessing little more than some drawings of rare birds and plants, I reached the tavern at Niagara Falls in such plight as might have deterred many an individual from obtruding himself upon a circle of well-clad and, perhaps, well-bred society.

Months had passed since the last of my linen had been taken from my body and used to clean my gun. I was, in fact, just like one of the poorer class of Indians, and was rendered even more disagreeable to the eye of civilized man by not having, like them, plucked my beard or trimmed my hair in any way. Had Hogarth been living, he could not have found a fitter subject for a Robinson Crusoe. My beard covered my neck in front. My hair fell much lower at my back: the leather dress which I wore had for months stood in need of repair; a large knife hung at my side; a rusty tin box contained my drawings and colors and, wrapped up in a worn-out blanket that had served me for a bed, was buckled to my shoulders.

To every one I must have seemed immersed in the depths of poverty, perhaps of despair. Nevertheless, as I cared little about my appearance during those happy rambles, I pushed into the sitting-room, unstrapped my burden, and asked how soon breakfast would be ready. No one knew who I was, and the landlord, looking at me with an eye of close scrutiny, answered that breakfast would be on the table as soon as the company would come down from their rooms. I approached this important personage, told him of my avocations, and convinced him that he might feel safe as to remuneration.

We talked a good deal of the many artists who had visited the falls that season, and he offered such accommodations as I might require to finish my drawings. He left me, and as I looked about the room I saw several views of the falls, by which I was so disgusted that I suddenly came to my better senses. "What!" thought I; "have I come here to mimic nature in her grandest enterprises, and add my caricature of one of the wonders of the world to those which I here see? No: I give up the vain attempt. I will look on these mighty cataracts, and imprint them where they alone can be represented—on my mind!"

---o---

CHARACTER OF WASHINGTON.

NO matter what may be the birthplace of such a man as WASHINGTON, no climate can claim, no country can appropriate him: the boon of Providence to the human race, his fame is eternity; his residence creation. Though it was the defeat of our arms, and the disgrace of our policy, I almost bless the convulsion in which he had his origin: if the heavens thundered and the earth rocked, yet when the storm passed, how pure was the climate that it cleared; how bright in the brow of the firmament was the planet it revealed to us! In the production of Washington, it does really appear as if nature was endeavoring to improve on herself, and that all the virtues of the ancient world were but so many studies preparatory to the patriot of the new.

Individual instances no doubt there were; splendid exemplifications of some single qualification: Cæsar was merciful; Scipio was continent; Hannibal was patient; but it was reserved for Washington to blend them all in one, and like the lovely masterpiece of the Grecian artist, to exhibit in one glow of associated beauty, the pride of every model, and the perfection of every master.

As a general, he marshalled the peasant into a veteran,

and supplied by discipline the absence of experience.
As a statesman, he enlarged the policy of the Cabinet
into a comprehensive system of general advantage
and such was the wisdom of his views, and such the
philosophy of his counsels, that to the soldier and the
statesman he almost added the character of sage.

A conqueror, he was untainted with the crime of blood;
a revolutionist, he was free from any stain of treason; for
aggression commenced the contest, and a country called
him to the command; liberty unsheathed his sword;
necessity stained, victory returned it. If he had paused
here, history might doubt what station to assign him;
whether at the head of her citizens or her soldiers,
her heroes or her patriots. But the last glorious act
crowned his career, and banished hesitation. Who like
Washington, after having freed a country, resigned her
crown and retired to a cottage rather than reign in a
capitol!

Immortal man! He took from the battle its crime,
and from the conquest its chains; he left the glory of
his self-denial to the victorious, and turned upon the
vanquished only the retribution of his mercy. Happy,
proud America! The lightnings of heaven yielded to
your philosophy! The temptations of earth could not
seduce your patriotism!

COMPOSITION.

Write in three ways:

(a) Washington exhibited in one glow of beauty the pride of every
model, the perfection of every master. *(b)* A conqueror, he was
untainted with the crime of blood. *(c)* Liberty unsheathed his sword,
necessity stained, victory returned it. *(d)* Washington, after having
freed a country, resigned her crown and retired to a cottage rather
than reign in a capitol.

Memorize second and third paragraphs.

THE RIVER.

RIVER! River! little River!
　Bright you sparkle on your way,
O'er the yellow pebbles dancing,
Through the flowers and foliage glancing,
　Like a child at play.

River! River! swelling River!
　On you rush o'er rough and smooth,
Louder, faster, brawling, leaping
Over rocks, by rose-banks sweeping,
　Like impetuous youth.

River! River! brimming River!
　Broad and deep and still as time,
Seeming *still* — yet *still* in motion,
Tending onward to the ocean,
　Just like mortal prime.

River! River! rapid River!
　Swifter now you slip away;
Swift and silent as an arrow
Through a channel dark and narrow,
　Like life's closing day.

River! River! headlong River!
　Down you dash into the sea;
Sea, that line hath never sounded,
Sea, that voyage hath never rounded,
　Like Eternity.

Questions: — What is said of the river, in first stanza. To what is it compared? Explain the comparison. Why is the river like impetuous youth? Give difference between two uses of word *still* in third stanza. How is the river like an arrow? How like Eternity? What is a "sounding line" called?

| foliage | impetuous | prime |
| brawling | lending | rounded |

ANALYSIS.

AGREEABLE EXPRESSION.

"Pay close attention to the emotions or feelings the selectioi suggests."

"Give due attention to the vocal tones called for by the selection."

"Lay special stress on those points that are to attract the attentioi of an audience."

What are the emotions suggested by "The River"?

In the first stanza, a feeling of innocent mirth, requiring "full lively and elastic" expression.

"The River" is here personified, and is to be addressed in the usual joyful, colloquial tones. Thus,

> River ! River ! LITTLE RIVER !
> Bright you sparkle on your way
> O'er the yellow pebbles DANCING,
> Through the flowers and foliage GLANCING,
> LIKE A CHILD AT PLAY.

The last line contains the pith of the stanza, hence "a tone-coloring should call attention to" this "figure of speech, that might otherwise pass unperceived."

In the second stanza we have the idea of combat or struggle, requiring bold, defiant tones. Thus,

> River ! River ! SWELLING RIVER !
> ON YOU RUSH O'ER ROUGH AND SMOOTH,
> LOUDER, FASTER, BRAWLING, LEAPING
> OVER ROOKS, by rose-banks sweeping,
> LIKE IMPETUOUS YOUTH.

The third and following stanzas suggest solemnity, warning, counsel, and require "grave and sustained tones." Thus,

> "BROAD, AND DEEP, AND STILL AS TIME"

should be given with fulness of voice, slow, deliberate utterance, and a marked pause between each member of the line.

The lines

> "Swift and silent as an arrow
> Through a channel darkly narrow"

require "accellerated motion, to conform to the requirements of imitative harmony."

In the lines

> "Down you dash into the sea"

a certain force of voice is required, while

> "Sea, that line hath never sounded,

> Sea, that voyage hath never rounded
>   Like Eternity, "

being in the nature of a climax, the voice must be gradually raised
till " rounded " is reached, when a short pause, and a change to solemn
tone is required for

> "Like Eternity."

————o————

SEBASTIAN ; OR, THE ROMAN MARTYR.

SCENE IV.—THE EMPEROR'S COURT—MAXIMIAN—THE PREFECT OF
THE CITY—CORVINUS—FULVIUS—SEBASTIAN—QUADRATUS, AND
GUARDS.

Maximian.   Well! of this enough.
We lavish favors freely upon all,
But from how few can we expect true service?
From soldiers only.   Men true to the death.
Men such as thou, Sebastian!   (SEBASTIAN *bows*.)
But from the gownsmen who frequent a court,
Fawning for favors, they are a base tribe.
Are they not, noble Fulvius?
   Fulvius (*drops on one knee*.)   Sire, your reproach is just,
But not to me.   I know, I've ill requited
Your divinity's many liberal subsidies ;
But now, at last, I can redeem my pawned faith.
I have found the foulest treason, the most fell conspiracy
About your majesty's most sacred person!
   Max. How, sirrah! about our person?
Speak! or the words shall be drawn
From you with iron pincers—
   Fulv. Sebastian is a Christian !
   Max. Thou liest, thou dog !   The captain of my guard,
The very keeper of my inmost trust—
Thou shalt prove thy word, thou wretch !
Or die, as Christian scoundrel never died !
                    (SEBASTIAN *steps forward*.)

Sebastian. My liege, I spare you all trouble of proof;
I am a Christian ! I glory in the name.

Max. Oh ! ye gods, hear this ! Was ever man
So served ? Was ever prince so betrayed ? One—one
Honored above all others, to join these infidel
Dogs who dishonor Rome, tear down our edict,
Undermine the state, plot against our very person.
One raised to honor, to trust, to the first rank !
Oh, ingrate ! viper ! scorpion ! what shall I call thee
Vile or bad enough ?

Seb. Hear me, my liege. In that I am a Christian,
You have the best bond of my fidelity!

Max. Ingrate!

Seb. Listen, most noble emperor. Where is fidelity?
'Twas this you asked me a moment since.
I'll answer. Go to the prisons, strike the iron off
The Christian's limbs; he is enchained fidelity.
Go to the courts, unload the groaning rack.
From the arena and the tiger's jaws snatch
The maimed Christian,—maimed man, but whole
In faith. Believe me, sire, no legion in your pay
Can count as many loyal hearts as languish
In Roman prisons, charged only with their faith.
And further, this : they never can be true
To king or state, who do not, above all,
Fear, honor, and obey the King of kings.

Max. Folly and madness ! I'd rather have a body guard
Of wolves than Christians. Your treachery is enough —

Seb. No traitor am I, royal emperor. By night and day,
Guarded, unguarded, I had access to you.
If I were a traitor, the traitor's opportunity
Offered at every hour—

Max. Yet you concealed your creed.
You feared the bitter death due to your crime.

Seb. No, sire! Coward no more than traitor.

I had a duty to my brethren—for them I lived;
But hope had almost died within me.
Fulvius, I thank thee!
Thou hast spared me the sad choice
Of seeking death or bearing still a life
I earnestly desire to give away.

Max. Ho! here, Quadratus! Arrest your tribune!
Do you hear? What! you hesitate?

Quadratus. My liege, I, too, am a Christian.

Max. What! more of it! Here, seize me that centurion!
Bear him away to instant execution.

(They take out QUADRATUS.)

But for this chief offender, take him to Hyphax,
The captain of my sure Numidian bowmen.
Bid them in Adonis' grove tie up this traitor,
And send an arrow into every joint,
And draw the treacherous blood from every pore,
And kill him sense by sense, and joint by joint,
Leaving the heart and brain to beat and burst
Until the last drop ebbs from out his veins.
Begone! and answer with your lives for his.

Questions:—Mention the characters in the scene. What men are true to death? Use another word for ingrate. What was Sebastian's best bond of fidelity? What did Sebastian call the Christian? Who lavished favors freely?

pawned	ingrate	fidelity	languish
requested	scorpion	groaning	centurion
conspiracy	scoundrel	treachery	opportunity

————o————

BOYS WANTED.

BOYS of spirit, boys of will,
　　Boys of muscle, brain, and power,
Fit to cope with anything—
　　These are wanted every hour.

Not the weak and whining drones,
That all trouble magnify ;
Not the watchword of '' I can't,''
But the nobler one '' I will.''

Do whate'er you have to do
With a true and earnest zeal ;
Bend your sinews to the task,
Put your shoulder to the wheel.

In the counting-house or store,
Wheresoever you may be,
From your future efforts, boys,
Comes a nation's destiny.

Questions :—What boys are wanted ? Give some reasons for persons not succeeding in what they undertake. What should be our watchword? What is a watchword ?

| muscle | sinews | shoulder |
| country | future | destiny |

---o---

PASSING CLOUDS.

Adelaide Ann Proctor, born in 1825; died in 1864. She became a convert to the Catholic faith in 1853.   Like Mrs. Hemans, her poems have enjoyed a wide popularity on account of their Christian elevation of sentiment, their sympathy with the feelings of the heart, and their grace and melody of expression. The '' Legend of Bregenz;'' ''The Tomb in Ghent;'' ''The Angel of Death;'' ''The Doubting Heart,'' and ' One by One'' are among the best known of her verses.

WHERE are the swallows fled ?
Frozen and dead,
Perchance upon some bleak and stormy shore.
O doubting heart!
Far o'er the purple seas.

They wait, in sunny ease,
The balmy-southern breeze
To waft them to their northern home once more.

Why must the flowers die?
Prisoners they lie
In the cold tomb, heedless of tears or rain.
O doubting heart!
They only sleep below
The soft, white, ermine snow,
While winter winds shall blow,
To breathe and smile upon you soon again.

The sun has hid his rays
These many days;
Will dreary hours never leave the earth?
O doubting heart!
The stormy clouds on high
Veil the same sunny sky,
That soon (for spring is nigh)
Shall wake the summer into golden mirth.

Fair hope is dead, and light
Is quenched in night;
What sound can break the silence of despair?
O doubting heart!
The sky is overcast,
Yet stars shall rise at last,
Brighter for darkness past,
And angels' silver voices stir the air

COMPOSITION.

Give the substance of the poem in your own words, and explain the last stanza as fully as possible. Tell the meaning of: "hope is dead," "light is quenched in night." Why shall the stars be "brighter for darkness past"? Show, by familiar examples, when we notice light, and feel it most.

　　　perchance　　　　　heedless　　　　　quenched

15

ANALYSIS.

The main idea running through these beautiful lines is, that however dark and cheerless our course through life may be, yet faith can see a silver lining on every dark cloud. The swallows have disappeared, only to return with the advent of genial weather. Flowers die only to spring up afresh, when winter is past. The sun hides himself behind the clouds, only to burst forth with renewed splendor. Hope seems lost; but from the silence of despair, angels' silver voices will stir the air.

------●------

COUNSELS FOR THE CONDUCT OF LIFE.

DECISION.

IT is but a truism to say that there can be no success in life without decision of character. Yet this quality cannot be created by human effort. Like vigor of body, it is a gift, and can be increased only through personal endeavors, aided by the help of God. But every man has within himself the germ of this quality, which can be cultivated by favorable circumstances and by motives presented to the mind.

Let no one despair because he has often broken his resolution. It has been well observed that nothing is more destructive of character than for a man to lose all faith in his own resolutions, because he has so often determined, and again determined, to do that which, nevertheless, he has never done. Here, as elsewhere, "the stature of the perfect man" is attained only by slow gradations of study, effort and patience. The whole armor cannot be put on at once. The first victory will render the succeeding ones easier, until the very combat will be desired for the luxury of certain conquest.

The intellect is but the half of a man; the will is the driving-wheel, the spring of motive power. A vacillating man, no matter what his abilities, is invariably pushed aside in the race of life by the man of determined will It is he who resolves to succeed, and who at every fresh rebuff begins resolutely again, that reaches the goal The shores of Fortune are covered with the stranded wrecks of men of brilliant ability, who wanted faith, courage and decision, and therefore perished in sight of more resolute but less capable adventurers, who succeeded in making the port.

The fact is, as Sydney Smith has well said, that " in order to do anything in this world that is worth doing, we must not stand shivering on the bank, thinking of the cold and the danger, but jump in and scramble through as well as we can. It will not do to be all the time calculating and adjusting nice chances: it did all very well before the Flood, when a man could consult his friends upon an intended publication for a hundred and fifty years, and then live to see its success for six or seven centuries afterwards. But at present a man waits, and doubts, and hesitates, and consults his brother and his uncle, and his first cousins, and his particular friends, till one day he finds that he is sixty-five years of age, — that he has lost so much time in consulting first cousins and particular friends, that he has no more time left in which to follow their advice." Obstacles and perplexities every man must meet, and he must either promptly conquer them, or they will conquer *him*.

It has been truly said that the great moral victories and defeats of the world often turn on minutes. Crises come, the seizing of which is triumph, the neglect of which is ruin. This is particularly true on the field of battle. It was at such moments that the genius of Napoleon shone forth with the highest lustre. His mind acted like the lightning, and never with more

promptness and precision than in moments of the greatest
confusion and danger.   What confounded others only
stimulated him.   He used to say that one of the principal
requisites of a general is an accurate calculation of time ;
for if your adversary can bring a powerful force to attack
a certain post ten minutes sooner than you can bring
up a sufficient supporting force, you are beaten, even
though all the rest of your plans be the most perfect
that can be devised.

Of course there are occasions when caution and delay
are necessary, — when to act without long and anxious
deliberation would be madness.   All wisdom is a system
of balances.   It is well enough to be careful and wary
up to a certain point; but beyond that a hesitating
policy is as ruinous as downright rashness.   Thousands
of men owe their failures in life simply to procrastination.
They seem to act on the advice, " never do to-day what,
by any possibility, can be put off till to-morrow."   They
never know their own minds, but debate with themselves
during the whole journey which side of the road to
take, and meanwhile they keep winding from the one to
the other.

Dr. John Brown, in speaking of that form of decision
called " presence of mind," well observes : " It is a curious
condition of mind that this requires.   It is like sleeping
with your pistol under your pillow, and the pistol on
full cock ; — a moment lost, and all may be lost.   There
is the very nick of time.   Men, when they have done
some signal feat of presence of mind, if asked how they
did it, do not very well know, — they "just *did it.*"

It is hardly possible to conceive of a more unhappy
man than one afflicted with the infirmity of indecision.
It has been remarked that there are persons who lack
decision to such a degree that they seem never to have

made up their minds which leg to stand upon. "A man without decision," says John Foster, "can never be said to belong to himself: he belongs to whatever can make capture of him; and one thing after another vindicates its right to him, by arresting him as he tries to go on."

Not only is decision necessary, but promptitude also, without which decision loses half its value.

Again: besides promptitude, tenacity of decision is necessary to him who would make his mark in the world, or achieve rare success. When a certain commissary-general complained to the Duke of Wellington that Sir Thomas Picton had declared that he would hang him if the rations for that general's division were not forthcoming at a certain hour, the Duke replied, "Ah! did he go so far as that? Did he say he'd hang you?" — "Yes, my lord." — "Well, if General Picton said so, I have no doubt he will keep his word; you'd better get up the rations in time." When a man of iron will is thus known to be so tenacious in his adherence to his resolution, that, once declared, it is like a decree of fate, there is no limit to the good or the bad results which he may accomplish.

COMPOSITION.

Write in three different ways:

(a) Let no one despair because he has often broken his resolution. *(b)* The intellect is but the half of man; the will is the driving-wheel, the spring of motive power. (c) It is he who resolves to succeed, and who at every fresh rebuff begins resolutely again, that reaches the goal.

Write the fifth paragraph entirely in your own words, changing all nouns, verbs, adjectives, and conjunctions, where possible.

truism	rebuff	crises	failures
decision	goal	lustre	conceive
armor	stranded	stimulated	vindicates
succeeding	adventurers	deliberation	tenacity —

NO MORE.

Felicia Dorothea Hemans was born in 1793, died in 1835. Her poems have been very extensively read. Appealing as they do to the affections of our nature, depicting domestic love, lofty patriotism, serene hope and holy resignation,—they will always be turned to with pleasure by that vast body of readers who seek in poetry the perfect expression of their own hopes and longings, their own sorrow or happiness. They are pure, noble, and most Christian in sentiment, and graceful and elegant in expression. Many of the shorter lyrics are English gems.

NO more! a harp-string's deep and breaking tone,
 A last, low summer breeze, a far-off swell,
A dying echo of rich music gone,
 Breathe through those words, —those murmurs of farewell,
     No more!

To dwell in peace, with home affections bound,
 To know the sweetness of a mother's voice,
To feel the spirit of her love around,
 And in the blessings of her eye rejoice —
     No more!

A dirge-like sound! to greet the early friend
 Unto the hearth, his place of many days;
In the glad song with kindred lips to blend,
 Or join the household laughter by the blaze —
     No more!

Through woods that shadow'd our first years to rove,
 With all our native music in the air;
To watch the sunset with the eyes we love,
 And turn, and read our own heart's answer *there* —
     No more!

Words of despair! yet earth's, all earth's the woe
 Their passion breathes — the desolately deep!

That sound in Heaven — oh! image then the flow
   Of gladness in its tones, — to part, to weep —
                              No more!

To watch, in dying hope, affection's wane,
   To see the beautiful from life depart,
To wear impatiently a secret chain,
   To waste the untold riches of the heart —
                              No more!

Through long, long years to seek, to strive, to yearn
   For human love, — and never quench that thirst;
To pour the soul out, winning no return,
   O'er fragile idols, by delusion nursed —
                              No more!

On things that fail us, reed by reed, to lean;
   To mourn the changed, the far away, the dead,
To send our troubled spirits through th' unseen,
   Intensely questioning for treasures fled —
                              No more!

Words of triumphant music bear we on,
   The weight of life, the chain, the ungenial air,
Their deathless meaning, when our tasks are done,
   To learn in joy; — to struggle, to despair —
                              No more!

Questions: — What things no longer breathe through the murmurs
of farewell? What home and family pleasures are no more? In the
third stanza what is mentioned as being "no more"? Give the fourth
stanza in your own words. How shall we find ourselves in heaven,
as given in the fifth stanza? What is meant by "fragile idols, by
delusion nursed"? "Treasures fled"?

———o——

STUDY.

THE favorite idea of a genius, among us, is of one who
   never studies, or who studies, nobody can tell when,
— at midnight, or at odd times and intervals —. and now

and then strikes out, *at a heat,* as the phrase is, some wonderful production. This is a character that has figured largely in the history of our literature. "Loose fellows about town," or loungers in the country, who slept in ale-houses and wrote in bar-rooms, who took up the pen as a magician's wand to supply their wants, and when the pressure of necessity was relieved, resorted again to their carousals.

Your real genius is an idle, irregular, vagabond sort of personage, who muses in the fields or dreams by the fireside; whose strong impulses — that is the cant of it — must needs hurry him into wild irregularities or foolish eccentricity; who abhors order, and can bear no restraint, and eschews all labor: such a one, for instance, as Newton or Milton! What! they must have been irregular, else they were no geniuses!

"The young man," it is often said, "has genius enough, if he would only study." Now the truth is, as I shall take the liberty to state it, that genius will study: it is that in the mind which does study; that is the very nature of it. I care not to say that it will always use books. All study is not reading, any more than all reading is study. Study, says Cicero, is the voluntary and vigorous application of the mind to any subject.

Such study, such intense mental action, and nothing else, is genius. And so far as there is any native predisposition about this enviable character of mind, it is a predisposition to that action. This is the only test of the original bias; and he who does not come to that point, though he may have shrewdness, and readiness, and parts, never had a genius.

No need to waste regrets upon him, that he never could be induced to give his attention to anything, he never had that which he is supposed to have lost.

For attention it is — though other qualities belong to this transcendent power — attention it is that is the very soul of genius: not the fixed eye, not the poring over a book, but the fixed thought. It is, in fact, an action of the mind, which is steadily concentrated upon one idea or one series of ideas, — which collects in one point the rays of the soul, till they search, penetrate, and fire the whole train of its thoughts.

And while the fire burns within, the outward man may indeed be cold, indifferent, and negligent, — absent in appearance; he may be an idler, or a wanderer, apparently without aim or intent; but still the fire burns within. And what though "it bursts forth" at length, as has been said, "like volcanic fires, with spontaneous, original, native force"? It only shows the intenser action of the elements beneath. What though it breaks like lightning from the cloud? The electric fire had been collecting in the firmament through many a silent, calm, and clear day.

What though the might of genius appears in one decisive blow, struck in some moment of high debate, or at the crisis of a nation's peril? That mighty energy, though it may have heaved the breast of a Demosthenos, was once a feeble infant's thought. A mother's eye watched over its dawning. A father's care guarded its early growth. It soon trod with youthful steps the halls of learning, and found other fathers to wake and to watch for it, — even as it finds them here.

It went on; but silence was upon its path, and the deep strugglings of the inward soul marked its progress, and the cherishing powers of nature silently ministered to it. The elements around breathed upon it and "touched it to finer issues." The golden ray of heaven fell upon it and ripened its expanding faculties. The slow revolutions of years slowly added to its collected treasures and energies; till in its hour of glory, it stood forth embodied in the form of living, commanding, irresistible eloquence.

The world wonders at the manifestation, and says, "Strange, strange, that it should come thus unsought, unpremeditated, unprepared!" But the truth is, there is no greater wonder in it, than there is in the towering of the pre-eminent forest tree, or in the flowing of the mighty and irresistible river, or in the wealth and the waving of the boundless harvest.

COMPOSITION.

Write a short sketch, showing the vulgar idea in regard to persons supposed to be geniuses. Take the first paragraph as your guide in this description. Show from what the lesson says, but in your own words, that the popular idea is false.

Show from the example of three geniuses, say a painter, a poet and a mechanician, that talent without study will not suffice.

intervals	abhors	spontaneous
loungers	eschews	decisive
wand	voluntary	Demosthenes
resorted	predisposition	dawning
carousals	bias	issues
muses	parts	eloquence
impulses	transcendent	manifestation
cant	concentrated	unpremeditated
eccentricity	penetrate	irresistible

———o———

SPIRITUAL ADVANTAGES OF CATHOLIC CITIES.

IN a modern city men in the evening leave their houses for a banquet; in a Catholic city they go out for the benediction. The offices of the Church, morning and evening, and even the night instructions, were not wanting to those who were still living in the world. The number of churches always open, the frequent processions, and the repeated instructions of the clergy, made the whole city like a holy place, and were, without doubt, the means of making multitudes to choose the strait entrance, and to walk in the narrow way. There are many who have no idea of the perfection in which great numbers, in every rank of society, pass their lives, in Catholic cities, not even excepting that capital which has of late been made the nurse of so much ill.

But wherever the modern philosophy has created, as it were, an atmosphere, that which is spiritual is so confined, closed, and isolated, that its existence is hardly felt or known. The world appears to reign with undisputed possession, and that, too, as if it had authority to reign. And yet there are tender and passionate souls who have need of being unceasingly preserved in the path of virtue by the reign of religious exercises, who, when deprived of the power of approaching to the sources of grace at the hour their inclinations may suggest, are exposed to great perils, and who, perhaps, sometimes do incur, in consequence, eternal death.

> "Ah me, how many perils do enfold
> The righteous man, to make him daily fall!"

House of Prayer, why close thy gates? Is there an hour in all nature when the heart should be weary of prayer? When man, whom God doth deign to hear in thee as his temple, should have no incense to offer before thy altar, no tear to confide to thee? Mark the manners, too, of the multitude that loiters in the public ways of every frequented town. See how it meekly kneels to receive a benediction from the bishop who happens to pass by; and when dusk comes on, and the lamp of the sanctuary begins to burn brighter, and to arrest the eye of the passenger through the opened doors of the churches, hearken to the sweet sound of innumerable bells, which rises from all sides, and see what a change of movement takes place among this joyous and innocent people.

The old men break off their conversation on the benches at the doors, and take out their rosaries; the children snatch up their books and jackets from the green in token that play is over; the women rise from their labor of the distaff; and all together proceed into the church, when the solemn litany soon rises with its abrupt and crashing peal, till the bells all toll out their last and loudest tone, and the adorable Victim is raised over the prostrate people, who then issue forth and retire to their respective homes in sweet peace, and with an expression of the utmost thankfulness and joy.

The moderns in vain attempt to account for the difference of manners in these Catholic cities and in their own, by referring to their present prosperity and accumulation of wealth; but these cities in point of magnificence incomparably surpassed theirs, and with respect to riches, these were far superior, for peace was in their strength, and abundance in their towers.

Questions:— What is meant by "the offices of the Church"? What does "life scholastic" mean? What is the meaning of "to choose the strait entrance," etc.? Give the paragraph of the Gospel in which this expression is used. Explain the first two sentences of the second paragraph. Does "the world" here mean the earth, or the people on the earth, or the kingdoms of the earth, or the pleasures and distractions of the earth? Does "passionate souls" mean "angry souls"? What does it mean? What is the lamp of the sanctuary? Write first paragraph, giving all the ideas in your own language.

| intellectual | atmosphere | inclination | distaff |
| monastical | isolated | consequence | incomparably |

BRINGING THE GOOD NEWS FROM GHENT TO AIX.

I SPRANG to the stirrup, and Joris, and he;
  I galloped, Dirck galloped, we galloped all three;
"Good-speed!" cried the watch, as the gate-bolts undrew;
"Speed!" echoed the walls to us, galloping through;
Behind shut the postern, the lights sank to rest,
And into the midnight we galloped abreast.

Not a word to each other; we kept the great pace
Neck by neck, stride by stride, never changing our place.
I turned in my saddle and made its girths tight,
Then shortened each stirrup and set the peak right,
Rebuckled the check-strap, chained slacker the bit,
Nor galloped less steadily Roland a whit.

'Twas moonset at starting; but, while we drew near
Lokeren, the cocks crew and twilight dawned clear;
At Boom, a great yellow star came out to see;
At Düffeld, 'twas morning as plain as could be;
And from Mechelen church steeple we heard the half-chime,
So Joris broke silence with: "Yet there is time!"

At Aerschot, up leaped of a sudden the sun,
And against him the cattle stood black every one,
To stare through the mist at us galloping past,
And I saw my stout galloper, Roland, at last,
With resolute shoulders each butting away
The haze, as some bluff river headland its spray;

And his low head and crest, just one sharp ear bent back
For my voice, and the other pricked out on his track;
And one eye's black intelligence — ever that glance
O'er its white edge at me, his own master, askance!
And the thick, heavy spume-flakes which aye and anon
His fierce lips shook upwards in galloping on.

By Hasselt, Dirck groaned; and cried Joris: "Stay spur!
Your Roos galloped bravely, the fault's not in her,
We'll remember at Aix"—for one heard the quick wheeze
Of her chest, saw the stretched neck, and staggering knees.
And sunk tail, and horrible heave of the flank,
As down on her haunches she shuddered and sank.

So we were left galloping, Joris and I.
Past Loos and past Tongres, no cloud in the sky
The broad sun above laughed a pitiless laugh,
'Neath our foot broke the brittle, bright stubble like chaff;
Till over by Dalhem a dome tower sprang white,
And "Gallop," cried Joris, "for Aix is in sight!"

"How they'll greet us!" and in a moment his roan
Rolled neck and croup over, lay dead as a stone;
And there was my Roland to bear the whole weight
Of the news which alone could save Aix from her fate,
With his nostrils like pits full of blood to the brim,
And with circles of red for his eye-sockets' rim.

Then I cast my loose buff-coat, each holster let fall,
Shook off both my jack-boots, let go belt and all,
Stood up in the stirrup, leaned, patted his ear,
Called my Roland his pet name, my horse without peer;
Clapped my hands, laughed and sang, any noise, bad or
   good,
Till at length into Aix Roland galloped and stood.

And all I remember is friends flocking round,
And I sate with his head 'twixt my knees on the ground,
And no voice but was praising this Roland of mine,
As I poured down his throat our last measure of wine,
Which—the burgesses voted by common consent—
Was no more than his due who brought good news from
   Ghent.

COMPOSITION.

On horses. Their courage, and their attachment to their masters. The horse is noted all through the pages of history for his courage and affection. Examples: Bucephalus, owned by Alexander; the well known story of the Arab and his steed; finally, we have a very striking instance of the horse's pluck and courage in the history of "How they Brought the Good News from Ghent to Aix." Give the distance between the two places. Make a small sketch showing the road, Letter the same, and indicate places mentioned in the story. Describe the start; first falter; anxiety of the other two riders; second mishap; all depends upon the third animal's heft; the second courier left behind wistfully glances after the last horse; the good steed makes his way into the town. The crowd surges about the noble animal. The rider is offered refreshment, but he first thinks of his faithful ally. "The best wine for the best horse," cries the rider, and "may it do the brave beast good," is in every one's mouth. "Will he die?" ask a hundred voices. In a few moments there is a struggle between exhausted nature and every one's desires. The public wish is satisfied. The good horse rises, shakes off the thick sweat, looks at his master, throws forward his ears, and with a neigh that sends gladness into every heart, seems to say: "Didn't we do it well?" A patting on the neck, then some choice little morsels which a fair lady allows to be nibbled from her palm, is the reward given to the brave steed that brought the good news to Aix.

abreast	slacker	heft	peer
girths	askance	haunches	galloped
postern	spume-flakes	roan	burgesses

ECONOMY OF TIME.

"Dost thou love life? then do not squander time, for that is the stuff life is made of."— FRANKLIN.

"Lost, yesterday, somewhere between sunrise and sunset, two golden hours, each set with sixty diamond minutes. No reward is offered, for they are gone for ever." — HORACE MANN.

ONE of the most important lessons to be learned in life is the art of economizing time. A celebrated Italian was wont to call his time his estate; and it is true of this as of other estates of which the young come into possession, that it is rarely prized till it is nearly squandered. Habits of indolence, listlessness, and procrastination, once firmly fixed, cannot be suddenly thrown off, and the man who has wasted the precious hours of life's seed-time, finds that he cannot reap a harvest in life's autumn. Lost wealth may be replaced by industry, lost knowledge by study, lost health by temperance or medicine; but lost time is gone for ever. In the long catalogue of excuses for the neglect of duty, there is none which drops oftener from men's lips, or which is founded on more of self-delusion, than the want of leisure. People are always cheating themselves with the idea that they would do this or that desirable thing, "if they only had time." It is thus that the lazy and the selfish excuse themselves from a thousand things which conscience dictates to be done. Now, the truth is, there is no condition in which the chance of doing any good is *less* than in that of leisure.

Go, seek out the men in any community who have done the most for their own and the general good, and you will find they are — who? Wealthy, leisurely people, who have abundance of time to themselves, and nothing to do? No; they are almost uniformly the men who are in ceaseless activity from January to December. Such men, however pressed with business, are always found capable of doing a *little more;* and you may rely on them in their busiest seasons with ten times more assurance than on idle men.

There is an instinct that tells us that the man who does much is most likely to do more, and to do it in the best manner. The reason is, that to do increases the power of doing; and it is much easier for one who is always exerting himself to exert himself a little more, than for him who does nothing to rouse himself to action. Give a busy man ten minutes to write a letter, and he will dash it off at once; give an idle man a day, and he will postpone it till to-morrow or next week. There is a momentum in the active man which of itself almost carries him to the mark, just as a very light stroke will keep a hoop going, while a smart one was required to set it in motion.

The men who do the greatest things do them not so much by prodigious but fitful efforts, as by steady, unremitting toil, — by turning even the moments to account. They have the genius for hard work, — the most desirable kind of genius. A continual dropping wears the stone. A little done this hour and a little the next hour, day by day, and year by year, brings much to pass. Even the largest houses are built by laying one stone upon another.

Complain not, then, of your want of leisure to do anything. Rather thank God that you are not cursed with leisure; for a curse it proves, in nine cases out of ten. What if, to achieve some good work which you have deeply at heart, you can never command an entire month, a week, or even a day? Shall you therefore stand still, and fold your arms in despair? No; the thought should only stimulate and urge you on to do what you can do in this swiftly passing life of ours.

Try what you can build up from the broken fragments of your time, rendered more precious by their brevity. It is said that in the Mint the floor of the gold-working room is a net-work of bars, to catch the falling particles of the precious metal; and that when the day's labor is done the bars are removed, and the golden dust is swept up, to be melted and coined. Learn from this the nobler economy of time. Glean up its golden dust; economize with the utmost care those raspings and parings of existence, those leavings of days and bits of hours — so valueless singly, so inestimable in the aggregate — which most persons sweep out into the waste of life, and you will be rich in leisure. Rely upon it, if you are a miser of moments, if you hoard up and turn to account odd minutes and half-hours, you will at last be wealthier in intellectual acquisitions, wealthier in good deeds harvested, than thousands whose time is all their own.

The biographer of George Stephenson tells us that the smallest fragments of his time were regarded by him as precious, and that "he was never so happy as when improving them." For years Benjamin Franklin strove, with inflexible resolution, to save for his own instruction every minute that could be won. Henry Kirke White learned Greek while walking to and from a lawyer's office. Livingstone taught himself Latin grammar while working at the loom. Hugh Miller found time while pursuing his trade as a stone-mason, not only to read, but to write, cultivating his style till he became one of the most brilliant authors of the day. *

The small stones that fill up the crevices are almost as essential to the firm wall as the great stones; and so the wise use of spare time contributes not a little to the building up of a man's mind in good proportions, and with strength. If you really prize mental culture, or are sincerely anxious to do any good thing, you *will* find time, or *make* time for it, sooner or later, however engrossed with other employments. A failure to accomplish it can only prove the feebleness of your will, not that you lacked time for its execution.

* Time, St. Alphonsus Liguori tells us, is of the same value as Almighty God, for in a moment we may lose or gain the possession of that infinite Being.

Questions: — What art is one of the most important in life? What did a celebrated Italian call his time? What is true of that, as of other estates? Wherein does lost time differ from lost wealth? For what is want of leisure a common excuse? Why is it a bad one? Who are the men in any community who do most for the general good? Why is it that the man who does much is likely to do more? How do men who do the greatest things do them? What is the most desirable kind of genius? What does leisure prove, in nine cases out of ten? To what should the thought of the impossibility of finding leisure stimulate you? Describe the floor of the gold-working room in the Mint. What is the object of this? What lesson may be learned from this? Mention instances of great men who made good use of their spare moments. What are almost as essential to the firm wall as the great stones? How is this applied to time?

COMPOSITION.

Give three or four sayings or proverbs in regard to time. You may select the two at the head of this lesson, and two other. Take any one of these, and explain it by illustrations. Show from the life of Washington, as a boy, how he valued time. Show from the wars of Napoleon how victory or defeat often depended upon a few moments availed of, or neglected. Show how, in banking business, for instance, a few moments too late in payment of a note may destroy a merchant's reputation. How in china work, a few moments' delay or forgetfulness may destroy the finest coloring of works, etc.

economizing	dictates	inestimable
estate	instinct	aggregate
listlessness	brevity	hoard
procrastination	parings	acquisition

HONESTY THE BEST POLICY.

JEAN Baptiste Colbert, when a boy of fifteen, was sitting one morning in the shop of his master and godfather — Monsieur Certain, a rich woollen-draper of Rheims — when he was requested by him to execute a commission.

"Lay aside your paper, and listen to what I am going to say. Here is an invoice, directed, you see, to M. Cenani, of the firm Cenani and Mazerani, bankers of Paris. Set off now to the hotel where the banker is staying, take the invoice to him, and at the same time show him those cloths. Come here, sir, and remember the prices: No. 1 is marked three crowns a yard; No. 2, six crowns; No. 3, eight crowns; and No. 4, fifteen crowns. It is dear enough, but it is the very finest Saxony."

"Am I to make any abatement, godfather?" asked Baptiste, taking a card to which little patterns of cloth were fastened, while Moline, the porter, loaded himself with several pieces similar to the specimens.

"The full price, and ready money. Not a penny less Remember."

Baptiste and Moline quickly reached the hotel.

"I wish to see M. Cenani," said Baptiste to the person in attendance.

"The first staircase to the left, Nos. 8 and 10," said the waiter. And, still followed by Moline, the young woollen-draper knocked at the door to which he was directed, and was quickly ushered into the presence of a very young man, in a dressing-gown of bright green damask, richly flowered with red.

"I come from M. Certain," said Baptiste, bowing.

"Here are several pieces of cloth for you to choose from," added Moline, placing his parcel on a table.

The young banker merely said: "Let me see them;" and, putting one aside, said: "I like this best; what is its price?"

"Fifteen crowns a yard," answered Baptiste. Moline made a grimace, which neither seller nor buyer remarked.

" **Very** well," said the latter; "it is for making hangings for my study in the country. How many yards are in this piece?"

" Thirty yards," said Moline, looking at the mark; ' and if you wish me to measure it before you, sir"—·

" It is quite unnecessary, my friend; I may trust M. Certain. Thirty yards at fifteen crowns make four hundred and fifty crowns: here they are;" and going with a careless air to an open desk, he took out a handful of money, which he gave to Baptiste.

" Do you know how to write, my little friend?" said he to him.

" Yes, sir," said the young apprentice, blushing, deeply mortified by the question.

" Well, give me a receipt."

Baptiste gave the required receipt, and took the money; then bowed and retired.

" Well?" said the master of the Golden Fleece, perceiving, from his station on the step before his door the approach of his godson and his shop-boy. — "Well?"

" Here we are at last," said Moline, throwing his bale upon the counter.

M. Certain opened it eagerly. " You have made no mistake, I hope?" said he.

" I don't think I have," said Baptiste, quietly.

" But I think you have," said Moline, with a smothered laugh.

" Do you think so, Moline? — do you think so?" cried the old woollen-draper, examining the cloth. "But, indeed, I might have expected this; the little rascal could not do otherwise. But I warn you, if you have

---

* A woollen-draper's sign; at one time all tradesmen hung a sign over their door, as innkeepers do now.

made a mistake, you shall go to M. Cenani to ask from him the surplus money; and, if he refuse to give it, you shall pay it out of your wages. No. 3 is wanting: No. 3 was worth — it was worth six crowns; no, eight crowns."

"Eight crowns' — eight crowns!" cried Baptiste, astounded. "Are you sure of that, godfather?"

"Perhaps you would like to make out, you little rascal, that it was I who made the mistake. I tell you No. 3 was worth eight crowns. I am half dead with fear. I will lay a wager that the fellow sold it for six."

"On the contrary, godfather, stupid creature that I am, I have sold it for fifteen; but" —

"Fifteen! — fifteen!" interrupted the woollen-draper, trying to disguise his joy; — "fifteen! You are a fine boy, a good boy, Baptiste; you will one day be an honor to all your family; and I, your godfather, congratulate myself on having stood sponsor for you. Fifteen! — I could almost cry with joy! Fifteen crowns —fifteen crowns for a piece of cloth not worth six! Thirty yards at fifteen crowns instead of eight — seven crowns profit; thirty yards, two hundred and ten crowns — six hundred and thirty francs * profit. O happy day!"

"How, godfather; would you take advantage?" said Baptiste, drawing back instead of advancing.

"Oh, perhaps you would like to go shares," said the dishonest shopkeeper. "Certainly; I agree to let you have something."

"Godfather," interrupted young Colbert in his turn, composedly taking up his hat, which he had put down on entering, "I cannot agree to any such thing"—

"Bravo! bravo, my boy! Well, give it all to me."

---

* Three francs to a crown.

"And I will go," said Baptiste, "to the gentleman whom I have treated so badly, to beg of him to excuse me, and to return him the money he overpaid me."

And with these words young Baptiste, who had, while speaking, been gradually approaching the street door, cleared the threshold with a single bound, and rushed out.

"Can I see M. Cenani?" asked the breathless Baptiste, of the servant who had opened the door to him a quarter of an hour before.

"He is not yet gone out; but I do not think you can see him," replied the valet: "my master is dressing."

"I beg of you, sir, to let me see him immediately," said Baptiste.

"I will go and inquire," said the valet; and he opened his master's door, without perceiving that Baptiste had closely followed him.

"What is the matter, Comtois?" asked the gentleman.

"It is the young woollen-draper, who was here just now, who wants to see you, sir," replied the valet.

"He cannot see me now," said M. Cenani. "My sword, Comtois."

"Oh, pray, sir, one word," said the imploring voice of Baptiste.

"What brings you here? What do you want? I paid you, did I not?" asked the banker, turning angrily to Baptiste. "I am engaged. Go."

With that fearlessness which is given by extreme youth and the consciousness of doing right, Baptiste, instead of going away, advanced a few steps into the room.

"Sir," said he to the banker, whose astonishment at his boldness for a moment checked the order already on his lips to turn him out, "I have imposed upon **you** — unintentionally, it is true — but that does not make you the less wronged." Then, advancing still farther into the room, he emptied his pocket on a table, adding: "Here are the four hundred and fifty crowns that you gave me just now; be so good as to return me the receipt I gave you, and to take your money. The cloth that I sold to you, instead of being worth fifteen crowns a yard, is only worth eight. Thirty yards at eight crowns make only two hundred and forty crowns. You are to get back two hundred and ten crowns. There they are, sir. Will you see if it is right?"

"Are you quite sure of what you say, my friend?" said the banker, quickly changing his tone. "Are you certain there is no mistake?"

"You have the piece of cloth still, sir; is it not marked No. 3?"

"It is," said Comtois, going to examine.

"The No. 3 is marked at eight crowns, sir; I do not mistake. I beg your pardon, sir, for having made my way in in spite of you; but, if you had found out the mistake before I did, I should never have forgiven myself. Now, I have the honor of wishing you good morning."

"Stay a moment!" cried Cenani to Baptiste, who was retiring with a bow. "You might have easily kept this money for yourself."

"I never thought of that, sir," replied the young apprentice, with great simplicity.

"But if you had thought of it?" again inquired the elegant Parisian.

"It was quite impossible, sir, that such an idea could ever have come into my head. You might as well ask me if I had thought of carrying off all that you have here;" and a smile, as if at the absurdity of the idea, lighted up the boy's countenance.

"Suppose I were to make you a present of this money that you have returned to me?"

"What right have I to it, sir? and why should you give it to me? I would not take it, sir," said Baptiste, without hesitation.

"You are a fine fellow, and an honest fellow," said the young banker, going towards Baptiste, and taking him by the hand — "you are a fine fellow, and an honest fellow," repeated he. "What is your name?"

"Jean Baptiste Colbert, at your service," replied Baptiste.

"Colbert, Colbert," repeated M. Cenani, as if trying to recall something to his memory. "Is it possible that you are a relation of the Colberts of Scotland?"

"The barons of Castlehill are the common ancestors of the Scotch and French Colberts, sir." *

"And how comes it that your father, a descendant of such an illustrious family, is a woollen-draper?"

"My father is not a woollen-draper, sir; but he is very poor; and it is to relieve the family of the burden of my support that I became apprentice to my godfather, M. Certain."

The servant entering the room to say the carriage was ready, the young banker let go the hand of the boy with regret, and dismissed him, saying: "We shall meet again, Baptiste; we shall meet again."

Baptiste ran down the staircase of the hotel, and was bounding into the street, when he was seized by the collar with a powerful and threatening grasp. It was that of his enraged master, who had followed him, and

---

* There had always existed a very close connection between France and Scotland.

now abused him in a frantic manner for having returned the money. All remonstrances from poor Baptiste were in vain.

"Get from my sight and from my employment. Go, I say, and follow the advice that I now give you, — it is my last. Never come within reach of either my arm or my tongue. There is my blessing for you; take it, and good-by to you."

Slowly and sorrowfully Baptiste left his godfather, and bent his steps to his father's house.

It was seven o'clock in the evening, and M. Colbert was already seated at supper with his wife and youngest son, a child of six years of age, when the parlor door opened, and Baptiste appeared. A cry of astonishment broke from the lips of both father and mother, alarmed by the confused and sorrowful air of the boy. "What is the matter? Why have you left the shop on a week-day? Is your godfather ill? Or are you-- Speak! What is the matter?"

"I have been dismissed by M. Certain," simply said Baptiste.

"You have been about some folly then, sir," said M. Colbert.

"I will leave it to you to decide, father," replied Baptiste, modestly.

"What do you mean?" demanded M. Colbert.

"With your permission, my dear father, I will relate to you all that occurred to-day, and then you can tell me if I have done wrong; but I do not think I have; for, notwithstanding the grief that I feel in appearing before you after being dismissed, yet, if it were to do over again, I would act as I have done."

"Go on," said his father, while his mother looked encouragingly at him. Baptiste related all that you already know, quite simply and candidly, and, though he heartily disapproved of it, tried even to find excuses for his godfather's conduct. "M. Certain is so fond of money," said he; "and then, is a woollen-draper; perhaps he did not understand my conduct. To sell a little over the value, or a great deal, is the same thing to him, perhaps. If one may charge twopence profit on the yard without being called a rogue, why may not one as well charge a hundred francs if one can? What do you say, father? Have I done wrong?"

"Come and embrace me, my son," said M. Colbert, extending his arms to Baptiste, who threw himself into them — "come; you are indeed my son: you have behaved well, and I am heartily pleased with you."

"Yes, you have indeed behaved well, my beloved Baptiste," added Madame Colbert, also holding out her arms to her son; "you have done right. Sit down here near me; you must be hungry! You shall never return to that man, I promise you."

"I cannot remain a burden to you, however," observed Baptiste.

"We will think of that to-morrow," replied M. Colbert; "to-day we will only think how we can best entertain the welcome guest that God has ordained that the woollen-draper should send us."

"Sir," said the one solitary servant of the house, quietly opening the parlor door, "a gentleman in a post-chaise wants to speak to you."

"Let him walk in," said M. Colbert, rising from the table to meet the visitor.

At the first glance of the stranger Baptiste colored deeply.

"Sir," said the stranger, bowing to Baptiste's father, and stopping to bend almost to the ground before

Madame Colbert, "I beg a thousand pardons for having thus forced my entrance; but I leave to-morrow, and the business which brings me to you would not admit of delay. I am M. Cenani, of the firm Cenani and Mazerani, of Paris. This youth is your son, is he not, sir?" inquired he, pointing to Baptiste, who blushed still more deeply.

"Yes, sir, thank God."

"You have cause to thank God, sir: this child acted towards me this morning in a truly noble manner."

"Only as he ought, sir, — only as he ought," said Madame Colbert, hastily.

"Nobly, madame. I see that you know the history, but, as you have probably heard it from your son, his modesty has undoubtedly left you ignorant of that which has most delighted me. I went to M. Certain's for a second piece of cloth, and was informed of all that had passed by the shop-boy. Your admirable child, madame, refused to divide with his master the overcharge on the cloth."

"Excellent, excellent! Quite right, quite right! Oh, my dear, dear boy!" said Madame Colbert, with happy pride, embracing Baptiste, who stammered:

"It would not have been honest."

"You are aware, sir," said M. Colbert, addressing the banker, "that on account of his conduct my son has been dismissed from M. Certain's."

"I know it, sir; the shop-boy told me so; and on that account I came here to ask you, since you have already suffered your child to enter into trade, if it would suit you to place him, honest and honorable as he is, in our banking house, where, in a larger sphere, he must make his fortune."

Baptiste, who had hitherto listened in silence, and

who now only began to understand M. Cenani's intention, cried suddenly: "If to make a fortune I am to leave my father and mother, I must decline it, sir."

"But I do not decline it for you, Baptiste," said his father, tenderly but seriously. "We are very poor, my son; and I should think myself guilty did I not accept the brilliant prospects which M. Cenani so generously offers you. Go, Baptiste, with this gentleman; in all that concerns the business of your calling, listen exclusively to his advice, and follow it; when the principles of integrity and of honor are involved, add to his counsels those of your own heart."

Baptiste wept while he listened to his father, but no longer made any objection.

Thanks to the natural buoyancy of his age, and also to the change of scene and place, Baptiste felt a new life spring up within him as he was whirled along in a comfortable carriage, with a young and gay companion.

He served the banking house of Cenani and Mazerani faithfully and well, and, whilst serving it, obtained that complete knowledge of business and finance that enabled him thereafter to be so useful a servant of the State.

In 1661 he was made Minister of Finance to Louis XIV. On his appointment to the office he found bribery and cheating going on on all sides, and the State yearly robbed of millions of crowns. To the difficult task of reforming these shameless abuses, he brought, with extraordinary abilities and energy, the same courageous and unbending truthfulness which had distinguished him as a boy.

COMPOSITION.

Write a short story, embracing the chief items in Jean Colbert's tale. Change names for those of individuals and bankers of your vicinity.

Take streets, dwellings and other data to make the sketch answer a home description. Let distances, money values, etc., be in keeping with the circumstances. Close your story by quoting some few words or lines, in prose or poetry, illustrating the principle that " honesty is the best policy."

draper	study	remonstrances
invoice	disguise	prospects
abatement	composedly	exclusively
specimens	consciousness	buoyancy
ushered	unintentionally	finance

HAMLET'S SOLILOQUY.

TO be — or not to be ! — that is the question -
Whether 'tis nobler in the mind to suffer
The stings and arrows of outrageous fortune,
Or to take arms against a sea of troubles,
And, by opposing, end them ? — To die — to sleep.
No more ! — and, by a sleep, to say we end
The heart-ache, and the thousand natural shocks
That flesh is heir to — 'tis a consummation
Devoutly to be wish'd. To die — to sleep —
To sleep ? — perchance to dream ! — aye, there's the rub
For, in that sleep of death, what dreams may come,
When we have shuffled off this mortal coil,
Must give us pause. — There's the respect,
That makes calamity of so long life:
For who would bear the whips and scorns of time,
Th' oppressor's wrong, the proud man's contumely,
The pangs of despised love, the law's delay,
The insolence of office, and the spurns
That patient merit of the unworthy takes,—
When he himself might his quietus make
With a bare bodkin? Who would fardels bear

To groan and sweat under a weary life,
But that the dread of something after death —
That undiscovered country, from whose bourne
No traveller returns — puzzles the will,
And makes us rather bear those ills we have,
Than fly to others that we know not of?
Thus, conscience does make cowards of us all:
And thus, the native hue of resolution
Is sicklied o'er with the pale cast of thought;
And enterprises of great pith and moment,
With this regard, their currents turn awry,
And lose the name of action!

COMPOSITION.

Copy selection " Who would fardels bear . . . . . . we know not of."
Write sentences taken from the Old or New Testament, containing
the following words: *bear* (one another's burdens); *proud* (God
resisteth); *come* (Thy kingdom . . . . . .); *death* (it is appointed)
dreams (Joseph's); *suffer* (little children); *country* (The prodiga.
went afar . . . . . .); *consummated* (All is); *will* (Thy will be
. . . . . .), and mention in what circumstances the expression was
used; *conscience* (The worm of . . . . . .); *lose* (If ye . . . . . .
what better are ye than they ?)

outrageous	contumely	bourne
consummation	quietus	pith
shuffled	fardels	awry

———o———

THE COUNTENANCE AND CHARACTER.

THE countenances of men are more diverse than
their features. Some men have a lofty countenance, some have a lowering countenance, or a worldly,
ostentatious, vain-glorious countenance, or a scorn-
ful countenance, or a cunning and dissembling countenance.

We know men by their looks; we read men by looking
at their faces—not at their features, their eyes, their
lips, because God made these; but a certain cast and
motion, and shape and expression, which their features
have acquired. It is this that we call the countenance.

And what makes this countenance? The inward and
mental habits; the constant pressure of the mind; the
perpetual repetition of its acts. You detect at once
a vain-glorious, or conceited, or foolish person. It is
stamped on their countenance. You can see at once
on the faces of the cunning, the deep, the dissembling,
certain corresponding lines, traced on the face as leg-
ibly as if they were written.

As it is with the countenance, so it is with the
character. God gave us our intellect, our heart, and
our will; but our character is something different
from the will, the heart, and the intellect.

The character is that intellectual and moral texture
into which all our life long we have been weaving up
the inward life that is in us. It is the result of the
habitual or prevailing use we have been making of
our intellect, heart, and will. We are always at work,
like the weaver at the loom; the shuttle is always
going, and the woof is always growing. So we are
always forming a character for ourselves.

It is a plain, matter-of-fact truth, that everybody
grows up in a certain character; some good, some
bad, some excellent, and some unendurable. Every
character is formed by habits. If a man is habitually
proud, or vain, or false, and the like, he forms for
himself a character like in kind. It is the permanent
basis formed by continually acting in a particular
way; and this acting in a particular way comes from

a continual indulgence of thoughts and wishes of a particular tendency. The loom is invisible within, and the shuttle is ever going in the heart; but it is the will that throws it to and fro.

The character shows itself outwardly, but it is wrought within. Every habit is a chain of acts, and every one of those acts was a free link of the will. There was a time when the man had never committed the sin which first became habitual and then formed his abiding character. For instance, some people are habitually false. We sometimes meet with men whose word we can never take, and for this reason: they have lost the perception of truth and falsehood; the distinction is effaced from their minds; they do not know when they are speaking truly and when they are speaking falsely. The habit of paltering, and distinguishing, and concealing, and putting forth the edge of truth instead of showing boldly the full face of it, at last leads men into insincerity so habitual, that they really do not know when they speak the truth. They bring this state upon themselves. But there was a time when these same men had never told a lie.

The first they told was only with half an act of the will; but gradually they grew to do it deliberately; then they added lie to lie with a full deliberation; then with a frequency which formed a habit; and when it became habitual to them then it became unconscious.

Questions :—How do we know men? What makes the countenance? How can we have a pleasant countenance? Give a description of what character is?

habitually   distinguishing   unconscious

THE HIDDEN GEM.

Scene IV.—*The Atrium.*

Enter Alexius *and* Carinus.

Car. Edessa, then, has been your chief abode,
  During your Eastern pilgrimage. You loved it?

Alex. Dearly ; it is a city of much beauty,
  Its houses stately, and its churches gorgeous.
  And then, besides, it is in truth a place
  Of gentle breeding, and of courtly manners.
  Nor is this all. The East does not possess
  A seat of learning more renowned than that.

Car. I well remember that, in Syria, youths
  Who panted after knowledge oft would say,
  "I will to famed Edessa, there to study."

Alex. Truly, because each nation hath a home
  Within its walls. Syrians, Armenians, Persians,
  There pass their youth in quest of varied lore.
  From many fountains elsewhere issue rills
  Of letters and of science ; some will creep,
  Winding along the plain, and dallying
  With flowers of enervating fragrance ; some
  Bound sparkling and impetuous from the rock,
  And threaten rudely delicacy of faith.
  But in Edessa these all flow alike
  Into one deep yet crystal cistern.

Car. How marvellous must be this graceful blending
  Of the two wisdoms into one design.
  But say, Ignotus, could a boy like me,
  With nought else gifted but *desire* to learn,
  There profit gain ?

Alex.   You measure profit ill.
  The vaunt of youth lies not in ready wit,
  Shrewdness of thought, or sprightliness of speech,—
  Torrents in spring that leave dry summer beds,

Trees that yield early, but ill ripening fruit.
The grace of youth is in the open brow,
Serene and true ; in blooming cheeks, that blush
Praise to receive, but glow with joy, to give ;
In eye that drinks in, flashes not forth, light,
Fixed on the teacher's lips, as hope's on heaven ;
In the heart docile, unambitious, steadfast.—
A youth with these may bind a smaller sheaf,
But every ear contains a solid grain,
Which heaven's sun and dew have swelled and ripened—
Bread of the present life, seed of the next.

Car. It cheers me, so to hear you talk, Ignotus.
But in my heart deep lies a secret thought
To man yet unrevealed. Your words so sweet
Would charm it from its nest—

Alex.   Perhaps unfledged.

Car. Yet soon must it have wings. Tell me, Ignotus,   .
Can it be wrong in one so weak as I
To fly at lofty heights, sublimest aims ?

Alex. [*surprised.*] What ! is ambition creeping in already,
To torture your young heart ? So needless, too !

Car.   Nay, judge me not
So meanly, Ignotus ; higher far I soar.

Alex. Higher than Rome's first Senator ? What ! child,—
O, no ! it cannot be !—You cannot dream
To match your flight against the Roman Eagle's,
Snatch the world's sceptre, and usurp a purple
Then surely doubly dyed. O no, Carinus.

Car. O, dear Ignotus, this would be to fall,
With broken pinion, lower ; not to rise.
Earth's gifts while scorning, can I love its crimes ?

Alex. Then solve me your enigma, dearest child.

Car. A nobler name than " Cæsar " or " Augustus "
I covet : such commands I long to issue
As angels execute, and demons dread :

To wear no purple, but what once He wore—
The King that ruled o'er Pilate's mocking court:
To stand before an altar, not a throne.

ALEX. O, loved Carinus, how my fears have wronged you!
May heaven's bright blessing beam on your resolve!
Have you weighed well its sequences, conditions,
Its difficulties, sacrifices, loss?
Euphemian binds to you, as its first link,
The chain of long succession to his name,—
While you would close it.

CAR.   But how gloriously
The priest, like the apostle, *ends* his line,
However proud its nobleness, more nobly;
As the sun's furnace yields at eve its gold.

ALEX. How tell Euphemian this?

CAR.   There is my trial.
And yet to-morrow it must needs be told.
Will you not help me?

ALEX.   Yes, dear boy, I will.
So noble is your thought, so sweetly told:
So dovelike is your nestling, yet beyond
The eaglet I had deemed it, that if e'en
It needed for its growth my heart's best blood,
There, like the pelican, I'd feed it willingly,
Till thence you drew it forth.

CAR.   O speak not so;
To-morrow you shall help me to disclose
My so long burrowing purpose. And perhaps
You then will tell me your own history.
Ignotus—pardon—you are not what men
Take you for. 'Neath that coarse dress, and in that
    spark
Of noble nature, and of brilliant fire,
Oh, tell me who you are!

ALEX. Yes, yes; to-morrow!

CAR. To-morrow ! Everything on that dark day !
  It looks to me like a storm-laden cloud,
  Embosoming blight, fever, dark dismay.
  And yet athwart it darts one precious beam
  Of glory, shooting from the deepest hue ;
  It bears your name, Ignotus, and it shines
  Upon my future way.
ALEX.   Blest be its omen !
  But you are wanted—so farewell, my child!
CAR. Farewell—who knows? Yes, yes, we meet again !
ALEX. 'Twill not be terrible when next we meet,
  When our eyes glass themselves in one another's;
  Tears will be wiped from them ; mourning none,
  Nor pain, nor sigh, will be: first things are passed.
CAR. Farewell ; I'll try to dream, then, of that bright to-
  morrow.

---o---

GONE.

Like drooping, dying stars, our dearly loved ones go
away from our sight. The stars of our hopes, our am-
bitions, our prayers, whose light shines ever before us,
suddenly pale in the firmament of our heart, and their
place is left empty, cold, and dark. A mother's steady,
soft, and earnest light, that beamed through wants
and sorrows ; a father's strong, quick light, that kept
our feet from stumbling in the dark and treacherous
ways ; a sister's light, so mild, so pure, so constant,
and so firm, shining upon us from gentle, loving eyes,
and persuading us to grace and goodness ; a brother's
light, forever sleeping in our soul, and illuminating
our goings ; and a friend_ light, true and trusty, is
gone out forever, to shine beyond the stars, where
there is no night and no darkness forever !

THE MOTHER OF THE MACHABEES.

Callanan was born in Ireland in 1795; died in 1829. During his life he was one of the popular contributors to "Blackwood's Magazine."

THAT mother viewed the scene of blood;
　　Her six unconquer'd sons were gone;
Fearless she viewed; beside her stood
　　Her last, — her youngest, dearest one;
He looked upon her and he smiled;
Oh! will she save that only child?

"By all my love, my son," she said,
　　"The breast that nursed, the womb that bore,
The unsleeping care that watch'd thee, fed,
　　Till manhood's years required no more;
By all I've wept and pray'd for thee,
Now, now, be firm and pity me.

"Look, I beseech thee, on yon heaven,
　　With its high field of azure light,
Look on this earth, to mankind given,
　　Array'd in beauty and in might,
And think, nor scorn thy mother's prayer,
On him who said it, — and they were!

"So shalt thou not this tyrant fear,
　　Nor, recreant, shun the glorious strife:
Behold! thy battle-field is near;
　　Then go, my son, nor heed thy life;
Go, like thy faithful brothers die,
That I may meet you all on high."

Like arrow from the bended bow,
　　He sprang upon the bloody pile;
Like sunrise on the morning's snow,
　　Was that heroic mother's smile;
He died — nor fear'd the tyrant's nod —
For Judah's law and Judah's God.

COMPOSITION.

Give the mother's words to her youngest son. Try to make your expressions as forcible, yet as simple as hers.

Next describe the alacrity with which the noble youth went to court death. This is specially narrated in the last stanza.

viewed   **array'd**   **recreant**

———o———

WASHINGTON'S ANSWER TO THE ROMAN CATHOLICS OF THE UNITED STATES.

Gentlemen:—While I now receive with much satisfaction your congratulations on my being called to the first station of my country, I cannot but duly notice your politeness in offering an apology for the unavoidable delay. As that delay has given you an opportunity of realizing, instead of anticipating, the benefits of the general government, you will do me the justice to believe that your testimony of the increase of the public prosperity enhances the pleasure which I would otherwise have experienced from your affectionate address.

I feel that my conduct, in war and in peace, has met with more general approbation than could reasonably have been expected ; and I find myself disposed to consider that fortunate circumstance in a great degree resulting from the able support and extraordinary candor of my fellow-citizens of all denominations.

The prospect of national prosperity now before us is truly animating, and ought to excite the exertions of all good men to establish and secure the happiness of their country in the permanent duration of its freedom and independence. America, under the smiles of Divine Providence, the protection of a good government, and the cultivation of good manners, morals, and piety, cannot fail of attaining an uncommon degree of eminence in literature, commerce, agriculture, improvements at home, and respectability abroad.

As mankind become more liberal, they will be more apt to allow that all those who conduct themselves as worthy members of the community are equally entitled to the protection of civil government. I hope ever to see America among the foremost nations in examples of justice and liberality; and I presume that your fellow-citizens will not forget the patriotic part which you took in the accomplishment of their revolution and the establishment of their government, or the important assistance which they received from a nation in which the Roman Catholic faith is professed.

I thank you, gentlemen, for your kind concern for me. While my life and health shall continue, in whatever situation you or I may be, it shall be my constant endeavor to justify the favorable sentiments which you are pleased to express of my conduct; and may the members of your society in America, animated alone by the pure spirit of Christianity, and still conducting themselves as the faithful subjects of our free Government, enjoy every temporal and spiritual felicity.

Questions:—What is it, to realize anything? Give the definition of the word animating. When is the government of a country good? How are good manners cultivated? What part did the Catholics take in the achievement of American independence? Give some examples of favorable sentiments.

reasonably	entitled	eminence
liberality	protection	agriculture

THE BELLS OF ST. MARY'S.

The Cathedral of St. Mary's, Limerick, is a large, gloomy looking building, with a very high tower, from which one can get a magnificent view of the surrounding country. In this tower is a very melodious chime of bells, about which there is told a pretty and touching story, which I do not doubt is true.

Once there lived in Italy a skilful artisan, who was celebrated for founding bells. No founder in all Europe could equal him—no chimes in all the world were so grand and sweet-sounding as his. At last he made a chime for a convent, which proved to be finer than any he had cast before. He had spent years upon them; they were his great work; he was very proud of them; he even seemed to have fallen in love with them, for he could not live out of the sound of their melodious ringing. So he purchased a little villa near a lovely seaside, beneath the lofty cliff on which the convent stood, and every night and morning he had the happiness of hearing the solemn silver chiming of his own dear bells, which, when sounding at that height, almost seemed to him God had taken and hung in the clouds, to call him and his children to prayer and to heaven.

But after a few bright, peaceful years, there came a dark and troubled time of war and pillage. The good Italian lost all in the terrible struggle—home, family, even his beloved bells, for the convent on the cliff was destroyed, and they were carried away to some distant land. At last he was released from a miserable dungeon, to find himself old, infirm, poor, and alone in the world. Then a great longing came to him and grew at his lonely heart to hear his bells once more before he should die. So he became a wanderer over Europe, searching for them everywhere. He would be told of wonderful chimes in this and that city, and go many weary leagues to hear them; but as soon as they sounded on his ear, he would sadly shake his head, his eyes would fill with tears, and he would turn to go on his way.

When, at length, he heard of the sweet bells of Limerick, he was very old and feeble, but he set out at once on what he knew must be his last pilgrimage. The vessel on which he sailed went up the Shannon, and anchored opposite the city. The old Italian took a boat to go on shore, at the close of a calm and beautiful day. He was very weak and ill, and reclining in the stern of the boat, looked longingly at St. Mary's Cathedral. Suddenly from the tall tower rang softly out the vesper chime. The Italian started up joyfully at the sound. Then he crossed himself, looked upward, and murmured: "I thank thee, Blessed Mother of Jesus! *I hear my bells at last!*" Then he sank back, and closed his eyes, and listened. The men, resting on their oars, were charmed at their solemn tones.

The Italian seemed to hear in his bells more than their own melody; all the music of his happy home: the deep murmur of the sea below the convent cliff, the sighing of the winds in the cypress and olive trees, and sweeter and dearer than all, the voices of his wife and children. *They* seemed to be softly calling his pious soul to leave the trouble and weariness of earth for the blessedness and rest of God. And his soul obeyed the call, for when the bells ceased their ringing, and the boatmen rowed to land, they found that the aged stranger was dead.

Questions:—Give a synopsis of the story in your own words.

ASCENSION HYMN.

Lift up, ye princes of the sky,
Back on your golden hinges fly :
  For lo, the King of glory waits,
And he shall enter in with shouts of victory.

  Who is this King of glory? Tell
Ye who can sing his triumph-song so well.

The Lord of strength and matchless might ;
The Lord all-conquering in the fight :
Lift, lift your portals, lift them high,
Ye princes of the conquered sky ;
  And you, ye everlasting gates,
Back on your golden hinges fly:
  For lo, the King of glory waits,
And he with shout and choral song
Shall enter in, leading his train along

SELF-RELIANCE.

OF all the elements of success none is more vital than
   self-reliance, — a determination to be one's own
helper, and not to look to others for support. It is the
secret of all individual growth and vigor, the master-key
that unlocks all difficulties in every profession or calling.
"Help yourself, and Heaven will help you," should be
the motto of every man who would make himself useful
in the world. He who begins with crutches will
generally end with crutches. Help from within always
strengthens, but help from without invariably enfeebles.

It is said that a lobster, when left high and dry among
the rocks, has not instinct and energy enough to work
his way back to the sea, but waits for the sea to come
to him. If it does not come, he remains where he is,

and dies, although the slightest effort would enable him
to reach the waves.   The world is full of human lobsters.
— men stranded on the rocks of business, who, instead
of putting forth their own energy, are waiting for some
grand billow of good fortune to set them afloat.

There are many young men, who, instead of carrying
their own burdens, are always dreaming of some
Hercules, in the shape of a rich uncle, or some other
benevolent relative, coming to give them a "lift."   In
ninety-nine cases out of a hundred, pecuniary help to a
beginner is not a blessing, but a calamity.   Under the
appearance of aiding, it weakens its victims, and keeps
them in perpetual slavery and degradation.

Lord Thurlow refused a lucrative office to Lord Eldon,
when poor, saying it was a favor to Eldon to withhold
it.   "What he meant," says Eldon, "was, that he had
learned that I was by nature very indolent, and that it
was only want that could make me very industrious."

Nothing, indeed, can be more unwise than the anxiety
of parents to accumulate property for the support of
their children after their own death.   Read the history
of the rich and the poor in all ages and countries, and
you will find almost invariably that the "lucky ones,"
as they are called, began life at the foot of the ladder;
while the "unfortunates," who flit like scarecrows along
life's path, attribute the very first decline in their
fortunes to having been propped up by others.   It is a
proverb, that rich young men, who begin their fortunes
where their fathers left off, too often leave off where
their fathers began.

The world, though rough, is, after all, the best
schoolmaster; for it makes a man his own teacher, and
gives him that practical training which no schools nor
colleges can ever impart.   It cannot be too often repeated,

that not helps, but obstacles, and not facilities, but difficulties, make men. Beethoven said of Rossini, that he had the stuff in him to have made a great musician, if he had only been well flogged when a boy, but that he had been spoiled by the *ease* with which he composed.

While it is true that all men cannot become Raphaels or Shakespeares, it is equally true that each mind may contain some germ, the development of which may exert an important influence over the whole world. Was not Kepler the son of a publican? Was not he an obscure man, who, by the invention of printing, revolutionized the whole intellectual aspect of society?

There are some men, who, instead of making the best use of the means within their reach, are always speaking of what they might do "under happier circumstances." Under happier circumstances!—as if the very seal of greatness were not precisely the regal superiority to circumstances which makes them aids and ministers of success; as if it were not the masterful will that concentrates twenty years of untiring but unappreciated labor on a great invention. Indeed, the "circumstances" on which so many faint-hearted men dwell, should be regarded as the very tools with which one is to work, — the stepping-stones by which one is to mount.

Let every young man have faith in himself, and take an earnest hold of life, scorning all props and buttresses, all crutches and life-preservers. Instead of wielding the rusted sword of valorous forefathers, let him forge his own weapons; and, mindful of the Providence over him, let him fight his own battles with his own good lance.

COMPOSITION.

Write out the different examples cited in this lesson, of persons who showed great self-reliance. In a separate paragraph, give the substance of what is said in eighth paragraph of lesson Give two instances, say the Presidents of the United States, who by self-reliance became distinguished men. Show that self-reliance is more likely to succeed in America than elsewhere.

vital	indolent	precisely
invariably	anxiety	concentrates
enfeebles	accumulate	unappreciated
Hercules	scarecrows	buttresses
lucrative	facilities	wielding

THE BLUE AND THE GRAY.

BY the flow of the inland river,
  Whence the fleets of iron have fled,
Where the blades of the grave-grass quiver.
  Asleep are the ranks of the dead;—
    Under the sod and the dew,
      Waiting the judgment day;—
    Under the one, the Blue;
      Under the other, the Gray

These, in the robings of glory,
  Those, in the gloom of defeat,—
All, with the battle-blood gory,
  In the dusk of eternity meet;—
    Under the sod and the dew,
      Waiting the judgment day;—
    Under the laurel, the Blue;
      Under the willow, the Gray.

From the silence of sorrowful hours,
  The desolate mourners go,
Lovingly laden with flowers,
  Alike for the friend and the foe;—

Under the sod and the dew,
　　Waiting the judgment day;
Under the roses, the Blue;
　　Under the lilies, the Gray.

So, with an equal splendor,
　　The morning sun rays fall,
With a touch, impartially tender,
　　On the blossoms blooming for all;
　　　Under the sod and the dew,
　　　　Waiting the judgment day;
　　　Broidered with gold, the Blue;
　　　　Mellowed with gold, the Gray.

So, when the summer calleth,
　　On forest and field of grain.
With an equal murmur falleth
　　The cooling drop of the rain;—
　　　Under the sod and the dew,
　　　　Waiting the judgment day;—
　　　Wet with the rain, the Blue,
　　　　Wet with the rain, the Gray.

Sadly, but not with upbraiding,
　　The generous deed was done;
In the storm of the years that are fading,
　　No braver battle was won;—
　　　Under the sod and the dew,
　　　　Waiting the judgment day; --
　　　Under the blossoms, the Blue.
　　　　Under the garlands, the Gray

No more shall the war-cry sever,
　　Or the winding rivers be red;
They banish our anger forever,
　　When they laurel the graves of our dead

Under the sod and the dew,
Waiting the judgment day; —
Love and tears, for the Blue,
Tears and love, for the Gray.

COMPOSITION.

Give a short account of "Decoration Day." Tell what is usually
said, and quote from the various articles on death, in this Reader, to
help you. Describe some special grave of some brave man whose
actions distinguished him in the battle where he was killed. Name
some Catholic soldiers or officers thus distinguished.

quiver	desolate	mellowed	sever
robings	impartially	upbraiding	laurel
gory	broidered	garlands	dew

DEATH OF THE VENERABLE DE LA SALLE.

THE Venerable De La Salle was nearing his final hour.
Under his instructions, the holy viaticum was
brought, the garden avenues through which the most
Blessed Sacrament was to be carried having been
decorated by his order.

Like a valiant soldier, the saintly Founder wished to
die arms in hand. His faith gave him supernatural
courage. What was the astonishment of the pastor, his
fellow-priests, and many persons distinguished for their
piety, when they beheld the dying man, not in his bed
of suffering, but prostrate on the floor to receive his God!
A short thanksgiving, made in the same posture, was
more than the patient could bear; he was again placed
in his bed, where he continued his secret conversation
with the Spouse of his heart. He had already received
the bread of angels; he was soon to hear their songs.

On Holy-Thursday night, after prayer, the most honored Superior, with the Brothers of the community and the members of the novitiate, assembled around the bed of the dying patriarch. "We are your children," sobbed the Superior; "we come to implore a father's blessing." "May God bless you all!" said the Venerable, in reply. Like Jacob of old, he beheld the Joseph of his heart at his feet. He had not lands to divide, nor wealth to distribute, but, like the divine Master he had so faithfully imitated, he gave his children the whole world as the field of their labors: they were to teach all nations that "sweet is the yoke and light the burden of those who truly serve God."

Towards midnight he entered into his death-agony. At two in the morning he rallied for a moment, and murmured: "Mary, Mother of grace, of sweetness and of clemency! Protect us against our enemies, and receive us at the hour of death!"

For many years these words had closed each day for the Venerable; they were among the last he uttered. A moment before his death he was asked if he willingly accepted all the sufferings he was then enduring. "Oh, yes," he replied, "in all things I adore the will of God in my regard."

With this profession of faith, the last embers of life were faintly glimmering. Making an effort as if to rise and meet one whom he wished to embrace, Jean-Baptiste de La Salle breathed his soul into the hands of the Creator. The world had lost one of its greatest benefactors, the Church one of her most faithful sons, and the Institute of the Christian Schools its Founder. Heaven had welcomed the valiant warrior, who had fought the good fight. The steward who had been at first faithful in few things, and was afterwards placed

17

over many, had entered into the joy of the Lord. It was Good-Friday morning.

JOMPOSITION.

Write the second paragraph in your own words, changing all the verbs, adjectives and participles.

viaticum	rallied	glimmering
thanksgiving	profession	steward

————o————

MARK ANTONY'S ORATION.

FRIENDS, Romans, countrymen! lend me your ears!
 I come to bury Cæsar, not to praise him.
The evil that men do, lives after them;
The good is oft interred with their bones.
So let it be with Cæsar!— Noble Brutus
Hath told you, Cæsar was ambitious, —
If it was so, it was a grievous fault;
And grievously hath Cæsar answer'd it!
Here, under leave of Brutus, and the rest—
For Brutus is an honorable man!
So are they all! all honorable men —
Come I to speak in Cæsar's funeral.
 He was my friend, faithful and just to me —
But Brutus says he was ambitious, —
And Brutus is an honorable man!
He hath brought many captives home to Rome,
Whose ransoms did the general coffers fill;
Did this in Cæsar seem ambitious?
When that the poor have cried, Cæsar hath wept:
Ambition should be made of sterner stuff!—
Yet Brutus says he was ambitious; —
And Brutus is an honorable man!
You all did see, that, on the Lupercal,

I thrice presented him a kingly crown,
Which he did thrice refuse: was this ambition?
Yet Brutus says he was ambitious; —
And sure he is an honorable man!
I speak not to disprove what Brutus spoke;
But here I am to speak what I do know.
You all did love him once; not without cause:
What cause withholds you, then, to mourn for him?
O judgment! thou hast fled to brutish beasts,
And men have lost their reason! — Bear with me;
My heart is in the coffin there with Cæsar;
And I must pause till it come back to me!
But yesterday, the word of Cæsar might
Have stood against the world, — now lies he there,
And none so poor as do him reverence!
O masters! if I were disposed to stir
Your hearts and minds to mutiny and rage,
I should do Brutus wrong, and Cassius wrong, —
Who, you all know, are honorable men!
I will not do them wrong, I rather choose
To wrong the dead, to wrong myself and you,
Than I will wrong such honorable men! —
But here's a parchment with the seal of Cæsar —
I found it in his closet — 'tis his will!
Let but the commons hear his testament —
Which, pardon me, I do not mean to read, —
And they will go and kiss dead Cæsar's wounds,
And dip their napkins in his sacred blood;
Yea, beg a hair of him for memory;
And, dying, mention it within their wills,
Bequeathing it, as a rich legacy,
Unto their issue! —
    If you have tears, prepare to shed them now.
You all do know this mantle! I remember
The first time ever Cæsar put it on:

'Twas on a summer's evening, in his tent,
That day he overcame the Nervii!
Look! in this place ran Cassius' dagger through!
See what a rent the envious Casca made!
Through this, the well-beloved Brutus stabb'd!
And, as he pluck'd his cursed steel away,
Mark how the blood of Cæsar follow'd it!—
As rushing out of doors, to be resolved
If Brutus so unkindly knock'd, or no;—
For Brutus, as you know, was Cæsar's angel!
Judge, O ye gods, how dearly Cæsar loved him!
This, this was the unkindest cut of all,
For when the noble Cæsar saw him stab,
Ingratitude, more strong than traitor's arms,
Quite vanquish'd him.   Then burst his mighty heart,
And, in his mantle muffling up his face —
Even at the base of Pompey's statue,
Which all the while ran blood!—great Cæsar fall
Oh, what a fall was there, my countrymen!
Then I, and you, and all of us, fell down;
Whilst bloody treason flourish'd over us!
Oh, now you weep, and I perceive you feel
The dint of pity: these are gracious drops!
Kind souls! what! weep you when you but behold
Our Cæsar's vesture wounded? look you here!
Here is himself — marr'd, as you see, by traitors!—
Good friends! sweet friends! let me not stir you up
To such a sudden flood of mutiny!—
They that have done this deed, are honorable!
What private griefs they have, alas, I know not,
That made them do it: they are wise and honorable,
And will, no doubt, with reason answer you.
I come not, friends, to steal away your hearts:
I am no orator, as Brutus is;
But, as you know me all, a plain, blunt man,

That loves his friend, — and that they know full well
That gave me public leave to speak of him;
For I have neither wit, nor words, nor worth,
Action, nor utterance, nor the power of speech,
To stir men's blood: I only speak right on!
I tell you that which you yourselves do know;
Show you sweet Cæsar's wounds, poor, poor, dumb mouths!
And bid them speak for me. But, were I Brutus,-
And Brutus Antony, there were an Antony
Would ruffle up your spirits and put a tongue
In every wound of Cæsar, that should move
The stones of Rome to rise and mutiny!

COMPOSITION.

Write a short sketch of Mark Antony's speech, from the following points:

Cæsar has been murdered by Brutus and others. The hour for burial is at hand. Mark Antony comes to mourn over his friend's body. The people call for a speech. Mark Antony tells what a man Cæsar was -- how generous, brave, ambitious. The people become excited. Desire to attack the murderers. The people are asked to examine the rent mantle formerly worn by Cæsar. The wounds are shown. Compared to mouths. Cæsar's will is discovered and read. Antony tells what he would do, were he in the place of his enemies, and guilty as they. Describe the murderer as hiding away, and Antony as carried by the grateful people. Say a few words about the true character of Cæsar, and show that he was not great in the Christian sense of the word. None can be truly great who are not truly good.

coffers	parchment	napkins	Nervii
Lupercal	closet	bequeathing	marr'd
mutiny	commons	legacy	utterance

———o———

I hold this thing to be grandly true:
    That a noble deed is a step toward God,
Lifting the soul from the common sod
    To a purer air and a broader view.

ST. GREGORY AND THE ENGLISH SLAVES.

IN the slave-market in Rome some twelve hundre
years ago, were English youths waiting to be sol(
At the opposite end of the square on which the mai
ket stood there was an ancient church, which, traditio
said, had once been a pagan temple, and before long
bell from its lofty summit gave warning of the hour o
prayer.

The crowd that had gathered to look at the slave
soon became smaller, but there were many who wer(
in no hurry to leave, while the near approach of thre(
strangers in monastic habits attracted attention.

" That the eldest and darkest of them is the Deacor
Gregory, I know," said a man to his friend beside
him.

" And has he really taken orders ? " asked the other.

" Yes, and it is said that he intends to live in the
new monastery of St. Andrew that he has built, when
ho takes possession of his father's inheritance."

Gregory came to the man who had charge of the
slaves and inquired from what country they had been
brought.

The keeper answered politely that they came from
Britain, and, that beautiful as were the youths in the
market-place, the island from which they came possessed others as beautiful.

" And do they hold the faith ? ' asked Gregory eagerly.

" No, they are pagans," answered the keeper.

" What is the name of the country ? ' inquired Gregory.

" The name of the country is Anglia, or the land
of the Angles."

" Angles do you call them ? Say rather angels, if
they but professed the Faith of Christ." Then Gregory, with a mournful countenance, turned to one of
his companions and said :—

" Brother Augustine, the sight of these youths, so fair
and beautiful, fills me with sadness. Oh! that they
possessed the truth! How I long to procure the conversion of their nation. I will give no sleep to mine
eyes till I have obtained permission to spread the light
of truth in their pagan home, and if God and our Holy
Father judge me not worthy of such a labor I hope
that some one else will be appointed to do the work.

The monk addressed appeared a year or two younger than Gregory. Augustine listened to Gregory's
remarks without making answer. He then gently
touched Gregory's arm, as if to remind him that the
church-bell had ceased and that they must not delay
if they wished to take part in the service.

Gregory hastened to obey, and after whispering a
few words to the slave-keeper that had answered his
inquiries, he followed his companion into the sacred
building.

The great St. Gregory—for it was he that had
spoken to the slave keeper, did not forget the pagan
youths he had seen. He was not permitted to go
himself, but when he was called to the chair of Peter
he sent Augustine with several other monks to
preach the word of God to the English nation.

Questions: —What is a slave? Who abolished slavery in the United
States? What is a deacon? Mention some celebrated monk. Give
the name of some celebrated monastery.

waiting	summit	ceased	remind
ancient	inquired	procure	inquiries

MORNING HYMN OF ADAM AND EVE.

These are Thy glorious works, Parent of good,
Almighty!   Thine this universal frame,
Thus wondrous fair!   Thyself how wondrous, then!
Unspeakable, who sitt'st above these heavens,
To us invisible, or dimly seen
In these Thy lowest works ; yet these declare
Thy goodness beyond thought and power divine.
Speak, ye who best can tell, ye sons of light,
Angels ; for ye behold him, and with songs
And choral symphonies, day without night,
Circle his throne rejoicing—ye in heaven!
On earth join, all ye creatures, to extol
Him first, Him last, Him midst, and without end.

Fairest of stars, last in the train of night,
If better thou belong not to the dawn—
Sure pledge of day, that crowned the smiling morn
With thy bright circlet—praise Him in thy sphere,
While day arises, that sweet hour of prime.
Thou sun—of this great world both eye and soul—
Acknowledge Him thy greater ; sound His praise
In thy eternal course, both when thou climb'st,
And when high noon hast gained, and when thou fall'st.

Moon, that now meet'st the Orient sun, now fliest
With the fixed stars, fixed in their orb that fly,
And ye five other wandering fires, that move
In mystic dance, not without song, resound
His praise who out of darkness called up light.
Ye mists and exhalations that now rise
From hill or steaming lake, dusky or gray,
Till the sun paint your fleecy skirts with gold,
In honor to the world's great Author, rise ;
Whether to deck with clouds the uncolored sky

Or wet the thirsty earth with falling showers,
Rising or falling, still advance His praise.
His praise, ye winds, that from four quarters blow,
Breathe soft or loud ; and wave your tops, ye pines,
With every plant, in sign of worship, wave.
Fountains, and ye that warble, as ye flow,
Melodious murmurs, warbling, tune His praise !
Join voices, all ye living souls ; ye birds,
That singing up to heaven-gate ascend,
Bear on your wings and in your notes His praise.

Ye that in waters glide, and ye that walk
The earth and stately tread or lowly creep,
Witness if I be silent, morn or even,
To hill or valley, fountain or fresh shade,
Made vocal by my song, and taught His praise.
Hail, universal Lord ! be bounteous still
To give us only good ; and if the night
Have gathered aught of evil, or concealed,
Disperse it as now light dispels the dark.

COMPOSITION.

Give a synopsis of each stanza.

———o———

LOVE OF HOME.

The traveller from his native land,
The veriest wanderer neath the sun,
When from his glass of life the sand
Has nearly its full volume run,
Turns to the land that gave him birth,
Things banished from his mind for years,
And sighs to see that spot of earth
That knew his childhood's smiles and tears.

WALTER MASON.

I HAD in my younger days many friends, and some who were very dear to me ; but I had no friend so thoroughly dear to me, none for whom I ever felt a love that was at once so deep, so reverent, and so full of pure and elevating influences, as Walter Mason.

His very presence seemed somehow to soften and exert a mild and gentle influence upon all the boys of our circle. We seemed to speak more guardedly and with more reserve, when he was with us ; and I can say for myself that the rough jest and the thoughtless word were always repressed when he was leaning on my arm, or speaking to me in his low and sympathetic voice.

He possessed a wonderful power of moving and of thrilling the souls of those who listened to him, as he spoke on subjects which excited either his pride or his enthusiasm.

I asked in my boyish days no greater treat, no higher bliss, than to sit at his feet and in loving silence look up into his kindling face, and watch his flashing eyes, as the charming words came pouring from his lips.

In the midst of many temptations, he never lost any of the freshness and the innocent simplicity of his guileless nature. I did not know then, but I know now, that God had great designs upon him ; and so, as he brought the three children safe out of the midst of the fiery furnace, did he, by the exercise of the same omnipotent power, bring this dear soul safe out of the perils and influences of a large school, never ceasing to watch over him with the same paternal love and care.

Walter was his uncle's heir, but he had received a call which he gladly obeyed. He had experienced many difficulties in following out his vocation, and it was not likely that he would be turned from it by the first serious temptation. When obstacles had stood in the way, he remembered how he had prayed that they might be removed; and he remembered, too, how his heart had swelled almost to bursting, when at length the way was opened before him, and he was free to follow it; and was he to falter now, when more worldly prospects were presented to his gaze? Walter was very holy, and he was very devoted, but still, he was only human, and these things did arise before him once or twice in the shape of a temptation, but he quickly shook them off, and he never wavered.

When his uncle came to see him, and pleaded long and earnestly—pleaded, indeed, till the tears began to run down his face—Walter did not speak, but taking his hand, led him to the chapel. It was not until they had both knelt in prayer that Walter turned to speak to his uncle. "He that loveth father or mother more than Me, the same is not worthy of Me," was all that Walter whispered in his uncle's ear. His uncle's head sank lower on his breast, and for some time his frame shook with emotion. At length Walter, who knelt close at his side, heard him say: "Thy will be done, my God! Thy will be done!" and he rose to go away. When they were outside the door, the uncle turned towards his nephew and took his hand, and told him that he consented.

Walter had scarcely commenced his ecclesiastical studies when God filled him with a great desire of laboring for the salvation of souls thousands of miles away from his native land. During his whole collegiate course he never faltered in his choice. Towards the end his health began to fail, but still he persevered.

After his ordination, he spent a few weeks with his sorrowing friends. The time soon arrived for his departing, and he went calmly and cheerfully to the mission of his choice. For a short space he labored among the children of his desire, and his services met with a warm response in the grateful hearts of his people. His zeal never flagged. Sinners turned to God, and the careless and indifferent obeyed his command, because his command was never anything but a mild and loving persuasion. So he trod his holy way for one short year, and then the yellow fever came again. It struck down its victims on the right and on the left, and although it made no distinction of classes, still, it was amongst the poor that it raged most terribly.

Like an angel of consolation, Father Mason moved on the track of the destroyer, and for a long time escaped. The fever was at length visibly on the decline, and every one that escaped it was thankful.

One morning, there arose a louder and more bitter wail than had ever been heard, even when the fever was at its height ; for it went abroad that the young priest had been struck down at last. People gathered in crowds in the churches, and the prayer went up to God that He would spare him. He lingered on for two or three weeks more, edifying all by his resignation and by his fervent desire to receive his crown ; and then, with a gentle smile upon his face, and a word of love upon his lips, went away to God, ere six and twenty summers had passed over his head.

COMPOSITION.

Describe the character of Walter.

WISDOM AND KNOWLEDGE.

William Cowper (1731 - 1800) is one of the first poets whose writings give striking evidence of the change in poetic taste which set aside the artificial style and sentiment of the school of Dryden and Pope for themes drawn from nature and the sympathies of humanity. "The Task" and "Table Talk" are a series of social and moral reflections, interspersed with satire, descriptive of natural and domestic scenes. Of his shorter poems, the droll "John Gilpin's Ride," and the lines "On Receiving my Mother's Picture," are the best known. Cowper will always be popular, as he is essentially a domestic poet. There is a sort of a comfortable and prosaic morality in his poems, which is peculiar to all Protestant (especially Church of England) writers for the great middle class of readers. They seem to say, "Be good because it is the most convenient!" Their idea is crystallized in the natural axiom, "Honesty is the best *policy*." Catholic moralists are "made of sterner stuff."

KNOWLEDGE and wisdom, far from being one,
   Have ofttimes no connection. Knowledge dwells
In heads replete with thoughts of *other* men;
Wisdom in minds attentive to their *own*.
Knowledge, a rude, unprofitable mass,
The mere materials with which Wisdom builds,
Till smoothed and squared, and fitted to its place,
Does but *encumber* whom it seems to *enrich*.
Knowledge is proud that he has learned so much;
Wisdom is humble that he knows no more.

———o———

THE IDOLS OF THE AGE.

LOOK around, my brethren, and answer for yourselves.
   Contemplate the objects of this people's praise,
survey their standards, ponder their ideas and judgments,
and then tell me whether it is not most evident, from
their very notion of the desirable and the excellent,
that greatness and goodness, sanctity and sublimity,
and truth, are unknown to them; and that they do not

only not pursue, but do not even admire those high attributes of the Divine Nature. This is what I am insisting on, not what they actually do, or what they are, but what they revere, what they adore, what their gods are. Their god is mammon. I do not mean to say that all seek to be wealthy, but that all bow down before wealth. Wealth is that to which the multitude of men pay an instinctive homage. They measure happiness by wealth, and by wealth they measure respectability. Numbers, I say, there are, who never dream that they shall be rich themselves, but who still at the sight of wealth feel an involuntary reverence and awe, just as if a rich man must be a good man.

They like to be noticed by some extremely rich man ; they like on some occasion to have spoken to him ; they like to know those who know him, to be intimate with his dependants, to have entered his house, or, to know him by sight. Not, I repeat, that it ever comes into their minds that such wealth will one day be theirs ; not that they see the wealth, for the man who has it may dress, and live, and look like other men; not that they expect to gain some benefit from it: no, theirs is a disinterested homage, it is a homage resulting from an honest, genuine, hearty admiration of wealth for its own sake, such as that pure love which holy men feel for the Maker of all; it is a homage resulting from a profound faith in wealth, from the intimate sentiment of their hearts, that, however a man may look, — poor, mean, starved, decrepit, vulgar, yet if he be rich, he differs from all others; if he be rich, he has a gift, a spell, an omnipotence, — that with wealth he may do all things. Wealth is one idol of the day, and notoriety is a second. I am not speaking, I repeat, of what men pursue, but what they look up to, what they revere. Men may not have the opportunity of pursuing what still they admire. Never could notoriety exist as it does now in any former age of the world; now that the news of the hour from all parts of the world, private news as well as public, is brought day by day to every individual, I may say, of the community, to the poorest artisan and the most secluded peasant, by processes so uniform, so unvarying, so spontaneous, that they almost bear the semblance of natural law. And hence notoriety, or the making a noise in the world, has come to be considered a great good itself, and a ground of veneration. Time was when men could only make a display by means of expenditure, and the world used to gaze with wonder on those who had large establishments, many servants, many horses, richly-furnished houses, gardens, and parks : it does so still, but it has not often the opportunity, for such magnificence is the fortune of the few, and comparatively few are its witnesses. Notoriety, or, as it may be called, newspaper fame, is to the many what style and fashion, to use the language of the world, are to those who happen to be within their influence; it becomes to them a sort of idol, worshipped for its own sake, and without any reference to the shape in which it comes before them. It may be an evil fame, it may be the notoriety of a great statesman, or of a great preacher, or of a great speculator, or of a great experimentalist, or of a great criminal; of one who has labored in the improvement of our schools, or hospitals, or prisons, or workhouses, or of one who has robbed his neighbor of his wife. It matters not, so that a man is talked much of, and read much of, he is thought much of; nay, let him have even died justly under the hands of the law, still he will be made a sort of martyr of.

His clothes, his handwriting, the circumstances of his

guilt, the instruments of his deed of blood, will be shown about, gazed on, treasured up as so many relics; for the question with men is, not whether he is great, or good, or wise, or holy, — not whether he is base, and vile, and odious, but whether he is in the mouths of men, whether he has centred on himself the attention of many, whether he has done something out of the way, whether he has been, as it were, canonized in the publications of the hour. All men cannot be notorious; the multitude who thus honor notoriety, do not seek it themselves; nor am I speaking of what men do, but how they judge; yet instances do occur, from time to time, of wretched men, so smitten with the passion for notoriety, as even to dare in fact some detestable and wanton act, not from love of it, not from liking or dislike of the person against whom it is directed, but simply in order thereby to gratify this impure desire of being talked about and being looked at. "These are thy gods, O Israel!" Alas! alas! this great and noble people, born to aspire, born for reverence, behold them walking to and fro by the torch-light of the cavern, or pursuing the wild-fires of the marsh, not understanding themselves, their destinies, their defilements, their needs, because they have not the glorious luminaries of heaven to see, to consult, and to admire!

COMPOSITION.

Copy first ten lines of third paragraph.

Give the following sentences in your own words:

(a) It matters not so that a man is talked much of, and read much of, he is thought much of; nay, let him have even died justly under the hands of the law, still he will be made a sort of martyr of. (b) Notoriety, or a making a noise in the world, has come to be considered a great good in itself, and a ground of veneration. (c) The question, now-a-days, is not whether a man is great, or good, or wise, or holy, — not whether he is base and vile and odious, but whether he has done something out of the way, whether he has been, as it were, canonized in the publications of the hour.

contemplate	involuntary	notoriety	centred
survey	dependants	community	smitten
ponder	disinterested	artisan	cavern
attributes	homage	secluded	marsh
mammon	intimate	spontaneous	defilements
instinctive	decrepit	speculator	luminaries

———o———

THREE DAYS IN THE LIFE OF COLUMBUS.

ON the deck stood Columbus ; the ocean's expanse,
  Untried and unlimited, swept by his glance.
"Back to Spain!" cry his men: "put the vessel about!
We venture no farther through danger and doubt."
"Three days, and I give you a world!" he replied;
"Bear up, my brave comrades, three days shall decide."
He sails, but no token of land is in sight;
He sails, but the day shows no more than the night;
On, onward, he sails, while in vain o'er the lee
The lead is sent down through a fathomless sea.

The pilot in silence leans mournfully o'er
The rudder that creaks mid the billowy roar;
He hears the hoarse moan of the spray-driving blast,
And its funeral wail through the shrouds of the mast.
The stars of far Europe have sunk from the skies,
And the great Southern Cross meets his terrified eyes;
But at length the slow dawn, softly streaking the night,
Illumes the blue vault with a faint crimson light.
"Columbus! 'tis day, and the darkness is o'er."
"Day! and what dost thou see?" "Sky and ocean — no more!"

The second day ends, and Columbus is sleeping,
While Mutiny near him its vigil is keeping.

"Shall he perish?"   "Ay, death!" is the barbarous cry;
"He must triumph to-morrow, or, perjured, must die!"
Ungrateful and blind! shall the world-linking sea
He traced for the future his sepulchre be?
Or shall it to-morrow, with pitiless waves,
Fling his corse on that shore which his patient eye craves?
The corse of an humble adventurer, then;
One day later — Columbus, the first among men!

But hush! he is dreaming; and sleep to his thought
Reveals what his waking eyes vainly have sought;
Through the distant horizon — oh rapturous sight! —
Fresh bursts the New World from the darkness of night;
O vision of glory! ineffable scene!
What richness of verdure! the sky how serene!
How blue the far mountains! how glad the green isles!
And the earth and the ocean, how dimpled with smiles!
"Joy! joy!" cried Columbus, "this region is mine!"
Thine? not e'en its name, wondrous dreamer, is thine.

Again the dream changes.   Columbus looks forth,
And a bright constellation illumines the North.
'Tis the herald of empire!   A people appear,
Impatient of wrong, and unconscious of fear:
They level the forest, they ransack the seas;
Each zone finds their canvas unfurled to the breeze.
"Hold!" Tyranny cries; but their resolute breath
Sends back the reply, "Independence or death!"
The ploughshare they turn to a weapon of might,
And, defying all odds, hurry forth to the fight.

They have conquered!   The people, with grateful acclaim,
Look to Washington's guidance from Washington's fame;
Behold Cincinnatus and Cato combined
In his patriot heart and republican mind!
O type of true manhood! what sceptre or crown
But fades in the light of thy simple renown!

And, lo! by the side of the hero, a sage,
In freedom's behalf, sets his mark on the age;
Whom Science admiringly hails, while he wrings
The lightning from heaven, the sceptre from kings!

But see! o'er Columbus slow consciousness breaks —
"Land! land!" cry the sailors; "land! land!" — he awakes —
He runs — yes! behold it! — it blesses his sight —
The land! O dear spectacle! transport! delight!
O generous sobs, which he cannot restrain!
"What will Ferdinand say? and the Future? and Spain?
I will lay this fair land at the foot of the throne —
The king will repay all the ills I have known;
In exchange for a world what are honors and gains
Or a crown?" But how *is* he rewarded? With chains!

Questions: — Explain "the ocean's expanse, *untried* and *unlimited;*"
"no *token* of land is in sight;" "The lead is sent down through a
fathomless sea;" "*spray-driving* blast;" "Southern Cross;" "perjured,
must die;" "Fling his corse on that shore *which his patient eye craves?*"
"Thine? not e'en its name, wondrous dreamer, is thine!" "A people
appear, impatient of wrong and unconscious of fear;" "defying all
odds."

COMPOSITION.

Write the eighth stanza in your own words, and give names of other
discoverers or inventors who were ill-treated.

expanse	barbarous	ineffable	Cincinnatus
lead	perjured	serene	Cato
wail	corse	constellation	republican
shrouds	adventurer	herald	spectacle
mutiny	rapturous	canvas	transport

———o———

PHILANTHROPY AND CHARITY.

Orestes Augustus Brownson (1803-1876), a distinguished convert to
Catholicism, and one of the ablest defenders ever enlisted in the
cause of the faith. His contributions to literature have been chiefly

ın the form of articles in the Boston Quarterly, Democratic, and Brownson's Reviews, the latter being the vehicle of his Catholic sentiment. Whether religious, controversial, political or otherwise, they are all marked by a great fearlessness and independence of adverse criticism, by definite, philosophical and practical views expressed in a style that is natural, direct and plain, and devoid of any attempt at elegance or brilliancy.

THE natural *sentiment* of philanthropy is, at best, only human love. This answers very well, when the work to be done is simply to concoct grand schemes, make brilliant and eloquent speeches, or when there are no disagreeble duties to be performed, no violent natural repugnances to be overcome; but it fails in the hour of severe trial. Your philanthropist starts off with generous impulses, with an ardent enthusiasm; and so long as there are no great discouragements, no disgusting offices in his way, and he has even a small number of admiring friends to stimulate his zeal, applaud his eloquence, flatter his vanity, and soften the rebuffs which a hard world gives him, he may keep on his course, and continue his task.

But let him find himself entirely alone, let him have no little public of his own, which is all the word to him, let him be thwarted on every point, let him be obliged to work in secret, unseen by all but the All-seeing Eye, encounter from mankind nothing but contradiction, contempt and ingratitude, and he will soon begin to say to himself, Why suffer and endure so much for the unworthy? He who loves man for man's sake, loves only a creature, a being of imperfect worth, of no more worth than himself, — perhaps not so much; and why shall he love him more than himself, and sacrifice himself for him? The highest stretch of human love is, to love our neighbors *as* we love ourselves; and we do injustice to ourselves, when we love them more than we do ourselves.

Nay, philanthropy itself is a sort of selfishness. It is a sentiment, not a principle. Its real motive is not another's good, but its own satisfaction according to its nature. It seeks the good of others, because the good of others is the means of its own satisfaction, and is as really selfish in its principles as any other of our sentiments; for there is a broad distinction between the *sentiment* of philanthropy, and the *duty* of doing good to others, — between seeking the good of others from sentiment, and seeking it in obedience to a law which binds the conscience.

The measure of the capacity of philanthropy, as a sentiment, is the amount of satisfaction it can bring to the possessor. So long as, upon the whole, he finds it more delightful to play the philanthropist than the miser, for instance, he will do it, but no longer. Hence, philanthropy must always decrease just in proportion to the increase of the repugnances it must encounter, and fail us just at the moment when it is most needed, and always in proportion as it is needed. It follows the law so observable in all human society, and helps most when and where its help is least needed. Here is the condemnation of every scheme, however plausible it may look, that in any degree depends on philanthropy for its success.

The principle the Associationists want for their success is not philanthropy — the love of man for man's sake — but divine charity, not to be had and preserved out of the Catholic Church. Charity is, in relation to its subject, a supernaturally infused virtue; in relation to its object, the supreme and exclusive love of God for his own sake, and man for the sake of God. He who has it is proof against all trials: for his love does not depend on man, who so often proves himself totally unamiable and unworthy, but on God, who is always and everywhere infinitely amiable and deserving of all love. He visits the sick, the prisoner, the poor, for it is God whom he visits; with tenderness he clasps the leprous to his bosom, and kisses their sores, for it is God whom he embraces and whose wounds he kisses. The most painful and disgusting offices are sweet and easy, because he performs them for God, who is love, and whose love inflames his heart. Whenever there is a service to be rendered to one of God's little ones, he runs with eagerness to do it; for it is a service to be rendered to God himself.

"Charity never faileth." It is proof against all natural repugnances; it overcomes earth and hell; and brings God down to tabernacle with men. Dear to it is this poor beggar, for it sees in him only our Lord, who had "not where to lay his head;" dear are the sorrowing and the afflicted, for it sees in them him who was "a man of sorrows and acquainted with infirmity;" dear are these poor outcasts, for in them it beholds him who was "scorned and rejected of men;" dear are the wronged, the oppressed, the down-trodden, for in them it beholds the Innocent One nailed to the cross, and dying to atone for human wickedness.

And it joys to succor them all; for in so doing, it makes reparation to God for the poverty, sufferings, wrongs, contempt, and ignominious death which he endured for our sakes; for it is his poverty it relieves in relieving the poor, his hunger it feeds in feeding the hungry, his nakedness it clothes in throwing the robe over the naked, his afflictions it consoles in consoling the sorrowing, his wounds into which it pours oil and wine, and which it binds up. "Inasmuch as ye did it unto the least of these, my brethren, ye did it unto me."

It does all things for God, whom it loves more than men, more than life, and more than heaven itself, if to love him and heaven were not one and the same thing. This is the principle you need; with this principle, you have God with you and for you, and to fail is impossible. But with this principle, Association is, at best, a matter of indifference; for this is sufficient of itself at all times, under any and every form of political, social, or industrial organization. He who has God can have nothing more.

COMPOSITION.

Write the sixth paragraph, and give two synonymes for beggar, sorrowing, rejected, infirmity. Write three short sentences showing a different use for these same words.

philanthropy	encounter	repugnances
schemes	ingratitude	plausible
repugnances	selfishness	leprous
impulses	sentiment	tabernacle
thwarted	capacity	reparation

---o---

FATHER MATTHEW.

SEIZE the pencil, child of art,
  Fame and fortune brighten o'er thee!
Great thy hand, and great thy heart,
  If well thou do'st the work before thee!
'Tis not thine to round the shield,
  Or point the sabre, black or gory;
'Tis not thine to spread the field,
  Where crime is crown'd, where guilt is glory.

Child of art! to thee be given
   To paint, in colors all unclouded,
Breakings of a radiant heaven
   O'er an isle in darkness shrouded
But, to paint them true and well,
   Every ray we see them shedding
In its very light must tell
   What a gloom *before* was spreading.

Canst thou picture dried-up tears,
   Eyes that wept no longer weeping;
Faithful woman's wrongs and fears,
   Lonely nightly vigils keeping,
Listening ev'ry footfall nigh,
   Hoping him she loves returning?
Canst thou, then, depict her joy,
   That we may know *the change* from mourning?

Paint in colors strong, but mild,
   Our Isle's Redeemer and Director.
Canst thou paint *the man* a *child,*
   Yet shadow forth the mighty VICTOR?
Let his path a rainbow span,
   Every *hue* and *color* blending,
Beaming "peace and love" to man,
   And alike o'er ALL extending!

Canst thou paint a land made free,
   From its sleep of bondage woken;
Yet, withal, that we may see
   What 'twas *before* the chain was broken?
Seize thy pencil, child of art,
   Fame and fortune brighten o'er thee:
Great thy hand, and great thy heart,
   If well thou do'st the work before thee.

QUESTIONS AND COMPOSITION.

How will the artist prove himself gifted with a great hand and great heart? What is the work before the artist? How is Ireland, as an island, in darkness shrouded? What rights has the true freeman? What mistake is often made about liberty and libertinism? How is the artist to represent "weeping eyes"? What marked contrasts must be shown in this picture? Name four persons who took a share in liberating Ireland from unjust, penal laws. How does the writer wish our divine Lord painted? In what double character? What special chain did Father Matthew seek to break?

Copy the second stanza. Then form sentences in which "art" will become a verb, "true" and "well" adverbs and adjectives, respectively. Give the expression—

> "In its very light must tell
> What a gloom *before* was spreading" —

in three or four different forms.

Commit the lines from Very Rev. D. O'Reilley's "Men as We Need Them," on intemperance. If convenient, write the sense of the same in three ways on the blackboard.

art	sabre	shrouded	depict	woken
shield	radiant	vigils	span	withal

ANALYSIS.

AGREEABLE EXPRESSION.

"Pay close attention to the emotions or feelings the selection suggests."

"Give due attention to the vocal tones called for by the selection."

"Lay special stress on those points that are to attract the attention of an audience."

Examine the selection carefully. What is its character? What the task given the painter?

The reader is then *to speak to the artist*. A conversational tone is therefore needed. Before reading with rhetorical effect, give yourself a thorough appreciation of the piece. Answer the questions fully, and *after* this exercise endeavor to realize the author's idea.

> "SEIZE the pencil, child of ART,
> FAME and FORTUNE brighten o'er thee !
> GREAT thy HAND, and great thy HEART,
> If WELL thou do'st the work before thee !
> 'Tis not thine TO ROUND THE SHIELD
> OR POINT THE SABRE, BLACK OR GORY '

'Tis not thine TO SPREAD THE FIELD,
　Where CRIME is CROWNED, — where GUILT is GLORY."

Strive to bring out the antithesis between "crime,"—"crowned,"
and "guilt," — "glory."

In the second stanza, the last four lines call for special attention

"True," "well," "every ray," "very light," "gloom,"

call for a tone-coloring that will bring out the full meaning of
those well chosen adjectives.

The other stanzas should be treated in same way, the antithetic
thoughts being made to give forth all their saliency.

———o———

SOUND AND SENSE.

THAT, in the formation of language, men have been
much influenced by a regard to the nature of the
things and actions meant to be represented, is a fact of
which every known speech gives proof. In our own
language, for instance, who does not perceive in the
sound of the words *thunder, boundless, terrible,* a something
appropriate to the sublime ideas intended to be conveyed?
In the word *crash* we hear the very action implied. *Imp,
elf,*—how descriptive of the miniature beings to which
we apply them! *Fairy,*—how light and tripping, just
like the fairy herself!—the word, no more than the
thing, seems fit to bend the grass-blade, or shake the
tear from the blue-eyed flower.

Pea is another of those words expressive of light,
diminutive objects; any man born without sight and
touch, if such ever are, could tell what kind of thing a
pea was from the sound of the word. Of picturesque
words, *sylvan* and *crystal* are among our greatest favorites.
Sylvan!—what visions of beautiful old sunlit forests,
with huntsmen and bugle-horns, arise at the sound!
Crystal!—does it not glitter like the very thing it
stands for? Yet crystal is not so beautiful as its own

adjective. *Crystalline !*—why, the whole mind is lightened up with its shine. And this superiority is as it should be ; for crystal can only be one comparatively small object, while crystalline may refer to a mass — to a world of crystals.

It will be found that natural objects have a larger proportion of expressive names among them than any other things. The *eagle,* — what appropriate daring and sublimity! the *dove,* — what softness! the *linnet,* — what fluttering gentleness! "That which men call a rose" would *not* by any other name, or at least by many other names, smell as sweet. *Lily,* — what tall, cool, pale, lady-like beauty have we here! *Violet, jessamine, hyacinth, anemone, geranium !* — beauties, all of them, to the ear as well as the eye.

The names of the precious stones have also a beauty and magnificence above most common things. *Diamond, sapphire, amethyst, beryl, ruby, agate, pearl, jasper, topaz, garnet, emerald,* — what a caskanet of sparkling sounds! *Diadem* and *coronet* glitter with gold and precious stones, like the objects they represent. It is almost unnecessary to bring forward instances of the fine things which are represented in English by fine words. Let us take any sublime passage of our poetry, and we shall hardly find a word which is inappropriate in sound. For example :

> The cloud-capped towers, the gorgeous palaces,
> The solemn temples, the great globe itself,—
> Yea, all which it inherit, shall dissolve,
> And, like this insubstantial pageant faded,
> Leave not a rack behind.

The "gorgeous palaces," "the solemn temples," — how admirably do these lofty sounds harmonize with the objects!

The relation between the sound and sense of certain

words is to be ascribed to more than one cause. **Many**
are evidently imitative representations of the things,
movements, and acts, which are meant to be expressed.
Others, in which we only find a general relation, as
between a beautiful thing, and a beautiful word, a
ridiculous thing and a ridiculous word, or a sublime idea
and a sublime word, must be attributed to those faculties,
native to every mind, which enable us to perceive and
enjoy the beautiful, the ridiculous, and the sublime.

Doctor Wallis, who wrote upon English grammar in
the reign of Charles II., represented it as a peculiar
excellence of our language, that, beyond all others, it
expressed the nature of the objects which it names, by
employing sounds sharper, softer, weaker, stronger, more
obscure, or more stridulous, according as the idea which
is to be suggested requires. He gives various examples.
Thus, words formed upon *st* always denote firmness and
strength, and are analogous to the Latin *sto*, as, stand,
stay, staff, stop, stout, steady, stake, stamp, etc.

Words beginning with *str* intimate violent force and
energy, as, strive, strength, stress, stripe, etc. *Thr*
implies forcible motion, as, throw, throb, thrust, threaten,
thraldom, thrill; *gl*, smoothness or silent motion, as
glib, glide; *wr*, obliquity or distortion, as, wry, wrest,
wrestle, wring, wrong, wrangle, wrath, etc.; *sw*, silent
agitation, or lateral motion, as, sway, swing, swerve,
sweep, swim; *sl*, a gentle fall or less observable motion,
as, slide, slip, sly, slit, slow, slack, sling; *sp*, dissipation
or expansion, as, spread, sprout, sprinkle, spill, split,
spring.

Terminations in *ash* indicate something acting nimbly
and sharply, as, crash, dash, rash, flash, lash, slash;
terminations in *ush*, something acting more obtusely and
duly, as, crush, brush, hush, gush, blush. The learned

author produces a great many more examples of a like kind, which seem to leave no doubt that the analogies of sound have had some influence on the formation of words. At the same time, in all speculations of this kind, there is so much room for fancy to operate, that they ought to be adopted with much caution in forming any general theory.

COMPOSITION.

Copy the sixth paragraph. Give four words beginning with *st*, showing strength, and give sentences in which these words will be employed.

Give the subjoined sentences in three different ways:

"In all operations of this kind, there is so much room for fancy to operate, that they ought to be adopted, with much caution, in forming any general theory."

| appropriate | caskanet | gorgeous | dissipation |
| diminutive | instances | meant | analogies |

ANCIENT AND MODERN WRITERS.

THE classics possess a peculiar charm, from the circumstance that they have been the models, I might almost say the masters, of composition and thought in all ages. In the contemplation of these august teachers of mankind, we are filled with conflicting emotions.

They are the early voice of the world, better remembered and more cherished still than all the intermediate words that have been uttered; as the lessons of childhood still haunt us when the expressions of later years have been effaced from the mind. But they show with most unwelcome frequency the tokens of the world's childhood, before passion had yielded to the sway of reason and the affections. They want the highest charm of purity, of righteousness, of elevated sentiments, of love to God and man.

It is not in the frigid philosophy of the Porch and the Academy that we are to seek these; not in the marvelous teachings of Socrates, as they come mended by the mellifluous words of Plato; not in the resounding line of Homer, on whose inspiring tale of blood Alexander pillowed his head; not in the animated strain of Pindar, where virtue is pictured in the successful strife of an athlete at the Isthmian games; not in the torrent of Demosthenes, dark with self-love and the spirit of vengeance; not in the fitful philosophy and intemperate eloquence of Tully, not in the genial libertinism of Horace, or the stately atheism of Lucretius. No: these must not be our masters; in none of these are we to seek the way of life.

For eighteen hundred years the spirit of these writers has been engaged in weaponless contest with the Sermon on the mount, and those two sublime commandments on which hang all the law and the prophets. The strife is still pending. Heathenism, which has possessed itself. of such siren forms, is not yet exorcised. It still tempts the young, controls the affairs of active life, and haunts the meditations of age.

Our own productions, though they may yield to those of the ancients in the arrangement of ideas, in method, in beauty of form, and in freshness of illustration, are immeasurably superior in the truth, delicacy, and elevation of their sentiments: above all, in the benign recognition of that great Christian revelation, the brotherhood of man. How vain are eloquence and poetry, compared with this heaven-descended truth! Put in one scale that simple utterance, and in the other the lore of antiquity, with its accumulating glosses and commentaries, and the last be the light and trivial in the balance. Greek poetry has been likened to the song of the nightingale, sitting in the rich, symmetrical crown of the palm-tree, trilling her thick-warbled notes; but even this is less sweet and tender than the music of the human heart.

COMPOSITION.

Change adjectives and common nouns in third paragraph, leaving balance as written.

Write the following sentence in three ways:

Heathenism still tempts the young, controls the affairs of active life, and haunts the meditations of age.

peculiar	Alexander	siren
intermediate	athlete	exorcised
haunt	Isthmian	yield
sway	Demosthenes	benign
Academy	libertinism	accumulating
Socrates	Horace	glosses
mellifluous	stately	commentaries
Plato	atheism	symmetrical
Homer	Lucretius	warbled

————o————

HUMILITY.

THE bird that soars on highest wing
   Builds on the ground her lowly nest;
And she that doth most sweetly sing,
Sings in the shade when all things rest.
The saint that wears Heaven's brightest crown,
In deepest adoration bends;
The weight of glory bows him down,
Then most when most his soul ascends;
    Nearest the Throne itself must be
    The footstool of Humility.

THE FELLOWSHIP OF CATHOLICITY.

"My spirit yearns to bring
    The lost ones back — yearns with desire intense —
And struggles hard to wring
    The bolts apart, and pluck thy captives thence."

                                                BRYANT.

MAN possesses powers which extend far beyond the visible world, into the realms of the unseen, for he is essentially a spiritual being. One of the deepest yearnings of his soul is to communicate with those of the spirit world.

"That the dead are seen no more," says Dr. Johnson, "I will not undertake to maintain, against the concurrent testimony of all ages and of all nations. There is no people, rude or learned, among whom apparitions of the dead are not related and believed. This opinion, which prevails as far as human nature is diffused, could become universal only by its truth; those who never heard of one another, would not have agreed in a tale which nothing but experience can make credible. That it is doubted by single cavillers, can very little weaken the general evidence; and some who deny it with their tongues, confess it by their fears."*

"Let us then not imagine," says the celebrated Dr. Channing, "that the usefulness of the good is finished at death. Then rather does it begin. Let us not judge of their state by associations drawn from the stillness and silence of the grave. They have gone to the abodes of life, of warmth and action. They have gone to fill a larger place in the system of God. Death has expanded their powers. The clogs and fetters of the perishable body have fallen off, that they may act more freely and with more delight in the grand system of creation.

* Rasselas.

It would be grateful to believe that their influence reaches to the present state, and we certainly are not forbidden to indulge the hope."*

It is not only consoling to believe thus, but so deeply rooted is the conviction, that there are moments when it asserts its vitality, in spite of our creeds or ourselves.

In Dr. Johnson's journal of March 28, 1753, we find : " I kept this day as the anniversary of my Tetty's death, with prayers and tears in the morning. In the evening, I prayed for her conditionally, if it were lawful."† And in a prayer which he wrote, he supplicates that he may " enjoy the good effects of the attention and ministration of his departed wife."‡

Here is a true expression of a secret and spontaneous instinct of the human heart ; for who believes, when kneeling by the grave of the loved and lost, that the sacred ties of friendship and affection, eternal as the laws of his being, are wholly severed? Does he not rather, at that hour, become aware, for the first time, how close were the bonds that bound him to the departed, and exclaim, in grateful relief: The living and the dead indeed make one communion!

Dr. Channing, in writing to a friend on the death of his child, says : "Our child is lost to our sight, but not to our faith and hope, perhaps not to our beneficent influences. Is there no means of gratifying our desire of promoting his happiness? The living and dead make one communion." §

The religions of all nations, with each individual consciousness, witness to the belief of mankind in a communion between the soul and spirits, between the living and the departed. The ancient religions of Egypt China, Greece, Rome, the Britons, Australians and

---

* Memoirs, p. 276.　† Boswell's Life.　‡ ibid.　§ Memoirs, p. 228.

American Indians, give the same testimony. Also the belief in magis, soothsaying, necromancy, and other superstitious practices which place us, as is supposed, in secret relations with the inhabitants of another world.

The demon of Socrates, the spectre of Brutus, the guardian of Cæsar, give the same confirmation. The histories of Mahomet, Cromwell, Napoleon, Jacob Bœhme, Swedenborg, Rousseau, Fourrier, and the works of all the celebrated poets, both ancient and modern, are stamped with strong evidence of the working of this instinct in the soul; and they owe much of their genius and popularity to its strange workings and fascinations.

One of the highest purposes of Religion, if it means anything, is to reveal to man the invisible world, and bring him into closer communion with its inhabitants, by teaching him to live more completely under its spiritual influences, because he is destined to move in its sphere, and there, amidst its glorious spirits, enjoy perfect bliss. Religion must do this, for, if she fails. men seek the gratification of this instinct elsewhere.

COMPOSITION.

Write the last paragraph in two different ways, and give a list of substitute words for: purposes, invisible, communion, inhabitants, teaching, completely, glorious, bliss.

essentially	vitality	conjurations
yearnings	spontaneous	fascinating
concurrent	soothsaying	communion

DEATH.

Lacordaire, Jean Baptiste, the most famous French pulpit orator of this century, was born in 1802; died in 1861. He studied law with most brilliant prospects, but suddenly abandoned it to enter the

priesthood. In 1835 he began his famous "Conferences" in the
Cathedral of Nôtre Dame, in which he discussed the religious social,
political and philosophical questions that were then agitating the
minds of France. These sermons were distinguished for their literary
excellence, their religious fervor and enthusiasm, their insight into all
the intellectual and moral temptations which beset the youth of the
present age. They gave their author a wonderful influence over
young and cultivated minds. Besides these "Conferences," his
admirable "Letters to Young Men" have been translated into English.

YOUNG men, I turn towards you. It is an old habit
which you must forgive in me. I have so often
called you to the road of great things, that it is difficult
for me to keep your remembrance and your name from
my words. You have a long career before you; but if you
prefer life to justice, if the thought of death troubles
you, that career which you paint so brightly, will sooner
or later be darkened by weaknesses unworthy of you.
Citizens, magistrates, soldiers, a time will come for you
when contempt of death is the sole source of good in
word or action, when private virtues no longer shelter
man, but when it is needful to possess the fearlessness
of a soul which looks above this world, and which has
placed there its life with its faith. If that faith be
wanting to you, in vain will truth and justice look down
upon you from heaven, their eternal abode; and in vain
will Providence bring under your feet events capable of
immortalizing your life. Glory will pass before you,
offer you its hand, and you will be powerless to call it
even by its name. But what is glory? Times are
greatly changed since it had altars. The future of
truth, of the universal expansion of justice in the
world, is henceforth the question amongst us.

Christianity has opened ways to us which antiquity
knew not; all is enlarged,—right, duty, responsibility,
man, and the world. Consequently higher virtues are

required, greater sacrifices, and more virile souls. When the three hundred Spartans awaited the innumerable horde of effeminate barbarians at Thermopylæ, they knew well that they must die, and one of them, desiring to leave an epitaph upon the tomb of his fellow soldiers, with the point of his spear cut upon the rock the famous inscription: "Traveller, tell Sparta that we died here to obey her holy laws." This, from whatever point of earth or heaven it may be seen, is an heroic spectacle, and the Christian ages have not refused to it their admiration.

But they had nearer to them another Thermopylæ, a Thermopylæ bathed with purer and more plenteous blood. Like Greece, Christianity has had its barbarians to conquer, and the narrow passes of the catacombs were the Thermopylæ where its faithful ones saved it by their death. Surely they also might have graven upon the rock an inscription worthy of their martyrdom; and it would not have been, "tell Sparta," but, "tell the human race that we died to obey the holy laws of God!"

But he for whom they died had taught them that modesty of which ancient heroism knew nothing. They died then without pomp, unknown to Greece and to themselves, and at length, when glory sought them underground, it found only their blood.

Here, gentlemen, you will perhaps stop me: you ask me where is the happiness whose name charmed your ear at the beginning of this discourse, as the object of your life and the final end of man? We have come to blood, to martyrdom, to sacrifice, under the most austere form. Is not this a strange road? Strange, if you will, but I do not swerve from it. In the glorious path where the course of ideas has led us, I feel, like you, the thorns which threaten or wound my flesh; they are sharp, they form a road of which you may say all, save that it is not the road of heroes and saints, the road of all those who have honored their nature, immortalized their life, saved their brethren, and respected God.

COMPOSITION.

Write the following sentence in four ways:

"If you prefer life to justice, if the thought of death troubles you, that career which you paint so brightly, will sooner or later be darkened by weaknesses unworthy of you."

Write sentences containing the following words : death, brightly universal, expansion, virtues, required.

difficult	barbarians	Catacombs
Christianity	Thermopylæ	heroism
responsibility	epitaph	martyrdom
consequently	inscriptions	sacrifice
horde	Sparta	immortalized

THE PURIFICATION.

BLESSED are the pure in heart,
　For they shall see our God;
The secret of the Lord is theirs,
　Their soul is Christ's abode.

Might mortal thought presume
　To guess an angel's lay?
Such are the notes that echo through
　The courts of heaven to-day.

Such the triumphal hymns
　On Sion's Prince that wait,
In high procession passing on
　Towards his temple gate.

Give ear, ye kings; bow down,
　Ye rulers of the earth!

This, this is he, your priest by
   Your God and King by birth

No pomp of earthly guards
   Attends with sword and spear,
And all defying, dauntless looks,
   Their monarch's way to clear;

Yet are there more with him
   Than all that are with you;
The armies of the highest heaven,
   All righteous, good and true.

Spotless their robes and pure,
   Dipped in the sea of light,
That hides the unapproached shrine
   From men's and angels' sight.

His throne, thy bosom blest,
   O mother undefiled!
That throne, if aught beneath the skies,
   Beseems the Sinless Child.

Lost in high thoughts — "whose son
   The wondrous Babe might prove,"
Her guileless husband walks beside,
   Bearing the hallowed dove.

Meet emblem of his vow,
   Who, on this happy day,
His dove-like soul — best sacrifice —
   Did on God's altar lay.

But who is he, by years
   Bowed, but erect in heart,
Whose prayers are struggling with his tears ?
   "Lord, let me now depart.

" Now hath thy servant seen
  Thy saving health, O Lord,
'Tis time that I depart in peace,
  According to thy word."

Yet swells the pomp, one more
  Comes forth to bless her God:
Full fourscore years, meek widow she
  Her heavenward way hath trod.

She who to earthly joy
  So long had given farewell,
Now sees, unlooked for, heaven on earth,
  Christ in his Israel.

Wide open from that hour
  The temple gates are set,
And still the saints, rejoicing there,
  The Holy Child have met.

Now count his train to-day,
  And who may meet him, learn.
Him childlike sires, meek maidens find
  Where pride can naught discern.

Still to the lowly soul
  He doth himself impart,
And for his cradle and his throne
  Chooseth the pure in heart.

Questions: — In what sermon of Christ are the first words in first
stanza found? What question is asked in second? Give the fourth
in your own words. How was Christ attended (fifth)? What invisible
attendant present (sixth)? How do they appear to spiritual eyes
(seventh)? What was the most fitting earthly throne for Christ
(eighth)? What question is Mary's guileless husband (Joseph) asking
himself? What vow had been made? Who made it? Who is spoken
of as " by years bowed "? In what part of the Testament do you find
"Lord, let me now. . . . . word"? Who else appears? Who are in the

Holy Child's train? To whom does this Child impart himself? Where does he find a cradle and a throne? Connect the first and last stanzas, and see their co-relation.

Sion's	guileless	score
dauntless	erect	set
righteous	struggling	discern

———o———

THE FLIGHT INTO EGYPT.

Frederick William Faber (1815–1863), one of the converts of the famous "Oxford movement," which brought into the Catholic Church Newman, Manning, Bowden, and so many other gifted English minds. Shortly after his conversion in 1845 he was ordained priest, and joined the Oratorians of St. Philip Neri. Of a singularly contemplative and poetical mind, he turned his abilities to the devotional and meditative aspects of religion, and poured forth the inexhaustible treasures of his soul in those marvellous works, "All for Jesus," "Growth in Holiness," "Bethlehem," "The Blessed Sacrament," "The Creature and the Creator," "The Conferences," and "The Foot of the Cross," works which have become fountains of refreshment for devout souls in every land. Wordsworth said of him that "Nature lost a great poet when Faber became a priest." Nature lost, but Religion gained; and the muse that had so sweetly sung the praise of Nature in the "Cheswell Water-lily," "Sir Lancelot" and the "Styrian Lake," chanted the mysteries of divine love in those beautiful *Catholic Hymns* which shall cause the name of Faber to be remembered as long as the English language shall be spoken.

THE night was dark and tranquil over the town of Nazareth, when Joseph went forth. No commandment of God ever found such alacrity in highest saint or readiest angel as this one had found in Mary. She heard Joseph's words, and she smiled on him in silence as he spoke. There was no perturbation, no hurry, although there was all a mother's fear. She took up her treasure, as he slept, and went forth with Joseph into the cold starlight, for poverty has few preparations to make. She was leaving home again. Terror and hardship, the wilderness and heathendom, were before her; and she confronted all with the calm anguish of an already broken heart. Here and there the night wind stirred in the leafless fig trees, making the bare branches nod against the bright sky, and now and then a watch-dog bayed, not because it heard them, but from the mere nocturnal restlessness of animals. But as Jesus had come like God, so he went like God, unnoticed and unmissed. No one is ever less missed on earth than he on whom it depends.

The path they took was not the one which human prudence would have pointed out to them. They returned upon the Jerusalem road they had so lately trodden. But, avoiding the Holy City, they passed near Bethlehem, as if his neighborhood should give a blessing to those unconscious babes that were still nestling warmly in their mothers' arms. Thus they fell into the road which leads into the wilderness, and, Joseph going before, like the shadow of the Eternal Father, they crossed the frontier of the promised land, far on until they were lost to the eye, like specks on the desert sand. Two creatures had carried the Creator into the wilderness, and were taking care of him there amid the stony sands of the unwatered gullies. Sunrise and sunset, the glittering noon and the purple of midnight, the round moon and the colored haze, came to them in the desert for many a day. Still they travelled on. They had cold to bear by night, and a sun from which there was no escape by day. They had scanty food, and frequent thirst.

They knew whom they were carrying, and looked not for miracles to lighten the load they bore. Old tradition said that one night they rested in a robber's cave. They were received there with rough but kind hospitality by the wife of the captain of the band. Perhaps it was her sorrow that made her kind; for it is often so with women. Her sorrow was a great one. She had a fair child, the life of her soul, the one gentle, spotless thing amid all the lawlessness and savage life around. Alas! it was too fair to look at; for it was white with leprosy. But she loved it the more, and pressed it more fondly to her bosom, as mothers are wont to do. It was more than ever her life and light now, because of its misfortunes. Mary and Jesus, the robber's wife and the leprous child, together in the cave at nightfall — how fitting a place for the Redeemer! How sweet a type of the Church he has founded! Mary asked for water that she might wash our Blessed Lord, and the robber's wife brought it to her, and the Babe was washed. Kindness, when it opens the heart, opens the eyes of the mind likewise. The robber's wife perceived something remarkable about her guests. Whether it was that there was a light round the head of Jesus, or that the mere vicinity of so much holiness strangely affected her, we know not: but, in much love and with some sort of faith, the mother's heart divined — earth knows that maternal divination well. She took away the water Mary had used in washing Jesus, and washed her little leprous Dimas in it, and straightway his flesh became as rosy and beautiful as a mother could desire. Long years passed. The child outgrew its mother's arms. It did feats of boyish daring on the sands of the wilderness. At last Dimas was old enough to join the band; and though it seems that to the last he had somewhat of the mother's heart about him, he led a life of violence and crime, and at length Jerusalem saw him brought within her gates a captive. When he hung upon the cross, burning with fever, parched with agony, he was bad enough to speak words of scorn to the harmless sufferer by his side. The sufferer was silent, and Dimas looked at him. He saw something heavenly, something unlike a criminal, about him, such perhaps as his mother had seen some three-and-thirty years before.

It was the child in the water of whose bath his leprosy had been healed. Poor Dimas! thou hast a worse leprosy now, that will need blood instead of water! Faith was swift in its works. Perhaps his heart was like his mother's, and faith a half natural growth in it. He takes in the scene of the crucifixion, the taunts, the outrages, the blasphemies, the silence, the prayer for their pardon, the wishful look cast upon himself by the dying Jesus. It is enough. Then and there he must profess his faith; for the mother's prayers are rising from beneath, and he is being enveloped in a very cloud of mercy. Lord! remember me when thou comest into thy kingdom! See how quickly he had outrun even some of the Apostles. He was fastened to the cross to die, and he knew it was no earthly kingdom in which he could be remembered. This day shalt thou be with m↴ in paradise! Paradise for thy cave's hospitality, poor young robber! And Jesus died, and the spear opened his heart, and the red stream sprang over the limbs of the dying robber, like a fresh fountain, and though his mother from the cave was not there, his new mother was beneath the cross, and she sent him after her first-born into paradise, the first of that countless family of sons who through that dear blood should enter into glory.

COMPOSITION.

Describe the cave into which Jesus, Mary and Joseph enter. The rough walls, the instruments of war and of strife scattered about. A little child is in a corner. Give the supposed questions addressed by the robber's wife to the Holy Family. The answers given by Mary and Joseph. Mary's request for water. The washing. The robber's wife uses the same water. Her joy at the sudden change in her little boy's skin. He is healed. Go on thus, and conclude by showing that our dear Lord, who has promised reward even for a *cup* of cold water given in his name, doubly rewards Dimas, whose mother had kindly furnished a *basin* of water to wash the Infant God.

alacrity	prudence	gullies	hospitality
perturbation	trodden	purplo	lawlessness
heathendom	unconscious	haze	type
nocturnal	frontier	tradition	vicinity

———o———

AFFLICTION.

Count each affliction, whether light or grave,
God's messenger sent down to thee : do thou
With courtesy receive him ; rise and bow,
And ere his shadow pass thy threshold, crave
Permission first his heavenly feet to lave ;
Then lay before him all thou hast : allow
No cloud of passion to usurp thy brow,
Or mar thy hospitality ; no wave
Of tumult to obliterate
The soul's marmoreal calmness : grief should be
Like joy, majestic, equable, sedate,
Confirming, cleansing, raising, making free ;
Striving to consume small trouble, to command
Great thoughts, grave thoughts, thoughts lasting to the end.